EXIT WOUNDS

"With considerable wit and wisdom, Lewis DeSimone joins the ranks of Stephen McCauley, Andrew Holleran, Michael Cunningham, and Patrick Gale in vividly bringing to life gay characters coping with middle age in all its effronteries and affordances. *Exit Wounds* focuses on a tight-knit group of older gay friends in San Francisco who face change on every front: from aging bodies and waning desires to an assimilated younger gay generation ("even fags are straight now") and a transforming cityscape where independent bookstores, like the one run by the narrator, don't stand a chance. What survives is the love that binds these friends to each other and to a city that, despite its sometimes alienating transformations, remains alive, beckoning, fabulous: in a word, home. Writing with heart-felt sentiment but without sentimentality, DeSimone has crafted a glowing anthem to a place and to the possibilities of personal transformation amid inevitable change."

—Joseph Allen Boone, author of *Furnace Creek* and *Conditions of Precarity*

EXIT WOUNDS

LEWIS DeSIMONE

REBEL SATORI PRESS
New Orleans & New York

Published in the United States of America by
REBEL SATORI PRESS
www.rebelsatoripress.com

Chapters 1 and 2 originally appeared, in different form, in *Saints and Sinners: New Fiction from the Festival*, ed. Tracy Cunningham and Paul J. Willis (Valley Falls, N.Y.: Bold Strokes Books, 2020).

Cover photograph by Rosangela Perry
Cover design by Sven Davisson

ISBN: 978-1-60864-313-4

for Harvey

Only one is a wanderer.
Two together are always going somewhere.
—Kim Novak in *Vertigo*

Mr. Widdicombe, there's no such place as San Francisco.
—Rosalind Russell in *Auntie Mame*

CHAPTER 1

MESOPOTAMIA

Everything fell apart at once, but I may as well start with Oscar's birthday party.

I was still fumbling in the kitchen when the doorbell rang. The clock over the refrigerator said 6:35, so I immediately knew who it was. Brendan had an unfortunate habit of arriving early for everything.

I buzzed him in and double-checked the oven. The cassoulet was simmering gently, the smell of duck fat lingering in the air as I closed the door. Everything was under control, so I could relax for a few minutes, until the others arrived.

Brendan greeted me with a bottle of Côtes du Rhône. "I wasn't sure what you were serving," he said with a shrug, apologizing for bringing a $50 bottle of wine.

"This will be perfect," I said. "Shall I open it now?"

"Maybe just decant it. It could stand to breathe."

As Brendan settled into one of the armchairs, I headed toward the bar and looked around for a decanter. I found my favorite, in the shape of an inverted lily. The wine rode along the sides of the neck and then flowed out in an enticing swirl.

Settling the decanter at the center of the dining table on the far side of the room, I asked, "What would you like while we're waiting?"

"Campari and soda, if you have it."

I went back to the bar and searched through the rows of bottles. The alcohol was organized according to frequency of use—gin and vodka in front, a variety of whiskeys and rums next, and everything else cluttered haphazardly in the back.

Behind me, I could hear Brendan relaxing into the chair. "It's got good bones, this place," he said, an odd gruffness in his voice.

I finally found the Campari, the bottle mottled like it had caught a case of glass-borne measles, still half full of potent red booze. It looked like cherry cough syrup but, as I remembered, tasted more like arsenic. I was surprised I even had any. It must have been a host gift someone had brought ages ago (someone with very peculiar ideas about party cocktails). I mixed his drink and made myself a gin and tonic. When I turned back, drinks in hand, I found Brendan gazing around the room, neck contorted to take in the far corners of the ceiling.

"Have you ever had it appraised?" he continued.

"What, the apartment?"

"I could easily get you 800 for it. The market's insane right now."

A one-bedroom on the edge of the Castro, worth that much? I shook my head in disbelief and took a seat. "I only paid 200."

"Yes," Brendan said, "twenty years ago. It's a whole other world these days."

Handing Brendan his drink, I studied the crown molding above his head, the still gleaming hardwood floor beneath our feet. I'd installed the brass curtain rods myself—half a day spent standing on a chair with an electric drill in my hand and a pencil between my teeth for marking the holes. That had been my first major household chore when I'd bought the place. Now I was a regular at Home Depot, a handyman manqué. Owning property had turned me into my father.

"I couldn't sell," I said. "Where would I go? If this place is worth that much, so is everything else. It's not like I can afford to upgrade." My eye strayed to the side of Brendan's chair, the ragged fabric marking Elsa's favorite scratching spot.

Brendan gazed sheepishly into his glass. His dark hair was still thick and curly. At this point, he was probably fixed for life. "I could find you something. Believe me."

Brendan had stumbled into real estate at the perfect moment, just when the city was starting to recover from the dot-bomb. He'd been a bartender and before that, a teacher, but the kids got worse each year and he was never going to get rich off an annual cost-of-living increase that barely kept up with his rent. The tips in the bar were no better, so eventually he quit and started working at a real estate firm in Noe Valley, mentored by an old friend. While the techies of the era were fleeing in droves, Brendan was studying at night for his license. It was, he said, the best decision of his life. Even in the off years, when commissions were thin, he at least enjoyed his work, and no one at the office was shooting spitballs at his back.

"Maybe not in this neighborhood," he said, gesturing toward the window with his drink. The Campari caught the light and glowed in his hand like nuclear waste. "The demand's pretty high here, but there are other spots where things are a little slower. Potrero Hill, the Inner Sunset."

"The Inner Sunset?" I repeated, trying not to scowl too obviously. The name sounded like a euphemism for death, and the architecture confirmed it. "Are you serious?"

"There are some great places out that way." Brendan squinted thoughtfully. "I'll take you for a drive some Sunday, see a few open houses. And who knows," he added, "you might need a bigger place if things work out with … what's his name?"

"Damien. And it's far too soon to be thinking about that." My glass was sweating; I wiped my hand on my pants and gazed over Brendan's shoulder, looking for anything that might be out of place.

"This isn't a surprise party, is it?" he asked, thankfully changing the subject.

"No," I replied. "You can't surprise Oscar. He knows all. And besides, he would kill me if I put him on the spot."

Still standing, I checked the table again—silverware in the right order, gold chargers gleaming. "As a matter of fact," I said, taking a seat across from Brendan, "maybe we should downplay the whole thing. As much as Oscar loves attention, he's a little shell-shocked about turning 50."

"How do we pretend it's not his birthday?"

"Just don't use the word," I said.

"*Birthday?*"

"No. *Fifty.*"

"1969 was a long time ago. Maybe he'll forget." He laughed. "You know how they tell you to get a colonoscopy when you turn 50, just in case? It took me three years to schedule mine. I was not in the mood to admit my age."

Oscar was the youngest member of our little crew, the last to cross over into seniorhood. His birthday had actually been a week ago, but dinner had been a scheduling nightmare, with six calendars to contend with. When we were all younger, evenings together could happen at the drop of a hat; now it required a spreadsheet to coordinate everyone's availability. Thankfully, the gods had aligned around tonight: Oscar had been scheduled to go to court, but the case was unexpectedly settled. Rafe had recently finished designing a loft for the latest Internet billionaire, and John closed the office early on Fridays. I didn't really know what Wayne was up to, but, despite John's protestations of true love, I suspected he was only a temporary member of the club and therefore dispensable.

Brendan went to the bathroom and I used the opportunity to obsess over the table—realigning silverware, sliding each glass to the exact upper corner of its placemat. I knew it was pointless, that all I was doing was moving things out of place so I could slip them back in, but I couldn't resist. My mother had always taught me that if you finish a task early, you should check it over. There was always room for improvement.

"You sure spruced up for company," Brendan said as he returned. "That bathroom smells as bleachy as a sex club on a Sunday morning."

"Thanks," I said, straightening up from the table. "I think."

"It's nice of you to cook," Brendan said. "I thought we were going out. Rafe keeps saying he wants to try that new place, what's it called?"

"You'll have to be more specific."

"You know, the one on Market that used to be Italian."

"Now it's Japanese."

"Yeah, that one."

"It's closed."

"Again?"

"What can I tell you? The space is cursed." I looked at my watch. It was nearly 7:15. "So where are they?" I asked the window, hoping the lights in the distance might answer.

"Maybe John's having trouble getting a babysitter."

"What are you talking about?"

"Oh, is he *bringing* the boy?"

I laughed. "So I was told."

"I just hope his heart can stand shtupping a 30-year-old."

"From what I've seen, Wayne seems pretty good for his heart."

"Aww, how sweet." He shook his head. "May-December romances never work, my friend. Just watch."

I took a sip of my drink. Not enough gin. Not nearly enough gin.

It was Oscar who had taught me about gay time. But in his version, there was a science to it: Come too early and you'll look desperate. Come too late and you're just being rude. For cocktail parties, that meant arriving in the second hour, once things had gotten started but before they petered out. For dinner parties, though, he was stricter, striving to be precisely seven minutes late. Just like the theater, he would say. Curtain is always at seven minutes past the hour.

I was back in the kitchen, taking the cassoulet out to cool, when the doorbell rang again. "I'll get it!" Brendan called out.

I settled the Dutch oven on the stove and pulled the salad out of the refrigerator. I began mixing the vinaigrette.

The kitchen had shrunk on me over the years. When I'd first moved in, I wasn't much of a cook, so room to boil pasta and toss a frozen entree into the microwave was perfectly sufficient. But over the years, my tastes had changed, along with my desire to entertain. I'd become remarkably skilled at utilizing the tiny workspace between the stove and the fridge. Cassoulet was the perfect dish for a party: it looked impressive, but all the real work was done long before anyone arrived. My guests would have no idea of the chaos that had preceded them.

Brendan pulled open the door, and suddenly voices were overlapping and echoing all over the place. Wiping my hands, I went out to greet them.

"We ran into each other on the street," John was saying, juggling a wine bag from hand to hand as he pulled himself out of a caramel suede jacket.

Wayne, his head emerging from a black mock turtle, was squeezed between John and the bookcase. He looked shorter than I remembered, until I realized that he was slouching a bit. Behind them, Oscar and Rafe were having their own conversation.

"It was hilarious," Oscar said loudly.

"What?" I asked, helping him off with his jacket. Beneath it, his white shirt pulled honey tones from his skin.

"Manspreading," he said, eyebrows arched excitedly.

"Sounds like a sexual position." Brendan shut the door behind them.

"Oh no," Oscar replied, leading everyone into the living room, "it's not nearly as much fun as that. It's all the rage these days: complaints that men spread their legs out to take up extra space on the subway."

"Like Larry Craig's wide stance?"

"Kind of," Oscar said. "But again, not as much fun."

"This is a new phenomenon?" John asked with a skeptical tone.

"Everything's new to millennials. They're barely out of diapers and busy creating the world, one reinvented wheel at a time."

I instinctively glanced over at Wayne, but he was too busy looking at his phone to register offense.

"Who wants a drink?" I asked loudly and made my way to the bar.

"What's everyone having?" asked Rafe.

"I have a gin and tonic, and Brendan's working on his Jim Jones Kool-Aid."

Smiling mischievously, Brendan held up his glass, fire-red.

"I'll stick to wine," said Rafe. He winked and tilted his head so that a thick lock of salt-and-pepper hair fell over one eye. Rafe was the sharpest dresser in the group. Tonight he wore striped slacks and a pink shirt that highlighted his broad shoulders.

There were nods all around. I picked up the decanter from the table and poured out the glasses. Oscar took one without looking as he continued his story.

"Much to my surprise, I actually snagged a seat on the M line tonight. Then, at Van Ness, a woman got on and took the adjacent seat, between me and a white guy. She was thin as a rail, but made quite a production of it, as if she was literally being squeezed in. Wriggling into the seat, she gave a scowl to the other guy—determined to let him know he was in a no-manspreading zone, even though his knee was a good six inches from hers. Then it was my turn. And suddenly the annoyance drained from her face. She actually smiled awkwardly. I could see the calculation going on: by pulling herself in tight, she was decrying the sins of manspreading, but if she pulled too far away from me she was demonstrating fear of a black man. Her woke signals were firing in every direction. It was like a bad sitcom."

"*Were* you manspreading?" John asked.

"Of course not. I'm a lawyer: I always stay within the lines."

I shook my head. "I don't know how you have the nerve to do these things."

"Jealous," Oscar hissed through a broad smile. "You wish you had the nerve, farm-boy."

I laughed. "I was raised to be polite. And afraid of conflict."

"Passive aggressive, you mean."

"That, too. But fortunately, I was very sheltered. Hell, I was 12 years old before I met my first brunette."

"How far you've come."

That was Oscar, ever the provocateur, destroyer of shibboleths. He fed off other people's hypocrisy like Popeye with a can of spinach.

Once we were settled around the table, Rafe turned to Wayne, who had put his phone away and was now gazing into his wine, bereft of ones and zeros. "So, what's new in your world?"

"Very exciting stuff," John said quickly, before Wayne had a chance to respond. "There are some VC guys who are interested in investing in his company."

"Viet Cong?" Brendan asked.

Oscar rolled his eyes, but Wayne just smiled. Turning to me, he said, "I thought you were inviting Damien tonight."

"Oh no, he's still away on his trip."

"What trip?" asked John. John loved nothing more than travel.

"A business trip to Chicago. Some convention."

"Sounds dreadful," Brendan said. "And cold."

"It's nearly May, darling." I said. "Even Chicago has spring."

"Just barely." He gazed back down at his plate to scrape the meat off a duck bone. They were all used to my excuses for Damien.

"Venture capitalists," Wayne said, bringing the conversation back. "We're deep into negotiations. With money from them, we can really get the company off the ground—hire the right people, fine-tune the product, do all the necessary market research. It's a godsend."

All I knew was that Wayne had cofounded some techie startup with someone he'd worked with at Google. Until recently they'd been working out of Wayne's living room.

"What exactly is the product?" I asked.

Wayne's eyes lit up as he launched into an answer—a speech

dotted with gigabytes, apps, and processing speed, all of which flew directly over my head. It was easier just to focus on Wayne's flawless skin, his thick head of hair, remarkably devoid of gray.

Wayne wasn't just new to our little circle. By most standards, Wayne was new to planet Earth. While the half-century mark had already slapped everyone else at the table, Wayne bore nary a wrinkle. Even his beard seemed to be growing in an adolescent's uneven patches.

I ran into the kitchen for another bottle of wine, and Wayne was still talking when I returned. "So, if all goes well, we'll soon be moving into a new space in SoMa." He touched John's hand perfunctorily before picking up his wine glass. He'd barely touched his cassoulet so far, mostly picking around the duck and sausage for the occasional scoop of beans.

"How long have you guys been together now?" Rafe asked.

"Nine months," John said, swirling his glass and looking for legs.

Like a baby's age, I thought, marked by months.

"The world certainly moves fast these days," I said.

"Too fast," said Rafe. "It's the Internet."

"What does the Internet have to do with it?" I asked.

"It fucks with our sense of time. Things are vanishing before we have time to make sure the new stuff is good and safe. I mean, for all its alleged benefits, social media is what gave us that asshole in the White House. I'd rather see the glaciers melt."

"Exactly," said Brendan. "When everyone has a voice, all you hear is noise."

You could say that we were just a bunch of curmudgeons—a small, cantankerous circle of middle-aged men trying to stave off their impending irrelevance. On any given evening, the conversation might touch on a dozen or more grievances—everything from vegetarianism to the effects of Grindr on old-style cruising. An eavesdropper would probably say that we believed culture had stopped developing around the turn of the century and that nothing good had happened since. That included—in fact, centered around—the Internet. Just as everything else in the world had been reduced to electrons, we feared that our own fate would be even worse—virtual, invisible, finally nonexistent. Change—which is inevitable, and which we had embraced when it was our turn to break the rules—had become the enemy, with the knowledge that one day it would erase us and the era we called our own. Those days were already fading from memory. Soon, they'd be relegated to history, diminished over time and then, eventually—and at some point not too far in the future—gone forever.

John smiled. "Remember when we had to go to the library and flip through card catalogs?"

"Or engage with a human being at the bank?" Oscar offered.

"Or browse actual books at a bookstore?" I said.

"How *is* business?" John asked.

"I think I counted 40 customers in the store today."

"That sounds good."

"Not really. Most of them browse the shelves, decide what they want, and then go home to order it on Amazon."

"Bastards," Oscar said in his best Joan Crawford.

Wayne cast a quizzical look around the table, as if we were all speaking a foreign language. "Don't you guys like what technology has given us?"

"Sure," Oscar replied. He dangled a fork over his plate, deciding whether to stab a tomato or an olive. "We're just concerned about what it's taken away."

Wayne laughed. "That's probably what people said about Henry Ford, too, when they looked around and couldn't find a horse and buggy."

"Yes," Brendan said with a sneer, "I'm sure it is." He swiveled his head toward Oscar and Rafe. "So, how's the renovation coming?"

"The new kitchen is going to be gorgeous," Rafe said. "I can't wait for our first dinner party."

I hadn't noticed anything wrong with the kitchen, but they had insisted on an upgrade. As a designer, Rafe was always up for experimenting with the latest styles, using his own home as a laboratory for his work. That was one thing they had in common: though dubious about technology, Oscar was all about steady progress. As long as something could be improved, it would be. Change was a constant for him. Enough was never enough. In the old days, that had been his calling card, but then it had referred to men, drugs, parties. Oscar loved excess. He was determined to experience as much as possible as quickly as possible. In those days, no one knew how long anything would last.

Small talk dominated now, the safe monotony of home design and the latest episode of *Pose*. It was all so civilized: an elegant dinner, designer clothes, fresh manicures, mostly polite, anodyne conversation. Twenty years ago—even 10—the setting would have been completely different. Back then, we would be clumped together in a corner of some bar, talking about how much we hated our jobs or who we longed to fuck. Back then, it was all about what was going to happen next. Now it was about where to put the dishwasher.

"So how's life in the 'hood?" Rafe asked.

Oscar and Rafe had been among the first couples to get married in 2004, when it was suddenly legal before it was suddenly illegal before it was suddenly legal again. But they'd been together for years by then, so nothing much changed in their lives. The wedding was largely an excuse for a grand party, and a slap in the face to Oscar's Baptist roots. They had moved to St. Francis Wood a few years back, seeking a quiet neighborhood and more space. Fog be damned, they wanted space.

"Shrinking," I said glumly.

"Well," said Oscar, "that's never a good thing."

"What do you mean?" asked Wayne, apparently oblivious to the double entendre. "There are places opening up all the time. Have you been to that new bar on Church?"

"Exactly," I replied. "*Straight* bars. We're being squeezed in every direction. The gay section of the neighborhood is now limited to four square blocks."

And that was the end of the small talk.

Brendan nodded. "I was just telling Craig he should take advantage of this crazy market and sell this place."

Instinctively, everyone else started looking around, assessing the room, searching for cracks in the walls.

"And do what?" I asked. "Where would I go?"

"Palm Springs?" John offered.

I sighed. "That heat would destroy me."

Oscar was nodding. "The Castro's dying," he said. "I knew it was over when I saw the first baby stroller."

"The Castro is not dying," Rafe retorted. "If anything, it's younger than ever."

"Point taken," Oscar said. "It's the culture that's dying." He leaned toward me, shoulder massaging mine. "Men our age belong in the suburbs."

"Hey, *we're* practically in the suburbs," Rafe said. "Come down to our neighborhood."

"I could never afford that," I said. "Can you picture me there, anyway—in a gated community? It's not quite the same thing."

"St. Francis Wood isn't exactly a gated community."

"The gates may be invisible, darling, but they're there."

John shook his head. "If San Francisco can't sustain a gay neighborhood, then what city can?"

"Why do you need one?" Wayne asked.

Brendan glared.

Oscar to the rescue. "You know how you can tell the city's gone straight?" he said, ignoring Wayne. "The gym. The place I go to is in the heart of the Financial District. When I started going, the locker room would be the cruisiest spot in town. No action, of course, but lots of wanton looks. Nobody looks anymore. They're too busy talking. Sports and IPOs, that's the extent of it."

"Sports?" I said incredulously.

Oscar nodded. "You'd be amazed how talkative they can be while squirming out of their BVDs under a towel. And it's not just the straight guys—though I will admit they used to be only 25% of the clientele and now they're easily 50. No, it's the gay guys, too. I'm telling you, the world has changed: even fags are straight now."

"God help us," said Brendan, reaching for a piece of bread. "We were freer when we were outlaws."

Wayne pursed his lips, contemplating his glass. "Seriously," he said, "aren't things better now? It's like you guys are nostalgic for inequality."

"There's a difference," Brendan said, "between equality and cultural integrity."

"Cultural integrity?" Wayne chuckled. "Like what, drag queens and leather bars?"

"You owe everything you have to drag queens," Brendan hissed, leaning in over his plate.

"Nostalgic memories of Stonewall aside—"

"Memories?" Rafe interrupted, laughing. "Just how old do you think we are?"

Brendan sighed. "I'm not talking about the Middle Ages," he said. "Gays have had a place at the table, in this town at least, for 40 years. The difference is that, until now, we weren't expected to conform in order to be treated like equals. We didn't have to turn into Ward and June Cleaver to get respect."

"What are you losing?" Wayne asked. "What's the trade-off?"

"We're losing everything that made us special."

"Hell," Oscar said, "even straight people do anal these days."

I nodded. "As Romanovsky and Phillips said, 'it's getting hard to tell the breeders from the queers.'"

"Who?" Wayne asked.

"Google 'em."

Wayne grew quiet, close-set eyes focusing on the salt shaker as if to will it, Carrie-like, to fly off the table.

I broke the tension by scraping my chair away and announcing dessert.

"Nothing for me," said Oscar, patting his belly, and the others followed suit.

I sighed, picturing a half-gallon of ice cream going right into my own stomach.

Someone needed to break the silence. "I got a summons for jury duty," I said.

"Oh dear." John's face fell. I might as well have said I needed a biopsy.

"Actually, I'm kind of looking forward to it. I hope I get further than the phone call this time. 'Thanks for playing, we don't need you. Bye.'"

"And you've always hated rejection," Brendan said snidely. He picked up his glass and drained the wine. "Well," he said, "if we're forgoing dessert, how about a nightcap?"

Oscar made a show of looking at his watch. "It's getting late," he said, tilting his head to one side. I remembered the gesture from our bachelor days, when Oscar was letting some flirt down easy.

"No no no," Brendan said, "it's barely 9:00. You can't get out of it with a yawn."

I started clearing the table. "You know the ritual, Oscar. We've been through it enough times."

Wayne crossed his knife and fork on his plate. "The ritual?" he asked, looking up.

"Every time one of us turns 50, we have cocktails at the Glass Coffin."

"It's kind of like rehearsal," Brendan said. "And hey," he added, turning a scowl toward me, "weren't we avoiding that word?"

I ignored him and caught Wayne's eye. His expression read confusion—Dian Fossey observing lesser primates. He turned haplessly to John, who rose from his seat quickly and announced, "I'm in."

Meanwhile, Oscar was hemming and hawing in the corner. "It won't kill you," I said. "It's not like we're going to announce your age to everyone in the place."

Brendan's lips curled up in imitation of the Grinch. "Now there's a thought."

"Don't you dare," Oscar warned, gritting his teeth.

Rafe helped me gather the remaining dishes and, from the kitchen, we finally heard Oscar's sing-song "Okay, one drink."

Everyone was putting their jackets on and draining their wine glasses when we reemerged into the living room. Brendan led the way out the door and down the stairs.

We reached the sidewalk as an oversized limo stopped at the corner, the blue glow of computer screens shining through its darkened windows. The bus's streamlined nose looked like something Sigourney Weaver should have been attacking with a flamethrower.

A young woman stepped out, tightening the straps of a backpack against her shoulders. As she approached, I recognized her as my upstairs neighbor, so I held the door open as the others made their way to Castro Street. We'd never introduced ourselves, though we had passed on the stairs or found each other at the mailboxes from time to time. Somewhere in her twenties, she was renting her unit from Kirk, who had been the longest resident in the building until he'd moved to wine country with his new husband. We'd never spoken, and when she passed she would toss me a perfunctory, closed-lipped smile. I'd never been able to determine whether she was shy or just rude, but I kept testing her—smiling broadly, saying hello only to be greeted by a brief nod.

She did it now as she reached the door, dipping her head, most of her face hidden behind a straight curtain of dark hair, fumbling with the heavy backpack as a nonverbal excuse. She passed into the lobby, hand never touching the door. I felt like a doorman in my own home, but tamped down my resentment. It was her parents' fault, I told myself. My generation, perhaps because we'd been spoiled ourselves, had ended up making terrible parents.

I caught up with everyone at the corner, falling in line behind Oscar and Rafe. We passed by a storefront where a figure was huddled under a rough blanket, an assortment of his possessions tucked against the wall—a small plastic bag spilling food wrappers, a wadded-up newspaper, holes in the kicked-off shoes. The person's face was invisible, only the long stringy hair at the back of the head showing above the blanket. He might have been a garden gnome or a fire hydrant for the attention his presence garnered.

I'd gotten used to the homeless on the street, as much fixtures of the city as the Transamerica Pyramid or the Bay Bridge. And over the years I'd learned how to evade their eyes. I'd given money to a few now and then, even ran into a McDonald's once just to buy someone a sandwich. But I couldn't help them all, and after a while it became easier to just pretend they weren't there.

But as I gazed at this nameless, faceless figure curled upon itself in the storefront, a dirty foot peeking out the edge of the blanket, a sudden sadness washed over me. One life, I thought. Like all of us, he had been given one life, and this was how he was spending it. In one of the wealthiest cities in the world, this was his life. I couldn't blame him, of course. I had no idea how this had come to be his life, to what degree it was mental illness or addiction or simple surrender.

Now, at middle age, I'd become sensitive to my own choices—the steps I'd taken in life, the ones I'd avoided—and their irrevocability. I had one life, too, and it wasn't one I'd imagined. But there was no turning back, and as time went on, there were fewer and fewer forks in the road, fewer opportunities to choose another way, to fix what was broken, to chase another dream. The dreams themselves were less vivid, less crucial. In the beginning, dreams were everything, they alone gave meaning to life. Now, it was just life.

I turned away and, moving into the center of our pack, continued down the hill.

"Here," Brendan said, leaning in with a half-whisper, "I want to show you something." He pulled me toward a real estate office, its windows collaged with flyers advertising various places for sale around the city. "Look," he said, pointing, "one bedroom, one bath, 600 square feet—just like your place. Asking price of 790 grand. Which means it'll fetch at least 900."

The flyer included three photographs—bedroom, living room, kitchen—all taken from tricky angles to exaggerate the size of the space. "My kitchen is nothing like that," I said, noting the sparkling appliances, gray marble countertops, cabinets galore.

"It doesn't have to be just like that," Brendan said. "It has the *potential* to be like that, that's the important thing."

I turned my eye to the description, the flowery euphemisms I'd always found so amusing in these listings, where *cozy* meant Lilliputian and *quiet* meant that the trucks whizzed by every 10 minutes instead of every 5.

"Where is this place?" I asked, giving in to the urge to play dumb. "It says Eureka Valley."

Brendan laughed. "It's just around the corner," he said, pointing at the address. "I think that's 19th and Diamond."

"You mean the Castro. Why doesn't it say that?"

"Because the real name of the neighborhood is Eureka Valley, that's why." He shook his head with a smirk, dismissing the apparent idiocy of the question.

"The 'real' name?" I pursued. "Or just the old name?"

"What do you mean?"

I rolled my eyes. "No one has called this place Eureka Valley since the sixties. It's like referring to Iraq as Mesopotamia."

"Not quite," Brendan said as we maneuvered into the crosswalk. "Technically, the Castro is a subsection of Eureka Valley."

"Technically," I echoed, "The word *Castro* scares away straight buyers."

Brendan sighed and started walking faster. "The world is a

dynamic place, Craig. You have to learn to embrace change."

"I'm sure that's what the dinosaurs said when they saw the asteroid flying through the air. And besides, aren't you the one who was just giving Wayne shit for proclaiming the virtues of change?"

"Well," Brendan said with a dramatic sigh. "Just don't tell him."

We snaked past a line outside the theater and made our way to the corner. Across the street, an enormous rainbow flag ruffled in the wind, spotlit by the glow of a streetlamp.

His hand on the door to Twin Peaks, Rafe turned around and smiled at Oscar. "Are you ready for your close-up, Miss Desmond?" he asked.

Oscar sneered and caught the door as Rafe glided through. Brendan followed and held the door for me. As I stepped inside, I felt a lack of pressure on the door and looked behind. Wayne and John were standing by the bus stop, huddled in conversation. I made my way inside alone.

CHAPTER 2
THE CURMUDGEON CLUB

Twin Peaks was the place you went when you wanted a cocktail, Brendan used to joked, rather than just cock. Once known solely as the haunt of gay men past their prime, it had recently grown more popular. Tourists came through with regularity, checking it off their list like Coit Tower or Fisherman's Wharf.

Fortunately, a group was leaving just as we arrived, so we were able to grab a table by the windows.

"Where are John and Wayne?" Rafe asked.

I smiled offhandedly. "They're chatting outside."

"Is something wrong?"

We were all spared from discussing it by the appearance of the waitress, who took our orders with a matter-of-fact look, a smile or nod hardly worth the energy. Within a few minutes, she laid six nearly overflowing Manhattans before us. Brendan bent over and sucked the first sip off the rim of the glass. "Some things never change," he said with a wink.

"Thank God for that," I replied. Braver, I picked up the glass by the stem, but it spilled a quick dribble on its way to my mouth.

"Remember how hard it was to cross that threshold the first time?" Brendan asked, gesturing toward the door.

I laughed. For years, I had passed by the place with disdain, rattling off its many nicknames to anyone I happened to be with.

No, I'd said, I'd never be ready for the Wrinkle Room. I'd have to be dragged kicking and screaming into the Crystal Casket. Aside from the cruel ritual of my elders' birthday parties—first Brendan, then John and Rafe—I'd barely set foot in the place. And then, on my own 50th birthday, Brendan and Oscar had bracketed me, one holding each arm, and practically carried me past the plate glass windows, up to the door.

Since then this spot had indeed become a kind of home. It was the go-to place when I wanted to just sit at a bar and not be bothered, when I wanted to have a quiet chat with a friend. And I'd grown a little ashamed of my youthful willfulness. Aging, I came to understand, was all about losing your arrogance. Along with everything else. Now this bar struck me as an oasis: though its huge windows looked out on a constantly changing world, the place itself was gracefully frozen in time.

I was wiping up my spill when John appeared beside the table.

"Where's Wayne?" Rafe asked as John pulled a chair over.

"He has an early meeting in the morning, and still has some prep to do. He needed to get home." He dropped a white bag on the table as he sat. "Happy birthday," he said.

With a quizzical look, Oscar peered into the bag and removed an oversized chocolate chip cookie. "Aw," he said with a laugh, "you shouldn't have."

He broke off a piece and passed it around.

"Body of Christ," Rafe said, lifting his triangle of cookie in the air.

"Ooh," purred his husband, "you are most assuredly going to Hell."

The rest of us lifted our pieces in an echoing chorus.

"Cup of salvation," I added, raising my glass.

John laughed along with everyone else, his eyes bright, the mysterious drama of the street corner erased for the moment.

"Guess what I got in the mail today," Oscar announced, placing his glass delicately on the table.

"The latest International Male catalog?" I offered. What is it, I wondered, that makes Manhattans go down so easily?

"Close," he said. "My AARP card."

Brendan laughed. "I've been getting their crap for years. Frankly, I'm kind of grateful. My mailbox would have cobwebs otherwise."

I laughed. When my own card had arrived in the mail a year ago, I'd opened the envelope cautiously, as if it might be full of anthrax.

"How do they even know I'm 50?"

Brendan fished the cherry out of his glass and drained it. "They know all," he said.

"Well, anyway," Oscar said, "thank you all for sharing in my encroaching decrepitude."

A screech went up from the next table, a mixed group who wouldn't see their own AARP cards for at least 20 years. A handsome bearded man was flanked by two women, one of whom had been the screecher. I could overhear only snippets of the conversation, just enough to make out that the bear was telling the girls about his latest conquest. He caught my eye with a look half conspiratorial, half desperate—a facetious cry for help. I looked away abruptly, at the pedestrians zigzagging their way through the intersection.

They had widened the sidewalks a few years ago, but the construction project had taken so long—endless months of walking past gaping holes in the ground—that by the time it was over I couldn't sense much of a difference. A small group was gathered at the bus stop now, while others streamed in both directions, arm in arm, heads thrown back in laughter, the familiar gestures of a night out with no objective other than nonspecific fun.

"What happened?" I asked the table, still gazing out at the sidewalk. The light had just changed, and a gaggle of people dashed across the street toward the subway.

"Where?"

"Here," I said, gesturing with my glass. There were still a couple of sips left. "To us."

"To us." The others hoisted their glasses, as well, and I laughed.

"No," I said, "I wasn't toasting. I was asking: what happened to us?"

Brendan shook his head. "Oh hon, I don't have that much time. So much has happened. Most of which I can't remember. What are you getting at?"

"How did we go from that," I said, gesturing out the window, "to this?" I placed my empty glass down with a decisive ring. Right on cue, the waitress passed by and Brendan signaled another round.

"To what? Sitting in God's Waiting Room and waiting for the undertaker?" Oscar asked.

"Well, I wasn't feeling quite that morbid, but … yes. When did we become middle-aged?"

"I don't know," John said. "It just happens. It creeps up on you. One day you're out and about, running around, thinking about the future. And the next you're counting gray hairs in the mirror."

"Just like that. So I didn't miss anything? It's not like I slept through the moment?" I tried to laugh. "I guess I always thought it would be like driving through the Robin Williams Tunnel, you know? You're in this darkened space between worlds, and suddenly you emerge out the other end and—boom—there's the Golden Gate Bridge in all its glory."

"You thought middle age would be glorious?" asked Rafe.

"I thought it would be something."

Brendan chuckled. "Oh, it's something all right. Ask my aching back." He laughed and turned toward Oscar with an ironic smile. "Not to scare you, hon, but this one's different: 30 and 40 are fabulous, like the entry points for exciting new phases of life. But 50?—50 is the beginning of the end."

"Gee, thanks, guys, you're really making this a fun birthday." Oscar plucked the cherry out of his drink and bit it off the stem.

"We just want to prepare you," I said.

"Prepare me? Jesus, it sounds like *you're* more upset about my age than I am."

I guess I was, in a way. Oscar was the youngest one in our group, so if he was old, it meant we all were.

It wasn't just the physical, though I knew what Brendan was talking about. I'd been going to the gym for years now, but suddenly I'd begun to notice that my energy level wasn't what it had been. Somewhere along the way I'd reached a plateau, and now the best I could do was maintain. The problem was that I no longer cared very much about looking fit. The problem was that I no longer cared very much about anything.

"What about sex?" Oscar asked. "I suppose you're going to tell me that goes, too?"

"Hardly, thank god." Brendan's eyebrows lifted humorously. "The need may not be as pressing and the equipment's a little tired, but once I get started, I'm 25 again."

"I get headaches," John said. "Sex headaches."

"Is that a thing?" Rafe asked.

"Oh yes. They're like ice cream headaches, only pounding."

"That's appropriate," Oscar mused.

"The only real problem," Brendan said, "is that sex really exhausts me now. More than it used to. Like any fine piece of meat, I suppose, I need to rest after I come out of the oven."

The waitress came back in the middle of that last line. With remarkable dexterity, she laid more brimming glasses on the tabletop and took away the empties. Brendan gave her a fifty and told her to keep the change. That was the other thing we loved about this place—the drinks were large and cheap.

"Where did this come from?" John asked, looking at the new glass before him as if it were Macbeth's ghostly dagger.

"Magic," Brendan said. "Just drink it."

"Well, I have patients in the morning, better have my wits about me."

"Yes," Oscar said with a laugh, "one can't have an optometrist show up for work blind drunk."

John, gazing down, wrapped both hands around the stem of his glass. He cleared his throat loudly. "So," he began after a long pause, "I wanted to tell you guys something. Now that Wayne's gone."

His tone was oddly heavy. Brendan and I shared a look, but he seemed as clueless as I was.

Finally, John lifted his head. "I'm thinking of asking him to marry me."

Brendan's face fell, and I could feel his knee twitching under the table. We were all silent as John sheepishly shifted his gaze to each of us in turn.

It was up to Rafe to break the awkward stillness. "That's great!" he said with at least a simulacrum of genuineness. With Rafe, kindness always came first, so you could never quite tell when he was horrified.

Oscar was less enthusiastic. "Don't you think maybe you should move in with him first?"

John smiled nervously, one corner of his lip trapped between his teeth. "I don't know," he said at last. "Do you guys think it's too soon?"

Brendan's expression softened. "Just because you *can* get married doesn't mean you should," he said. "There's nothing wrong with a little cohabitation. It's like renting instead of owning."

John laughed half-heartedly. "Maybe you're right," he said. "He's got so much going on, this might not be the right time."

Maybe in another ten years, I thought—when Wayne's grown up and John's the one in diapers.

When you can't say something nice, I thought, ask a question. "Do you love him?"

For a long moment, John hid his face behind his drink. "Of course."

"Well."

Oscar met my gaze. Like Harold in *The Boys in the Band*, preparing to eviscerate his host. "Do you think he's ready to settle down?"

John's eyes widened. "I hope so."

"Who's ever ready for major events?" Rafe said. "Moves like this require a leap of faith. Don't you think, guys?" He looked around the table like an evangelist preacher searching for an *Amen*.

I felt like I was back in the Midwest, where everyone was afraid to speak the truth, even when their lies were completely transparent.

"Don't ask me," I said. "I can't decide between a *grande* and a *venti* at Starbucks."

I cradled my drink and gazed out at the street again as the parade passed by. Young men laughing, falling onto one another's shoulders, lesbians in baseball caps, a couple of thirtyish guys with thick beards and plaid shirts nearly bursting with muscle. No drag queens yet, but the night was young.

I was impressed with how well Oscar was handling things. On my fiftieth, I'd been a bit of a basketcase, but he was sitting here calmly, treating it like just another day. Then again, Oscar had always been better at hiding his feelings, tamping down any semblance of insecurity or disappointment in public. To most others, his life looked like a smooth upward trajectory. His closest friends—Rafe and I—knew the despair that would hit from time to time, the difficulty he had handling his own imperfection; but the rest of the world was oblivious. That was how he wanted it. I, on the other hand, had never mastered a poker face.

"I should have baked you a cake," I said when I caught Oscar's eye again.

He laughed. "Maybe we can just stick a candle in my cocktail."

"That'd set the place on fire," said Rafe.

"So would 50 candles on a cake."

The evening was winding down, at least for us. In the past, our nights out had been an adventure—always on the lookout for the unexpected, staying out until it happened, until serendipity had its way, usually in the form of a flirtatious stranger or the entertaining spectacle of drunken people behaving badly. One or the other was inevitable if we waited long enough. But now, going out was the event itself—almost scripted. After all these years, we were our own entertainment. The rest was scenery.

John was the first to call it quits. As we stood to say good night, Oscar and Rafe used the opportunity to leave, as well. As the door thwacked shut behind them, Brendan and I sat back down and looked at each other. He raised his eyebrows.

"Sad," he said when the others were gone. "John was never particularly interesting, but even *he* can do better than that."

"I'm sure he thinks he's done quite well," I said. "Wayne's smart, handsome ..."

"Young."

"There is that."

"So what's with Damien?" he asked.

"I told you. He's at a convention."

"Have you talked to him?"

I gazed down at my glass. "No. I'm sure he's really busy."

Brendan tapped a finger against the table, drawing my eyes back up to his face. "Are things going okay?"

"With Damien? Sure. It's only been a few months, but I think we're doing great."

"You should bring him out sometime, with the gang. I feel like I've seen him only, what, once?"

I nodded. "Sure."

I'd never been particularly good at uniting the pieces of my life. When I was a teenager, I'd dreaded friends calling the house or running into them when shopping with my mother. I was two different people, depending on the circumstances. I didn't know how to behave otherwise, how to integrate. Some things never change.

"So what now?" Brendan said abruptly, pushing his empty glass toward the center of the table. "It's barely 11:00. I say we go somewhere else."

"I couldn't," I said. "Not tonight." I was picturing crisp sheets, the new book on my bedside table.

"Come on," Brendan coaxed. "Just one more drink."

[29]

In the old days, I could be easily persuaded. In the old days, I would say *yes* before the question had even been asked. I'd gotten a lot better at giving *no* for an answer, and Brendan, surprisingly, had gotten better at accepting it. "Just walk me to 440," he said.

We crossed the street together and stopped in front of the bar. A burly man in leather pants sat on a stool just outside, checking the occasional ID while a few stragglers smoked at the edge of the sidewalk. Loud music blared into the night. The place was crowded. I had once liked crowds.

Two slender boys emerged from the bar. "Screw this place," one of them said loudly. "Too many bears for my blood. Let's go to Box."

"Box?" said his friend. "Where's that?"

"Up on Market. Next to that seafood place." And they were off.

"Oh my lord," Brendan said, rolling his eyes.

"What?"

"*Box?*" Brendan repeated. "They mean Beaux."

"Education is wasted on the stupid."

Brendan smiled. "Sure you don't want to come in? The place just got more appealing."

"No, thanks."

He leaned in for a kiss. "Good night, buddy."

He slipped past the bouncer—no need to check for ID—and was absorbed into the crowd. I smiled and made my way down the street.

It had usually been Oscar who directed our evenings out. He had a fail-safe itinerary, a specific order for the pub crawl. We would start at the Midnight Sun—cocktails over music videos and old *Golden Girls* clips to loosen us up for the evening. Next, Badlands—before its hip reinvention. We'd huddle in the back, where we could easily scope the crowd if we were in the mood to cruise, or simply enjoy one another's company if we weren't. The evening could easily end there, but if anyone felt like giving in to a darker impulse, there was always the Detour, the Edge, Daddy's. There were ample choices. All that was before the online world replaced human beings with headless images.

I tried to remember what this street had looked like then, when it was all new to me, as new as it was for the kids who now skidded past with an enthusiasm I could barely recall. The bars replaced by storefronts, the space on the corner that had changed hands every two years like clockwork. Sometimes, perhaps, location wasn't everything.

I'd met Oscar at Badlands, Barry at the Sun, Peter and Garrett and Jake at one place or another in the neighborhood. Friends or lovers, it didn't matter. It was all about the excitement of novelty. We were young and free and just figuring out who we were. And most of all, who we wanted to become. We thought in the future and lived in the present. But the hierarchy of the tenses had shifted long ago.

Once again, walking past these markers of memory, I was drawn into the slipperiness of the past, even the worst moments coated in an undeserved nostalgia that makes them untouchable, makes them seem like something they never were. You can't win against the past. That's why the best course of action is to ignore it.

As I stepped onto the rainbow-striped crosswalk, I remembered the potholed black one it had replaced. I saw Barry standing in front of the pizza joint, grabbing a mid-evening slice of pepperoni to absorb the beer and give him energy to keep going. I heard Oscar singing a few bars of "Don't Leave Me This Way" when anyone threatened to call it a night.

So much of it was about romance in those days—the fantasy of connection, finding the right man, if only for a night. My sex drive was still fine. I just seldom felt inclined to deal with the baggage it entailed, the effort of getting there. Damien came as a relief. Even if we didn't see each other that frequently, he was there. He took away the need to search.

I'd noticed it, too, the daddy syndrome that had captured John. Somewhere in my mid-40s, it became harder to get the attention of men I was interested in. Only gradually did I notice that I was getting looks from a whole different demographic. After half an hour spent trying to make eye contact with my usual type—the hairy men around my own age who had always been my preference—I would look away to find a young guy staring at me. At first, I figured these boys were hustlers, the type who hung around older men less for what was in their jeans than for what was in their jeans pockets. Once or twice, I'd welcomed the chat, even flirted along—if only to keep in practice. Inevitably, the conversation petered out when our stockpile of common interests came to an abrupt end. After a while, it became a game. I would make cultural references that dipped increasingly into the past—from Gaga to Madonna to Liza, and beyond. By the time I got to Judy their eyes had gone dull with incomprehension, and I could safely call it a night.

The crowd thinned out after Harvey's, and I made my way toward 19th Street on a nearly empty sidewalk.

Back at the apartment, I hung my coat in the closet and looked around the room. The dining table was a shambles—wine glasses empty but stained red at the bottom, crumbs everywhere, wadded-up napkins, candle wax pooling into a hard medallion on a placemat. I carried glasses, two crisscrossed in each hand, into the kitchen.

Twenty years ago, I'd fallen in love with this place at first sight. It was all potential then, of course. I'd had the carpet ripped up to put in a hardwood floor, repainted all the walls. And over the years, as each appliance broke down one by one, I'd replaced them with the latest model. For a time, nothing had matched—the new stainless steel refrigerator calling attention to the avocado porcelain stove that belonged to another era, the dishwasher that rattled so loudly I would run it only during the day, while I was at work. Looking around now, I realized that Brendan was right: what had first attracted me to the place was the bones. I had added the flesh myself, over time.

I'd never lived anywhere longer. Even my childhood home had held me for only 18 years, before I ran off to college. I'd chosen Stanford less for its academics than its proximity to San Francisco, a city that somehow called to me even before I'd set eyes on it. When the plane touched down and I'd gotten my first glimpse of the Bay (in my naïveté I mistook it for the Pacific Ocean), I'd wept. When school was over, there was no question of returning to Minnesota. I was already home.

I'd had a few apartments in my first years in town—the Mission, Diamond Heights, the Lower Haight, circling the Castro until I'd finally found the right spot. And now, 20 years filled this place, 20 years of people and life. They were evident everywhere. Barry had helped me pick out the bed—and break it in. Mario, who was spending a summer in the city between semesters at art school in Milan, painted a portrait of me that still hung beside the bookcase. I could barely recognize myself in the image now—35, with a full head of hair and a slim build. The credenza held an eclectic assortment of souvenirs from various trips—a cheap vase from Mexico, a tiny replica of the Colosseum, a collection of stones from a beach in Maui.

They were just mementos, I thought, insignificant in themselves. In the end, it didn't seem to matter what I had accumulated, or accomplished. I'd lost sleep over that for too long—the missteps, the missed opportunities, the things I'd left undone, the things I should never have attempted. I'd lost sleep, but in the end, sleep is all you have.

Looking back over it all, there was still nothing better than those Monday nights when Oscar would come over to my place in the Mission for our weekly ritual before the TV: Oscar, a blender of margaritas, and Heather Locklear wreaking havoc at Melrose Place.

I was older than I'd ever expected to be; maybe that was part of it. When I'd first moved to San Francisco, there were no 50-year-olds in the Castro. The 50-year-olds were already dead.

I craved a glass of brandy, but decided against it. I'd had enough to drink for one night. Better to just curl into bed with a book and put the whole evening behind me. I went into the bathroom and brushed my teeth.

I had a love/hate relationship with the bathroom, despite the retiling that had obsessed me a few years ago. The white fixtures were impossible to keep clean. I wiped down the sink. Behind the faucet, the sponge caught a few short black hairs. They still turned up now and then—hiding behind the fixtures, embedded in every sponge. The cat had been dead for months, but her hair, her hair was everywhere.

Gazing in the mirror, I rubbed a hand over my buzz-cut. Keeping it this short ironically helped make its encroaching thinness less glaring. What was it about men's hair, I wondered. It disappears from where you want it and grows in abundance where it never used to be—clogging your nostrils, curling out of your ears, turning to steel wool in your eyebrows. Too much and not enough at the same time.

I'd just crawled into bed when I heard the voices. It hadn't been around for weeks, the straining a cappella of the boys on the street. They would march through the neighborhood now and then, a small group of black teenagers, singing pop songs—Whitney, Beyoncé, Mariah. I'd watched them from the window once or twice. They couldn't have been more than 16 years old—just kids, playing, trying to outdo one another with the high notes. There were no black families in the neighborhood, hardly any families at all, so clearly they'd come from elsewhere—Bayview, perhaps, the Western Addition, places where it wasn't so safe to call each other "girlfriend" and sing love songs. Oscar, visiting one evening a few months ago, had christened them the Dreamgirls. Sitting in the window, he sang softly along with them in a lovely, whispered falsetto.

They sang tonight in delicious harmony. I laid my book down on the bed, leaned back against the headboard, and closed my eyes. I let the music swim around me. I wanted to hear every note.

CHAPTER 3
BRUNCH AT TIFFANY'S

I never had an answer when people asked what I wanted to be when I grew up. Even as a kid, I sensed the absurdity of the question. Even then I knew that work was something you *did*, not something you *were*.

So while my classmates spent their college years planning careers—taking classes that would appeal to recruiters from Chase and IBM; building résumés to get them into professional school—I majored in English because I liked reading novels, because I felt they taught me something about life. I naively bought into the notion, on its last legs in those days, that college was meant to develop your critical thinking skills, not just teach you a trade. I wanted to be an educated person who was able to analyze the world before me and manage a conversation at cocktail parties. I didn't really care what I did for a living as long as it supported the living.

After years of jumping from one dysfunctional corporation to another, I finally landed at the bookstore, and the searching stopped. I'd already amassed enough money to buy the condo and create a nest egg, so I could manage the pay cut.

At the store, I felt like I was back in college, surrounded by books. Home. Here, surrounded by shelves and shelves of literature and history and even self-help, I could forget, at least from time to time, the corporate behemoths that lay behind it all. In this narrow space, I could pretend that the world still cared about the life of the mind. In my little corner of the world, at least, that could still be true.

Cassandra was rearranging books at one of the display tables when I got back from a late lunch.

"Hi," I said in my jauntiest manager voice. I still struggled to find the right balance between approachable and authoritative. Every employee I'd ever had seemed to require something different. Cassandra had a bit of a chip on her shoulder, so I erred on the approachable side with her.

"Hey," she replied, still looking down at the books. She had a stack of Gertrude Steins leaning into the latest Allan Hollinghurst, who was squeezed on the other side by Zora Neale Hurston. Cassandra liked to arrange the displays around a theme—lesbian poetry, lesbian erotica, lesbian fiction, or, when she was feeling particularly angry, feminist theory. I was afraid to ask how Hollinghurst fit into today's selection.

I gazed toward the back, looking for customers. "Pretty quiet now, I see."

"Yep." Cassandra always dressed in black from head to toe. The only splash of color was her lavender hair.

"Oh well, it's still early."

She turned at that and gave me the look. Cassandra had several expressions, but only one constituted "the look." The look was reserved for sarcastic irony. Her lips curled into a wavy pattern (I marveled at her ability to move each side in a different direction) and her eyes opened wide, sending a mirroring wave through her forehead. She gazed up at me through her bangs, the fluorescent light glinting off her nosering. I imagined a caption running beneath her face—*Really?* and *Gimme a break* were the top contenders. When it wasn't *Jesus, Dad, you're embarrassing me.*

Cassandra moved on to the next table and straightened out an assortment of cocktail napkins. My favorite featured an image of Rosalind Russell sipping a martini above the tagline *Auntie needs fuel.* I typically had to dig that one out of the bottom of the pile; Cassandra kept burying it.

In keeping with America's declining literacy rate, we had started carrying a variety of trinkets ages ago—penguin-headed swizzle sticks, Mitch McConnell voodoo dolls, and candles so fragrant I had to stand back if anyone punctured the cellophane. A while back, we had found the perfect solution in porn. The entire southwest corner of the store had been full of DVDs, bare chests and leather vests for days. But once everyone started streaming porn—or making it themselves—we had to look elsewhere for moneymakers. Now, in addition to the generic tchotchkes, we carried San Francisco memorabilia—refrigerator magnets, Ghirardelli chocolate, tiny cable cars. It was only a matter of time, I thought, before books occupied the smallest table in the store.

Joel was hovering by the gift cards in the back, rearranging. By the end of the day, the display was usually a mess, customers pulling a card out of one slot and dropping it carelessly into another.

"Hey, boss," he said, as was his habit. He must have thought it was a term of endearment.

I always found myself being especially gentle with Joel. I had the impression that anything less would scare him to death. He was in his early twenties and had arrived in town only a few months ago, from somewhere in the South—Fayetteville, Arkansas or Fayetteville, North Carolina, I couldn't remember which. Whatever it was, it had clearly done a number on a sensitive gay boy.

In my office, I checked my cell phone. Still no reply to my text to Damien, or my voicemail. He should have been back for a couple of days now, but he'd always been notoriously slow to respond to messages. Damien preferred to do things on his own schedule. Pushing would get me nowhere.

I decided to call Angela to let her know I might be on jury duty soon.

"What's up, Craig?" She sounded more clipped than usual. I imagined her juggling papers poolside, or spooling through her stock portfolio on a laptop. "What can I do for you?"

It was best just to jump in. Angela didn't like wasting time. "I have to report to jury duty," I told her.

"What? You can't get out of it?"

"We'll see," I said. "Jury selection is on Thursday. I'll let you know right away. I'm sure the staff will be fine minding the store."

There was a long pause. I could hear her breathing, tapping her fingernails against a table. "Angela?" I asked cautiously.

She sighed so loudly I was startled and pulled the phone away from my ear for a moment. "Listen," she said, "I have some news of my own."

Angela always had news, but it usually took her a while to articulate it, so I began scrolling through emails, not quite following what she was saying.

The most recent email was from an unfamiliar address, someone named Hardesty. Tiffany Hardesty. A realtor.

The word echoed in my ear. "Her name is Tiffany," Angela was saying.

"Tiffany Hardesty."

"Yes. Do you know her?"

"No. I just got an email from her. She wants to come to the store today."

"Well, isn't she on the ball."

"What's going on, Angela?"

"I thought I'd told you about this." Now I heard a tinkling through the phone, like a glass being set down.

"About what?"

"Well," she said, "it must have slipped my mind. But you know how hot real estate is in San Francisco these days, and it's no surprise that the store hasn't been doing particularly well. No reflection on you, of course, Craig. You've been wonderful. But people just don't read anymore. How many bookstores are left in that town, anyway? Meanwhile, other businesses are just clamoring for space, and our store is in a prime location."

"You're selling the store?"

She paused, no doubt to catch her breath after that monologue. "We'll see," she said. "It depends on what kind of interest there is. But Tiffany's optimistic."

I leaned back and took in the room—books on every surface, in towers on the floor.

"Don't worry, Craig. Nothing will happen quickly, you know how these things go."

Exactly. Back in the old days, I'd been through enough corporate takeovers to know how these things went—painfully, cruelly, inefficiently. That was why I'd left that world.

"What should I tell the staff when they see her here?"

She practically shrieked. "Nothing! The last thing we want is for people to panic at this stage. Tell them we're considering some renovations, maybe. You can come up with something."

"I don't want to lie, Angela."

"Oh, you don't have to *lie*, Craig. Just don't tell them what they don't need to know, until they need to know it."

I responded to Tiffany's invitation and made a mental note to be standing in the doorway at the appointed hour, lest she find Cassandra first. It wasn't as if I hadn't seen it coming, but Angela had never expressed disappointment about the performance of the store. She'd always seemed content to plod along, as long as we broke even or made a slight profit. She left me to my own devices almost entirely, particularly since moving to Palm Springs. In the end, I didn't think it was the store's performance that bothered her. She was moved more by the ridiculous state of San Francisco's real estate market. She was sitting on a gold mine, and it was unfortunately covered in books.

I decided to get my mind off things by jumping into work. If I did end up on jury duty, my in-box would be overflowing before long. I might as well leave it as empty as possible in anticipation.

On my first message, my fingers kept tripping into typos. Clearly, I thought, the prospect of Tiffany (I was picturing a pale blue dress with a white bow) was making me nervous. I seldom look at the keyboard—the way, I suppose, a runner doesn't look at his feet. I'd learned to type in high school, when it was a class that only kids on the college track or wannabe secretaries took. Everyone else thought it was a waste of time. And now kids were typing in nursery school, and doing it all with their thumbs by 13, proving that evolution can indeed work backward.

I had barely made a dent in the in box when I decided the gods were telling me I should take a break. I still had an hour before Tiffany's arrival, so I decided to run across the street for a latte.

It was a typical San Francisco spring day—the sunny side of the street warm and inviting, the shady side like a Minnesota winter. Fortunately, we were in the sun for now. The store felt bright and open, bathed in an almost yellow light. I walked slowly through the room, tidying up the displays here and there, running my hand across the spines of books on the shelves to create a more uniform appearance.

I had loved bookstores and libraries since I was a kid, overwhelmed by the sheer number of volumes, an entire world of possibility. In college, I preferred to study in the silent carrels of the library, with only fluorescent lighting and the musty odor of old pages to define the space. I would willfully get lost in the bowels of the building, making my way through the maze, but with no idea what the endpoint looked like. And in bookstores I took a similar approach. Even if I had come on a mission to find a particular volume, I wouldn't leave until I'd perused every section of the store, hoping for the unexpected find that would make the trip worthwhile. The best discoveries, I'd always believed, are the ones you make on your own. There are no algorithms for exploration.

It was still possible to browse in some bookstores, the ones that weren't overloaded with children's books passing as adult fare and the usual illiterate best-sellers. In laying out this store, I'd tried to provide rewards for browsers—deserving but otherwise unheralded titles on full display beside the latest empty-headed vampire love story. I sprinkled them throughout the store, assuming that putting all the good stuff together would serve no purpose other than to create a literary ghetto that people would ignore. Instead, while pondering various romance titles, the shopper might stumble upon a classic and be introduced to a new perspective on life. Nothing pleased me more than ringing up a customer and finding John Fowles in among the bodice-rippers.

It wasn't always so easy, of course. In the past, a customer had once returned to announce that my recommendation of *Moby-Dick* had gone unappreciated. "I gave up halfway through," the man said. "Three hundred pages and still no whale! He's the title character—what's he waiting for?"

Outside, I jogged across the street toward the café. A motley group of hipsters were lined up on Castro, wool hats against the sun, earbuds shutting out the world. In the old days—before my time, but I'd been told—all those corners, indeed most of the street, would have been occupied by men in jeans and cut-offs, flanneled or shirtless, leaning against walls, watching each other, waiting.

A Bauer bus pulled up, "Mtn View" emblazoned in tiny yellow lights above the driver's head, and the hipsters marched listlessly, silently on board. Among the many things millennials had disrupted was the standard work schedule. Still clutching to adolescent habits, they stayed up late and slept even later. By the time this bus arrived at its destination, they could head straight to the office food hall and have their pick of avocados and M&Ms.

I would settle for strong coffee and a chocolate croissant. I settled at one of the tables the café had set out on the sidewalk. As usual, I had to fight with the San Francisco wind to keep my napkin from blowing away and, in a serious gust, taking the pastry with it, but it was worth a little diligence to be able to watch the show.

I was constantly amazed by the amount of activity in this neighborhood between rush hours. The cafés were always full of people, commandeering tables as makeshift desks, laptops open before them, smartphones neatly at their side. There was barely room for the coffee. I preferred it out here, where the sun cast too much glare to make screens very useful.

You could work anywhere these days. It was a blessing and a curse. At least I was spared heading into an office—god forbid, one of those open workplans that had recently become so popular, probably because they reminded everyone of a nursery school, with designated play and nap areas in every corner. But other people, it seemed, thrived on always being available, never having to stop sharing their brilliance, usually as loudly as possible. They carried weighty expressions worthy of an oncologist or prime minister, as if the placement of a logo on a website or the precise phrasing of a code would save lives and determine the fate of the free world.

I bit into the croissant and found the rough edge of a single slab of chocolate—semihard, unmelted, as though it had been slipped into the cooked pastry after the fact. Still, it was good enough. In the San Francisco sunshine, anything was good enough.

My phone buzzed as I was washing the bite down with the latte. I looked around. A couple of tables over, a pair of tourists were poring over a map, too engaged to be disturbed by a stranger's conversation. I pulled the phone out of my pocket, Oscar's photo on the screen. I remembered taking the picture in Sonoma. He was holding a champagne flute, toasting the camera, a field of grape vines in the distance.

"Hey, what are you doing tomorrow night?" Getting right to the point, as usual.

With most people I might have paused, pretending to look for my calendar. "Nothing," I said. "What's up?"

"One of my colleagues just gave me opera tickets. She had some sort of family crisis and can't go."

"What about Rafe?"

Oscar laughed. "I have a hard enough time getting Rafe to watch *Carmen*. There's no way he's going to sit through five hours of *Parsifal*."

"*Parsifal*?"

"Not you, too."

"No," I said, "it's one of my favorites."

"Depressing as hell," Oscar added, "but fabulous. It starts at 6:00, so no time for dinner. We'll have to grab a nosh at the opera house during intermission. See you in front at 5:30?"

"Sure."

I was impressed that he could leave the office that early. Oscar was a hard worker, but that seemed to come with the territory. When we met, he was working at a bank and couldn't stand it. Law school was his ticket out. He needed the direction of a career with a clearer trajectory. He ended up loving the work, which was fortunate. I'd known too many people in college who had gone to law school simply because they didn't have any specific passion, and the law seemed like a sure path to financial success. But the more money they made, the less happy they seemed.

"How are you doing?" he asked, his voice betraying distraction.

"Fine," I said. "Some shit at work, but I can tell you all about it later."

"Great." He paused. "I have to prepare for a deposition now, so see you tomorrow night." Oscar didn't waste time at either end of a conversation. His hours were billable.

■

Tiffany was everything her name implied, plus 30 years. I spotted her when she was still half a block away, long blond ponytail bouncing from side to side as she made her way toward me. When she got closer, the tightness of her pale skin became clearer. I'd never understood plastic surgery. It didn't seem to make people look younger—just old with fewer wrinkles. Age, I thought, revealed itself in too many ways to succumb to anything we tried to do to hide it. It wasn't just in the skin, but the eyes, the hairline, the neck, the shoulders, the way we carried ourselves. It was experience as well as decay, and there was no point in pretending you could have one without the other.

I positioned myself just ahead of the store, in the center of the sidewalk. I might as well have been wearing a sandwich board.

"Craig?" she asked.

"Hi."

She stretched out a stiff arm, bare skin under a yellow cap sleeve, and French-manicured fingers shook my hand.

I smiled. "I thought we'd meet out here first. The staff doesn't know anything about this."

"Of course." She scrunched her pert nose, the smile turning into a sympathetic pout.

I gave her a little background on the store as she assessed the sidewalk traffic, and then we moved inside. I kept close to her, whispering casually, to give the staff the impression that she was just a friend I was showing around. We stopped in the middle of the store and she made a subtle pirouette to check out the space. I saw her mentally measuring the ceiling, every nook and cranny in the place.

"How long have you been here?" she asked, gazing toward the front, where Joel was ringing up a sale.

"Me? Seven years now." I turned away for a reconnoiter of my own.

"Do you like it?"

I gazed up at the posters that lined the wall space just above the bookcases—oversized portraits of writers, from Austen to Roth. "Yes," I said. "I love it."

Tiffany crossed her arms and moved toward the back.

We finished our meeting in the office, where she barraged me with questions about foot traffic, the neighbors, maintenance issues. I was sure Angela had filled her in and provided all the necessary paperwork, but I was the one who knew the space best. I lived in it on a daily basis.

Finally satisfied, she shook my hand again. "I'll be in touch," she said.

"Do you think it will take long?"

She smiled and shook her head. "Oh no. There's pent-up demand. This place is going to sell like hotcakes."

I'd never been particularly fond of hotcakes. I silently led her back through the store and watched until she vanished around the corner onto Castro.

CHAPTER 4
THE INNOCENT FOOL

Our seats for the opera couldn't have been much better—center orchestra, just a few rows back from the pit. We were close enough to see the singers' facial expressions, which in my usual dress circle seats had to be left to the imagination.

Of course, hardcore opera buffs always claimed that the sound was better the higher you sat: Physics had decreed a trade-off between sight and sound. And since opera, for them, was all about the music, they gladly climbed as high as possible. Having sat in the rear balcony more than once myself, the stuffy confines where oxygen was in even shorter supply than legroom, I always thought they were exaggerating to hide the fact that their real concern was price.

Oscar had arrived with only a few minutes to spare. Standing outside the main entrance, I saw him jogging up from Market Street. He met me on the steps, a bit out of breath, forehead glistening. Apologizing, he dug into his pocket for the tickets and pressed his hand against my back to lead me through the doors.

We didn't have time to chat before the orchestra settled in and the performance got under way. Within minutes, though, I could see the transformation on his face. He looked increasingly relaxed, which I imagined had as much to do with the languorous sweep of Wagner as it did with the chance to sit down and cool off.

By the first intermission, I was telling myself I would never sit anywhere else in this theater. We grabbed ready-made sandwiches at the bar and made our way upstairs to the balcony overlooking Van Ness.

"Amazing, isn't it?" he said.

"The opera?"

"No," he replied. "That." He gestured across the street. City Hall was lit up beautifully tonight, as always—its gray walls almost silver against the deep blue of the sky. In June, it would vibrate in rainbow colors for Pride. "You have to love this place." I studied his profile, the high cheekbones that had always given his face a regal quality, the determination of his gaze.

After a contemplative moment, he turned his back to the street and looked at the people filtering through the balcony. A muscular guy stood by the door, thick arms straining against his sport coat. He was talking to a woman in jeans and a polo shirt. Another thing I loved about San Francisco: you could seldom be over- or underdressed.

"So," I said with a sigh, "we haven't had a chance to talk about John's news."

"What is that boy thinking?"

"Which one?"

He shook his head. "I'm not concerned about Wayne. He can take care of himself. As soon as he figures out who he is. But John. This is not going to go well for him."

"Maybe he'll be one of the lucky ones. Beatty and Bening. Woody and Soon-Yi."

"It's not just the age," Oscar said. "They're so different. And I'm not sure John even realizes it. I mean, do you honestly get the slightest vibe from Wayne that he's relationship material?"

"To be honest, I think John's the real wild card. He's so tentative about it. When you propose to someone, you should know the answer. This isn't the fifties."

Oscar shook his head. "I don't think John's ever felt comfortable being single. He takes life too seriously. And believe me, nothing is more serious than marriage. So the older he gets, the more desperate he becomes. Maybe he thinks Wayne is his last chance."

"That's no reason."

"Well," he said, "a man has to make his own mistakes."

"Seriously? You think we should just say nothing?"

Oscar squinted. This was getting serious. "Nobody wants to hear someone rain on their parade."

"But we're good friends."

"All the more reason."

∎

Inside, I fell back into the music, the luscious melodies that seemed to embrace the hall. The plot, what little there was of it, was carried less by the singers than the orchestra. *Parsifal* had always cast a kind of spell on me. It painted the world as bleak and hopeful at the same time. It did for me what religion was supposed to do and never had. It healed.

When the curtain finally came down, we lingered in our seats for a moment. There was a distinct hush—inevitable with *Parsifal*—before the audience burst into thunderous applause.

It was late, most people rushing in every direction—trains to the south, parking lot to the west. Oscar pulled away from the crowd. "Drinks?" he asked, flicking his head toward Hayes Valley.

"Of course."

We ended up sitting at a bar on Gough, nursing Sazeracs.

"Jury selection tomorrow," I said. "Think I'll get picked?"

Oscar smiled. "You really want to?"

"I'm looking forward to it," I said. "Don't ruin the glamour for me."

"Oh," he said with a laugh. "Right, the glamour!" He lifted his glass. "So have you told Damien about it—jury duty?"

"I left him a voicemail."

"A voicemail? Haven't you talked to him since his trip?"

I had both hands around my drink, watching the oversized ball of ice swirl like a planet on its axis. "We've been playing phone tag."

He nodded.

"You don't like Damien, do you?" I asked.

A nervous smile now played on Oscar's lips. His eyes were inexpressive, but behind them, I knew, he was thinking of what to say.

When he finally spoke, his voice was soft and the words came out carefully, in a deliberate cadence, like a poet reading his work aloud. "Craig, it doesn't matter what I think. If John is in love with Wayne, if you're in love with Damien, that should be all that matters."

"What a cop-out." I leaned back and smiled. I had to admire his slyness.

Behind him, the bartender clamped a strainer over the shaker and, arm raised high, poured a pale pink concoction into a chilled martini glass. He carried the glass to the far end of the bar and settled it before a blond woman.

Oscar caught my eye as I glanced away from the bartender.

[51]

He swirled his glass.

"So tell me, then: how *are* things with Damien?"

"Are you cross-examining me?"

"No," he said. "I would charge for that. I'm just psychoanalyzing you."

I drank.

"Is the sex still good?"

"That's what it always comes down to, is it? Even at our age?"

He smiled lasciviously. "Yes," he said. "It is."

"It's fine. I mean, he's very understanding."

"Understanding? About what?"

I gazed down at the drink again, the nearly black bartop distorted by the glass. "I'm not as young as I used to be."

"Oh. You can't get it up?"

I looked up quickly. "No, that's perfectly fine. I just have trouble coming."

"Oh honey, we all do, now and then."

I shrugged. "The doctor says it's a normal side effect of my anxiety medication. It takes a while."

"Is this a problem when you're with Damien?"

"No, it doesn't bother him at all." I took another sip. I got a sudden smattering of absinthe, the licorice flavor coating my tongue. "I'm not sure he even notices."

"Aha."

"Aha what?"

"How can he not notice?"

"I don't know," I said. "He's distracted. It's sex."

Oscar nodded again, his eyes never breaking their hold on mine. "What are you getting?" he asked at last.

"Getting?"

"From the relationship."

I gave him a blank stare, or tried to, but instinctively my eyes drifted away.

"Look," he said, "I don't mean to criticize. I barely know the guy. I've met him what, twice?"

"It takes a lot to get Damien to cross the bridge."

Oscar laughed. "That's why I've always advocated dating in your own area code."

Of course, there was more to it than that. "I don't think he feels comfortable with our crowd."

"Comfortable? You mean he doesn't *like* us."

I turned back from the window, prepared to defend Damien, but caught myself, lips closing around an inaudible *No*. "He has a hard time relating. Damien's never been into this whole world."

"And what world would that be?" Oscar's cheeks were carved with what seemed like extra dimples.

"He's a little more … restrained than most of my friends."

Oscar laughed. "You know, for a literary guy, you're being awfully imprecise with your language. How many euphemisms can you put into one conversation?"

"What do you mean?"

"Restrained? Or uptight?"

I smiled, if only to cut the tension. "He would say restrained."

"But you're the one who's doing the talking."

"Okay. Uptight. He has a hard time with the stuff we talk about."

"Like what?"

"Art, literature. He's a tech guy; he's not too well versed in all that. And he feels very self-conscious, worried he's going to say the wrong thing."

"So he's afraid he'll disparage Sondheim and we'll jump him in an alley?"

"Something like that. He's just not into all the trappings of gay culture."

"Ah." Oscar's eyes opened wide as he threw his head back. "Now it all makes sense."

"What?"

"He's a homosexual."

I laughed. "Duh."

"And we're gay."

"What do you mean?"

"*Gay* is a cultural thing. *Homosexual* is just biology. It's just about who he's attracted to, who he fucks. *Gay* is much bigger." He flicked his hands, palms out to take in the room.

"So what's wrong with that? There are all kinds of gay people. There are all kinds of straight people."

"Sure. To each his own. But this—" he swiveled his head back and forth for a wide view of the bar, the scattered couples fresh from the opera, as many gays as straights—"is *your* kind."

I had a sudden image of Damien the first time we'd gone out together in the Castro, stopping in his tracks at the corner to give wide berth to a drag queen. Towering over us—seemingly half her height derived from high heels and a bright yellow bouffant—she did command attention, but Damien's expression was less appreciative than terrified.

"We complement each other," I said. "The last thing I want to date is a mirror."

"Yeah. Black and white complement each other, too. But without shades of gray you don't have much of a picture." He played with his cherry stem. "Do you have many shades of gray, Craig?"

I sighed. "I have nothing *but* shades of gray."

"You're too hard on yourself."

"It's one of my charms."

His eyes grew abruptly sober. "No," he said, "it isn't."

CHAPTER 5

CIVIC DUTY

There are three things people are most anxious to avoid: death, taxes, and jury duty. But jury duty is the only one you actually stand a chance of escaping.

In San Francisco, it seemed, everyone got called annually, like clockwork. It was as predictable as the Folsom Street Fair, or the closing of half the restaurants that opened in a year. Shortly before my most recent summons, a friend posted on Facebook that he had been called and was seeking advice on how to get out of it. *Tell them you think everyone's guilty,* someone suggested. *Tell them you're racist,* said another.

Tucked between Civic Center and the Tenderloin, the federal building was completely unfamiliar territory. I had probably passed it numerous times, but it had never registered. Its stone and glass dull in the morning mist, the building was suitably imposing. I passed a line of heavy posts that separated the sloped entrance from the sidewalk and wondered if they had been erected as a defensive measure after 9/11 or Oklahoma City.

The cavernous lobby, no less cold and impersonal than the bland exterior, completed the Kafkaesque effect. I had the feeling I was about to enter a space I might never get out of. Passing through the security check, I had a sudden panic that I'd forgotten my boarding pass.

The guard pointed me toward the elevators and I made my way to the jury room, where color finally entered the picture. Although the rows and rows of chairs gave the space the look of an oversized train station waiting room, there was at least a human scale to the surroundings—carpet to absorb the sound, a lower ceiling, and wooden furniture. The room was already crowded with dozens of people, some looking with vague interest at their phones, others staring blankly into space.

After a brief wait, my group of about 50 people was summoned to the courtroom. Wood paneling framed slabs of granite on the walls. We made our way onto the benches just inside the door in a hush. Squeezed between a gruff-looking middle-aged woman and a young guy with green hair, I gazed around the room. The lawyers' tables were positioned on the right side of the room, just beyond the railing that bisected the space. At the far one, closer to the wall, two well-dressed men flanked a young man in shirtsleeves with a dark ponytail who seemed as uncomfortable in his clothes as he was in the room. Directly behind him, bordering a narrow door in the middle of the wall, sat two burly men who must have been security guards, though like everyone else, they were in suits rather than scary uniforms.

The judge's desk was on a rise toward the back of the room. She peered down at us through wire-rimmed glasses as we settled in, a practiced inscrutability in her gaze. Just before her desk, on a level with the lawyers, the court stenographer sat behind a desk of her own with a computer screen before her and a pile of papers on one side.

"Thank you all for being here," the judge said at last. Her voice was softer than I expected, almost maternal. "I'm Judge Reilly. Just to give you some context, you are here for a criminal trial that is scheduled to begin next week. We will be in session for 4 hours a day, from 9 to 1. All told, the trial is expected to take two weeks. I'm confident that we will have it all wrapped up in that time. We will begin today by identifying any hardships you may have that would preclude you from serving at this time. Now, does anyone have any concerns about your ability to serve? If so, please line up before the bench."

Almost instantly the line began to form. The gate in the railing squeaked noisily as each person passed through. Impatient, none of them held the gate open for the next person, forcing us all to endure the noise repeatedly, echoing through the chamber.

By the time everyone was standing, the line snaked all the way back into the gallery.

The judge addressed the first person in line. "What is your name, madam?"

The woman whispered inaudibly.

"Speak up, please."

"Miriam Wilson," she said.

"Very well, Ms. Wilson, what is your hardship?"

"I can't serve, Your Honor," she said. "I take care of my elderly mother."

"Who's taking care of her now?"

"I am." I couldn't see her face, but at that moment her back arched, as if height would make her sound more credible.

The judge smiled. "I mean who's with her at the moment, while you're here talking to me?"

"Oh," the woman sputtered, and her shoulders gave way a little. "My sister."

"And does she often take care of your mother?"

"Yes," the woman said, "but in the afternoons."

"Does she work in the morning?"

"In the morning?" Her tone grew shrill.

"Yes. Does she have a job or any other obligation?"

"Not that I know of."

"So you take care of your mother in the morning, and she takes care of her in the afternoon."

"Yes."

"Well, what if you switched shifts?"

"Switched shifts?" As the woman twisted her shoulders, the oversized flowers on her print blouse danced jerkily.

"Yes," pursued the judge. "While the trial is proceeding, could she take the morning shift?"

"But I have the morning shift."

The judge scowled and took a deep breath. "Ms. Wilson, as I stated, the court day will end at 1:00. If your sister takes care of your mother in the morning, you will be available to take her shift in the afternoon. Is there any reason you could not do that?"

The woman paused. "Oh," she said finally, "I would have to ask her."

It went on like this for several minutes, one person after another approaching the bench with a sob story, most of which were as poorly thought out as Miriam Wilson's. Several people claimed they often had to travel on business, but they couldn't point to any travel plans in the next month. Others, like Ms. Wilson, simply couldn't comprehend that court would be in session only in the morning.

Whenever the judge showed impatience with a juror's excuse, one or two other people would pull out of the line. Original excuses were apparently in short supply.

"I'm happy to serve, Your Honor," said a middle-aged woman in a shapeless dress, "but it's a bad time for me."

"I take this duty seriously," said a tall young man in glasses, "and I wish I could serve. I'll be happy to serve the next time."

They blended together after a while, the people and the excuses, and a theme emerged. Jury duty, I began to see, was something people dreaded because they were supposed to. It was spinach for adults. Few people questioned their disinclination, assuming the prospect of jury duty was objectively distasteful. But at the moment, I was enjoying it immensely. Watching these people squirm was the most fun I'd had in weeks.

The judge called a 20-minute recess, and people dashed out like panicked travelers in search of a lifeboat. I decided to linger in the hallway and check messages on my phone. Just an ad for the touring company of the latest jukebox musical and a request to renew my ACLU membership. After the election, I'd joined every progressive organization I could find, but the constant emails became as exhausting in their way as the monster they were all trying to fight. I put the phone away and dug a Sudoku book out of my bag.

I had a method for Sudoku, going through each square one number at a time, marking the spots where there were limited options for each. I exhausted the obvious possibilities quickly and now tapped my pen against the page, hoping for inspiration.

I had to hold the book nearly at waist level to make out the puzzle clearly. I'd noticed the change in my vision only recently, though I realized it had come on gradually, as books and computer screens moved farther and farther from my eyes over time.

"I think I'd try a four over there."

I turned toward the voice: a thirtysomething woman with chunky glasses and a mane of strawberry blond hair. "Sorry," she said, "I get nosy when I'm bored."

I laughed. "No problem," I said. I looked back at the puzzle, pondering.

"Aren't you going to do it?"

"Do what?" I turned back, withholding my annoyance.

"The four. Right there in the first cell."

I studied the square, the lines and numbers suddenly just a jumble before my eyes. "But that could be anything."

"Yeah, but I think it's a four." She smiled mischievously.

I hesitated, still gazing at the puzzle. "The thing is," I said at last, "I don't like to guess. I like to be sure of each move. If you make one mistake, it can screw everything up pretty quickly."

She chuckled. When I looked back, she was shaking her head. "You're never going to get through it without guessing at least once," she said. "Take a leap of faith."

I folded the book, using my pen as a marker. "It's hard to concentrate around here," I said.

"I know what you mean." She gave a loud exhale and arched her back. "Can you believe we've been here for two hours and we still don't even know what the trial is about?"

"You think that would help?" I asked with a smile. "Maybe if they told us it was a nice juicy murder, people would be less inclined to get out of it."

Her sharp laugh echoed loudly in the cavernous space, and she quickly clamped her mouth, eyes wide with embarrassment. "I certainly would."

"So I take it you've never done this before."

"No," she said, "but it's fascinating already, even though nothing's happened."

"I think it's fascinating *because* nothing's happened. There's a surreal quality to it all."

"So what do you think?" she whispered. "The defendant looks pretty sleazy to me."

"I don't think we're supposed to talk about that."

"No, I guess not." She leaned against the wall, lips pursed.

He did look sleazy, I thought. There was a deadness in his eyes, and he was jittery, as though allergic to the collared shirt his lawyers no doubt had forced him into. I remembered the friend who had said most arrested people are guilty. If not of the crime they're charged with, then certainly something else. Al Capone went to prison for tax evasion, after all.

The bailiff came out to call us, and everyone filtered back into the courtroom. As the judge proceeded to read a series of names, people began to shift anxiously in their seats.

Finally, she paused and looked out over the top of her glasses. "If I have called your name, you are excused. Thank you for your service. Please check in with the bailiff on your way out."

A couple of dozen people rose from the benches and scurried toward the door, some with alacrity, others feigning dutiful disappointment.

When they were gone, the room seemed even larger, and an ominous air took over. It was about to get real. I glanced toward the far wall and spotted the Sudoku lady. She arched her eyebrows, apparently open for adventure.

"All right," the judge said. "Now that it's just us." She paused for effect and the lawyers dutifully chuckled. The joke seemed to settle the nerves of the potential jurors, most of whom laughed along. "Let me tell you a bit about the case you have been asked to help us with. The defendant, Raul Vasquez, has been charged with possession of a firearm. Mr. Vasquez is a convicted felon. The reason for his felony conviction is irrelevant to this case and will not be discussed and should have no bearing on your deliberation. However, it is illegal for a convicted felon to be in possession of a firearm. Your responsibility is to determine whether he was indeed in possession of the gun in question. If you find beyond a reasonable doubt that he was, you will find him guilty."

She paused like a lecturer waiting for a point to sink in, and then introduced the attorneys, who stood and gazed in the jury's direction as the judge told us their names. The prosecutors gave us close-lipped smiles, the man bouncing a bit on his heels while the woman stood stock still, hands folded before her. The defense team might have been the leads in a buddy movie—one older and a bit overweight, the other young and spry, with a crown of curly brown hair falling over his forehead. He had an aquiline nose just the right size for his face and, though he tried to look serious, his restrained smile still revealed perfect rows of bright teeth. The defendant sat between them, looking down at the table, suggesting that the lawyers were as new to him as we were.

Introductions done, Judge Reilly paused and turned her attention to each of us in turn. Satisfied that we were all still conscious, she went on.

"As I call your names," she said, "please come through the gate and take a seat." She indicated the jury box and explained how the seats were numbered: odd in the back row, even in the front. We were to fill the seats in numerical order, with the spillover sitting on the bench inside the gate.

At this point, the order seemed completely random. The jury box quickly filled with 14 people. I was among the last to be called and therefore relegated to the bench, where I found a sheet of paper with a number and a brief questionnaire.

"You don't need to fill anything out," the judge said, "just be prepared to answer these questions orally as your number is called."

I glanced at the list of questions. All fairly innocuous, I thought: name, profession, marital status, hobbies. It was like speed dating.

Hobbies? I supposed that would be the place to say something about torturing small animals.

I was surprised by my own nervousness, suddenly wracking my brain for a response. I wanted my hobbies to sound interesting but benign. Completely in my own head, I barely paid attention to anyone else's response, so my turn came with surprise.

"Craig Amundsen," I said. "I'm a bookstore manager, unmarried." I looked down at the form and heard the unconvincing tone in my own voice. "Hobbies? I read a lot, and I subscribe to the opera."

There you go, I thought: interesting and slightly highfalutin. Me in a nutshell.

My number was 25. I glanced to my right and counted the remaining people. There were 32 of us in all. At this rate, even I wasn't likely to be picked. The last person in the row might as well get up and go home now.

"Thank you," the judge said. "Now I'm going to ask a series of questions. Please raise your hand if any of these apply to you."

Everyone sat up in their seats. We were entering the *Jeopardy* phase of the day.

"How many of you have served on a jury before?"

A smattering of hands went up. The judge called on each person one by one. "Please don't tell us any details about the case. Just state whether it was criminal or civil, and whether you reached a verdict."

We got through that question quickly, and the judge moved on. With her next question, I could tell we were getting somewhere.

"Do you think you'd have a problem giving the testimony of police officers the same level of credence as anyone else, not more or less?"

She dispensed with that one expeditiously, as well. "Now

then, onto our next question. The defendant has the right not to testify. Would you have trouble accepting his choice to take advantage of that right?"

A couple of people raised their hands and indicated that the defendant's silence would make them suspicious. The judge probed and got them to agree to let it go. I was beginning to see how she'd gotten this job: between the maternal tone and the deft logic, she was impossible to argue with.

"Could you give equal weight to direct and circumstantial evidence?" She had to explain this one. The jurors puzzled over it for some time, but only one raised her hand.

"Yes, Juror number 27."

"I think I would have a problem with that, Your Honor."

I looked to my right. I remembered this woman from our round robin with the demographic questions. She'd said she was a pastor.

"Please elaborate."

"I think I would have a hard time trusting circumstantial evidence. I trust eyewitness evidence more. Direct evidence."

All this time I'd been trying to avoid revealing facial expressions, but now I found myself squinting in disbelief. This woman was a pastor. She believed in God. And she would trust only direct evidence. This day could not get better.

Until it did.

"Do you or anyone close to you own or have experience with guns?"

If we were in Texas, that question would probably have kept us busy for the rest of the day, but in San Francisco it was less of a problem. A few people raised their hands. I sat quietly, arms folded, until, suddenly, I remembered Oscar telling me about the revolver he kept in an upstairs closet. My hand shot up with a start. I wasn't sure it counted. Oscar was just a friend, not a lover; and he lived all the way across town. But I didn't want to be accused of holding anything back. And, frankly, I was tired of just watching the show from a distance.

◘

When the questioning was over, the dynamics of the room shifted subtly. All the prospective jurors were asked to return to the main seating area, where we took seats randomly. While we sat silently and the judge looked down at her papers, the prosecution and defense tables became beehives of activity.

From my vantage point, I could make out a large piece of paper spread out on the prosecution table, with yellow post-it notes placed in rows upon it. The defense table was less visible, but they appeared to be using a similar technique. Clearly, each post-it represented a prospective juror. The lawyers whispered to each other as they shifted the notes around the page. They might have been arranging the seating chart at a wedding.

Now and then, one lawyer would write something down on a separate piece of paper and carry it over to the other table. The opposition lawyer would draw a line through a name, perhaps add a new one, and pass it back. This process continued for several minutes.

Finally, all the lawyers made their way to the bench and conferred with the judge. They passed her a single sheet of paper and returned to their seats.

"Thank you for your patience," the judge said, looking out at the jury pool. "We have settled on 12 jurors and 2 alternates. When I call your name, please take a seat in the jury box as directed by the bailiff."

Drum roll, please.

Judge Reilly called people out in numerical order, skipping over several. Number 2 was the first pick, then it jumped to number 8. The woman beside me now, who had been number 4, smiled briefly but then thought better of it, lest the order be just a coincidence.

There were 10 people in the box when the judge called Nancy, the Sudoku lady, number 19. I was 6 people away, with only 4 spots left. Suddenly, what I feared most was not being picked for the jury, but being picked as an alternate—having to sit through the trial only to be sent away before deliberations began. It would be too anticlimactic.

"Juror number 25." I felt like I was being called to the principal's office. The 12th spot, just in the nick of time.

I passed through the gate and around the front of the jury box to take my seat, the sixth one in the front row. The alternates were then called, one beside me and the other behind him.

The seats were even more comfortable than I'd imagined, with lots of legroom and space between. The alternate beside me was already settling in, prepared to sleep the trial away.

"Everyone else, thank you for your service. You are now dismissed."

And 18 people on the benches rose as one and quickly filed out. When the door closed again, it felt like a private club, and the gravity of the situation began to descend. As ludicrous as this case appeared—all these people here just because some guy had or had not held a gun—we were now embarking upon something together, something we had to take seriously, something that would greatly affect the life of a person, the man in the uncomfortable shirt who now looked out at us, assessing us all, the peers who had been called upon to judge him.

Turning toward the jury box, the judge smiled broadly. "Thank you all again for being here. If you haven't served on a jury before, I think you're going to find it a very rewarding experience."

Dismissed, we exited the box in single file, first one row and then the other. It reminded me of the end of a church service in childhood, when we would have to wait for the people in front to march down the aisle ahead of us.

The door at the end of the box led to a narrow hallway and directly across, a conference room, anchored by a long table and twelve chairs, far less comfortable-looking than the ones in the courtroom.

The bailiff stood before the table with a pile of lanyards. As we each approached, he checked our names off a list and handed us a lanyard, at the end of which dangled a blue card with the word *Juror* printed in large letters.

Well, I thought, at least it comes with jewelry.

CHAPTER 6
TRIGGER WARNING

People say I have a way with words. I can twist them, wrap them around one another, layer them like the buttery swirls of a croissant—grab just the right metaphor, the image that will most clearly illustrate my point. I can use words to explain, to persuade, to seduce. Once, whispering in a prospective lover's ear, I strung together a series of unrelated French words—not a sentence at all; I've never been able to think in French, so when I'm actually trying to speak it, the words come forth slowly, translated one by one from the English in my head—and watched all resistance spill from his body, bones surrendering to flesh.

I have a way with words, but words have their limits. Sometimes they just aren't enough. Words can make a mess of things, spill out too much of what's inside, like a dog slobbering over you when you walk through the door at the end of the day. But sometimes words are cats: they just won't come when you really need them.

My phone buzzed as soon as I got out of the subway, riding up the narrow escalator at Castro station, faint rainbow lights gleaming on the walls that bracketed the steps. Stuck behind a hipster in a shirt the color of money, I pulled out the phone as the stairs chugged slowly along. It was Damien.

"You little devil," I said. It was a joke that never got old.

"Hi. How was jury duty?"

The 24 bus was just pulling up as I got to the surface, and the person behind me made a run for it, jostling me in the process. I watched her go, heels lifting from the sandals that flapped against the sidewalk, canvas bags hanging from both shoulders on long straps that swayed around her like the scales of justice.

"It was fine," I said. I strolled slowly down the street and got past the bus while the hurried woman was still waiting in line at the curb. I hoped she would see me and realize that her rush had been unnecessary. But she was as oblivious to me now as she had been a minute ago. Whatever was at the other end of the bus was the only thing on her mind.

"They picked me."

"What? I never thought that would happen."

"Well, somebody has to get picked."

"I suppose so, but … well, it's like the lottery. You never think it's going to happen to someone you know."

"Kind of like getting hit by the proverbial bus," I added, gazing back at the frantic woman who was finally flashing her Fast-Pass in the driver's face.

"What is it?" he asked.

"The trial? I can't tell you."

"Oh, right."

"I'd have to kill you."

A young guy emerged from the Thai restaurant with a plastic bag in his hand, and I realized I was hungry. I tried to remember what was in the fridge that I could throw together. Once I made it home, I knew I would be in no mood to head back out to the grocery store. I would have to get creative with whatever was available. One night I had made a meal out of broccoli, marshmallow, and beans. My life sometimes resembled an episode of *Chopped*.

"What I can tell you is that the trial should take only a couple of weeks. I'm kind of looking forward to it. It might be interesting."

"Well, good luck."

"Thanks." I was at the corner. It was do-or-die time: turn right for Mollie Stone's and the certainty of dinner, or straight ahead and risk chaos on a plate. I opted for the store.

Already, in the comparative quiet of 18th, it was easier to talk. "How was your trip?" I asked.

"It was fine."

"Nothing eventful?"

"Not really." Sometimes Damien was about as communicative as a teenager.

The automatic doors hissed open. On my right was a large display of flowers, chockablock to the pastry counter. One-stop shopping for date night.

"So what would you like to do this weekend?"

As I grabbed a basket, there was a long pause, followed by a series of *ums*. "I've been thinking," he said at last.

"Always a good practice." I made my way into the produce aisle, avoiding the overpriced organic section in favor of pesticides.

He stuttered a laugh. "What if we just slowed it down a bit? I mean, it's only been a few months, and we're spending every weekend together."

"You don't want to see me?"

"No, it's not that. I just … it's a lot. I think we're going kind of fast, and … I'd like to slow down, have more time to myself."

This is where I ran out of words. I found a spot at the end of the aisle and froze in place, the empty basket dangling from my hands.

"I see," I said, though I didn't. It was just easier than actually processing the information and coming up with something to say. It was what I'd always done when surprised or disappointed: I shut down, assuming there was a proper response and I just needed time to figure out what it was. I let the silence ride for a minute, hoping something would come to me. I couldn't say the first thing that popped into my head, which in similar situations was something like, *What have I done?* That was where my mind went first—my own flaws, my own mistakes. More than once, I had actually gotten the dreaded response *It's not you, it's me,* or a variation thereof. So clearly, that line of questioning went nowhere. It was better to shut up.

My therapist had always used silence as a way to get me to talk. As soon as I took my seat across from him, he'd smile politely and stare at me for as long as it took until I became so uncomfortable that I started blurting out the most embarrassing things. For once, I took a page out of his book and controlled myself, if only to see how it felt from the other side of the conversation.

"Are you still there?" Damien asked at last.

A tall woman glided past me with a small dog on a leash. As she turned to inspect the organic lettuce, an Adam's apple bobbed above her necklace. "Yes, I'm here."

"I'm sorry," he murmured. I pictured him pacing the floor of his apartment, the phone pressed to his ear, searching for something to say. I was the verbal one in this relationship. Damien did not have a way with words.

He went on, a series of sentence fragments and blips. It was as if the cell reception were going in and out, except that I heard every word and verbal tic as clear as a high note from Natalie Dessay. "Well, I don't. ... It's not that I don't want ... I just need a little time. You know what I mean, right? Or maybe I'm just ...

I don't know."

I made a mental note to remember this conversation. One day, I knew, I would look back on it and laugh. I'd talk about it at parties. I'd use it as a case study when I became a speech therapist.

In the past, with previous boyfriends, I would push back against this moment. I'd crave a full dialogue about what was going on, I'd want to dredge up feelings and probe for explanations and misunderstandings, try to worm my way back in, twist reality to match my fantasy. I would vow to fix whatever he didn't like about me, whatever behavior might have precipitated his change of heart. When I was younger, I saw rejection as an indictment of my being. And I could never trust any of the excuses. Even now, I refused to believe that Damien just needed a break. It was safer to assume this was just his cowardly way of breaking up with me.

In the past, I would have humiliated myself for the chance of love, because every chance at love might be the last. An advantage of being older is that it's easier to just let things go—because you know that, in the end, everything does.

A man in a suit, broad-shouldered with a slight paunch, entered the aisle from the other end. He pondered the oranges for a moment before taking in the length of the display. His eyes widened as he dipped his head. I followed his gaze and spotted the dog—a hairy terrier small enough to be stuffed in a purse—its head angled upward, sniffing at the food while its owner, riffling through the kale, remained oblivious.

"I understand," I said to Damien, less to allay his discomfort than to make sure I didn't have to listen to any more of his inarticulate babbling. "Call me when you want."

"Um … okay." He wasn't expecting that. Another thing I'd learned: Sometimes they expect you to fight. Sometimes this whole "let's slow it down" conversation is simply a test. I couldn't tell now whether I had passed or failed.

"Have a nice weekend," I said.

"Yeah, you, too. And good luck with the trial."

"Thanks. Maybe I'll throw the book at him." Or someone, I thought.

He laughed nervously and we hung up.

In the meantime, the man had moved closer and was now openly staring at the animal, whose tongue darted out suddenly to spite him.

"Is that a service dog?" he asked.

The owner twisted her neck toward him with a practiced sneer. "Not that it's any of your business, but yes."

"Really?" he said. "What service does it perform?"

She pulled away, dropping a bunch of greens into her basket. "She does my taxes."

"I wish I'd met her in April," he said. "But last I heard, being a CPA doesn't get a dog into a grocery store."

She hardened her stance and met him eye to eye. "You're not from around here, are you?" she said, her voice deeper than before.

"*Not from around here?* What, are there different rules for hygiene and civic responsibility in this zip code? But just so you know, *Marjorie*, I moved to this neighborhood back when you were tearing apart Tonka trucks."

"Pig," she said and began to walk away.

"That's in aisle 5. By the way, I hope that dog's ass is organic, because it was licking the grapes!"

As she vanished around the corner, he turned to me and rolled his eyes.

I wasn't feeling hungry anymore. I went into an adjacent aisle and grabbed the first Merlot I could find.

Outside, I decided to take a walk before heading home for my liquid supper. I trudged slowly up the hill, each step a deliberate statement, a rebuke to middle age. When I'd moved to San Francisco after college, my eyes fell in love with the hills, and my legs barely noticed them. For years, I'd marched up and down as a matter of course, whether neighborhood hills like this one or its more intense cousins like Nob and Telegraph. But after a while, I began to question the old maxim about the shortest distance between two points being a straight line and learned to maneuver my way around with detours that skirted the steepest hills. To get to Noe Valley, I would take Diamond Street instead of Castro, for example. The addition of a couple of blocks would actually save me 15 minutes and a lot of huffing and puffing.

And then, at the stroke of 50—my own personal New Year's Eve, albeit without the balloons and fireworks—even those diversions became problematic. I became conscious of the slightest incline, my legs and lungs complaining in unison. But I didn't curse San Francisco. Instead, I cursed my legs and lungs. I cursed my age. I cursed the simple fact that with age comes wisdom, but its price is decay.

But tonight I needed the exercise, so I kept on—beyond the turn for home.

I stopped again at the aptly named Hill Street to take a breath, and turned. From this vantage point, all of the Castro was laid out before me, a few blocks of colorful houses ending abruptly at 19th to make room for wall-to-wall commercial buildings. And there were rainbow flags everywhere, from the tiny banners that lined the sidewalk to the immense rippling beacon at Castro and Market. From this distance, all you could see was color—rainbows on the flags and the sidewalks, rainbows in the bright paint of the buildings and the clothing of the people strolling across the street, from here just dots of color like traveling elements on a Seurat canvas. From here, nothing had changed. The Castro was all rainbows all the time. The corner of Queer and Gay, as a visiting friend had once called it, admiring the view from my living room window. To a visitor looking for paradise, that was how it seemed. Unlike those of us who had lived here for decades, they didn't know what it had once been. They had no idea just how bright a rainbow could be.

In the age of cell phones and text messages, nobody spontaneously shows up on your doorstep anymore, but when I realized I was in front of Brendan's place, I decided to go rogue.

Brendan lived on the lower level of a Victorian a couple of doors in from Castro. His unit had a separate entrance, through a side gate. I rang the bell at the gate and, a moment later, heard a rustle on the other side.

The gate swung open and Brendan was standing before me, a corkscrew in one hand. "Am I interrupting something?" I said with a laugh.

"No, you're just in time. We were about to open a bottle of Pinot." He backed up and led me in.

I pulled the Merlot from my bag. "In case we run out," I said.

"Oh, is it one of *those* nights?"

I managed a perfunctory smile. "I got picked for jury duty."

"Oh my, it *is* one of those nights!"

The fence, tall gray planks worn by the weather, protected an overgrown side garden, with lush shrubbery and a colorful assortment of flowers sprinkled here and there. The entrance to Brendan's unit was several yards away, at the top of a couple of concrete steps. Just beyond stood a wrought iron table and chairs.

"Keep Bette company while I deal with this," he said, darting toward the table to fetch the aforementioned Pinot.

Bette, auburn hair like a lion's mane, was standing on the far side of the garden. "Nice to see you again, Craig."

"You, too." We embraced, a faint minty smell wafting around me. I held the hug a second too long. When I let go, I'd have to think about Damien again.

Bette lived upstairs, in the rental unit, but they had known each other for far longer. When her husband died, she wanted to downsize, so when Brendan's tenant moved out, he'd rented the place to her. I hadn't seen her very often. Most of my time with Brendan was spent in restaurants and bars, boys' nights only. Bette's presence had always been a special treat, typically reserved for my visits to his place and this garden, a respite from all the rest.

"It's been ages," she said, settling back into her seat. "You must have stories to tell."

"No," I said, feeling my skin redden. "But I long to hear some of yours." Bette was quite the raconteur. It was a requirement for keeping up with Brendan.

I joined her at the table. The iron was cold against my fore-arms.

"Well," she said with a laugh, "if our host here can ever get that cork out of the bottle, you'll hear a lot more."

On cue, there was a sudden pop and Brendan's arm flew off to the side, cork intact. He placed the bottle on the table. "Let me run inside for another glass," he said, disappearing up the steps to the kitchen.

Bette was pouring when he returned with the third glass. He held it out to her.

I swirled the wine just to watch the legs form. "I hope you two weren't about to dig into some scandalous dirt I can't share.

I don't want to cramp your style."

"Of course we were about to dig into dirt," Brendan said, taking a seat. He lifted his glass. "So, jury duty, hunh?"

"Yeah, the trial should last a couple of weeks, according to the judge."

"Sounds exciting," Bette said.

"That remains to be seen."

"So what else is going on?" asked Brendan.

"How do you feel about service animals?" I asked. I launched into the story, glad I had something to report that was even newer than Damien.

When he finished laughing, Brendan began to shake his head in disbelief. "They're taking over everything," he said. "Vegans and trannies."

"Brendan!" Bette scolded.

"I'm sorry," he said. "I know they have their problems, but they're not *my* problems. Trans is totally different from gay."

"How so?"

"Look," he said, "I was born gay. I don't need to alter my body in order to express my sexuality."

"Neither do they," Bette said, "It's not all about surgery."

"Then what's the big deal? They keep telling us gender is an artificial construct—and I completely agree. It's absurd, the rules we have about what men can do and what women can do. If you want to wear a dress, wear a dress. But *sex* is not a social construct. It's a physical reality."

"Well, to many of them it's the wrong reality."

"The wrong reality? Do you hear yourself? You sound like Kellyanne Conway."

She threw her head back, laughing. "Don't you dare!"

Brendan laid his arm out in front of us. "Look, if I told you that I don't like my arm, that I really don't think I was meant to have it, and that I plan to cut it off, you'd lock me up in the nuthouse, wouldn't you? But if you say the same thing about your dick, they give you a special spot in the Pride parade."

"It's not the same thing."

"Really? Why not? If there's a disconnect between your brain and your body, why assume it's the body that's wrong? Of course, I'm a cis-gender man, whatever the fuck that means, so I don't get to have an opinion."

"Don't you mean sissy gender?" I asked.

"Let's talk about something nice," Bette said. "What was the gossip you were threatening to unleash?"

"Well," Brendan said, settling back in his chair, "there's always John Wayne."

"John Wayne?" Bette asked. "I had no idea you were into cowboys."

"I'm not," he said. "John Wayne is hardly a cowboy."

"I'm confused," Bette said, shaking her head.

"In fact," Brendan went on—he was on a roll now, I could tell—"if this were a movie, it wouldn't be a cowboy picture. It would be some farcical mystery: *The Story of the Shortsighted Optometrist.*"

I chuckled. The quickest remedy for your own pain is to think about someone else's.

"Please," Bette said, feigned panic in her eyes, "spill!"

Brendan sighed. "You know my friend John. The optometrist?"

"John Keppler? Who doesn't? I'm one of his patients."

"Oh, right. I forgot about that." Brendan seemed to hesitate. "In fact, John told me about your first visit."

"My first visit?"

"Don't you remember?"

"No, it was years ago."

Brendan, eyes alight, turned to me. "Well, according to John, when he was ready to see her, he came out of his office and, gazing at her chart, called out—"

"*Betty!*" Her hand waved in the air as she smiled broadly. Remembering, she turned to me. "At first, I didn't react. You've probably never experienced this, Craig, but when someone mispronounces your name it takes a second to realize who they're talking to. When I finally figured it out, I rose from my seat, looked him in the eye and said—as haughtily as I could—'It's pronounced *Bet*. As in Midler, not Davis.' He broke into a wide grin and we were instant friends."

"Well," I said, "there are two kinds of queens—Davis queens and Midler queens. You're lucky he was the right one."

She tossed her curls and I suddenly got a distinct Divine Miss M vibe. "So what's the story?" she asked.

"Well," Brendan continued breathily, "John's getting married."

Bette turned to me for confirmation.

"To Wayne," I said.

"Ah. So together they make a cowboy?"

"No." Brendan and I, in perfect sync.

"Although," Brendan continued, "to be fair, Wayne is just a few years away from *playing* Cowboys and Indians."

"Cowboys and Native Americans," I corrected.

"Yes," Brendan said, "of course."

"What does that mean?" Bette asked.

"He's 12."

Bette laughed heartily, letting go the stem of her glass to avoid spilling it.

I jumped in. "And by 12, he means 30."

"Same difference. It's all dog years to me."

"Tell me about him," Bette said. "Is he worthy of our optometrist?"

"God no," Brendan said. "Hence the 'shortsighted' part of our title."

"Right. I forgot." Bette relaxed into a smile. "Well, we've all made mistakes in love, haven't we?"

"Indeed."

I'd never brought Damien here. I couldn't quite picture him in this quiet space, this pastoral oasis surrounded by the noise of the city. I wondered what he would think of Bette and her flowery skirt, the hippie-ish curls going gray that spilled haphazardly over her face when she laughed. I saw him now at a gathering at my place when we'd just started dating, an impromptu cocktail party designed to introduce him to my core group of friends. After the niceties were done and the conversation began to dance from old stories to our usual obsessions—movies, gossip, books, Oscar's latest politically incorrect observation—Damien could be spotted silently nursing his drink in a corner of the room, the armchair swallowing him more and more every time I looked.

"What boggles my mind," Bette said, "is that love seems to be the one area of life where I never learn. I don't touch a hot stove anymore. I don't go to a science-fiction movie thinking, *Yeah, this time I'll really enjoy it.* But when it comes to men ... it's like I'm always just starting out. Every single time I fall for the romance. I forget that it's fleeting. I forget that men are—"

"Pigs," I said.

"I was going to say children, but that'll do."

She was clearly an expert on the topic, full of stories that felt at once specific and sadly universal. The early love who bought her flowers on a regular basis and then vanished overnight, the one who kept promising that his marriage was over and all she had to do was wait. For eternity.

"You know the old saying," she said, "Men play at love to get sex, and women play at sex to get love."

"Present company excepted, of course," Brendan said.

Bette laughed. "What about you?" she asked, turning to me. "Do you play at love or at sex?"

"Well, to be perfectly honest," I said, sliding back against the chair, "sometimes one, sometimes the other."

"Ah, versatile," Bette replied drily.

As the sky darkened, so did the conversation. The jokes and gossip were soon eclipsed behind an oddly soothing blanket of melancholy.

Bette had met Brendan when he was visiting a friend at an AIDS hospice. She was an administrator, in charge of admitting new patients and making sure their needs were met through to the end. She made the rounds every few hours and began to notice Brendan, visiting George every day. She struck up a conversation with him at the bedside while George was sleeping. She asked him what George was like before he got sick. Brendan relished the opportunity to talk about him, to remember the lively person he had known before, to balance out the thin, pale man in the bed, the body wasting away, the spirit vibrant still, if only through his words.

"She was an angel," Brendan said now, retelling the story. It was one of his favorites.

"It was an amazing place," Bette said. "I had the most transformative experiences of my life there. But I left after three years. That was enough death for me. That was when I started working at the bank—I found safety in numbers."

I was sometimes embarrassed by how protected I'd been. I was barely ten years younger than Brendan, but that was enough for my experience of the epidemic to be dramatically different. By the time I arrived in San Francisco in the early nineties, things were changing. My generation knew how to protect themselves; safety had been drilled into us, condoms as much a part of being gay as Madonna or cockrings. I knew people who were dying, but they weren't my peers. They weren't people I had known for years, people who were healthy when we'd met, people I'd shared my youth and dreams with.

No gay man in those days was free of the terror, the uncertainty, the fear that you'd forgotten about a sore in your mouth, a paper cut on your finger, that the tiniest thing would be the death of you. But I didn't know the depth of grief that still showed on Brendan's face. I'd been spared. And listening to him, I felt ashamed of having gotten away scot-free.

Brendan had told me all about those years, sitting right here over bottle after bottle of wine. The world had been different then. In Brendan's stories, it was glorious and tragic all at once. I sometimes looked with envy at the richness of his life, so much more intense than mine, but he had paid for it.

"Things have changed a lot since then," I ventured.

Bette, reaching for a pretzel from the bowl on the table, scrunched her chin. "Yes and no," she said. "The drugs were a game changer, and the whole culture around safer sex had quite an impact. But it looks to me like the biggest difference is demographic. People are still dying, but they're racial minorities now, not sexual ones."

"Maybe not for long," Brendan said, swirling his wine. "These kids don't get it, if you ask me. They don't see it in front of their faces like we did—young men who look old, wheelchairs, canes, lesions. They don't see it, so they're not afraid of it. And they're being less careful as a result."

"Well," Bette added with a sigh, "young people always think they're invincible."

"It's not just that," Brendan went on. He was growing more animated. "This crowd has no sense of history. They think the world began with them."

"Doesn't every generation?" said Bette.

Brendan shook his head and smiled, but his eyes were still raging. "You know, every morning I wake up and I'm baffled to be alive. I appreciate each day, but all day long I see ghosts on every street corner. They're all still young—as young as Wayne—and that's how I know I'm imagining things. I wonder sometimes what they would look like now. With gray hair. Or no hair. With wrinkles and paunches and arthritic limbs."

I watched Bette watching him, her eyes soft but not wet, blending empathy with reason, emotion with pragmatism, without trying.

"Bartending was supposed to be a temporary gig for me," he went on, his voice quieter now as dusk settled around us. "After I gave up teaching. I was going to tend bar—casual, part-time, no stress—while I figured out what to do next. But then, when so many friends started getting sick, I couldn't do it. My heart wasn't in the search and I couldn't spare the time. I kept tending bar every night, even though the crowds got smaller and smaller, because I was spending my days at someone's bedside. Too many someones."

Bette reached a hand across the table and grasped his fingers. "And you were wonderful at it. They needed you and you were there." Her voice rose, lifting the mood gently. You were there, she was saying, and now you're here.

"You know how I think of it," she said, turning her gaze to some middle spot between Brendan and me. "I think we're here to teach. When you've lived through something that other people need to know about, it's your duty to tell them. I don't think we get anywhere by criticizing them for not knowing something they haven't been taught."

"But they have," Brendan persisted. "How can they not know? I didn't live through World War II, but I know what happened."

"Then we need to make sure they understand."

He frowned. "You can't really understand unless you've been there. Unless you see the real world with your own eyes. But the only world that counts these days is virtual. People don't get sick and die on the Internet."

"Actually," I said, "doesn't that keep them safer? I've heard that young people don't have sex anymore. At least not like we did."

Brendan laughed. "Well, who has sex like we did?" He leaned on an arm of the chair, the other hand still clutching his glass by the bowl. "Or me, at least."

Bette waited for the laughter to die down, her lips now curled in a gentler smile. "I'm serious," she said. "Young people need to be taught, mentored. It's unfair to criticize them just for being young. Did you ever have a mentor, Craig?"

I tried to remember. It wasn't something I'd ever thought of. "My high school English teacher encouraged me a lot," I said at last. "But other than that … not really. And as far as gay life goes, I feel like my friends and I discovered things on our own."

Suddenly I was back at the Midnight Sun, barely out of college, afraid to look anyone in the eye, with no clue of what to do if someone approached me.

"People have to make their own mistakes," Brendan said.

"Some mistakes are more dangerous than others," Bette responded. "We know that all too well." She paused. "I try not to look upon aging as a problem. It's more of a gift. Just think of the wisdom we've all accumulated. Like community elders."

"Elders?" Brendan cried. "Speak for yourself."

She glared at him, only half facetiously. "You've been here a long time, as long as me."

"1978," he said. *"Annus horribilis."*

I'd heard only snippets of this story before, how he'd moved to the city for college but spent most of his time in the Castro, absorbing everything he could about gay culture.

"Just in time for Jonestown and the assassinations," he said.

I was in grade school then, halfway across the country, and San Francisco was as exotic to me as Japan. But somehow, watching the drama unfold on TV, I had a sense that I was peering into my own future. That was probably my first memory of this city, grainy images on the nightly news. Now, every time I passed City Hall, I couldn't help reconstructing its history in my head—wondering which of those basement windows Dan White had climbed through to snake his way upstairs for his killing spree; transposing an image from television onto the doorway as I walked by, Dianne Feinstein breaking the news to a press of cameras and crying citizens. It was a glorious building, but it would always be shrouded in death.

In the aftermath, Harvey's name reached all the way to Minneapolis, and for the first time, I saw images of men walking arm in arm down a street on the far side of the world, as I thought of it then. A street that I now walked along myself, every day of my life.

"You look a little like him," Bette said softly to Brendan.

"Who?"

And, in the dimming light, I saw it myself—something in the slope of the nose, the high forehead.

"Harvey Milk."

Brendan laughed. "Please, Sean Penn *as* Harvey Milk!"

An odd silence suddenly settled around us. When Brendan spoke again, his voice was smoother, the tone darker. "Those days," he said. "They changed me. It was like I grew up overnight. I didn't want to waste a minute, and I refused to be quiet. I think I came out to my parents the next day." He smiled. "And I haven't shut up since."

Bette reached across the table and grabbed his hand. "So much wisdom," she said. "Even if we're not in the thick of things, marching in the streets like we used to, we have a lot to contribute."

"I write checks," Brendan said.

"That, too."

"What about you?" I asked.

She chuckled. "Sometimes I feel like I've sold out, working at the bank all these years. So I do a lot of volunteer work now. It's less stressful, being on my own schedule."

"AIDS?"

She shook her head. "Homelessness."

"Still a saint," Brendan piped in from the shade of the acacia by the side fence. The sun had sunk behind the hill.

"Hardly." Bette smiled. "But I do what I can do."

"What can anyone do?" Brendan asked. "It's an intractable problem."

I could tell that the difficulty didn't matter much to Bette. In the fading light, her eyes were still glowing. She was a believer. In her long skirt and the orchestra of noisy bracelets on both wrists, she advertised her idealism. And I was grateful for it, glad someone still believed in improving things, no matter how impossible that seemed to the rest of us.

"What about you, Craig?" Bette seemed eager to change the subject. The reference to sainthood had made her blush—whether with flattery or irritation, I couldn't be sure. "How's the store?"

"The owner's selling it," I said.

"Oh no! I love that place!"

"Glad somebody does."

"I'm just glad somebody reads," Brendan said, getting up from the table.

"Then business isn't good?"

I tried not to laugh. "Well, the few people who still read anything longer than a tweet these days seem to buy everything online, so the store can be a pretty lonely place."

"I told you to stock more porn," Brendan said.

"I had to show the place to a realtor the other day."

"Who?"

"Tiffany Hardesty."

A guttural sigh emerged from the darkness.

"That bad, hunh?"

"No," he said. "Not from Angela's standpoint, at least. Tiffany's a pit bull."

"Charming."

"But what about you?"

Outside, the fog was settling over Twin Peaks—the other one. "I have no idea. It may be time to reinvent myself. Again."

Brendan laughed. "Hey, reinvention keeps you young."

I didn't want to talk about the store any more than I wanted to talk about Damien. If it were just Brendan and me, all that would no doubt be coming up now. I'd be spilling my worries and my dirty laundry all over the garden. Bette's being here was a blessing, an excuse to put all that away in the back of my mind. She exuded a sense of calm in the quiet way she sat and listened, in the alto tones of her voice. And her eyes, in the dimming light, suggested an abiding joy that had survived everything and still refused to surrender.

Suddenly an orange light broke through and cast a lovely glow on the yard. I turned to see Brendan in the doorway, arm reaching in toward the light switch. As he stood there, a slinky gray cat padded between his feet and made its way down the steps.

"Little Edie!" I cried and made the automatic but always futile clicking sound with my tongue. She ignored me every time, but still I tried. Ignoring people was Little Edie's greatest pleasure.

Brendan looked down at the touch of fur on his bare ankle and smiled. He turned his gaze back into the house, toward the floor. "Well," he asked, "are you coming, too?"

And in a moment, Big Edie—fatter than her sister and twice as furry—found her way out. She turned in a circle at the foot of the steps and then plopped onto the grass and began licking her paw.

Meanwhile, Little Edie had already vanished under a bush by the fence. She would emerge again in a moment and begin her perambulation through the yard. Eventually, when you'd forgotten she was even in the vicinity, she would settle at your feet and begin a soft cry for petting. But only when it was least convenient.

Distracted by the cats, I didn't notice at first that Brendan had vanished into the house. I was trying to coax Big Edie to get off her fat ass and join us at the table when the door suddenly slammed and Brendan appeared, practically dancing through the yard. He had a joint between his lips and another balanced on the ashtray in his hand. He settled the equipment on the table and resumed his seat.

He pulled a lighter out of the ashtray and lit up. Inhaling deeply, he held the joint out toward Bette.

She grabbed it eagerly. "Ah, the luxury of legality," she said. "No need to hide the smell behind closed doors."

At least some things had improved recently, I thought, taking the joint in turn.

CHAPTER 7

MILLENNIAL APPROACHES

Somewhere in my forties, I gave up on love. It wasn't a decision, really. It wasn't even a reaction to heartbreak. One Sunday morning I woke up alone and realized that I was perfectly content. The only breath I heard besides my own was coming from Elsa, curled up at the foot of the bed, dreaming about squirrels.

I have strangely vivid memories of that day. I walked down to the newsstand beside the movie theater to pick up a thick, unwieldy copy of the *New York Times*, then stopped at a café for an everything bagel and an oversized latte. At home, I spread the bagel with cream cheese and placed it on a china plate, beside a mound of ruby red strawberries, and settled everything on a small table by the window, where the moisture on the strawberries glistened in the sunlight. And I read the news, section by section, reveling in the crispness of the paper—a sound and texture you can never get from scrolling online—and felt completely at home in the world. My world.

I told myself that I'd wasted enough time in pursuit of some amorphous, quite possibly illusory vision of how my life should be, a coupled existence where two people can maintain their individuality while traveling through the world with a shared purpose, where you take turns being the nurturing one, the needy one, the strong one, the weak—calibrating your life according to the needs and desires of your beloved, free to be yourself with every virtue praised and every fault forgiven. It had never happened that way, at least not for long.

But that day, as I bit into a perfect strawberry and read about plays I'd have to fly across the country to see, I didn't have to do anything about it. I could just be. And, I told myself, when I wanted physical connection, I could get it. I was still young enough, still attractive enough, for the odd tumble, the innocent flirtation, the fun without the burden.

So I stopped looking. I went to bars to meet up with friends, or to pick up a stranger for the night. I went to the theater alone. I even treated myself to a fancy dinner more than once. I became a bit of a regular at a charming bistro deep in a quiet corner of the neighborhood, where a table for one was always available. I canceled my match.com membership, keeping only access to the occasional cruising site, where no one talked about their favorite books or their love of long walks along Ocean Beach. Intimacy became completely transactional—you do me, I'll do you, and we'll keep our hearts covered up, no matter how exposed our bodies may be.

That's what Damien was supposed to be—a body, a roll in the proverbial hay. And then, on the first night, while we were still lounging in bed after said roll, he smiled at me with his eyes. He asked questions about my life—who I was, what I wanted, what I'd been through. He seemed genuinely interested, and sweet. And he was so handsome. Not just a headless torso on a screen, but soft lips, a couple of days' growth of scruffy beard, and eyes, eyes that saw me.

And I fell. He wanted me. In that moment, at least, in those first few weeks, he wanted me. And that was enough for me to forget my resolution, enough to forget that I already had everything I needed to be happy. Enough to create a space for him, a hole that would quickly morph into a wound when he was gone.

It had barely been a week since Oscar's birthday, but he suggested a boys' night out at a new restaurant on Market Street. It occurred to me that he wanted to erase all memory of the birthday and quickly replace it with an evening of his own design. No jokey cards, no obligatory visits to God's Waiting Room.

Despite my best efforts, I was still a few minutes late. But when I peeked through the restaurant window, Oscar was sitting at a round table by himself. He waved coyly as I passed, fingers dipping one at a time like Liza Minnelli's at the end of *Cabaret*.

"Where is everyone?" I asked, snagging the chair to his right, to have a view of the sidewalk.

"They're gay," Oscar replied. He was already swirling the olive skewer in his drink.

Fortunately, the waiter was at my side before I had a chance to start drooling over Oscar's gin. "I'll have one of those," I said, pointing.

"One isopropyl martini coming up," Oscar whispered as the waiter scurried away.

"Are we embalming this evening?"

He laughed. "No. It's just been a long day. I was in court." He leaned in close, lips curling into a smile. "But you know all about that now, don't you?"

"Don't ask," I said. "I'd have to kill you." I'd texted him the news the night before, sitting at home alone, my whole body loopy from Brendan's pot.

"So," he said now, "are you going to at least tell me what the case is about?"

I sighed. He was a lawyer; he knew the rules. "All I know at this point is that the defendant is a convicted felon, and he was apparently found with a gun, or they think he had a gun. The charge is possession."

"Ah. Interesting."

"There is one funny thing I can tell you." I paused as the waiter came back and laid a drink in front of me. "The judge asked if any of us owned a gun or knew someone who did. I was all set to just sit it out until I remembered yours."

"Mine? God, that thing hasn't seen the light of day in years. I don't even go to target practice anymore."

"Exactly. I said that my best friend owned a gun."

"Aw," Oscar said, tilting his head. "I'm your best friend."

"Yes, wiseass. So the next question was, did you own the gun because you'd been the victim of a crime."

"Oh dear."

"I said no. So the defense lawyer asked why you had the gun, then."

Oscar pursed his lips thoughtfully, as if he wanted to hear the answer himself.

"I told him what you'd told me once, that you had it in case of the zombie apocalypse."

He laughed. "Oh my god, you didn't!"

"I did, and the whole courtroom burst out laughing. And then he asked, 'Does your friend think the apocalypse is coming anytime soon?'"

"I hope you said yes."

I smirked at him. "No. And that was that."

"And they still took you? They didn't think you were insane?"

I sipped the drink, momentarily stunned by the vermouth. I'd forgotten to ask for it dry. "The weirdest thing for me, though, was how reluctant people were to serve. Their so-called hardship stories were pretty sketchy."

"Civic responsibility at its finest."

"I had no idea, for example, how many people have to take care of their elderly mothers. It was half the room."

"You learn so much about the kindheartedness of people when you ask them to do something."

The drink had relaxed me enough to break my other news. Affecting a bright tone, I said, "I heard from Damien."

"And?"

The others were on their way. I decided to cut to the chase. "It's over."

"What? What happened?" Oscar straightened up, a clearheaded demeanor smoothing the contours of his face. I had shocked the gin out of him.

On the sidewalk outside, a straight couple passed by arm in arm. "I don't know."

"What, he broke up with you without a reason?"

"Oh, no." I turned to face him. "He didn't break up with me."

"You broke up with him."

I hesitated. "Not exactly."

Oscar blew out a breath and straightened up in his chair. "Okay, let's start again. What exactly happened?"

"Well, he got back from his *convention*," I said, trying to convey the air quotes through my tone rather than miming them with my fingers—it seemed gauche—"and decided that we were moving too fast and he wanted a break."

Oscar scrunched his chin thoughtfully. It was an exaggerated expression I'd seen many times before: he was trying not to look judgmental. "You do realize that that's not the same thing, right?"

"Oh please. When that conversation happens this early in a relationship, you're doomed. I know, it's happened enough. It's sad, though. I really did think it was different this time."

"Did you? Just the other day you were talking about how unsure you were."

"Of *my* feelings," I said, "not his."

"Oh Jesus."

Thankfully, the waiter chose that moment to return and replenish our drinks. I took a brief sip.

"Okay," I said, "I know how that sounds."

"Really? Do you?"

"Look, you can psychoanalyze my selfishness and immaturity later. First, I just need to wallow a bit and get a reality check."

"Okay." It was Oscar's humor-me tone, but I wasn't feeling picky at the moment.

"I know there were certain disconnects, we weren't always in sync, but overall, I thought things were going fine. Was I just deluding myself? It did seem to move pretty quickly. Do I always move this fast?"

"Yes," Oscar said, not missing a beat, "you do."

"So it's my fault? I chased him away? There was no sign from him that anything was wrong."

Oscar sighed. "Has it occurred to you that slowing it down might be a good thing? It's been what, three or four months, and you're spending every weekend together."

"Except this past one," I interrupted.

"Right. When he was on a business trip. Why *not* be more casual about it? Maybe see other people. Enjoy the moment instead of planning for the future. The future comes soon enough, believe me."

"I didn't make this all up, you know. You remember what it was like in the beginning, for both of us. I talked to you every step of the way." I had told him about the look on Damien's face, the glow when he saw me. "He was smitten, really smitten. And I specifically remember telling you how much that unnerved me. *Watch out,* I kept telling myself. *Don't fall into the trap. This one could be like all the others and just slip through your fingers.*"

"Too bad you weren't listening."

Damien had courted me in the beginning—phone calls after every date, flowers delivered to the store in the first week. And then he got me. And the courting stopped.

"I'm fine." I said. "It's all for the best."

"For the best. So you're just dumping him?"

"Well, I don't want to be harsh about it. I thought I'd just do what the kids do these days—I'll ghost him."

"Ghost him?"

"Yeah, like not return phone calls or messages. Pretend he doesn't exist."

"That's mature."

"*Au contraire,*" I said, "that's the new normal."

"There could be a happy medium."

"I've never been able to find one. Maybe I'm just more comfortable with the extremes."

"You're even more flippant than usual tonight."

"And I've barely begun to drink." I made up for that now. After another sip, my tongue grew numb. Heaven.

"Fuck him," I said and lifted my glass to toast to Damien's nonexistence.

"Fuck him?" Oscar held his martini aloft, but inches away. Our glasses were too full; any clinking would lead to a spill—alcohol abuse, in our parlance.

"Fuck him." I forced down another swig.

Oscar avoided my eyes as he settled the glass back down. "I think you should welcome the break. Take this time to figure out what you want at this point in your life."

"This point in my life?"

"Yes," Oscar replied. He twisted his lips thoughtfully, clearly pulling on all his lawyerly skills to come up with a diplomatic way to say something dangerous. "Haven't you been down this road before?" he asked. "With guys like Damien, I mean."

"Guys like Damien?" I felt like a parrot, but nothing was making sense. No, it made sense—but only if I scratched beneath the surface of the words. And I was in no mood to do that.

"The romance," he said. "You're acting like you're in love with him. You're not."

"How do you know what I'm feeling?"

"At this point, you're just infatuated. It's a necessary step, but it's not love. You know that." He looked at me in that way he had, the way there was no arguing with. Oscar knew me as well as anyone ever had. "Love takes time," he said.

I was feeling petulant. It was a chronic condition: once I'd taken a stand, the finest logic couldn't persuade me to give in. Even when I knew the other person was right, I refused to admit it.

"You've been in love before," Oscar said. "Compare that to this."

He was talking about Garrett, of course—one of the few I'd been with long enough to see the evolution. In the beginning it's all surface and fantasy. But after a while, when that territory is spent, there's room for a shift. I'd gone there with Garrett. After a while, it wasn't about how Garrett made me feel. It was about learning to see the world though his eyes, feel what he was feeling, know his vulnerabilities, know what he needed and what

[98]

made him hurt.

"You have to give it time," Oscar said. "And don't lose your-self along the way. I don't want to belabor it, but the one time we all got together, it was like you were a different person. Like you were just Damien's boyfriend."

"That's not fair. I was trying to introduce him to you. I didn't want to muck up the conversation with our private jokes."

"I would love to have heard some private jokes. It would have made you seem more like a couple."

I remembered that night well, the casual gathering that ended up feeling far less than casual. Damien had dutifully asked Oscar about his work, where he went to school, where he lived, and for a while he seemed genuinely interested. But once the question-and-answer session was out of the way, he seemed to withdraw from the conversation, his eyes dulled somehow, the muscles that had created his smile suddenly drooping, spent.

"It's just so embarrassing," I said, gazing down at the table. "I hate how this happens. Someone reels me in, and then, when he knows he has me, he pulls back and makes *me* feel like the needy one. Romance is a game of Gaslight."

"Craig, I don't think he was deceiving you."

But it was easier to believe that he was. It was easier to believe that this was just the way the world worked.

"You know," I said, "my parents used to fight a lot. In their true Midwestern way, of course, they held in the anger as long as they could. So when it did come out, things could get ugly." I felt Oscar leaning in closer, but I was just watching the olives in my glass swaying back and forth. "And one day, I was about 12, I guess, they were going on about something. Not so loud this time; it was just an argument. I guess a healthy argument, at least by their standards. There was no dishware sailing through the air, at least. Anyway, I was trying to get their attention. I'd been asking them about something—god knows what now, the details are irrelevant. All I remember is how it felt. They couldn't hear me, because all they could focus on was their argument, poking holes in each other's points, trying to have the last word. So I lost it. I yelled. I'd never yelled so loud in my life."

I held the glass before my eye. On the other side of it, the world looked blurry, like a dream sequence in a movie. "I got their attention. They stopped talking and just stared at me. And then they looked at each other and my mother actually rolled her eyes. Like, *Can you believe this kid? So emotional.* Here they are, my entire life acting like a couple of lunatics, and now they're accusing me of being overemotional."

"I get it," Oscar said. "But that was them. It's not Damien or anyone else. And it's not you."

"Right. I guess I don't really know Damien. Like you say, if this came as a surprise, then I wasn't paying attention."

I turned to the window, where Rafe, arm in arm with John, was waving at us.

The additional company brought with it a longed-for festive mood. The waiter had just delivered a round of drinks when Brendan came rushing in.

"Sorry I'm late," he said, squeezing in beside me. "I passed right by the place at first, didn't recognize it with all the new décor. What's this incarnation all about?"

"Healthy food, they say," Rafe replied.

Brendan grimaced. "I hope that doesn't mean kale is the only vegetable on the menu."

"Where's Wayne?" I asked.

"He'll be here soon," John replied, tapping the phone he'd just placed on the table. "Working a bit late."

A series of indifferent nods made their way around the table.

"By the way," John continued, "I haven't popped the question yet, so please don't say anything."

"Oh," I asked, "why not?"

"Cold feet?" asked Oscar brightly.

"No, I just haven't found the right moment."

Rafe shook his head. "There's never a right moment." He gazed at Oscar like a heroine out of *Masterpiece Theatre*. "Or a wrong one."

"Just do it!" Oscar said. "Rip off the bandage."

"Eeeww, honey," said Rafe, "it's love, not a wound."

Oscar lifted an eyebrow. "You're making my point for me."

"This obsession with food lately," Brendan said, returning to his own topic, "it's insane. I was on a flight recently where they made an announcement that, because someone had a peanut allergy, nobody could even open a bag of them. Nobody had food allergies when we were growing up. Now nobody can eat peanuts. What's up with that?"

Rafe looked up from his menu. "Helicopter parenting," he said.

"Exactly! Allergies come from things you haven't been previously exposed to. As a gay man who came of age in the eighties, I have great appreciation for a functioning immune system. And kids don't get a functioning immune system by staying indoors, avoiding other people, and refusing vaccines and peanuts. They get it from eating dirt."

"Did *you* eat dirt?" John asked with a grin.

Brendan smiled mischievously. "I still do, honey. But now it takes the form of gossip."

We were still laughing when Wayne appeared in the doorway, lips sealed inscrutably. Brendan leaned toward me and whispered in my ear, "Millennial approaches."

Wayne tapped John on the shoulder and slid into the seat beside him.

"Yay," Oscar said, "the gang's all here. Wayne, do you eat peanuts?"

Wayne cast him a flummoxed look. He stuttered out a "Yes. Why?"

"We were just talking about how nobody eats peanuts anymore."

"Or gluten," Brendan added.

"Thank god for alcohol," Oscar said. "It kills everything."

Settling the napkin in his lap, Wayne looked around the table, a smile threatening to break out on his face. "So how is everyone, allergies excepted?"

There was a round of *Fine*s before Rafe asked, "Did the Viet Cong come through?"

Wayne's smile broadened. "Yes," he said. "We're feeling a lot more stable now."

Sporadic small talk ensued as everyone checked out the menu. In a few minutes, the waiter returned to take our orders. John took the liberty of ordering a couple of bottles for the table—one white, one red. He was the resident wine expert, or at least the one most willing to take on the duty.

I was beginning to think Oscar had been right to arrange the evening, or maybe it was just that the gin had started to work. Without a celebration at the center of attention, we had an opportunity to be more relaxed, with no one on the spot. And by no one, of course, I mean everyone. If we all got a turn, none of us could take it personally.

"So," he said, gazing past me to Brendan, "I hope you haven't persuaded this guy to move to El Cerrito yet."

"I'm working on it."

"Please, no," I said. "I draw the line at the East Bay."

"You could always just move in with Oscar and Rafe," John said. "They have a few thousand square feet to spare."

"But sadly, no sense of flair," said Brendan. He turned to Rafe. "How are the capri curtains doing?"

Rafe laughed softly.

"What's so funny?" Wayne asked. "What are capri curtains?"

Brendan could barely contain himself. "You know about capri pants, right?"

"Yeah, the short ones."

"Precisely. Which no one, male or female, in whatever decade, should be caught dead in. Well, when they first bought the house, Rafe here decided to save a little money by reusing the curtains from their old place. Only that place was normal size. The mansion has 14-foot ceilings. The curtains ended up hanging six inches above the floor."

Rafe declaimed over the laughter, "They were temporary."

"Yeah, that's what I said about my virginity all through high school."

The waiter returned with the wine and displayed each label to John.

"This is what I love about you guys," Oscar said. "All this lighthearted banter. It's like *The Boys in the Band* before they start calling ex-lovers."

John nodded and watched the waiter begin to uncork the bottles. "I'll do the Cab," he said. "Wayne, would you taste the Chardonnay for us?"

"Look at that," said Brendan, "two sommeliers in the same family."

I kicked him under the table. "So Rafe," I said, desperate to change the subject, "I hear you've been awfully busy lately. More Silicon Valley billionaires adding extensions to their mansions?"

While Rafe launched into a discussion of his latest project—something to do with the death of another Pacific Heights doyenne and her heir's determination to get rid of every piece of chintz in the place—I watched the ritual taking place on the far side of the table. The waiter poured a taste of red wine out for John, who ceremoniously swirled it, lifted the glass up to the light to assess its legs and color, and finally, with a slight inhale, drew it into his mouth. His cheeks moved back and forth for a few seconds, as if he were gargling mouthwash, before he finally swallowed. He pursed his lips, looked up at the waiter, and smiled.

Now it was Wayne's turn, and the process went a lot faster. Barely gazing at the wine, which seemed rather pale from my side of the table, he spilled it into his mouth, washed it around a bit, and settled the glass back down. He gave a quick, matter-of-fact nod. If John's approach was ostentatious, Wayne's was pointedly reserved, suggesting a natural confidence. Wayne had nothing to prove.

The waiter refilled their glasses and then, carrying one bottle in each hand, made his way around the table.

We placed our orders, and the waiter dutifully penciled them down on his pad. "It's so refreshing to see a waiter write things down," Brendan said when he'd gone. "I can't stand the pretension in most places where they just nod at everything you say and come back later with the wrong entrée."

Oscar abruptly cut off the chitchat by raising his glass. He gazed around the table, waiting for the glasses to be held aloft. They went up like the wave at a football game.

"To friendship," he said. "And thanks for putting up with my pissy mood on my birthday."

There were chuckles all around as we drank.

"Well, to be fair," Brendan said, "a man doesn't turn 39 every day."

"Thank you," said Oscar with a polite nod. "You just became my favorite."

We usually tried to avoid politics. One on one, the subject was easier to handle, but when we were all together, it could easily get out of control, one negative comment feeding on the last, all leading to the same sense of hopelessness we'd started with. But inevitably, when the bar we'd all thought couldn't get any lower did just that, the subject of the world's collective wrath reared its ugly, nameless head.

"I keep saying," Oscar intoned, "he's not the disease; he's the symptom. This anti-intellectual, racist, greedy culture created him. Piece by piece, they put him together like Frankenstein's monster. They took Reagan's TV personality and mental defectiveness and grafted it onto Wall Street greed, then topped it off with the Christian right's hatred of anyone who isn't a straight white man. And presto, the bumbling monster who kills everything it touches. The only difference is that this monster is orange instead of green. What we need is a shitload of angry villagers with pitchforks." He stabbed a meatball and broke it in two.

Brendan, who had barely touched his dinner yet, swirled his wine. "I remember the first time I saw Sarah Palin, when she gave that obscene speech at the convention about pit bulls with lipstick. I literally wanted to climb through the TV cables and throttle every ounce of life out of her."

"It's sad how these people bring out such violent feelings in us genteel liberal homosexuals," Rafe said with a laugh.

"Bullies, plain and simple," Brendan said. "The only way they can feel better about themselves is by picking on their superiors.

I got beat up on more than one occasion as a kid. But it wasn't because I was gay. They didn't know I was gay. They called me a fag because I was smarter than them. Because I read books instead of hanging out on the corner. I was the good student, the one who was going to get out of that sad little place and leave them behind. And they hated me for it."

"In my case," I said, "there was no question. They called me a fag because they knew I was a fag."

Wayne gazed out from under bushy brows, his eyes narrowed sympathetically. "That sounds awful," he said as the laughter ebbed.

I felt myself smiling and instantly wondered why. "It was a long time ago."

He kept staring as at something he couldn't quite make out.

"Didn't anything like that ever happen to you?" Rafe asked.

"A little name calling here and there," he said, "but nothing serious. I did have a classmate who got picked on a lot. He was a little more … obvious than me, so—"

"So you had cover," Rafe said.

"I guess so."

Oscar turned to me, eyes probing. "So how faggy were you?"

"Well, I couldn't catch a ball to save my life. But I was good at math. In junior high, we had gym twice a week, and each quarter was eight weeks long, so I calculated I could miss five gym classes per quarter and still pass."

"What'd you do, play hooky?"

"Sometimes, I would just pretend to be sick in the morning—my mother was a real pushover. Or I'd feign a stomachache when I got to the gym. And once or twice I just spent the hour in the library, hiding behind a bookcase. Probably reading Jane Austen."

Oscar shook his head. "My my, still waters run deep. Did you ever get caught?"

"Worse," I said. "One time I miscalculated. The only *F* of my entire academic career. My father was apoplectic."

I hadn't thought about junior high in years. And suddenly, despite the laughter, I could feel it again. I didn't have to feign the stomachaches. Just the thought of stepping into that locker room, or someone passing me a field hockey stick, was enough to make my entire GI tract churn.

"Gym class was a nightmare," Rafe said. "I lived in abject fear of being skin instead of shirt."

"You?" John asked.

He laughed. "I wasn't always this gorgeous."

"Gorgeous has nothing to do with it," I said. "I was shy about being naked in front of the other guys, but they were indifferent to it. Even though I was too anxious to be turned on by it, I still saw nakedness—even just a bare chest—as being sexual somehow. And for them, it was just … changing their clothes."

"Exposure," Rafe said. "It was like we were revealing more than our bodies. Like our gayness would show on the skin."

"Exactly," I said. "I think the straight boys, for all their constant thoughts about girls, could compartmentalize sexuality better than we could. Sex wasn't just an urge for me. It was an identity."

"When did you get over that self-consciousness?" Wayne asked.

I thought for a moment. "Probably the first time I went to bed with another man. Stripping off my clothes for him was like bringing the two things together—lust and identity. For the first time, I was what I did, if that makes sense."

"You were in the zone," Oscar said with a laugh.

Rafe lifted an eyebrow. "Ironically, like an athlete."

"I played baseball in high school," Wayne said.

I tried to picture him in a uniform, the visor of a tight cap keeping his eyes in shadow, the way the tight pants captured his ass. "Did you enjoy it?"

"Yes. I wasn't bad."

"Beyond gym class, I completely avoided sports," John said, "but I wonder sometimes if I would have gotten better with practice. The thing was, I always felt like I was being watched, like every mistake was a sign of some defect."

I turned to Wayne. "Did kids throw the word *faggot* around when you were growing up?"

"Of course," he said. "But they said it to everyone. It was just a generic insult."

"Stemming from homophobia," Rafe said. "That's the problem. If you call a straight kid a fag, it just rolls off his back. Call a gay kid a faggot and he takes it to heart."

Across the table, Wayne was hunched over a bit, his brow painfully furrowing.

"What?" I asked, catching his eye.

"It's kind of sad," he said. "All these gender roles—what's masculine, what's feminine. It's ridiculous when you think about it."

"Yes," I said, "it is."

"It's different now, I suppose," Rafe said. "Your generation seems not to get as bogged down as we did."

Wayne shrugged. "Not as much. People don't categorize themselves so easily—male, female, gay, straight. We're just more open, I guess."

Brendan scowled. "Or unwilling to pick a side."

"Maybe there shouldn't be sides," Rafe argued.

Now Brendan laughed. "Wasn't it Woody Allen who said bisexuality is better because it doubles your chances of getting a date?"

As the laughter wound its way around the table again, I fell into the sound. This was how it had always been for us, through years and years of dinners and cocktails and dancing and cruising, but despite the levity, it felt now like something was fraying at the edges. Oscar and Rafe were already out of the neighborhood, and though their new place was only a few minutes' drive away, it seemed like another world—quiet streets full of large (for San Francisco) one-family homes and not a rainbow crosswalk in sight. And if John really were the next to get married, I could hardly imagine what that would do to the dynamic. Every time we got together, it felt like it could be the last time—which it was, in a way, because at every gathering things were a little different, the jabs a bit harsher, the silences a bit longer, the energy dimmer and dimmer, like a lightbulb whose filament was slowly dissolving, surrendering to time.

Silence reigned while we waited for the waiter to process a sea of credit cards. As the small talk resumed—something about pewter faucets and copper pipes—I found myself gazing absently over Wayne's shoulder, not focusing on anything. The rest of the room looked like smeared streaks of color, a vibrating Rothko.

CHAPTER 8
THE NIGHT IN QUESTION

Every day started with bad pastry and worse coffee. We gathered in the jury room, a windowless space that smelled faintly of mildew and fear. I had to wonder how many other juries had sat in here, around this table, and decided the fate of how many defendants. Lives were no doubt changed in that room, the lives of people who never set foot inside it. But right now, it was just a meeting place for 14 random strangers, grabbing caffeine and carbs to get through an experience none of us could really predict.

The bailiff had promised a continental breakfast. When I walked into the room, I found a box of doughnuts. If the continent in question was North America, they'd hit their mark.

On the first day, I was just biting into a glazed doughnut when Nancy sidled up beside me in pursuit of a cruller. "Good morning," she said, grabbing the last one from the box. It dripped a shocking amount of powdered sugar as she placed it on her napkin.

I nodded and swallowed quickly. "Good morning," I said and took a quick sip of coffee. It was like a rock was lodged in my throat and I had sent thin, tasteless water down to flush it out.

We moved away from the table to make room for someone else. Facing the wall, she said, "Are we ready for this?"

"Hard to say," I confessed. "It's kind of nerve-racking, to tell you the truth."

"I know!" Her eyes widened behind the glasses. "I kept waking up last night from the strangest dreams. Anxiety dreams—you know, like showing up for a test and realizing you haven't attended a single class or read anything on the syllabus."

A sixtyish man joined us, smiling over his coffee. Juror number 6, I recalled—one of the first ones picked. I was amazed that I remembered. But at this point, they were all just numbers to me.

"Good morning," he said. "I'm Don."

We shared introductions and nervous smiles. I was suddenly aware of a desire to keep a professional distance. Being too friendly with people might make the deliberation difficult. Like having an affair at the office.

"Have you ever done this before?" Don asked, squinting through wire-framed glasses. The glasses had fallen to the midpoint of his nose, which was wide and pinker than the rest of his face.

"No," Nancy and I responded in chorus.

"New to me, too," Don said. "Can't say I'm looking forward to it, either."

Nancy cocked her head to one side, lips curled. "Oh, I'm looking upon it as an adventure."

"Something to tell the grandkids," I added with a laugh.

"Exactly."

Don didn't seem amused. His bushy white eyebrows sank. "Well," he said, "the jury's still out on that."

"No pun intended," I said.

He looked at me quizzically for a moment before his eyes finally lit up. "Right," he said, chuckling hoarsely, "right."

We were still making introductions—Bonnie, the fortyish mother from Brisbane; Chet, the lanky marketing director; Madge, the secretary whose ready smile was belied by heavy eyes that screamed for escape—when the bailiff came in to fetch us. "It's time, people," he said politely. "Please follow me. And don't forget to take the same seats you had yesterday. You need to stay in the same seats for every session."

We followed him in single file down the cold beige hallway. It was a relief when he opened the door to the courtroom, whose shiny wood paneling and ornamentation gave me another frisson of excitement.

The tone for today was somber. The lawyers stood to greet us, thin-lipped smiles pasted on their faces. Between the defense attorneys, Vasquez gazed down at his hands. It gave me the chance to look closely at him without the discomfort of eye contact.

Whereas the benches beyond the gate had been full of prospective jurors the other day, they were now thinly populated, 10 or so people spaced apart. Near the front, directly aligned with the defense table, a fiftyish Latina sat solemnly beside a young man who resembled the defendant. I turned away abruptly.

Ms. Harmon, the lead prosecutor, rose from her seat and stood before the jury box, close enough for me to make out the fine stripes in her navy suit and the delicate gleam of the fabric. She was wearing a white silk blouse with a high, round collar, counterbalancing the masculine look of the suit.

"Good morning," she said. She smiled politely and scanned the jury, locking eyes with each of us in turn.

After the preliminary niceties—I was already growing tired of how many times we were told by one person or another how grateful they were for our service, as if we'd just come back from Afghanistan—she lifted her chin and paused for several seconds. The silence focused everyone's attention and brought a new seriousness to the proceedings. She was collecting herself, I thought, preparing for the tough part.

"Ladies and gentlemen," she said at last, "in the early morning hours of October 6th of last year, the defendant, Raul Vasquez, arrived at the ER of San Francisco General Hospital with a gunshot wound. Now that may not sound like such an extraordinary thing. Sadly, SF General sees gunshot wounds far too often. The legal question in this case centers on how Mr. Vasquez acquired his wound. The evidence will show that the wound was self-inflicted, that Mr. Vasquez accidentally shot himself."

Behind her, Vasquez lifted his head suddenly, as if he thought he was being called. His eyes were blank, indifferent.

Harmon stopped for a moment and her lips curled into a smile. Standing now near the middle of the space before the jury box, she decided to answer it. Again she went over what the judge had told us about felons and guns. And again she told us that we shouldn't care what his earlier crime had been.

"The only thing we're asking of you," continued Harmon, "is to determine whether the defendant was in possession of a firearm at the time he was shot. Now the defense will tell you he was shot by a stranger, that he never had his hands on a gun—even though a gun was found in the very vehicle that brought Mr. Vasquez to the hospital, a gun that the evidence will show was the one that wounded him."

She began to pace as she outlined the events of the night, or the prosecution's version of those events.

A friend of Vasquez's, she said, had driven him to the hospital that night. Vasquez had been shot in the leg—at close range. There were burn marks not just on the wound, but in the pocket of his jeans—proving, she said, that the gun was in his pocket at the time. Quickly stuffing the gun into his pocket as he ran, he accidentally fired it.

Her straightforward presentation only made the circumstances of the trial seem more bizarre. All the trappings of this room, and the associated resources—time, money, people—were dedicated to something as simple as a man shooting himself in the leg. It was an episode of *Law and Order* written by Samuel Beckett.

"The prosecution will show definitively that Raul Vasquez shot himself with the gun found in the car that brought him to the hospital. And we trust that you will hold him accountable for his crime."

Another dramatic pause. "Thank you," she added at last, then made her way back to her table and took her seat. She began to scratch notes on a pad of paper as the judge called the defense counsel to make his own opening argument.

Mr. Crews unspooled his legs from beneath the table and made his way toward the jury box. He was well over six feet tall, thin as a ballerina. His cheeks, shaved close, were almost concave.

"Good morning," he said in a firm, deep voice. "The prosecution tells an awfully good story, but I'm afraid the truth isn't quite as convenient as Ms. Harmon paints it. Yes, Mr. Vasquez arrived at the hospital with a gunshot wound. But Ms. Harmon got one crucial thing wrong: Raul Vasquez did not shoot himself." He chuckled briefly, dismissing the thought as absurd. "In fact, the evidence will show that Mr. Vasquez was the victim of a drive-by shooting, that he never had possession of any gun, let alone the one that shot him."

Beside me, Bruno the alternate was already slouching in his seat. Unless there was some unforeseen circumstance, he would be dismissed before deliberations began, so I suspect he didn't think it worth his while to pay much attention. Meanwhile, at the far end of the jury box, Don was leaning forward.

"Not a shred of evidence," Mr. Crews said, "convincingly implicates Mr. Vasquez in a crime. There is no physical evidence—no fingerprints, no DNA—to prove that Mr. Vasquez had even touched the gun in question, and no witnesses who saw him with it. In short, there is reasonable doubt everywhere. And where there is reasonable doubt, there can be no conviction."

Crews wasn't as fond of pacing as Harmon was. He took a position before the prosecution's table and stood stock sill, his height lending him an air of authority his speech might not otherwise merit. Vasquez, he said, was out with friends that night, at one of their favorite bars in the Mission District. As they were leaving the bar in the early morning of October 6th, a car sped by and a man pointed a gun out the window. This stretch of the neighborhood was known for gang activity, and Vasquez became the innocent victim of a drive-by shooting. The bullet hit him in the leg and a friend drove him to the hospital. Vasquez, he said, was the victim of a crime, not the perpetrator.

Throughout, Crews's tone was matter-of-fact, with none of the emotion and dramatic flair that had characterized Harmon's version of events. Even his description of the drive-by was cold, almost tentative. I suppressed an urge to raise my hand, to ask for clarification. His story was sketchy, missing too many elements to be convincing. Who was the intended victim of the drive-by? Had other shots been fired? Did they find blood in front of the bar? I just had to trust that everything would be revealed in time. I was skeptical, but already hooked.

I glanced again at Vasquez, sitting stock still on the other side of the room. His head had fallen toward the end of Crews's presentation and he was now staring at his interlaced fingers on the tabletop. His knuckles had dark markings on them—tattoos, I assumed, illegible from this distance.

The judge called a quick recess, and we filed back into the jury room.

I met Nancy by the coffee, picking up the last remaining crumb of a doughnut. "Can we vote now?" she whispered.

The coffee pot was empty, so I grabbed a water bottle from the mini-fridge.

The other jurors were scattered around the room, most standing, a few already seated at the table. Ellen, a young Type A, was furiously typing an email on her phone. Arnold, a young blond guy, was in the corner, lifting his hands over his head and stretching from side to side. His biceps bulged out as he moved. He was what Oscar would call a fireplug.

Directly before me, a woman whose name I couldn't recall crossed her arms on the tabletop and shrugged. She looked up at me through a tangle of frizzy curls and said with a deadpan tone, "Are we having fun yet?"

"Oh, I'm sure it will get more exciting than this."

She frowned. "If it does, I'm not sure I could stand it."

I was beginning to think that jury duty brought out the comedian in everyone.

"I'm Sandra," she said.

"Craig."

She nodded, but whether because she remembered my name or simply approved of it, I couldn't guess.

"First time on a jury?"

"Yes," I replied. "You?"

"Yeah. I'm just glad it's not an asbestos case. I hear there's millions of asbestos cases. Can you imagine how boring that would be?"

Sandra carried herself as if every moment were a chore. I had the feeling she would have found the O.J. trial boring.

In general, the talk was minimal at this point. The main topic on everyone's mind was the trial itself, and we were forbidden to discuss that. And we didn't know each other well enough to talk about anything else. It wasn't exactly a cocktail party, where you strike up a conversation and ask 20 questions to get to know a stranger. It was more akin to a condo association, I thought (being no fan of my own): you were friendly but showed no indication of wanting to be anyone's friend. That path was strewn with nothing but trouble.

Soon enough, the bailiff spared us the temptation, at least for today, by calling us back into the courtroom.

By the time we ended for the day, my head was swimming with details—tantalizing references to gun residue, fingerprints, and DNA, competing images of what had happened that night on a Mission street corner I'd never visited. As I left the building, I exhaled slowly, hoping to expel it all for the night. I decided to walk back to the Castro. It was only a half hour's hike, and depending on whether MUNI was having a bad day, I might even get there before the train.

The weight of the trial was getting to me already, hours of lawyerly pontifications and witness testimony. I thought of how after rigorous exercise my body would shut down, too exhausted to even tremble. That seemed to be happening to my brain now. Relieved at last of the pressure to pay attention, my mind was flitting all over the place, idly reacting to the world around me. I felt a vague hypersensitivity, as if the intensity of the courtroom had kept my nerves protected and now there was nothing between them and the outside world. Through my shoes, I felt the hardness of the pavement. I relished the warm sun on my face, the sweat just beginning to spill down my back.

I stopped at the corner of Grove and Van Ness, the opera house on one side, the symphony on the other, its huge rounded windows styled like piano keys. In a few blocks, as I rounded the corner onto Market, I passed the trash-laden sidewalk outside a doughnut shop, an empty lot behind a chain link fence strewn with colorful combination locks, and I marveled at the transition, one neighborhood giving way to another, the life of the city rising and falling along the stretch of its greatest boulevard. Behind me were the towers of downtown, beyond them the bay. And ahead, just before the street veered uphill and vanished into the horizon, was the Castro.

A few blocks down, just past Zuni Café (scene of my first date with Garrett, who'd raved that he'd never before had chicken that tasted so much like chicken), the freeway emptied onto Octavia Street under a huge, bright sky. When I'd first come to the city, this corner had been shadowed by a grungy overpass, which seemed to mark its eastern edge as the wrong side of the proverbial tracks. These last few blocks hadn't yet improved much, but the sense of division was no longer as clear, as unsubtle.

I climbed the gentle slope toward Safeway, whose parquet floor and gourmet stock had turned it into a suitable competitor for the Whole Foods that now dominated the opposite corner. In my college economics class, I'd been taught that competition tended to lower prices. Another rule of thumb torn to shreds by the 21st century.

I was passing Peet's when I spotted a familiar face in the window. Wayne looked up from his laptop, white earbuds dangling like misplaced Allen wrenches. I waved faintly, and his response turned into a beckoning gesture under a wide smile.

"How are you?" he said, sliding down from his stool as I entered the building. He placed his hands gingerly on my shoulders and came in for an air kiss.

"Welcome to my office," he said, pulling away. He was whispering, careful not to disturb the dozens of other people crouching over their own laptops, changing the world one app at a time. "What are you up to?"

He settled back onto his stool and I took the empty one beside him. "I'm just getting back from jury duty."

"How is that going?"

"Hard to say. They're just starting to build the case. Lots of very technical mumbo jumbo."

"Oh, right up my alley."

I chuckled. "Not unless you're into ballistics and blood spatter."

He scrunched his nose, as if he could smell the cordite. "Eeeww. Really?"

"It's a long story. I'll tell you all about it when it's over." I gestured to his screen, where half a dozen windows splayed around one another like playing cards. "What are you up to?"

He shook his head and closed the laptop. Military secrets, I presumed. "Oh, the usual. Building a business is all-consuming."

I didn't ask him to explain it. I'd long ago learned that doing something and describing it called upon two very different talents. It was like asking a writer what his book was about. Whenever I hosted a reading at the store, someone in the audience would inevitably ask what the writer was working on next, only to hear an incoherent, rambling reply that belied the articulateness on display the rest of the evening.

And besides, Luddite that I was, it was unlikely that I'd understand a word coming out of his mouth. So I changed the subject. "How's John?"

"He's good. I'm meeting him for dinner tonight." He dipped his head to one side with a soft smile. His beard had come in now. Unlike many of his peers', it was neatly trimmed—more Jeremy Irons than ZZ Top. He ran his finger along the side of the laptop, as though caressing a cat. "How long have you guys known each other?"

"Me and John?" I had to think for a moment. "About 10 years, I guess."

"Wow. I don't have any friends from that far back."

"And that would be what, grade school?"

He laughed. "College, actually. But I haven't stayed in touch. People are everywhere, doing all sorts of things. I can't keep up."

"It's funny," I said. "When you're young, you live for the future. When you're older, you live in the past."

"Can't we find a happy medium?"

"Like what?"

He smiled slyly. "I don't know—the present?"

"Touché."

Outside the sun pierced its way through a large cloud. "I have an appointment with John on Saturday," I said, bringing the conversation back.

He lifted his head, a nervous attentiveness returning to his expression. "Really? I didn't know you were a patient."

"I wouldn't let anyone else get that close to my eyes."

"Did you know his other boyfriends?" He dropped the question as casually as he might have asked *How did you meet?* or *What's your favorite color?*

"Some," I replied. "The more important ones, I guess."

[120]

"So what's his type?"

I laughed nervously. I suddenly felt like I was balancing on a tightrope. "I'm not sure John has a type."

"Doesn't everyone?"

"I thought you didn't believe in types," I said. "Didn't I hear you talking about sexual fluidity the other night? Do bisexuals have two types?"

"I didn't say I was bisexual."

"No, you didn't. But I just got this vibe that you didn't categorize so much. You seemed to suggest that our generation is too rigid."

He dipped his head again. It seemed to be his way of expressing a stance without having to commit to it.

"Why are you asking about John's type? Aren't *you* his type?"

"Sure." From his lips, it rhymed with *fur*.

"Is he yours?"

"I don't have a type," he said through a mischievous smile.

I leaned back in victory. "See?"

Someone at a nearby table looked up, annoyed. I'd forgotten to use my inside voice.

Wayne wore his youth like armor. The smooth skin, the well-coiffed hair, the wide-awake eyes—they were all barriers somehow to whatever was underneath. I remembered being that attractive once, but the inside had never matched the outside. Inside I was a tangle of insecurity and uncertainty. I was fumbling through life, trying things on one at a time to see which one fit, which one felt like me, whatever that even meant.

But when I gazed closely at Wayne—those light brown eyes that sparkled in the sunlight coming through the window—I had no idea what he was masking. Of course he wanted people to think he was as confident in his heart as he appeared to be on the surface. But he'd already given the lie to that stance, in his awkward tone of voice while asking about John's past. At some level, Wayne was as lost as the rest of us.

I sat silently beside him for a long moment, waiting.

"I just haven't had that much time for dating," he said at last.

"Really?"

"A few boyfriends here and there, but it's never been a priority for me."

I attempted a sympathetic smile to wipe the shock off my face. "So what, do you just hook up with guys? Like on Grindr or—" I stopped myself before the phrase *whatever the kids use these days* slid out of my mouth.

Wayne blanched. "Occasionally," he said, eyebrows coming together in a caterpillarish *V*. "It can be more efficient."

"Indeed," I said and smiled. "Cruising can certainly be a time suck. But when I was young"—here it comes, I thought—"I didn't feel I had much choice. The body wants what the body wants. Hormones are hormones."

Abruptly, he turned to gaze out at the street. "But they could get you into a lot of trouble in those days, right?"

"What do you mean?"

"Well, how did you deal with HIV when you were coming out?"

"I see. Well, by the time I came out, it was already here, so I never experienced life without that threat. Nevertheless, I decided I couldn't just shut myself up in a box out of fear. You learn to adjust. Everyone was very careful."

Meanwhile, Brendan was nursing his closest friends, watching them die.

Wayne's expression still hadn't changed. "I know a few guys who are on PrEP. They treat it like permission to do whatever they want."

I wondered if he blamed us—my generation, or even more, the ones who had come before. We had gone overboard. The very ones who had earned the community's freedom had, in short order, ruined it for everyone else. It was like greenhouse gases or income inequality—something to lay at the feet of an older generation, an older generation who, in younger eyes, had been shortsighted and self-centered.

They were no doubt right about climate change and racism and the rest; every generation had its role to play there. But I didn't buy the sexual part of the argument. Sex, to me, was the life force itself. I still clung to that notion, even as my own libido was beginning to fade. I'd chosen sexual partners randomly at times, desperate not to go home alone on a Saturday night. I'd spent a lot of hours in my youth just looking—checking out every man in the room, evaluating, selecting. I'd spent half my energy in pursuit of sex—thinking about it on the subway, at the grocery store, in line at the bank. I'd lain on a towel in the park on countless weekend afternoons, relishing the heat of the sun as it sank into my bare chest and imagining the sensation was from the hands of a passing stranger. I'd taken home, even dated, men I could no longer imagine myself with, men who had looked better in the dark, men who were unsophisticated or unkind or just boring. And now, on the other side of 50, with all that behind me and no idea what to replace it with, I didn't regret a thing.

"Well," I said at last, "I guess you're pretty picky about who you date, so John should count himself lucky."

"Yes." Wayne smiled, and the wall went back up. The smile—those broad, perfectly straight teeth—wiped away everything.

It was strange, I thought, back on the street, heading to the store. They'd been together for nine months, and this was the first time I'd had a one-on-one conversation with Wayne. It was the first time he'd spoken that much without an air of trying to defend himself. Our gang put every new lover through the wringer. Some, like Garrett, managed to charm them quickly enough to break through. But if they didn't claim their ground right away, it was a constant struggle. Damien had given up after a single try.

History had a way of creeping up on me. Memories came back more and more lately—filling the gaps in my thoughts, turning each day's quiet into a wormhole to the past.

Dead or alive, the ghosts were everywhere, popping up unexpectedly, hijacking the most ordinary moments. The smell of a newly sharpened pencil conjured Barry, the odd mix of graphite and cinnamon that wafted from his skin. Scratching an itch behind my ear, I would suddenly feel Jake's lithe fingers massaging the same spot, soft and warm as a silky bath. And the crest of a wave at Ocean Beach in the crepuscular light drew me once again into Garrett's eyes, that piercing blue that nothing else in the world could match.

I didn't live in those memories, but the past was adept at forcing its way into the present. It was more real somehow, perhaps because it was complete, no longer subject to the whims of the moment. It was fixed, and nothing I did or dreamed could change it.

Most of the time, that was a comfort. I could pull the memories out like books on a shelf, evidence that life had been full of joyful moments. Some of them still made me laugh: Joseph on Halloween, singing a Donna Summer tune in a cracking falsetto as he charged down the street, a Wonder Woman cape flowing in the breeze behind him. The look of befuddlement on Evan's face as he tried to teach me to rollerblade and instead had to watch me tumble to the ground over and over.

Those were fine—the relationships that had run their course, or had never really gotten off the ground. A few of them had broken my heart, but I could live with that, too, because in retrospect I could see that the end had been preordained. A fantasy had died, but I hadn't missed out on a reality.

And then there were the ones who were gone—some lost to the world, others just to me—and the few who remained on the periphery of my life in Christmas cards and Facebook posts, or a polite wave when we passed each other on the street.

Most, of course, were more decidedly gone—lost to my memory, as well. I used to keep a running list of them—all the men I'd slept with, or fumbled with for a few random moments at a party or a back room somewhere—but over time, the list became just a jumble of words. *Tony, Midnight Sun, 3/20/98.* He was a name, a place, a time, but I no longer had any idea what we had done or talked about, no image of what he looked like—how broad his shoulders, how big his dick. Or the color of his eyes.

Those names were just evidence, a catalog to prove that I hadn't been a hermit, that even if love continued to elude me, connection had not. The names, in a way, were my salvation. I wasn't ashamed of any of it.

It was the other type of regret that haunted me—the things undone, the ones I'd let slip out of fear or ignorance or insensitivity.

Damien was nothing, I told myself. Oscar was right: I didn't really know him. He couldn't really hurt me.

Now, it was rushing back to me again. Maybe it was the inevitability of loss, the vibe I got that Wayne would leave John before long, that the whole thing was an illusion on both their parts. Or maybe it was Wayne himself, the naïveté that reminded me of my own, long ago, when I believed there would always be time, that any mistake could be mended, any road exited.

CHAPTER 9
FLESH AND BONE

We'd heard from only one witness on the first day, a security guard at the hospital, who had testified about Vasquez's arrival. The guard had seen the car pull up, and the driver racing around to the passenger side to help Vasquez as he made his way toward the entrance.

This testimony served little purpose other than to paint a picture of the scene. I'd gazed over at Vasquez as the guard spoke, imagining him leaning against his friend, limping toward the hospital doors.

On the second day, the first witness was a police officer, a beefy man with a no-nonsense demeanor and a vocabulary right out of *Hill Street Blues*.

The cop had been called to the hospital when Vasquez came in for treatment of the gunshot wound. The prosecutor led him through the events.

"Officer Turner, why were you at the hospital that night?"

"I was called in response to the report of a person who was admitted with a gunshot wound. Whenever that happens, the hospital calls us because there may be a crime involved."

At the defense table, Crews grimaced and began to rise but caught himself.

"And what did you see when you arrived?"

"The first thing I noticed was a car directly in front of the entrance that was taking up two parking spaces. Both doors were ajar."

"Did you inspect the car?"

"Not at that juncture," Turner said, settling back in his chair.

"What happened next?"

"Inside the hospital, I spoke with the security guard on duty, who told me that Mr. Vasquez had arrived in the company of another gentleman, a Roland Talbott. Mr. Talbott was helping Mr. Vasquez walk because of the wound in his leg."

"And was Mr. Talbott still there?"

"Yes, he was in the waiting room. I interviewed him and ascertained that it was his car I had spotted in the parking lot."

"So he had driven Mr. Vasquez to the hospital."

"Yes."

"Did he tell you anything about the gunshot?"

Now Crews shot up. "Objection, Your Honor. Calls for hearsay."

"Sustained," said the judge.

Harmon stood back, lips pursed. "Did you inspect the car?"

"Yes. I told Mr. Talbott that the car would have to be moved, since it was taking up too much space. But, because there was a possible crime involved, I asked him if I could search the car first."

"Did he give you permission for the search?"

"Yes."

"And the car was registered to Mr. Talbott?"

"Yes, he confirmed that with the registration."

"Well then, what did you find in the car, Officer Turner?"

"Of relevance to the case, ma'am, I found blood stains on the passenger seat."

"Anything else?"

"Yes. On the back seat I found a handgun."

Harmon displayed a delicate smile that might have passed for a frown—lips sealed and curled delicately, eyes narrowed—and walked to her table. She dug inside a box and pulled out a gun. "Is this the gun, Officer?"

She laid it on the ledge in front of the witness chair, and Officer Turner looked it over without touching. "Yes," he said.

"This gun was found in Mr. Talbott's car."

"Yes."

"Did he explain why he had a gun?"

Crews shot up again. "Objection. Hearsay."

"Sustained." The judge looked down at the prosecutor. "Ms. Harmon, you can pursue this line of questioning when you call Mr. Talbott to the stand."

"Yes, Your Honor." She retrieved the gun and laid it gently back in the box. As she turned to face Turner again, she asked, "Officer, did you interview the defendant in the hospital?"

"Yes."

"What did he tell you about the incident?"

"Objection!" hollered Crews.

"Don't tell me," Harmon said, turning toward the defense table. "Hearsay?"

Before Crews could respond, the judge called them both up to the bench. They gathered at the far side of the room and the judge looked down from her chair as they spoke. Suddenly, a muffling sound came out of the speakers behind the jury box. At the bench, the three of them were mouthing words I couldn't make out at all.

The white noise went off as abruptly as it had begun once their private conversation was over. Turning back to the room,

Judge Reilly gazed down at Turner. "The witness may answer the question," she said.

"Could you repeat it, please?" the officer asked.

"Certainly," said Harmon. "What did Mr. Vasquez tell you about the incident that had brought him to the hospital?"

"He said that he'd been shot."

"Where?"

"In the leg."

A soft chuckle traveled through the courtroom.

"In what location did he say he was when he was shot?"

"Oh. In front of the Peppermill Bar, near Mission and 20th Street."

"How did he say he was shot?"

"It was a drive-by, he said. A car pulled past and ... someone shot him."

"Did he give you a license plate number?"

"No."

"Any description of the vehicle?"

"He said it was too dark."

"Too dark. On Mission Street."

"Yes, ma'am."

"So he didn't know who shot him or why?"

"He didn't indicate that he did, no."

"Did he mention any witnesses to this incident?"

"No. Other than the man who found him."

"And who was that?"

"Roland Talbott."

"Is that all?"

"Yes. He said they were with other people at the bar, but they had left before Mr. Vasquez and Mr. Talbott left and the shooting occurred."

Harmon nodded and folded her hands at her waist. "Officer Turner, did you conduct an independent investigation at the Peppermill, to confirm Mr. Vasquez's story?"

"I did. The next day."

"And what did you learn?"

"No one we spoke to at the bar or the adjacent businesses mentioned having seen or heard a shooting."

"Did you inspect the premises?"

"We checked the sidewalk and the storefront, but didn't find any evidence of a shooting."

"What kind of evidence were you looking for?"

"Blood. A shell casing. Bullet holes anywhere."

"And you found none of that."

"No."

"But there was blood in Mr. Talbott's car."

"Yes."

"Thank you, Officer. No more questions." Harmon made her way back to her table.

"Mr. Crews," said the judge.

Crews jumped up and began to talk on his way to the witness stand. He started with background questions, mostly reiterating what Harmon had already established. It felt like instant replay.

"You say you found the gun in Mr. Talbott's car." Now Crews crossed his arms before his chest and stood directly in front of Turner. "Did you pick it up?"

"Yes," Turner said. "With gloves."

"Was it warm to the touch?"

"Not particularly."

"Did you have any reason to believe it had been recently fired?"

"I couldn't say one way or the other, sir."

"So it may not have been fired that evening."

"Yes." Turner squinted. "Or it may have."

I couldn't make out Crews's expression, but his back arched subtly. "No further questions, Your Honor."

Turner left the stand and was replaced by the ER doctor who had treated Vasquez. The trial was turning into something out of Agatha Christie: lots of puzzle pieces laid out willy-nilly, with no sense yet of how they fit together.

Dr. Flagstad was a tall, rather broad-shouldered woman with red hair pulled back in a ponytail. She took the stand with a professional demeanor, though it was clear that this was not her milieu at all.

With a few preliminary questions, the prosecutor established that Flagstad was on duty the night of the incident and had treated Vasquez for his wound. But it was the wound itself that Harmon was most interested in.

"What was the nature of Mr. Vasquez's wound?" she asked.

Dr. Flagstad squinted, lips in a thoughtful pout. "There were two wounds, actually," she said.

"Two?"

"Yes. There was an entry wound in the thigh, and an exit wound in the shin, just below the knee."

"So there was no bullet."

"No. The bullet had gone right through."

Harmon entered another exhibit into the record—photographs taken at the hospital of Vasquez's leg. She held them up and walked slowly in front of the jury box, displaying them. The wounds were clean in the photos, no blood gushing anywhere, so they weren't quite as difficult to look at as I'd feared. One small hole in the thigh, a larger one below the knee, a dark jagged ring.

"Doctor, how can you tell which is the entry wound?"

Dr. Flagstad frowned—the look of a teacher being asked a stupid question by a particularly dull pupil. "Entry wounds are typically smaller and symmetrical. Once the bullet penetrates the skin, it's slowed by contact with internal tissue and does more damage on the way out. Exit wounds are therefore larger and"—she hesitated, searching for the right word—"messier."

Harmon nodded briefly. "What position would Mr. Vasquez's leg have been in to create these wounds?"

"Given the position, we could tell that his leg was not bent more than 30 degrees."

"So he may have been more or less standing still?"

"Yes."

"What does that mean about the position of the gun?"

"The gun would have to have been in an almost vertical position and, given the amount of damage we saw, very close to the entry point."

"Is the wound, then, consistent with a shot being fired from several feet away—say from the distance between a street and the sidewalk?"

Crews looked flustered. He stood up like a jack-in-the-box. "Objection! Dr. Flagstad is not an expert in bullet trajectory."

Harmon, I could tell, was doing all she could to keep from rolling her eyes. "The ER at SF General sees gunshot wounds every day."

Crews started to object again, but the judge cut him off. "I'll allow the question, but solely in that context. Be careful, Ms. Harmon."

"Thank you, Your Honor. Dr. Flagstad, given your experience with gunshot wounds, do you think it's possible that Mr. Vasquez was shot from a distance?"

Dr. Flagstad looked completely unflustered. She leaned toward the thin microphone in the witness box. "No."

"Thank you," Harmon said. "Your witness," she called out, not looking directly at Crews.

Despite his dramatic objection, Crews steered away from asking the doctor more about the nature of the wound. Instead, we got something akin to his approach to Officer Turner—a methodical restatement of what Harmon had already asked, his apparent goal merely to catch Dr. Flagstad in a lie. He dispensed with her pretty quickly. He was going through the motions, but knew he could get nothing from her that would help his case.

Dr. Flagstad was dismissed and, after a bit of haggling with the attorneys, the judge decided to call it a day. We all filed back into the jury room.

The bailiff instructed us to drop our notebooks on the table. As people began to file out, he scooped our notebooks into a pile, counting as he went. We had been told that the notebooks would be held, that we couldn't look at them outside of the court, probably to avert any chance that they fell into unauthorized hands. As a result, I didn't feel much ownership of my notes and found myself a bit hesitant, knowing they could be read by someone else. In lieu of written judgments, I stumbled upon the idea of using symbols for the credibility of witnesses and statements, up and down arrows that might come in handy later.

Except for the slapping of the books against the table, the room was silent. Everyone clearly tried to put on a game face, but Nancy did flash me a reassuring eyebrow lift on her way out the door. We were all still in the dark.

CHAPTER 10

GHOST STORIES

I took the afternoon off to decompress. When I got to the store at around 6:00, Joel was arranging the tented chalkboard on the sidewalk. He fiddled with the base to get it perpendicular with the door, and I peered over his shoulder as I approached:

Tonight 7:00
Derek Sweetwater
Author of Geoffrey's New York

"Nice," I said, gesturing toward the chalkboard with my coffee. "But you misspelled it."

He looked back at the sign, forehead crinkling. "Misspelled what?"

"His name. Didn't you check the book cover? It's D-e-r-i-c-k."

Joel turned to look through the doorway, where the books were stacked on the front table. He wiped away the errant chalk mark with his fingers. "Who spells it like that?" he sputtered.

"Derick does." I squeezed past him into the store.

Dave was in the back, arranging chairs for the reading.

"Looks great," I told him.

He turned toward me, a lock of dark hair falling over one eye. "How many people do you think will come?"

"No idea." Readings were unpredictable things these days. "Let's not jinx it, though. Set out about 15 chairs."

Dave aligned the chairs to create sight lines between the seats. A few bookcases had been pushed back toward the window to make room for the narrow podium. The microphone stand struck me as optimistic, but better safe than sorry.

In my office, I settled my bag beside the desk just as the phone rang.

"How are things going, Craig?" Angela, feigning concern, as usual.

"Great," I said, trying to infuse my voice with an upbeat tone. "We're having a reading tonight."

"Oh, how nice." She paused, waiting for her moment. "You made quite an impression with Tiffany."

"Did I?"

"Yes. And she loves the space. In fact, she's bringing a client over on Saturday to check it out."

On the opposite wall there was a framed clipping from the *Bay Area Reporter*—a gift from Oscar—an interview with me right after I'd taken over management of the store. I could barely make out the photo from here—a naively optimistic smile, unruly hair that had not yet vanished down the drain.

"Thanks for the heads-up." I cringed at the cliché, but it seemed more polite than what I really wanted to say: *Thanks for the warning.*

She didn't ask about the reading, or who the author was. For a bookstore owner, Angela had never expressed much interest in books. I wasn't even sure what she read herself. When I first started, before she'd moved to Palm Springs, she visited a few times, a copy of the *Times* best-seller list in her hand, and made sure all the listed books were prominently displayed. The rest of our collection was just window dressing.

By the time I got myself together and stepped out of the office, people were starting to filter in for the reading. Two or three chairs were already taken, and other customers were milling about, killing time by browsing. Though it was always stressful hosting a reading, since you could never be sure how many people would show up, it was also when the store seemed most alive.

I heard voices at the front and gazed down toward the doorway. I recognized Derick from the photo on the book jacket—handsome, late thirties, sporting the same shy, surprised smile.

He was looking at the display of his own books on the front table, whispering to a couple of friends, when I approached. "Hi, Derick," I said. "I'm Craig Amundsen. We spoke on the phone."

"Of course." His cheeks were flushed. "Thank you so much for doing this."

"My pleasure," I said. "I enjoyed the book."

"Oh, you've read it." He looked startled by the idea of other people reading his work. So many writers had told me just that: after spending years locked in with their own words, it was hard to get used to the idea that someone else was reading it while you were in a parallel universe, washing the dishes or making love or cleaning the litter box.

He introduced me to his companions—a tall blond with soft skin who stroked Derick's shoulder now and then, the way you calm a frightened cat in your lap; and Keith, a stout guy in a leather jacket who seemed closer to my age than theirs.

"How was your trip?" I asked, leading them toward my office.

"It was lovely. It's so nice to be here. I haven't visited San Francisco in quite a while."

"Keith is putting us up," Jared, the blond, said. "It's a reunion of sorts. We knew each other in New York."

Keith smiled. "I moved here several years ago, to get away from the chaos. I love it, but I have to admit, the timing was ironic. As New York gets cleaner, San Francisco gets dirtier. I think the rats followed me across the country."

As they settled their things in the room, I went through the routine with Derick. He began skimming through his copy of the book, which was heavily flagged with post-it notes.

"Do you know what you're going to read?"

"Yes," he said. "A bit from the beginning, and then a scene from a little later on."

"Good," I said. "Just enough to whet their appetite." I peered out the door. It was 7:05 and the seats were mostly filled. "Okay, let's go."

Derick smiled nervously. I caught him squeezing Jared's hand, the ring glinting on his finger. We all moved to the doorway, and I made my way alone to the podium.

It wasn't a bad turnout for a debut novelist—most of the seats filled, a few other people standing toward the back, positioning themselves to escape if the evening got boring. The audience was almost exclusively gay men, a few around Derick's age but most past 50. I recognized Gary, an older guy who always wore a flannel shirt, no matter the weather, and the same bushy mustache, now gray going on white, covering his upper lip.

"Thank you all for coming," I said, leaning toward the microphone. As the murmuring voices settled down, I found a light grip on the podium and sought out a pair of eyes to focus on—that had always been my trick for easing into public speaking: one person at a time. Angela's call fresh in mind, I realized that this might be one of the last times I stood here and hosted an event like this. I savored the moment, the view of the entire store afforded by the podium's position near the rear wall of the build-ing—the display tables, worn and scratched with age; the shelves I'd stained myself to brighten up the space; the armchair in a nook off to the side where, to my chagrin, some people tended to read for as long as an hour and then put the book back on the shelf.

"We're thrilled to welcome Derick Sweetwater here tonight, to read from his debut novel, *Geoffrey's New York*. Derick is an exciting new voice, and although the title of his book is very Big Apple, it has something to say to all of us, even on the Left Coast. Just check out the review in this week's *BAR*." I dug out a quote from the review and, holding up a copy of the book, read a couple of the blurbs on the back. "Now, please welcome Derick Sweetwater."

I stepped back as Derick approached from the sidelines to a smattering of applause. He was carrying his own copy of the book, the brownstones on the cover at an angle, as though a calamitous earthquake threatened to bring the whole neighborhood clatter-ing to the ground. Once he was settled at the podium, I slinked back the way I had come and took a spot leaning against the wall.

After a brief introduction, he cracked open the book. He paused for a moment before beginning to read.

Some new lovers have romantic dinners or spend all day in bed. Geoffrey liked to walk. In those first weeks, we scoured the town like cu-rious nomads. We would meet at a familiar spot—the Great Lawn, the Chrysler Building, the Stonewall Inn—with no agenda other than to explore. Geoffrey would close his eyes and spin around a few times, one arm extended, and wherever his finger was pointing when he stopped became our route. The goal was to keep going until we got lost, until the landmarks fell away and we were left with indistinct streets, peculiar storefronts, a world where both of us—natives of this oversized metrop-olis—could feel like tourists, invaders. We stumbled around, searching

for novelty, while the real natives—the people who lived in the neigh-
borhoods that seemed so exotic to us—went steadily about their busi-
ness, fully aware of where they were and where they were going. As
they brushed past, Geoffrey's smile widened: he was in his element. The
ineffable mystery, this unknown land, was Geoffrey's New York.

And I followed him through it, peering down alleys as if they were
Alice's keyhole. I told myself at first that it was a way to expand my
knowledge of the city. But gradually, Geoffrey taught me that we were
exploring time as much as space. As we moved from one block to an-
other, life went on behind us, everything kept changing. We would walk
down the same streets in six months and find them just as strange as
they'd been on our first visit. In our own neighborhoods, we saw the
changes happening, step by step, so that by the time the scaffolding was
removed from a new building we had no memory of the skeletal struc-
ture it had once masked, the hole in the ground before that, the empty
lot, the houses that had been torn down to make way for progress. We
saw only what was now there, and in some deep part of our brains we
imagined that it always had been. It was only here, in the places we saw
so seldom, that change became visible. It was only here that transforma-
tion seemed real.

I scanned the audience. A couple of people looked puzzled, engaged in trying to figure out the story. One man off to the side was smiling brightly and nodding. But most faces were expressionless, inscrutable. I was reminded suddenly of my new daily ritual. This, too, was a kind of jury, taking in the evidence, sitting in judgment.

Derick read for 20 minutes or so, jumping as promised from the reflective opening section to a more concrete passage in the middle, an argument between the two main characters, and when he closed the book the audience applauded politely.

It wasn't the kind of book that sold well, not these days. Derick's story was not populated with girls on trains, or twinks in love with their own abs. It wasn't action-packed, jumping from one continent to another and leaving a body count on each shore. Derick replaced all that with heart and a youthful earnestness that would no doubt fade in time.

As the applause died down, I jumped up to join him at the podium.

"Thank you, Derick," I said. "We have time now for some questions, if anyone would like to start. …"

Derick dutifully parried questions for a few minutes, the usual litany about when he wrote, where his ideas came from. Questions that budding writers would ask, hoping to learn the secrets of success.

When the questioning was done, I pointed to a table set up in the middle of the store, copies of *Geoffrey's New York* stacked like a ziggurat on one corner, and invited the audience to get Derick's autograph.

Jared appeared suddenly at Derick's side and clutched his arm. "You were great!" he said. "Wonderful stage presence." He turned toward me. "I taught him everything he knows."

"Oh, really? Are you a writer, too?"

"No," Derick said. "He's a drag queen."

Jared threw his head back and gave me a side wink.

A ragged line began to form before the table. Derick glided toward it. Turning back, he said, "We're all going to go out for a drink later. Would you like to join us?"

"Sure," I said.

He sold seven or eight books and signed the rest of the copies we had on hand. I asked Joel to close up the store and then followed Derick and his friends outside.

Keith, the native, was in charge of the evening. He led us to the Mix, his favorite bar, a couple of blocks from the store. It was a place I had once frequented under a name I could no longer remember, but other than that it didn't seem to have changed much.

We commandeered a corner on the back patio, where the crowd was thinner and the music farther away. I offered to pay for the first round, but Keith was already waving his wallet in the air. He and Jared headed off to fetch beers while Derick and I chatted.

"Where else is the tour taking you?"

Derick laughed. "I wouldn't exactly call it a tour. My publisher can hardly afford to do marketing, let alone send me around the country. Aside from a couple of local spots in New York, the rest is just an excuse to visit friends."

"You got a pretty good crowd tonight."

"It was certainly better than the last reading. We were at a tiny dive in the Bowery. And by *we*, I mean me and three audience members—one of whom was Jared."

I smiled sympathetically. "Well, I can tell you from experience. The more important thing is the publicity—anything in the paper or online, and the mere fact that the bookstore people know who you are."

"Even if I embarrass them with a small showing?"

"Did any of those three people buy books?" He nodded. "Then they're happy, believe me. So what's next on the agenda?"

He leaned against the weathered wall. "Well, we're staying a few more days here, and then we head to L.A. Jared has a friend we can stay with who arranged for me to do a reading for his book club."

"Ah, so you've already sold them!"

"I hope so. An acquaintance of mine in New York said he'd

[142]

recommended it for his book club, and I was very excited. Then, a week later, he told me they'd decided against it because the library didn't have enough copies."

"What? They wanted you to come read to them and they couldn't even be bothered to buy their own?"

He smiled. "Well, five or six copies wouldn't exactly put me into a new tax bracket."

"That's irrelevant," I told him. "It's just rude. Maybe it's the bookstore guy in me, but aside from research, I think libraries are for children and poor people. If you can afford the damn book, then buy it. Especially if you know the author."

Suddenly Jared and Keith appeared, a beer in each hand. "Well," Jared said, "I'm not sure what that was about, but someone's passionate about something."

"Sorry," I said, "I'm just a little protective of my writers."

"Your writers."

"The lifeblood of a bookstore."

"Well," Jared said, lifting his beer. "To the lifeblood."

Four bottlenecks clinked.

"It must be exciting," I said to Derick. "Your first book."

He smiled cagily. "Well, it's the first time I've had my name on the cover, anyway."

"What do you mean?"

"I used to be a ghostwriter."

"Oh, that sounds like fun."

He scowled. "Not so much. I got tired of telling other people's stories. And the last one was a real dick."

"The last one?"

Derick shook his head and brough his fingers beside his lips to twist an imaginary lock. "I'll never tell."

"Well," I said, "you made the right choice."

We talked about the state of literature, the struggle of embarking on a new career. The conversation reminded me of the old days, when I was Derick's age, or younger—when conversations like this felt like philosophizing.

The crowd was mostly on the young side and very hip. No flannel shirts, no skimpy tanktops or crotch-outlining jeans, fashionable haircuts replaced by man buns. The stud earrings that my generation wore—left ear for top, right for bottom—had been replaced by huge plastic loops stretching the lobes out of shape. I imagined what their ears would look like when this trend had finally seen its 15 minutes. These presumably gay men looked no different than the straight hipsters strolling Valencia or swarming out of a SoMa startup.

It wasn't far from this spot that Garrett had approached me for the first time, his sly smile made brighter by his eyes. Lucky for me, Garrett didn't share my insecurity, the fear of rejection that often kept me riveted to one spot, eyes turned toward the floor, the wall, anywhere but the face of another man. But he saw through all that. He knew exactly what to say.

Gazing cynically out at the crowd, he said with a weary sigh, *Wouldn't you rather be at home reading a good book?*

I laughed loud enough to catch the attention of the whole group around me—me, the center of a circle, the spot where you plant the compass in geometry class. But when I lowered my voice to respond, they all faded away. There was only Garrett then. And when our flirtation finished, when it was clear what would come next, he moved in close, his breath—beer and spearmint—tickling my cheek. *I live just around the corner,* I said. *I hope you're not allergic to cats.*

Only the musical, he said. And I thought he'd won me for life.

Beside me now, Derick was beaming as he looked out at the

crowd. "Having a good time?" I asked.

"Absolutely. I'm still just shocked that I've actually published a novel."

"Even after all those ghost stories?" Keith asked with a smirk.

"Especially after all the ghost stories."

In this space, teeming with bodies, I imagined my own ghosts—two decades' worth of lovers and strangers all in one place. A mop of red hair in the distance, a bright poppy in a dark field, conjured up Garrett. A sudden turn of a head, firm jaw angling archly upward, was Barry contemplating the skyline. And so many others, names forgotten, faces little more than fractured images—all there, calmly colliding and drawing apart in the web of memory.

On nights like this, all those years ago, Oscar and I would go from bar to bar, checking out the vibe, searching for the proverbial Mr. Right Now, who was usually too easy to find. Looking back, I wondered how I'd ever had the time. I was no busier now—arguably less so—but I couldn't imagine keeping up that pace again. I decided that it had more to do with energy than time. The minutes ticked by more slowly when you were young, and time itself bent to your will.

CHAPTER 11
EYEWITNESS

"Better one, or two?"

The contraption clicked and everything grew a shade blurrier.

"One," I said, though we'd been at this for so long I could no longer be sure if the clarity was improving or if the brightness of the eye chart against the surrounding darkness was completely fucking with my vision.

A few more spins of the dial and John pulled the cold frame away from my face. He flicked on the light and started scribbling on a pad.

"Am I going to die?" I asked.

He snickered. "First of all, I'm an optometrist, not an M.D. And second, yes, you are going to die. We're all going to die." He looked up at me. "But at least you'll be buried in a fabulous pair of glasses."

There was a coziness to the exam room, crammed with mysterious equipment, hermetically sealed from the outside world. I'd come to look forward to these annual visits. They were a kind of ritual.

"However," John said with a dry tone that pulled my gaze back to him. "The time has come for progressive lenses."

I felt my brow furrowing.

"What your grandfather probably called bifocals," he said.

"Only without that nasty line across the middle."

"Why?" I asked.

"It happens," he said. "Your near vision is still strong—because of all that reading, no doubt. But the distance vision is getting worse. Everyone's eyes get less flexible with age."

"Great."

"You'll get used to them," he said. He grabbed an eyedropper from the table and moved closer. "Now look up," he said. "This will sting a bit."

"That's what they all say."

Deftly, he put drops in each eye and handed me a tissue. I dabbed the underside of my eyes and pulled the tissue away, noting the brightness of the material, like yellow chartreuse spilled onto a tablecloth.

"Okay," he said, "while we're waiting for the dilation, let's pick out your new frames." He rose from his chair and led me out to the reception area.

He put me in the hands of one of the young opticians. This, too, was part of the ritual. Even if he had time, John couldn't linger with me and look over various frames, lest another patient observe and wonder why they weren't getting the same attention.

Whenever my prescription changed, even slightly, I would get new frames. So for all intents and purposes, I was actually just adding to my collection rather than replacing. I had begun to wear eyeglasses like any other accessory—to match the rest of the outfit.

As always, there were too many choices. The optician, Ned, struck me as a wannabe *Queer Eye* host, excitedly pulling frames off the shelves and holding them against my face in an almost flirtatious manner. He gravitated toward chunky frames, which reminded me of Groucho Marx. "No," I said, "narrower." I wanted something subtle, not a pair of glasses that would enter the room before I did.

It was a sunny day, and bright light was streaming into the office, bouncing off the mirrors placed here and there so people could check out their frames. My eyes were dilating swiftly. I had only a few minutes before the whole experience became completely untenable.

"How about these?" I asked, pulling a pair of bright blue frames off the shelf. Unfolding them, I noted a purple tinge to the underside. I laid my own glasses aside and slid the new ones over my ears.

I was a bit startled by the image of myself staring back from the mirror. This new man seemed relaxed, confident—almost bold. His glasses were, at any rate. They were so not me.

"I'll take them," I said.

"Fabulous!" Ned replied. "Those are my favorites."

Something told me he had a lot of favorites.

Back in the exam room, John turned out the lights again and pulled another mechanism toward me.

"Eeeww," I said, "I hate this part." The glaucoma test was the only phase of an eye exam that made me truly uncomfortable.

"Just be glad I'm not a proctologist," John murmured.

Assenting, I settled my chin on the support. I felt like Anne Boleyn, waiting for the axe.

"Wayne's been working like a fiend lately," John said. A bright blue pen light shone toward me, leaving everything else pitch black. His voice took on a Darth Vader quality.

I was a captive audience, unable to respond because of the chin support—not to mention the poker within millimeters of my eyeball.

[148]

He adjusted the machine and rolled it toward my other eye. "I have to say, I really admire his chutzpah. Starting a business at his age. He's a very ambitious guy."

The probe moved closer, the blue light radiating. I could see scratchy lightning bolts on the periphery—reflections, I assumed, of the veins in my eye.

"I'm not quite sure what he sees in an old fart like me." He grunted and wheeled away from me, taking the machine with him. Caught by surprise, I was a second late lifting my chin and hit my head on the upper part of the frame.

"Why do you say that?" I asked, settling back in the exam chair.

"Our worlds are so different," he said, switching on the ceiling lamp. He adjusted the light with a dimmer switch to protect my eyes. "Don't get me wrong, it's exciting to be exposed to new things, and his energy is infectious. But sometimes it feels like we don't even speak the same language. There seems to be a bigger gap between this generation and us than there was between us and what came before. Hell, back in the eighties, anyone between junior high and the old folks' home was listening to Madonna. But now ... well, I have no idea what people Wayne's age listen to."

"Noise," I said. "They listen to noise."

"What about you?" John asked. "Are you still seeing Damien?"

"I don't know," I said. "I think we're on a break."

"You *think*?"

I shrugged. "We're on a break." Before he could ask for details, I added, "I ran into Wayne the other day, you know."

"Oh, where?"

"Peet's. He was working."

"As a barista?" His shocked look turned quickly into a laugh as he saw me struggling with the question.

"No. He was on his laptop."

"He brings that thing everywhere. Even to bed."

"Don't you tell him it's bad for his eyes?"

John smirked. "What it's bad for is sleep. That bright light just before bed is a terrible idea. But apparently he's immune. The boy sleeps like a rock."

"That'll be over soon enough. Before you know it, he'll be just like the rest of us, waking up at 3 a.m. to pee and then staring at the ceiling for the next four hours."

"So what did you guys talk about?"

"Besides you?"

"Uh oh. What did you tell him?"

I laughed. "Nothing. He should know everything by now, anyway, right?"

"You think I tell my boyfriends everything? What do you take me for, an idiot?"

"Have you popped the question yet?"

He adjusted his glasses with a poke on the bridge. "I'm working on it." He leaned forward now. "Do you think I should?"

"If you want to know where to place a semicolon in a sentence, then come to me. But for relationship advice?" I sealed my lips.

"Well, you just spoke to him. What do you think? Do you think he's ready?"

If I wasn't the expert, I could point him to Oscar, or Brendan. But he wasn't asking them. Probably because he knew what they would say.

"I don't know. He does seem a little …"—*lost*, I wanted to say, but *distracted* would do—"distracted."

"By work." He nodded and leaned back in his chair.

By life. "Yeah. I get the feeling he's still trying to find himself."

"Do people still do that?" John asked. "Look for themselves?"

"The smart ones do, yes." And suddenly I realized that I didn't just want to protect John from making a mistake. I wanted to protect Wayne, too.

"Well," he said with a sigh, "we'll see." He slapped his knees dramatically and rose from his seat. He handed me a packet of disposable wraparound sunglasses. "Now be careful, your eyes will be dilated for a while."

He said it in a tone clearly meant to shut down the conversation. I smiled wanly and got out of the chair.

On the way out, I strapped the flimsy glasses across my face, imagining that I looked like José Feliciano. Not that anyone on the street would have the first idea who José Feliciano was.

The world looked dark, as if night had fallen prematurely. Even with the shades, things were blurry and I found myself wobbling a bit as I turned the corner. I had only a few minutes before meeting the realtor at the store, not nearly enough time for the dilation to wear off. My timing was terrible. I could sense an *I Love Lucy* moment about to begin.

As I approached the store, I saw a couple of hazy figures standing in front. Tiffany was pointing at something above the windows, and another woman—older, but just as slender—followed her finger. I ripped the sunglasses off and a blinding blast of light assaulted my eyes. Stopping on the sidewalk, I squinted through the next moment to adapt to the pain. My only option was to rush them inside as soon as possible.

"Tiffany!" I said, approaching with an outstretched hand.

She came toward me, smiling perfunctorily. "Hello, Craig."

We shook hands and she introduced me to her companion, Yvonne. "Let's go inside," I said, barging through the doorway without waiting for a response.

Yvonne stopped in front of the cash register, where Cassandra was perched, gazing down at us. "It's lovely," Yvonne said. "Very nice layout."

"Thank you." I threw Cassandra a nod of greeting and continued toward the back. "Please follow me to the office. I have to drop off my things."

Reluctantly, Yvonne and Tiffany pulled away. I could hear their footsteps behind me. My hearing seemed preternaturally strong all of a sudden.

The darkness of the office was like a salve to my eyes. I breathed a sigh of relief and dropped my bag on the floor. "Please," I said, turning toward the doorway, "have a seat." I gestured toward the chairs in front of the desk.

"We just wanted to take a look around," Tiffany said, poised awkwardly behind the chair.

"Certainly," I said. "But I was hoping we could chat a bit first."

Yvonne, nonplussed, slinked into a chair and crossed her legs. I shut the door behind her.

"It's rather dark in here, isn't it?" Tiffany asked. I immediately wondered if she'd been named after the lamps.

"Oh, sorry," I said. I flipped on the desk lamp, which was more of a spotlight on my paperwork than a light fixture. Baby steps, I thought. "It can be so bright out in the store, I like to keep it a little cozier in here. Helps me concentrate."

Tiffany was visibly annoyed, but Yvonne threw her head languidly back and gazed up at the ceiling. She might have been a bat looking for a perch.

"Is that an original tin ceiling?" she asked.

"I think so, yes." I turned to Tiffany, concerned not to steal her thunder, or her pitch.

"This building has a lot of wonderful old features," Tiffany said dutifully. "Now—"

My brief respite in the dark would have to suffice. Time to grin and bear it.

"What are you hoping to do with the place?" I asked Yvonne as she unfolded herself and rose to her feet. Her hair was pulled up into a bun that seemed to add to her height.

"A yoga studio," she said.

"Do you teach?" It was like asking a tall man if he played basketball after seeing him dribble.

"Yes."

I opened the door, prepared to be blinded again, but it wasn't as bad this time. Behind me, Yvonne continued, "There's only one other studio in the neighborhood, but clearly the demand is greater than that. Or soon will be."

She was pulling a wayward strand of hair off her face, and I remembered the constant line of ponytailed young women streaming in and out of Soul Cycle every time I passed. She knew whereof she spoke.

Tiffany—who, as far as I knew, had seen the place for only the ten minutes she'd spent with me on her first visit—led the tour, pointing out the obvious as she made her way through the store. She stopped before the plate glass windows in back, highlighting the Southern exposure, the tiny patio. "Good for an outdoor class, perhaps?" she asked.

Yvonne, lips pursed, gave no reply.

I volunteered nothing as we made our way through the store. It was Tiffany's job to sell the place. I wasn't at all sure of my role, and not even sure I wanted to play one. I suddenly wondered if I should have deliberately messed up the place, gouged a few holes in the floor, shattered a pipe.

"What about the juice bar?" Tiffany asked suddenly, too loudly. My eyes darted toward the front, where Cassandra was standing guard and staring in our direction. I couldn't tell if Tiffany's words had caught her attention, or if she'd been watching the whole time.

"Up front, I should think," Yvonne replied. She was in her own world, swatting Tiffany's remarks away like flies.

The bookshelves came in for questioning. "How long have these been here?" Tiffany asked me.

"The shelves? Forever, as far as I know." Perhaps she'd misunderstood what the term *bookstore* meant.

"I'm just wondering what it looks like behind them." She turned to Yvonne. "You'll want to paint everything anyway, of course."

I felt a sudden pang, picturing the walls denuded of books. It seemed sacrilegious, like the burning of Alexandria.

Tiffany tried to rush through the space, but Yvonne kept holding her back, slowing her own pace and stopping every few feet. Her arms folded against her chest, she gazed around the room. I imagined that she was picturing the transformation, counting how many yoga mats could fit on the floor, how many leotarded butts could be raised at once in downward-facing dog. I could almost smell the sweaty nylon and wondered if my olfactory senses had improved along with my hearing.

"Is it quiet?" she said at last, as we neared the front of the store.

"Reasonably," I replied.

"No street noise once you close the door?"

"Not much. And the neighbors are fine."

She nodded, chin forward. "Good."

We were at the front now. Tiffany stood in the doorway, and

Yvonne slowly joined her. I had no choice but to face the street, the sun. Everything was yellow. Yellower than Tiffany's bleached hair.

"Well," she said with an air of dismissal, "thank you, Craig. We'll be in touch." She shook my hand again.

Yvonne's hand was warmer this time, a calming energy coming through her skin. Her smile seemed genuine, but anything would next to Tiffany. "Lovely to meet you," she said.

"Same here."

I didn't bother watching them go. I had to turn around as quickly as possible, back to the safety of artificial light.

"What was that all about?"

Cassandra was beside me, as though she'd silently teleported herself across the room. Her eyes were an unnatural blue today, like lapis. With alternating contacts, her eyes went from blue to brown so often I could never be sure what their real color was.

I fumbled. "Business acquaintances of Angela's," I said at last.

"What did they want?"

"She just asked me to show them around."

"Why? She's not selling the place, is she?"

I avoided her gaze. "Give me a sec," I said. "I need to make a call." I hurried back toward the office and closed the door, relishing the darkness.

If I had kept them in the office longer, I could have told Cassandra they were accountants, looking over the books. But I'd never learned how to lie. Every time I'd tried in the past, I would picture myself a complete exhibition of tells—blushing from my collar to the crown of my head, stammering out an incoherent jumble of words. I was incapable of making eye contact, certain my duplicity was written on my face and that my front would crumble if I were to see suspicion in the other person's eyes.

Now, so I could tell myself I hadn't lied to Cassandra, I picked up the phone and dialed. In the old days, I could have called the time, or the weather, just to hear an innocuous voice that wouldn't expect a response. Instead, I called the next best thing.

"Hi there, what's up?"

"Hi. I could use a drink."

"You're speaking my language," Brendan said. "When?"

The timing worked out perfectly. I stayed in the office until 4:30, when Cassandra left for her break. When I emerged, Joel was standing at the cashier station, checking out a customer. I smiled on my way out and he threw me a confused look in return. Cassandra had told him something. He, too, was convinced the sky was about to fall.

◘

I snagged a table under the overhang, protected from the late afternoon sunlight. My eyes had pretty well adjusted, but I didn't want to take any chances. I had just ordered a drink when Brendan entered.

"What are you doing in this obscurity?" he asked, settling his things on a spare chair. The waitress was still in the vicinity, so he ordered a drink before sitting down.

"I saw John today. My eyes are still dilated."

He laughed. "John'll do that to you." He ran a hand through his hair and looked toward the door. "Listen," he said, "I invited Bette to join us. I hope that's all right."

I liked surprises even less than Oscar, but after a momentary flutter of disappointment I let it go. Maybe Bette was just what I needed today. "Sure," I said. "The more the merrier. And I'm in the mood for some merry."

"What did you want to talk about?"

"Nothing," I said. It felt like a lie, the answer to a question I hadn't really considered. "We can talk about anything you want. The more trivial, the better."

"What's been going on?" he asked.

"It's just exhausting. Between the trial and all this stuff with the store, I'm pretty stressed out."

"How is Tiffany? Charming and lazy as ever?"

"Ooh, you guys are awfully competitive."

"It's a dog-eat-dog world, Craig."

"Well," I said, "it looks like all those lovely books are about to be replaced by yoga mats."

"*Another* yoga studio?"

I nodded. "With a juice bar. I imagine it'll be the new hot spot for kombucha."

"Yum. So what does that mean for you?"

"Who knows? Maybe I could be in charge of the changing closet. Which is probably what my office will become."

"Maybe this is just what you need, Craig. A good derailing."

"That sounds so dirty when you say it."

He laughed. "Everything I say sounds dirty. It's a gift."

Looking up from the glass, I spotted Bette near the doorway, scanning the crowd, looking more than a bit lost. As her eyes finally raked the alcove, I waved her in.

She arrived with a delicate chuckle. "Well, this is a cozy spot, isn't it?"

"Yes," Brendan said, pulling out a chair for her, "Craig is resting his eyes."

"What?"

"I just came from my eye exam."

"Oh." Her hair bounced gently against her shoulders as she settled into the chair. "With the famous shortsighted optometrist?"

"The very one," I said.

"Well, is everything all right?"

"With my eyes, yes. My mind is another matter, but this"—I raised my glass in the air—"is medicine enough for that."

"Speaking of which," Brendan said, rising, "what are you drinking?"

Bette curled her lower lip out before deciding on a white Russian.

"Coming right up." The waitress was on the far side of the room, so Brendan headed to the bar.

"I stand out like a sore thumb in here," Bette said, looking around.

"Women come in here all the time," I said with a laugh. "Of course, they're usually drunk out of their minds and wearing bridal veils, but that just makes you all the more special."

We made small talk for a few minutes. I told her about the store and as much of the trial as I rightly could.

"I suppose you'd have to kill me if you said more," she replied, peering at me through her curls.

"Yes!" I laughed heartily. For once, I didn't have to tell the joke myself.

"Are you seeing anyone at the moment?" she asked—out of the blue.

"Not really," I said.

"Oh, is that like being a little pregnant?"

"Maybe. I was seeing a guy named Damien, but we're on a break now."

"Your idea or his?"

I was spared from answering by Brendan's arrival, fresh with a creamy tumbler that he laid before Bette. "Cheers," he said.

Reading the moment well, Bette pivoted. "So how is our optometrist?" she asked. "Is he hitched yet?"

"No. I think he's pretty anxious about it."

Brendan rolled his eyes.

"Who wouldn't be?" he said. "I suspect Wayne is an acquired taste."

"He's not a bad person," I countered. "He's just different from us, that's all."

"Precisely," Brendan said. "Never mix generations or genders, that's what I always say."

"Do you?" Bette folded her arms in comic challenge.

"Present company excepted," he said. "I'm not sure you guys know John's history. He's always had a bit of a problem making up his mind."

"What do you mean?"

Brendan sighed. "I met him just as he was coming out." He lifted his glass dramatically. "Right after the divorce."

"Divorce?"

Pulling the glass away, he revealed sternly pursed lips. "Grad school sweetheart, apparently. This was when he was still in Chicago. You know he was raised in a very religious family. I guess he thought he could 'pray the gay away.'"

"Wow, I had no idea." I didn't know whether to be shocked that John hadn't told me or ashamed that I'd never asked.

"It didn't last long. A couple of years, maybe. To tell you the truth, I'm not sure he ever told her what the problem was. He just announced that it was over and hopped on a plane to San Francisco, and that was that."

"Cold."

"Well," Bette said, "it must have been extremely difficult. Good for him for dealing with it."

"So what exactly did he say?" Brendan asked. "About Wayne."

"I got the sense that he's having doubts. And it wasn't just him. I ran into Wayne the other day, and he actually asked me what John's type was."

Brendan's brow furrowed. "Very strange question to ask someone else about your own boyfriend."

"Maybe there's a sexual disconnect," Bette said.

"That would be ironic. Isn't an affair with a younger man all about sex?"

My head was starting to throb, and I realized I hadn't eaten since breakfast. "I don't want to spread rumors. I don't know anything for sure. I'm just a little concerned, that's all."

"Well," Brendan said haughtily, "they have nothing in common, so what else could it be but sex?"

"Don't be reductive," Bette scolded. "I don't know John well, outside of my annual exam, and I haven't met Wayne at all, but you never really know what makes a relationship work. They must fulfill each other's needs somehow."

"I felt a little sad for Wayne the other day," I said. "He seemed vulnerable."

"Vulnerable?"

"Yes. Like he was worried about John, their relationship. Maybe the age difference is getting to him, after all. We all wonder about our lovers' pasts, don't we? What about when your lover has 20 more years of past than you do?"

Bette nodded vigorously. "Gossip is great fun, of course, but in the end we can't do much more than support. People marry for all sorts of reasons. We don't need to know why, unless they want to tell us." She locked eyes with Brendan for a long moment. "My own marriage was quite unconventional."

I'd never heard much about her husband. He'd died long before we met, and I'd always been afraid to ask.

She pondered her drink now. The sunlight had shifted and caught her hair in a golden glow. Strength apparently gathered, she looked up and into my eyes. "Paul and I were friends. Close friends. Brendan knew him."

Brendan smiled, but let her tell the story.

"He was gay, so it wasn't a physical thing. But I loved him more than anyone else I've ever known. And when he tested positive, we were both terrified. I had very good insurance through the bank, but he was struggling. I didn't want him to lose everything just to pay for his healthcare, so we got married. Back then, that was the only choice."

She told me about the doctor's visits that turned into urgent hospital stays, the opportunistic infections that came one after another, seemingly feeding on each other.

"I came to think of them like bullies on the playground," she said, lobbing a faint smile at the analogy. "The bullies always pick on the weak kid, the one they know they can handle. They can't really exist unless they feed on someone defenseless, more vulnerable, less able to fight back."

She told the story simply, without emotion—rolling Paul over to prevent bedsores, counting the lesions on his skin, holding joints against his lips to calm his anxiety and increase his appetite. They were married, she said, legally and emotionally—everything but the sex.

"He was a wonderful guy," Brendan said. He reached across the table and took her hand.

Bette sighed and shook her head, as though to drive the past away. Her face grew softer, tranquil. "I don't know why I brought that up," she said.

Our eyes locked. "No," I said, "I get it. There are all kinds of love, aren't there?"

"Yes," she said, nodding. "All kinds."

Brendan leaned back with a dramatic, contented sigh. I could see that he was desperate to lift the mood. "And now we're a couple of confirmed bachelors."

"Bachelorettes," Bette said, "thank you very much."

"Such an old-fashioned girl." Brendan smiled. "And we're going to grow old together."

Bette laughed. "I'd say we've already started!"

CHAPTER 12

NO MIND

There was something about being on a jury that brought out my latent paranoia. Since I was supposed to sit in judgment of someone else, I wanted to make sure my own life was as blemish-free as possible. I set the alarm extra early every day, to give myself a cushion in case there was a delay with the subway.

I'm not sure what I was afraid of. Surely, you can't be arrested for oversleeping, or held in contempt for being late to court. The night before the first session, I dreamt about arriving at the bookstore at 10:00 a.m. and suddenly remembering that I was supposed to be in court an hour and a half earlier. As I scurried out the door, I was greeted by a couple of burly policemen, who dragged me into a car, thick hands burrowing under my arms. When I woke up with a hard-on, I realized the dream wasn't strictly about the trial.

The prosecution spent three days on a string of expert witnesses—mostly FBI experts in gunshots, blood, DNA, fingerprints. The information was highly technical, and after an hour or so I would find myself feeling grateful for the cold: it was keeping me awake.

I hadn't concentrated this hard since college, determined to follow every sentence, as if listening to a long poem, where any single word might be the clue to explaining it all. There was no time to let my mind wander. While I could get through everyday things—dealing with people at the store, talking to friends—while unconnected thoughts darted through my head, here I had to keep all that at bay. Whenever a stray thought entered my mind, I tried to ignore it and focus on what was happening before me. It was like meditation, that process where you acknowledge a thought and then push it away in order to cultivate "no mind."

I tend to be an active listener. Now I had to restrain my instinct to nod as I followed an argument, or to squint when I was unsure of something. I needed to affect disinterest, no obvious leanings toward one side or the other.

No bullet casings had been found outside the bar where Vasquez said the drive-by had happened, so they'd been unable to run a ballistics test. They had, however, scoured the gun for fingerprints and DNA, testing the trigger, handle, and barrel.

"Is this the gun you tested?" asked Harmon, settling the gun onto the shelf before the witness. She backed away and crossed her arms.

The fingerprint expert, a middle-aged woman with a rather firm demeanor, answered crisply. "Yes."

"What did you find?"

"We could not isolate a workable print."

"And what does that tell you?"

The witness frowned. "Nothing, really. It's not at all unusual. From my own experience, fingerprints are found on only about 10% of handguns."

"That few?" Harmon pursued. "Why is that?"

The witness sat up, visibly excited. This was her thing. "Mostly it's because of the nonporous surfaces. But this particular gun"—she held it up and pointed with the other hand—"has a textured surface on the handle. Lots of nooks and crannies, so there's really no spot big enough to capture a useful print."

"So you can't conclusively state that the defendant touched this gun?"

"No."

"Can you be sure that he did *not* touch it?"

The witness gave her a puzzled look, the first moment when her testimony didn't seem rehearsed. "No."

"Your witness," said Harmon, taking her seat.

Crews stood up but stayed behind his table. "No questions at this time, Your Honor. But the defense reserves the right to recall the witness at a later date."

Harmon didn't have much more luck with the DNA expert. While there were markers on the gun that matched the defendant, they weren't complete: they could as easily have been from thousands of other people.

"So it's not him," said Crews in his cross-examination, the question mark barely audible.

"I didn't say that," said the witness, a man this time, tortoise-shell glasses magnifying his eyes. "It's inconclusive."

"Can you say with certainty that my client's DNA was on that gun?" Crews said, his tone rising. He was looking for his Perry Mason moment.

"No."

The witness paused, and a cryptic smile crept onto Crews's face.

"But I can't say it wasn't, either." He was still gazing into the middle distance. Eye contact clearly wasn't in his repertoire. I might have given him a downward arrow for that one, until I realized that a little Asperger's was exactly what you wanted from someone in his field. Obsession with facts. Invulnerability to social cues.

Crews's eyes opened wide. He stood frozen before the stand. After a moment, his smile broadened into a passive-aggressive semicircle of teeth. "Thank you," he said softly. "No further questions."

I felt a sudden urge to raise my hand, to ask my own follow-up question. There were too many holes, and no one was bothering to fill them. Maybe, I thought, they wanted the holes to be there.

The gun was becoming a character in the story, this inanimate object that Harmon kept picking up with blue-gloved hands, as if it were contaminated. I noted that Crews never bothered; an indifferent look on his thin face, he would grasp the gun between bare fingers, flesh unafraid of metal. That, too, seemed part of the story: Harmon wanted us to see the gun as a dangerous object, the key to everything. Crews depicted it as trivial, an irrelevant prop. It was just something the police had found in the back of a car, as arbitrary as a gum wrapper.

Their dance followed a pattern that recurred throughout this phase of the trial—Harmon drawing detailed responses out of expert witnesses, Crews barely addressing the gist of their testimony. Even when it was damaging to his case.

Another FBI agent—not a technical analyst this time—testified that the gun had been traced to an owner in Arizona, who had reported it stolen. He spent only a few minutes on the stand. It was just another random detail we had to digest.

Subsequent testimony was less about the gun itself than the effects it left behind. Harmon called an outside expert who focused on the burn marks on Vasquez's leg and his jeans. Again, she showed us the photographs taken at the hospital. The witness pointed out the entry wound in his thigh—a small, almost clean round hole—and the exit wound, at the top of his shin. I forced myself to look more closely this time, despite the instinct to turn away from the gore. The exit wound was large, misshapen, in a kind of starburst pattern, the result of the bullet pushing through the leg—bone, muscle, flesh. As the ER doctor had noted, the real destruction happened on the way out, not the way in.

They spent a long time on the burn marks, the brown-black ring around the entry wound, remnants of gunpowder and cordite. The exit wound, by contrast, seemed to be marked only by blood. In addition, there was a semicircular abrasion on the entry wound, made by the gun itself rather than the bullet—evidence that the gun had been touching the skin when it went off.

"Is this wound," Harmon asked, "consistent with Mr. Vasquez being shot from a distance?"

"No," the witness said, shaking his head firmly. "Absolutely not."

Next she brought out Vasquez's jeans—blue denim between blue rubber fingers—and showed us the holes. There was one hole in the outer fabric, below the knee; and one in the pocket, the inside of which had been burned by the gunshot.

"What do these holes in the fabric tell you?" she asked the witness. Everything needed to be underlined.

"The gun was in the jeans pocket when it went off."

Again, Crews had nothing to say, but that didn't stop him from speaking. He tossed several questions at the witness, designed to draw out excruciating detail. His strategy now seemed to be to overwhelm us with technical information, to make the whole process look so complicated that nothing we saw could be trusted.

I sat back in my dangerously comfortable chair, and immediately had to reach out for the wall before me to stop the swivel. I practiced my poker face. I was a body in a chair, a pair of eyes, as indifferent as the evidence Crews wanted me to ignore.

On the other side of the room, Vasquez embodied the disinterested look I was struggling so hard to affect. He, too, was furniture. None of this was about him. Harmon was talking about someone else, an imaginary creature who had stuffed a gun in his pocket and blown a hole in his leg.

At each break we would leave the jury box in an orderly line, footsteps heavy on the creaking wood floor. Back inside the jury room, the air felt 20 degrees warmer. If the cold in the courtroom was intended to keep us awake, the heat in here must have had another purpose—perhaps our discomfort would encourage deliberations to go quickly. Already I had images of Henry Fonda sweating through his clothes, trying desperately hour after hour to steer 11 strangers his way.

As people moved through the room, gathering their things, no one spoke a word. They all seemed to be in a daze, and I wondered if I looked the same—if my eyes wore the same flatness, if my shoulders slumped with the same concession to gravity. I assumed it was just the relentless technical detail that did everyone in—the immersion in information that, outside, in our real lives, we had no reason to know anything about. In a few short mornings, I had learned how DNA analysis is done—the swabbing, the testing for how much DNA is on a particular spot of an object, the fact that it can be recognized as male or female, that the markers aren't always conclusive. I'd learned how fingerprints are lifted from an object—the "superglue" that's applied to hold the dye, the methanol used to remove the dye from the clean spots to leave only the fingerprints visible. I'd learned how the trajectory of a bullet is traced; what the elements of a cartridge are; the process by which a bullet is ejected from a gun.

And now, all of it was swimming in my brain, along with the

posturing of the lawyers, the weariness of the judge, and above all, cutting through everything, Vasquez's face. He sat there every day, expressionless, his head floating atop a white shirt whose collar was too big for his neck, the top edges riding his cheeks, the points at the bottom pulling away from his black tie. At one moment, when he turned to look at a witness, the collar shifted to reveal something dark, a black curve on his skin. Another tattoo. At this point, it was just a shape, a swoop of ink connecting to something beneath the collar, and I found myself wondering what the image might be, as if I were working on a jigsaw puzzle without the picture on the box as a guide.

When I got back to the store, Cassandra was lying in wait.

"That lady was here again," she said as she tailed me through the store, her platform shoes clattering across the floor. They were frightfully high, and I had visions of her tumbling off of them while reaching for a high shelf, burying herself under a pile of books. I wondered if our insurance covered footwear accidents.

"What lady?" I pushed open the office door and flicked on the light.

"The blonde. The realtor."

"Realtor?"

Cassandra rolled her eyes. "I couldn't help recognizing her, Craig. Her picture's on half the bus stops in town."

I feigned confusion with a squint.

"Ads, Craig. It's not like she's on the Most Wanted list or something."

"Oh." I nodded and settled in behind the desk.

"What's going on?"

I signaled for Cassandra to close the door and take a seat.

"Angela's thinking of selling the place."

"I knew it!" Pressing against the arms of the chair, she lifted herself slightly. "When?"

I raised my hands like a traffic cop. "Wait wait wait," I said. "Nothing's final. So far she's shown it to only one client."

"That you know of."

"Was there someone else with her today?"

"No. She didn't even come inside. I just spotted her on the sidewalk, checking things out."

"Maybe she was just checking out the neighborhood."

Cassandra was in no mood to hypothesize. She preferred to jump straight to panicked conclusions. "Should I start looking for another job?"

"Don't you already have another job?" I asked. She was at the store only part-time.

"Of course," she said. "You don't think I can afford to live in this town on one salary, do you?"

I booted up the computer. Consoling the hysterical has never been my strong suit.

"Do you think the new owners would keep us on?"

I clicked on my email server. "Not unless you can teach yoga."

"Yoga?!"

"That's one of the options, a yoga studio."

"What about the store? There are so few bookstores left in the city. …"

My in-box was nearly empty. I closed the laptop. "I know," I told her, elbows on the desk. "That's just where the world is these days."

"Well it's criminal," she said.

[170]

It was refreshing to hear someone Cassandra's age defending at least a piece of the old guard. I wouldn't want to debate her on veganism, but it was nice to be on the same side for once.

"Look," I said, "Angela promised to give us ample notice, and severance to tide everyone over. I was hoping not to have to tell you just yet. I didn't want to worry you."

"Worry me? Shouldn't I be worried? Don't you think it's going to happen?"

"Well, given the market, I tend to think she'll get an offer she can't refuse."

The reference escaped her, or she just wasn't in the mood for a game of movie trivia. Instead she smirked. "So you're not worried about worrying me. You're worried I'll leave before we close up shop."

I started to say no, but caught myself, tongue pressed against my palate. I had promised myself I would minimize the drama and the fear, but actually she was right. If she found out too soon, it would make my life difficult. I hadn't been thinking about what was good for her and the others.

"Well, I'm sure it'll be a while. First she has to find a buyer, and then there's all the paperwork of a sale. But I can understand why you might want to explore options ahead of time. As I said, Angela wants to provide a severance package, but if you don't want to wait, I get it."

Cassandra shook her head mournfully. Her purple locks were still trembling when she suddenly stiffened. "How much severance?"

"I don't know yet. I can ask."

"Thanks." She rose from her seat and moved toward the door. "Should I tell the others?"

"No," I said, "I will."

"Okay. Thanks."

She closed the door behind her and I pried open the laptop again. But I was in no mood to work. I found a real estate site that Brendan had told me about. "Just check it out," he'd said. "Get a sense of what's out there before you dismiss the idea out of hand."

I left the search wide open—condos or houses, one-bedroom minimum, the whole city as my search area. The only variable I cared about right now was the price range. I plugged in what Brendan had said I could get for the condo.

Nothing.

I went a hundred thousand dollars higher, two. Trying to calculate how much mortgage I could handle—if I got a new job, something that paid a lot more than the bookstore.

Nothing.

I had to shift to "Any Price" in order to see any dots at all appear on the screen. The only places that approached affordability were in neighborhoods near the ocean. Only in San Francisco would beachfront property be more affordable than inland.

"Okay, Brendan," I said aloud, "I tried."

CHAPTER 13

t l ; d r

Hills be damned, San Francisco is a city for walking. I left the store and headed south on Castro. The hill got markedly steeper at this point, but it was only for a couple of blocks. On the steepest stretch, I walked backward to relieve the pressure.

The hill crested in a long plateau toward Alvarado, where the street seemed to disappear into the sky. That demarcation had always struck me as appropriate, the dividing line between the Castro and twee Noe Valley. Noe had gentrified much earlier; by the time I'd moved to town it was already home to yuppies who swept up the quaint single-family houses just in time to start popping out kids and cluttering 24th Street with strollers. I had fallen in love with the neighborhood's charm right away. But most important, it was a mere hill away from the Castro—close enough that I could jaunt over whenever I wanted, but far enough that I didn't have to define myself by its in-your-face gayness. I was taking baby steps in those days, and Castro-adjacent was good enough.

I'd left Noe Valley ages ago. There wasn't much reason to come back on a regular basis. The shopping was no better here than in the Castro, and the restaurants were as hit-or-miss as those in any other part of town. But I did occasionally venture over the hill simply to walk the familiar paths, to give in to a bit of nostalgia, to remember those early days when everything was new and alive.

The valley came gradually into view, shoebox houses lining the hill in the distance. Dusk was approaching, casting a clarity to the landscape, highlighting the undular effect of the hills. This was always the antidote to doubt and second-guessing my life: standing at the top of a hill, witnessing San Francisco. I was still in love. With this, at least—in love with the city as the 49ers had seen it, I supposed, when it was just seven hills making their rolling way toward the ocean.

The southern slope was steeper, but gravity did half the work, pulling me quickly along the sidewalk, my feet planting solidly, my legs stretching different muscles than they had on the other side. After so many years here, I always knew exactly where I was, but I still liked to look at the street signs as I passed, if only because of the quaintness of the typography, the block letters framed by a dark rectangle with white rounded corners, as artful as the boldly painted Victorians behind them. The signs for Elizabeth Street and Castro were affixed perpendicularly to each other on a street post. Every time I passed I made a mental note: One day I would write a novel whose heroine was named Elizabeth Castro, and she lived right here, on this corner. She didn't even like the apartment, but she chose it and stayed there because of the name, because she believed in the destiny of geography. As Brendan would say, Location, location, location.

The momentum carried me swiftly down the last block, and I had to make an effort to slow down, lest someone be coming around the corner, past the Bank of America building. The light was red, so I stayed on the north side of 24th Street, resisting the urge to visit the bakery across the street, which I had frequented back in the days when I didn't care so much about carbs.

I remembered a dive bar a few doors away. That temptation was a little harder to resist. I didn't usually drink by myself, especially not at this time of day, but at least I didn't know anyone in this neighborhood anymore. I could sit quietly by myself and just think for a while.

On 24th, it had always seemed to me that the shops and the restaurants were the attraction. In the Castro, the commercial spots were merely a backdrop. Less effort was put into making the Castro storefronts appealing because there was no way to compete with the parade. You didn't go to the Castro to shop. Not for tchotchkes, anyway. You went to the Castro to people-watch. Or was that just a polite way of saying you went there to cruise?

Not that the Castro had a monopoly on cruising, certainly not in this town. When I'd moved to San Francisco, I was told that 40% of the men were gay. It was clearly an exaggeration, but not by much. Maybe it was just that I noticed only the gay ones, or that I tended to hang out in places where they were overrepresented, but I quickly learned that when in doubt as to a man's sexual orientation, it was safe to assume he was gay.

It was the same with age. When I was younger, I barely noticed it. The financial district was full of people, generic people as far as I was concerned. But now, when I walked through the same neighborhood, I couldn't help noticing how young they all were. Where had all the middle-aged people gone? Did they vanish into the ether when I wasn't looking? Or did they all just march to BART as soon as the workday was over so they could get back to their suburbs and their children as quickly as possible and leave the sidewalks to the young folk? Now that I was no longer one of those young folk, I saw only them. I was the outlier, so suddenly they were visible.

The bar was narrow, the outside walls coated in uneven black paint that stood out among the pastels defining the rest of the street. Inside, the darkness became the visual equivalent of comfort food, wood paneling vying with gleaming bottles and beer taps at the bar. I ordered a draft and carried it toward a counter by the window, where I could feel myself on the periphery between night and day, dark and light.

This was exactly the kind of place Damien would take me to—simple, quiet, where nobody bothered you, nobody was on the prowl.

Things had been moving too quickly, he said. He needed time to breathe. Four months. Like clockwork. That, I had learned long ago, was as long as it took for the romance to wear off. That was when you began to see each other as real people rather than fantasies made flesh. That was when it all turned to shit.

I had often probed Oscar for insight into how he and Rafe had lasted so long. The secret, he said, was making space for each other. They weren't enmeshed like other couples we knew, the ones who hold hands obsessively and steal kisses over dinner with friends, the ones who use the word *we* more than *I*—the ones who burn out as soon as the sex falls to less than five times a week. Oscar and Rafe had three lives—one for each of them, and one for the relationship. "It's like when you're making tea," he'd told me once, after a miserable break-up, when it was the last thing I wanted to hear. "One spoonful of leaves for each cup, plus another for the pot."

I knew Oscar was right. But still, I wanted love to be easy. I wanted it to be as easy as sex.

The beer was hoppy, thick on the tongue. I usually went for a wheat beer, but when in Rome, I thought. This was a sports bar. I should be glad I wasn't expected to drink Coors.

A straight couple raced by hand in hand, fresh faces bright and pink. I watched them cross the street just in time to catch the northbound bus. Headed downtown for the evening—dinner, theater, perhaps a romantic stroll along Union Street—whatever people did these days when they were young and in love.

One evening, ages ago now, Garrett had picked me up in his white Miata for a mysterious date. He wouldn't tell me where we were going and, to prevent any clues from escaping, wrapped his necktie around my eyes after I'd strapped myself into the passenger seat. I peppered him with questions along the way, throwing out guesses—rattling off names of fancy restaurants I hadn't yet visited, imagining a picnic in the depths of Golden Gate Park. At one point we slowed to a near stop, and Garrett grumbled about the traffic and cursed someone cutting him off—"Rich Marin bitch!" I laughed and suddenly became aware of the cool wind, the crisp, clean air most noticeable on the coast. As the traffic plodded along, I heard the rattle of tires on the pavement, felt the subtle sway beneath us. We were on the bridge, the most beautiful icon of the city, invisible to me through the dark silk of Garrett's tie. "French Laundry?" I asked teasingly. He'd talked about it endlessly as one of his favorite places. It all made sense now. He laughed and let me remove the blindfold, just as we passed under the north tower, rich orange plates piercing the sky.

Damien had never done anything like that.

The light was ebbing when I finished the beer and ventured back outside. Emboldened by the alcohol and a touch of nostalgia, I jaywalked across the street and stopped in front of the bakery. There was a model train set in the window, more a general invitation than an advertisement, something to catch the eye and draw it gently back to the display case, brimming with cakes and loaves of artisanal bread. A woman stood before the counter, a toddler struggling in her arms while she pondered the options. The empty stroller beside me, on the other side of the doorway, must have been hers.

In the old days, I might have given in to the temptation, strolled inside, and bought something sweet to spoil my appetite. But today I was just taking a walk through what had become a foreign landscape since my move, an anthropological expedition of sorts to see how the other half, they of the strollers and perpetual earbuds, lived.

Suddenly, behind the woman, I spotted a pair of eyes staring back at me. It was a man no more than 40, unshaven, with a diamond twinkling in his left earlobe. His brown hair was cut short, one stray lock dipping over his forehead. His gaze was expressionless but deliberate, daring me to look away.

Anthropologists are supposed to be the watchers, not the watched. My neck jerked back slightly before I caught myself, not wanting to be too obvious. I always felt uncomfortable when someone caught me staring at them: curiosity and admiration were equally suspect.

The woman with the toddler, holding a finger to her mouth indecisively, shifted out of the way and the clerk made a gesture toward the man, abruptly stealing his attention. I slunk past the stroller and continued along the sidewalk, feigning nonchalance.

Learning to cruise had given me a new perspective on people watching. Early on, I came to understand that the eyes are the last part of a man's body you should stare at. In the darkened bars of Castro Street, I would feel a man's eyes on me long before I'd see them, and I learned to study men from the feet up, with only a quick glance—a nanosecond on the periscope that took in the whole landscape with a slow turn—to confirm that the face would not be a disappointment, lest you fall too quickly in love with the waist and the guns.

So when the eyes were the first thing I spotted, it always threw me. Locking eyes right off the bat was a breach in protocol, a foreshortening of what should be a long procedure, its slowness carefully calibrated not just to give you time to assess whether you really wanted what you to saw but to increase the desire by building tension. It was all about tension in those days: the prospect of the fantasy falling apart before it could get off the ground was part of what made it special, a piece of the danger that made the whole thing worth pursuing.

Just past the public parking lot, I stopped at the ATM. I'd gotten so used to using cards for everything, I seldom realized when I was out of cash. The yellow wall of Wells Fargo was a reminder to check my wallet.

Down to 23 bucks. I dug out my debit card and stuck it in the slot.

A hundred dollars richer, I turned away to slide the bills into my wallet. The guy from the bakery was standing at the curb, one foot braced against a parking meter as he tied his shoe. A box from the bakery sat on the sidewalk beside him.

Cruising was a game. I loved the initial moment, when you wonder if each gesture is a coincidence, whether he's brushing past you in the bar, needing the restroom at the same time, or just turning up at the same spot on the street.

Careful not to repeat the sin of eye contact, I put the wallet back in my pocket and continued strolling. I stopped at one of the neighborhood's many indefinable boutiques, unrelated bric-a-brac competing in the window with candles and embroidered dishcloths. It was the kind of store I would venture into only at the holidays, or when I had to find a creative gift to bring to an open house. My mother's apartment was full of stuff like this—mismatched figurines, teacups with handles too small for an adult finger to fit through. Still, for show, I pretended to be interested.

I felt someone passing behind me. That was another skill I'd developed somewhere along the way—sensing beyond vision or hearing or touch. When I was walking down a sidewalk, I could always tell when someone was coming up behind me, even if they were silent. I would pull myself toward the buildings and let them go by. I came to think of it as a common skill, some cave-man sense intuitively ingrained into the species by natural selection, so that when I was the one walking behind someone else, someone who had no idea that there was anyone else in the vicinity, even when I was within inches of their back, I felt flummoxed and not a little furious.

As the sensation passed, I turned my head casually to the left and saw him strolling slowly ahead, the box cradled against his hip, gently grazed by the bottom of a black leather jacket.

He stopped in front of a restaurant and checked out the menu on display. Waiting.

This never happened anymore. This hadn't happened to me in years, certainly not to this extent, with this brazenness. It felt like we were a couple of 25-year-olds, playing our favorite game. This was what it had all been about when I first got to San Francisco. I could have spent the entire afternoon hopscotching down the street like this, no matter where it ended.

We continued for a while, him stopping in front of one window as I passed, me stopping at the next place and letting him go by. And the whole time, I saw only his back.

He moved with a kind of grace, long legs gliding nimbly past with just enough sway to the hips to suggest a self-conscious sexuality. He was letting me know that he was comfortable in his body, that for the moment, at least, the body was all that mattered.

The quaint shops of 24th began to peter out past Sanchez. The game was bound to change once we'd crossed the street. I stopped at the shoe store near the corner, the U-shaped windows with dozens of shoes arranged around me, an army of the suddenly raptured.

The familiar presence slid past, but only for a moment. I pulled away from the shop just as the guy disappeared into the flower shop next door.

This wasn't part of the game. Was I supposed to follow him inside? Or was I just misinterpreting the whole thing, after all? Perhaps he'd intended to get flowers all along. Perhaps the flowers and the baked goods, whatever they were, were for his lover, his husband.

I stopped in front of the display of flowers on the sidewalk, pretending to admire the tulips, and snuck a peek through the window.

He was chatting with the woman behind the counter, gesturing with one hand. I imagined him describing a bouquet, the perfect arrangement of flowers to surprise his husband with. In any case, the spell was broken. I peeled away.

The walk had been fortuitous. My previous apartment was just a block over—fate drawing me toward it, toward the past. For old times' sake, I decided to take a look, see how that particular stretch of the neighborhood had changed.

I turned down Sanchez and made my way onto Jersey, the almost suburban setting of my former life.

I'd always marveled at how such a quiet residential street could exist just a block away from the hubbub of the neighborhood's main drag. At this end, Jersey was a hodgepodge of styles, well-preserved Edwardians chockablock with more recent buildings that were not as well cared for. Multi-unit and single-family houses were mingled on the street, so I imagined that in the old days even the larger ones housed only a single family.

I walked along the north side, past a series of dull earth-tone buildings, Priuses of every color and the occasional BMW parked out front. Midway down the block, I gazed across the street and found the house, the window of my first-floor apartment just beside the front door. They had painted the place since, striving for a modified Painted Lady effect with two shades of blue and a gold trim. It was glossier now—in keeping, I supposed, with the new money pouring into the neighborhood from the latest IPO millionaires, but somehow missing something. You can't go home again, they say. The past remains off limits.

This time I felt a breeze as someone passed slowly behind me, heard footsteps skipping up a set of wooden stairs. I turned just as the sound stopped. He was standing there, halfway up the staircase, posing in three-quarter profile. The bakery box was still cradled in one hand, but the other now held a fairly large bouquet, tulips and freesia spilling out of the brown paper cone.

He held my gaze for a few seconds and finally let a sly smile curl onto his lips. He nodded his head toward the red door at the top of the stairs. "Would you mind helping me?" he asked, his voice surprisingly deep. "My hands are full."

Now I was beginning to believe in fate. Unless this was still part of the game—unless he had followed me onto this street, with a nail file in his pocket that he would use to pick the lock. Even without that, even if it was his house, there was something risky about this, walking into a building with someone who had shared less than 10 words with me. I felt a tingling of adrenaline and a boldness I hadn't experienced in years, back when lust was too strong and adventure too tempting to admit the notion of danger.

I nodded and followed him up the stairs. He held the box toward me and, as I took it, he dug into his pocket for a set of keys (so he wasn't a burglar, after all). The flowers tucked under his arm, he turned a key in the door.

His apartment was at the end of a long hallway. The door opened onto an open kitchen, a laminate counter separating it from the square living room. He dropped the flowers on the counter, and laid the box beside them. He turned to me, his head tilted down slightly. "So," he said, his tone rounder, even deeper in the confines of the space, "what's your name?" He unzipped his jacket and let it fall open, revealing a pink striped shirt I recognized from the sale rack at Banana Republic. I'd considered getting one myself, but they were out of my size.

"Craig," I said, aware that my own coat was still closed. I reached a hand tentatively up to grasp the zipper.

"Welcome, Craig." He leaned forward. My arm, the metal zipper cold in my fingers, was caught between us as he pressed his lips against mine.

The seduction had all happened on the street. There was no need to waste time now. As he pulled me into the living room, I glanced back at the flowers, wondering how long they could last without water.

The room was dominated by a sectional sofa that took up most of a side wall and half of the back, beneath a wide window that looked out onto a spartan garden.

We fell onto the fluffy seafoam cushions and the sofa seemed to ripple beneath us like an ocean wave lapping against the shore. His hair was soft against my skin, his hands firm upon my neck and the small of my back. His lips raked slowly across mine and continued along my check, around my chin, and glided toward the bottom of my neck, where they lingered, tickling, lightly sucking. I arched my neck to give him wider access.

We were naked within minutes, chest hair pressing together like Velcro, arms swimming up and down each other's sides. As he lifted his, a tuft of thick, almost black hair came into view and I flicked my tongue against it. He brought my head down upon his nipple and I felt him squirm beneath me.

It all came naturally, uncalculated, like an improvised dance— his limbs in sync with mine, his pleasure feeding my own and telling me what to do, where to touch him, how long to hold on, the precise pressure of fingers upon skin. I was always amazed by the connection that can happen between two people who don't know each other, two people who come to each other simply as bodies, with no history, no personalities attached. My passions, undifferentiated, undetermined by social rules and personal expectations, could be set free here, in this unfamiliar room, with this man who still hadn't told me his name, this man who had barely heard my voice. With a lover there was always baggage. I was always Craig, this Craig that I presented to the world or that was projected onto me. I was the man who loved Puccini and steak au poivre, or the one who talked endlessly about books and hid his tears at sappy movies. I was a personality, an identity, a specific human being relating to another specific human being. But here, on this couch I could freely imagine was a raft in the middle of the Pacific, I was something far more generic—just a piece of the universe, a body unencumbered by its own history or its attempt to be perceived in any particular way. Some people disparaged these couplings as *impersonal* sex, oblivious to the fact that that was precisely the point—stripping away the personal to make room for a more profound connection, allowing two small pieces of the torn universe to sew themselves back together. It was communion, unobstructed, unprogrammed, unjudged.

I'd known this feeling with lovers, too, from time to time, in discrete moments when we were able to shut everything else out, even our history together. I still remembered a night with Garrett when, waking up in the middle of the night, we had turned to each other and silently, our minds shut off, began making love, and I'd had the sensation that we were floating in space, high above the world, high above our lives, just floating and becoming one. And in the morning, we were Garrett and Craig again, and every day and night after that, until Garrett and Craig were no longer enough.

Fucking a stranger, I thought, as this man who had dropped his flowers for me scraped his fingers firmly down my back, was like meditation. It was freedom from the world, a momentary nirvana. Love was strangely complicated, sex strangely simple. It was when they came together that you really had a problem.

I heard two clocks—one I could see on the wall in the kitchen, the other perhaps in the bedroom off to the side—their rhythms just half a second off so that the ticking was in double time, lending a disco beat to our movements—life speeding up or on two separate tracks, marking two different places in time.

When he was ready, when he had put off the moment long enough, edging each of us closer and closer, then pulling away to savor the feeling, to reinvigorate the desire, when he was ready he rose onto his knees and looked down at me, alive and exhausted at once, and he came, long arcs shooting over me, my body suddenly and repeatedly awash in him, shards of him that I imagined would be imbedded in my chest hair for days, gummy orbs I would find each morning while showering. I would pull them off one by one, roll them in my fingers before flicking them away to sluice down the drain.

I tried to hide how impressed I was. I'd been able to do that once. I used to measure each shot, like a golfer striving to hit the ball farther and farther down the fairway. Now I was reduced to a weak dribble at best, middle age draining volume and power at once.

All of it seemed to have changed over time, my body's reaction to sex. There was something fuzzy about it now, as if my nerves had frayed with age, or my cock less a part of me than it once was. The sensation, though mild, was soothing, but still I craved the explosion, the sudden rush, the undeniable cataclysm. The little death.

He barely smiled. In that sudden rush of relief, he simply guided his body back to the sofa and lay beside me, one knee bent to curve over my leg, his head just grazing my shoulder. I waited for his breath to slow, for the hairs on my neck to grow less windswept against him. He handed me his t-shirt from the floor, soft white cotton that had pressed between his chest and the pink-striped shirt, and I wiped myself clean, or clean enough for now.

I was nearly fully dressed when he, still naked on the sofa, said, "So what were you doing outside? How did you know this was my house?"

"I didn't." I looked down at him, buttoning my shirt. "I used to live across the street. I just wanted to take another look at the old place."

"Wow," he said, "and I thought you were a stalker. That made it extra hot."

I laughed. He didn't seem to concern himself much with the coincidence, the minuscule chance that I would end up in front of his house just minutes after we'd followed each other down another street. His indifferent look, green eyes focused on my own

[186]

fingers as they slipped button into hole, button into hole, suggested that all of life was just something to take in, to accept and not question. He seemed to be onto something that remained a mystery to me, some organizing influence just beneath the surface, moving all the pieces into place—boxes of baked goods, white tulips and freesia spilling from a paper wrapping, bodies coming together as if they'd known each other all their lives and then drawing apart to make room for the next thing, the next moment of clarity that he was certain would come.

I pictured him 15 or so years hence, when the creases in his face would be deeper, when the soft brush of brown hair at his temples had, like mine, gone completely white.

The apartment looked familiar already, like a place where I'd spent months and not just 30 or so distracted minutes. I knew the bookcase beside the television, the set of Virginia Woolf that took up half a shelf. I knew the carpet, the dirty beige that once had been cream, still visible if you could lift away the foot of that leather recliner and peek. I knew the late morning streak of sunlight that spilled at a sharp angle through the window, just a sliver of brightness cutting a swath all the way to the kitchen counter.

I'd had all this once, or something like it. The small boxy space and no more possessions than could comfortably fit in it—a smattering of books, a couple of shelves of CDs, just enough room to be cozy, a space that would feel cramped only during a party, one of those rare events when the world seemed made of people and not things. I had spent a good chunk of my days here, snug and warm, waiting for life to begin and not realizing until too late that it was already in full swing.

It wasn't until the door was open and I had one foot in the hallway that he told me his name. "Goodbye, Craig," he said, lips parting in a soft smile, revealing the misaligned canine that had bit into my flesh.

"Goodbye …"

"James," he said.

"James." I kissed him gently, more like an old friend than someone I'd spent the last half hour tumbling around with, exploring every inch of his skin.

The door closed behind me and I made my way along the hall, down the steps, my old house across the street watching with those eye-like windows on either side of the door. The world seemed silent in the twilight, as if something had stopped the clocks, called everyone to rest. I heard only my footsteps on the sidewalk, until I finally turned the corner and returned to the bustling refuge of rush-hour 24th Street.

I crossed to the north side, still warm from the last rays of the sun. The strollers on the sidewalk had been displaced by commuters hustling in from the 24 bus or the J trolley, which bracketed the core blocks of the neighborhood. Briefcases and grocery bags in hand, they spun off 24th in all directions, eager to leave one part of the day behind and relax into the next.

I reached for my phone to check the time. A text stood out against the wallpaper—a picture of the Golden Gate Bridge, towers poking through the fog. Date-stamped half an hour ago, while I was in James's arms, it was from Damien:

I've been thinking a lot about us and
would like to talk. Want to come over
this weekend? I miss you.

I quickly put the phone back in my pocket and dropped my hands to my sides. I saw the bus coming and decided to hop on. I was going against rush-hour traffic and the trip was a short one, so there was nothing to lose.

The bus jittered on its way up the hill, chugging like an old man out of breath. I held onto a strap near the front, standing before a woman in stained khaki pants, a large plastic bag positioned on the floor between her feet. After bumping into it one too many times, I shifted down the aisle until I was standing in front of a teenager, skinny and curled up on herself, thighs firmly together, feet turned slightly inward, arms pinned against her sides, hands meeting before her to cradle her phone and type faster than a Katie Gibbs alumna, all the while her head bobbing gently with the music pumping from her earbuds, music so loud that I could hear the beat myself. I loathed texts, receiving them and feeling obliged to send them. My thumbs were too big for the keyboard on the screen, so I resorted to hunting and pecking with an index finger. Thirty years after learning to type, I was thrust back to my medieval days.

The bus crested the hill and I turned toward the front, peeking through the wide window until the theater sign finally came into view, the letters flashing one by one against the darkening sky. It was more a landmark than a theater these days. I hardly ever went to the movies now, preferring the coziness of my living room. The Castro was for film festivals and cult classics where you would go with a group of friends and howl when the Mother Superior called Julie Andrews a cunt-face.

I pulled the flimsy cord and the bus shuddered to a stop at 20th. I emerged onto the sidewalk, met by a sudden gust of wind.

There was no one at the mailboxes, no one on the stairs I had to make small talk with on my way home. I savored the silence. I didn't want to talk tonight. I tossed my backpack onto the couch and stripped off my clothes. I needed a shower. But as I lifted a hand to my face to scratch my beard, I caught a whiff of James's scent. I wasn't ready to wash that away, not just yet.

Instead, I walked over to the stereo and lifted the lid on the turntable. My friends often marveled at the collection of LPs that commanded two low shelves against the wall, mementos of my teen years. The LPs were now matched in number by CDs, but I drew the line at streaming music, as I had drawn the literary line at Kindle. Whatever it meant for the environment, I still liked *things*, real things made of elements from the real world, and above all, these slippery black discs with their too visible, too fragile grooves.

I pulled a favorite Joni Mitchell from its sleeve. The needle rode gently upon the record, and I remembered every crackle, anticipated every skip. The imperfections proved it was real.

CHAPTER 14

LANDFILL

"What did he want?" Oscar adjusted his sunglasses. Despite the dark lenses, I could read the shock in his expression—twisted lips, a furrow just above the gold-rimmed frames.

I shook my head and focused on maintaining a glacial pace around the park. "That wasn't clear. 'I miss you,' he said."

I was tempted to dig the phone out of my pocket to show him, but even if it came to that there was no need. I'd looked over the message countless times already and had it memorized like a childhood poem.

We were making our way around Salesforce Park, the trail snaking above downtown, manicured greenery surrounded by skyscrapers—an antiseptic knock-off of New York's High Line. I remembered loving the High Line. Built on the tracks of an abandoned elevated rail, it had an organic quality that was sorely lacking here: it integrated with its surroundings in a way that felt quintessentially New York. By contrast, this park proclaimed its solipsistic magnificence from the literal rooftops, belonging to everywhere and nowhere at once.

"Well," Oscar said, rounding the corner by a stand of prickly trees, "you haven't actually broken up, right? I mean, this was supposed to be a temporary break."

There was a fresh patch of grass on the side of the path, netting still visible around the edges. "I didn't take him seriously," I said, shaking my head. "I figured he was just trying to let me down easy."

"Easy? It came out of the blue on a phone call."

"Well, that's easy in Damien's book. He's not the most emotionally intelligent person."

A couple of hipsters brushed past, one in a lumberjack beard, the other less consciously disheveled. I heard something about launch dates and bugs. Not the kind of bugs that were jumping around the plants beside us.

"So what did you tell him?" Oscar asked.

"Nothing. I haven't responded yet. I'm not sure what to say."

Oscar stopped in a tiny patch of shade. "Well, you should at least find out what he wants."

"Why? Should I care?"

"Don't you?"

"I don't know."

And I didn't. I had assumed I'd never see Damien again. It had been safer to write him off, along with the few personal items I'd left at his house. The cost of doing business, I told myself. Cut your losses and run before it gets any more humiliating.

It was one of my unsung skills, wiping my mind of things I didn't want to think about. In my youth I'd made a complete mess of myself after every break-up, weeping on friends' shoulders (Oscar still hadn't forgiven me for ruining his suede coat) and walking around like a zombie for weeks at a time. In those days I assigned love a high priority: it superseded everything else. For the sake of a man, I would break plans with friends, reschedule job interviews, and—most pathetic of all—pretend to like things I didn't care about. I'd spent a summer researching a full itinerary for a trip to France, but when Barry suggested

Puerto Rico instead—muggy beaches and spicy food substituting for the Louvre and coq au vin—I chucked my guidebooks aside and bought a new swimsuit. Paris had to wait for the inevitable break-up.

Sometime after the third or fourth romantic nervous break-down, I learned to put all my feelings into a box, shut the lid tight, and move on. Most of the time, I didn't even wait for things to fall apart: at the first sign of trouble, I'd make my excuses and run. Sometimes I didn't even bother with the excuses. Saying anything at that point made me feel vulnerable. I didn't want to run the risk of appearing to care more than I did—or, at least, more than *he* did. I figured that serious problems at the beginning were a pretty good indication that wedding bells would never ring, so I had nothing to lose by cutting it short. I came to think of love as a reality game show: if you have to lip-sync for your life more than once, you are not going to win the title, so don't worry so much about staying in the game.

"It's only been a couple of weeks," Oscar said. "Are you feel-ing calmer about it?"

"Calm?"

"Yeah—maybe willing to start again with less pressure?"

I took in a deep breath. Something in the air, something bounc-ing off the trees, squeezed my nasal passages. "No," I said at last. "He ruined it."

"What do you mean?"

"Just the way he handled this whole thing, the spontaneous wall going up. All the feelings drained out of me in an instant. Self-protection, I know, but that's my M.O. It's kept me sane for years."

"I wouldn't go that far."

I wasn't ready to laugh. "And even when we were together, it was so circumscribed. I mean, he hardly ever met you, and you're my closest friend."

"Have you met his?"

"Yes," I said, recalling a very uncomfortable coffee date with Rupert, whose views on abortion and Hillary Clinton were less than enlightening. "I made sure that happened as seldom as possible."

We stopped at the eastern edge of the park. Oscar turned to the skyline, studying the Millennium Tower as if to decipher the tilt.

"We're on landfill," he said. "This whole amusement park is going to sink into the muck one day."

"Everything sinks into the muck eventually."

"Are we still talking about Damien?"

I laughed. "No. Just this whole fucked-up world. I'm tired of fighting it."

"You'll find him," Oscar said.

"Who?"

"The one who fits. But he won't be perfect. The relationship won't be perfect. That's what you have to understand."

"I'm not looking for perfection."

Oscar smiled. "Bullshit, Craig. That's exactly what you're looking for."

I closed my eyes for a moment against the sun. A breeze kissed my forehead. "I'm looking for Garrett."

When I opened my eyes, Oscar was gazing softly at me—the face no one else, no one but Rafe, ever saw. "But he wasn't perfect, either. No one is."

He'd seemed perfect at the time—perfect for me, at least. We'd had so much in common—theater, books. We'd read in bed together every night, feet gently entwined, a toe absently massaging an ankle while we both gazed intently at the books in our laps.

Oscar took a few steps and returned to the skyline.

"You have no idea," he said, "how many times I've fantasized about divorce."

"What?" I was flabbergasted.

"Relax. It's all in the past now, for the most part. But about once a month, for a couple of years, some little thing would happen—he'd snap at me over some minor disagreement, leave a cabinet open, be distracted and not pay attention to something I was saying—and I'd stop in my tracks and ask myself, *Do I really want this?*"

It was my turn to stop in my tracks, just under the shade of a tree that leaned protectively over us. "Seriously?"

"Yes. It was silly, most of it." He came closer, the two of us frozen on the path. "But I still would get these sudden feelings, this urge to run. His eyes would glaze over as I told him about an opera you and I had seen. Or he'd wake up in the morning all disheveled and I'd see how fat he was getting around the waist. Stupid, inconsequential things that had nothing to do with our relationship. But I would collapse into myself for a minute and this voice inside me would say, *Get out while you still can!*"

I didn't know how to react to any of this. So I didn't. My silence seemed to invite him to say more.

"And just as quickly as the thoughts came, they would leave. But I was worried because they came so frequently, because there was this piece of me that was so quick to surrender. I wondered if I really loved him. Once the feeling passed, though, I learned to pay more attention. And eventually I started noticing how many times I felt exactly the opposite. There were so many more moments when I would look at Rafe and feel—" His voice trailed off abruptly, and he turned away to look up at the tree, the intricate twists and turns of the branches splintering in innumerable directions so that you couldn't tell where one ended and another began. "I would feel this wave of awe. His face, the curve of a shoulder. The way he laughs. And I'd be so happy."

He plucked a leaf and spun it between his fingers, the edges dancing in the dappled light. "And I realized after a while that my feelings were completely normal, at least normal for me. It's not like you choose somebody and then you're done, you never have to think about it again. The truth, for me anyway, is that you make that decision over and over again. Like you choose to be alive. If you start thinking that you don't have a choice, then you end up feeling trapped. But if it's a constant decision, then you know you're in control. You know that you want it. And you have no excuses."

Oscar pulled away and continued on the path, dodging a young woman on her phone.

"I think part of it was just looking at how my life had changed over the years. Subconsciously I blamed Rafe. I was an old married man. That's why I didn't go out as much or have adventures. It's weird. I mean, I had acquired everything I wanted in life—the husband, the house, the great job. My bucket list was filling up. But I missed the days when everything was uncertain and new. I missed learning stuff about myself. I missed wondering what was around the corner."

"But you were happy."

"Oh yes," he said. "I was happy as this person—this person I'd always wanted to be. But it was a vision, something that was *going to happen*. When it actually *did* happen, it felt kind of foreign. I'd spent so much of my life planning for some future moment, and suddenly here it was. It took a while to realize that who I had become was who I'd always wanted to be."

A soft breeze blew between us. "I suppose there's a lesson for me in this somewhere."

"There's always a lesson." He turned away and headed toward the escalator. "Let's get out of here."

I followed him downstairs and onto the street. "We were supposed to have lunch," he said. "Do you want to grab something?"

"I'm not really hungry," I said.

We passed by a large construction site, pile drivers rattling the earth, workers milling about in hardhats. The noise was unbearable, so we found ourselves walking faster and faster just to get away.

Back on Market Street, we turned east, toward the bay. The Ferry Building stood at the end, capping the street, giving a point of focus to the canyon of skyscrapers. We moved steadily toward it, battling the cool breeze coming in off the bay.

Halfway down the block, a figure in jeans and a red t-shirt was waving broadly with both arms and bouncing from foot to foot, like a windsock character outside a car dealership. As we got closer, I could see bright blond hair flipping from shoulder to shoulder as she danced, clipboard in hand.

"Oh God," Oscar intoned. "Her again."

"You know her?"

"She's here every day. The financial district is full of them—goody-goodies who are trained to be saccharine sweet to guilt people into giving money to whatever they're shilling for on a given day. It's like Up with America, but for charity."

She was dancing in the middle of the sidewalk, so there was no subtle way of passing. "Can I have a smile?" she asked, latching onto Oscar's sneer.

"No," he said, glaring.

"What about you?" She reached a hand toward me. "Do you have a minute for the environment?"

Up close, I could read the logo on her shirt, an organization I'd never heard of with a picture of an owl perching on her left breast.

"Sorry," I said.

"Are you sure?"

"Come on," said Oscar, passing on the curb.

"Well," she sang, "the environment has a minute for you!"

Oscar whipped around. His grin now matched hers in width and insincerity. "Does this shit ever work?" he asked.

She looked at him, eyes wide, lips sealed.

"Does anyone ever fall for this cultlike behavior and actually give you money?"

"Sir"—and a faint smile began to grow.

"I care a great deal about the environment," Oscar said. "The Moonies, not so much. You might want to try a different tack."

"I'm just doing my job," she said softly.

"Your act, you mean."

As we passed, someone else was coming toward us. I looked back to find the girl returning to her dance, smile as broad as a toothpaste commercial. I turned to Oscar and we both burst out laughing.

"I've wanted to do that for months," he said.

"Fat lot of good it did."

"It's not as if there aren't plenty of other jobs in this town."

"Yeah," I said, "but most of them don't come with dance lessons."

"Ah," he cried, "San Francisco!"

We continued along the street, the sky seeming broader as we approached the open expanse before the Ferry Building.

Off to the side, cars whizzed by on the Bay Bridge. I always wondered why there weren't more accidents on the upper level, drivers distracted by the view of the city—Coit Tower holding court on Telegraph Hill, the Transamerica Pyramid piercing the sky, from azure to cerulean.

Most of the new construction was going on just south of us. Market was still basically the same street I'd known for 20 years. Any changes to it had been so gradual, I'd forgotten them. Buildings came and went one at a time, and usually the tear-downs were eyesores, so there was no nostalgia for them. In other parts of town, though, I felt nothing but nostalgia. It's always hard to accept when something you love changes, when the very parts of it that you fell in love with are suddenly ripped away.

CHAPTER 15

CLOSING ARGUMENTS

As a rule, I've always preferred public transportation—the convenience, the chance to relax and leave the driving to someone else. And I've always had a particular fondness for trains.

But I draw the line at trains that go under water. In earthquake country.

It added insult to injury, I thought, compounding the usual aspersions about the bridge-and-tunnel crowd with a soupçon of danger. I marveled at the thousands of people who boarded BART every morning and didn't bat an eye as the train entered the tunnel, knowing they would soon be 100 feet under the bay and back under it again on the way home. Twice a day—ten times a week—they tempted fate, or at least Poseidon, trusting that the earthquake wouldn't come in those few minutes of submersion, that the train wouldn't break down and trap them underground—underwater—as the earth shook not just underneath but all around them.

I suppose it's not much different from flying—which has always struck me as a leap of faith for those of us who aren't experts in aerodynamics, trusting that the rules of physics really can support a 50-ton aluminum can hurtling through empty air, all for the sake of finding London when the doors open.

Walnut Creek was no London, which made me wonder all the

more what I was doing on this rattling car, perched on an industrial fabric–coated seat that smelled vaguely of sweat and bleach. It beat the alternative, I told myself. Driving across the Bay Bridge and into the insane traffic on the east side was a fate worse than death, as far as I was concerned. The interlocking freeways splintered off in every direction but west, all of them flying past beige strip malls with little indication that any given turn would really matter all that much. Once you got past Oakland and Berkeley, with their self-consciously multicultural and antiestablishment ethos, everything looked pretty much the same. Suburbia, to me, was just a place where sidewalks went to die.

I had placed the overnight bag on my lap at Civic Center and pulled out my book, hoping to distract myself with images of Norwegian snow and the disconnects between men and women, the joy and burden of children—a foreign world that bore no resemblance to what I had just left or what I would find at the other end of the tunnel.

As the train idled at Embarcadero—last chance to escape before the deluge—I realized I'd been reading the same paragraph since I'd cracked the book open. I kept losing my place, unable to trace a verb back to its subject. It wasn't Knausgaard's fault. Today I would probably have the same struggle with Dr. Seuss.

I closed the book and held it loosely in my lap, thumbs grazing the cover, as the train began its descent through the tunnel, down into the waters of the bay. I couldn't help thinking of Persephone, heading back into the underworld for another six months. I should count myself lucky, I thought.

After talking to Oscar, I had finally, reluctantly, responded to Damien's text, trying to match his cavalier tone. *Sure,* I said, *let's talk. What's a good time?*

I had taken people back before. You might say I never let them go.

He responded within minutes. That was the first sign that something was up. Damien was not one to jump on messages. He seldom even answered the phone when I called him. I'd always worried that I was the one who responded too quickly. Availability—even with a text or a voicemail—was a sign of desperation. It was as if we were having a breath-holding context, and I was always the first one to swim up for air.

Come over around noon on Saturday, he said. *I'll make lunch.*

Damien making lunch. Now I knew I was in Bizarro World. He'd already let me down. He wasn't trying to break anything to me gently. Damien wasn't the type to go out of his way to convey bad news. No, I thought, he wanted something. But I still couldn't believe that what he wanted was me.

I was still daydreaming when the train pulled to a stop on the elevated platform in Walnut Creek. I would have missed it altogether if I hadn't thought to check the sign outside. In the suburbs, the outdoor stations were as nondescript as the underground, with precious few unique landmarks in what passed for a skyline. I quickly tossed my book into the bag, squeezing it between underwear and a sweatshirt, zipped up the bag and hurried to the doors just as they were huffing their way open.

Damien lived a few blocks from the station, which gave me a chance to enjoy the fresh air and hope it allowed me to think more clearly than I could in the stuffy confines of the train.

It was at least 20 degrees warmer here than San Francisco, with no fog or clouds or ocean breeze to compete with the glaring sun. The weather offered a lovely change of pace now and then— a chance to lie in the sun or take a quick swim in the pool on the edge of Damien's complex. But at the end of every weekend spent here, I'd been relieved to return home to the city's temperate vibe, the comfort of a leather jacket pulled tight.

Since we'd started dating, I'd made this trip at least a dozen times. Damien's forays into the city were mostly event-focused—theater tickets, a dinner reservation. He didn't think of the city as a place to relax, so if we didn't have plans I would come out here and we'd spend an evening or a quiet weekend—hiking at any number of trails nearby, watching a movie. I'd come to like the effortlessness of it. Being here with Damien was a chance to forget the stress of the city and just *be* for a couple of days.

It had never taken long for my relationships to get to the stage of spending weekends together. When I'd dated people who lived nearby, we could spend any night of the week together, but still weekends were special, almost a requirement. Even early on, when we barely knew each other, they were a chance to practice domesticity. In retrospect, now that I'd been burned more times than I cared to recall (some lessons need to be learned and learned again ad nauseam), I realized that those weekends had a tendency to create an artificial sense of bonding—forcing things together that might be better left apart.

His condo complex took up half a city block, a series of buildings connected by walkways, like a college campus. I made my way toward his and rang the bell. He buzzed me in without answering.

The hallway smelled of lavender, the artificial aroma of something recently cleaned. The carpet stretched for what seemed like miles. The place had the antiseptic quality of a hotel—the bold carpet, the muted blue walls, the absence of natural light.

Damien's door was propped open. I knocked lightly as I pushed it inward.

"Come in!" he called from the kitchen. Jazz was spilling softly from the stereo.

I closed the door behind me and was settling my bag discreetly in the foyer when Damien emerged, wiping his hands on a navy dishtowel.

"Hi," he said, smiling. His teeth were huge and straight, bright white despite his addiction to coffee. It was that smile that had first captivated me. His eyes grew wide, lines radiating around them, a dimple carving its way into one cheek. Damien certainly knew how to smile.

He came closer and leaned in to kiss me. Taken aback by the abruptness, I turned my head, and his lips delicately landed against the side of my mouth. His stubble scraped my cheek. He was around my age, but his skin was oddly rougher—probably from the fogless East Bay sun.

"How was BART?" he asked, backing up toward the kitchen.

I followed him around the corner. "Fine," I said. "Pretty quiet."

"Good." He hung the towel on a hook beside the refrigerator. "Can I get you anything? Mimosa?"

"Sure."

He nodded and pulled a bottle of champagne and a container of orange juice from the fridge. A couple of champagne flutes were already positioned on the counter beside an overflowing platter.

"I made a salade Niçoise," he said sheepishly.

"How festive." I marveled at the organization of the platter—green beans neatly aligned on the left, sliced tomatoes on the right, potatoes and hard-boiled eggs bordering a clump of tuna in the center, all over a bed of mixed greens. Damien was basically a meat-and-potatoes guy, his favorite meal hamburgers grilled on the patio.

He handed me a flute, bubbles coursing through the juice,

and led the way into the living room.

His place was somewhat larger than mine—a reflection of differing real estate prices on either side of the bay—but more spartan. Aside from a large painting on one wall—sailboats off Catalina, a gift from his parents—it was filled only with functional items. There were no tchotchkes holding court on tabletops, a minimal number of books on the shelves, mostly sci-fi titles or things he needed for work. I had actually envied the simplicity of his wardrobe. My own closet was jammed with clothes—shirts squeezed against each other on the rod, sweaters piled high on the shelves—so that each morning I was confronted with enough choices to paralyze my ability to dress myself, if I could even see everything hiding in the clutter. Damien, by contrast, had more focused taste, his idea of variety an assortment of plaid shirts in every shade of blue.

I chose the armchair by the window, gray cushions that I could sink into for protection. Damien sat on the edge of the sofa, directly across.

"So how have you been?" he asked.

"I'm good," I said, trying to make my expression match the words. "The trial takes up half my day now, so I spend less time at the store."

"The trial?"

"Jury duty, remember?"

"Oh yes," he said. "What's it like?"

"It's fascinating. I'm really glad to be there."

"Wow," he said with a chuckle, "you're a good citizen. Most people try their best to get out of it."

Bits of pulp danced in the mimosa. "They don't know what they're missing."

We made small talk for a while, exchanging stories about

work—the imminent sale of the store, his boss's demands on his time. It felt like a first date, strangers just getting to know each other. He was turning on the charm. It was evident in the number of questions he asked. Damien had a knack for steering the discussion toward himself, asking a question only so he could provide his version of a response as soon as his interlocutor was done. I thought of this as college freshman communication, a back-and-forth sharing of information about oneself without stopping to listen to what the other was saying, with no attempt to turn lines of dialogue into an actual conversation.

But he wasn't doing that today. Today he was asking about specific things in my life—the store, Oscar, my mother—without addressing his own version of each topic. He was making an effort to seem genuinely interested, to follow up on my responses in a way that kept the discussion moving, albeit stiltedly. It might have been pleasant if I had decided to play along, if I weren't so careful, so dubious, so self-conscious of every twitch of an eyebrow, every tap of a finger, if my stomach weren't churning, if I couldn't hear the voice in my head insistently asking what I was doing there.

The conversation was flowing so naturally, so blithely, I barely registered the sudden change in tone.

"I just needed a little time to regroup," he was saying when I realized I'd missed the shift. He could have been talking about work, the technical stuff that always went over my head, the kind of thing I'd gotten used to listening to with half an ear. "But the more I thought about it, the more I missed you."

I pressed my lips together flatly, pretending he was just reciting the weather report.

"I decided I'm happier with you than without you."

He meant it to be flattering, and at first that was how I read it. I took another sip, an excuse to shut my eyes as the bubbles floated down my throat. Though I'd never been fond of jazz, I tried to focus on the music, Ella scatting in the background.

I decided I liked my champagne more without juice than with it.

"I'm really glad you came," he said, smiling broadly. He rose from the chair. "Let me finish dressing the salad and we can eat."

The small talk continued over lunch, a well-laid table between us, lots of vegetables to distract us, mimosas continually refilled. He hadn't asked me for a reaction. In a conversation that had ranged through a dozen topics, this—the recommencement of our relationship—was the only one he hadn't asked my opinion of. He assumed the answer. After all, he'd been the one to call the break. Of course, I had spent the past couple of weeks on hold, just waiting for this moment. My own feelings couldn't have changed in the interim. I'd just been waiting for him.

Taking a break from eating, I laid my hands on my knees. As he related a story about work, a project he'd been struggling with, getting no support from colleagues, I became suddenly aware that my fingers were moving—typing out his words on my jeans, transcribing automatically, focused on the letters while my head missed the meaning.

I abruptly pulled my hands back to the tabletop and stabbed a tomato wedge. "Have you been seeing anyone?" I finally ventured to ask.

He had just brought a forkful to his lips. He struggled now to swallow it. "What do you mean?"

"Well, were you just sitting at home alone every night?"

He giggled in that way of his, the half-coughing, half-stammering sound I'd learned to associate with a spinning of the wheels, buying time to come up with a story. "You know I'm a bit of a homebody."

"Yeah."

Of course, I recalled, he preferred to order in. I was imagining the others who'd been here over the past couple of weeks—auditioning over dinner at this table, or cocktails in the living room, or blowjobs on the bed. Men he'd met online, torsos that acquired heads only in the flesh, like zombies stumbling through graveyards in search of spare parts. He'd compared them all to me, and they'd all come up short. So here I was. Bully for me.

He peered at me curiously. "Have *you*? Been seeing anyone?" A lock of dark hair fell over his brow, dangling just above one eye. That tip of his head, the half-smile: the same look as the face pic that had caught my attention on our first night of online flirting.

In all our time dating, we had seldom talked much about our romantic history. I knew about his childhood, his education, the job that had precipitated his move from Orange County, but I couldn't remember the name of a single previous boyfriend. Maybe he'd never mentioned them by name. Maybe he hadn't known any of them long enough to remember their names.

"No one special," I said.

He laughed, but his eyes weren't so sure. "So what *have* you been doing, you naughty boy?"

He was trying to make light of it, even turn it into something sexy, but his shoulders stiffened. He hadn't taken a bite for a couple of minutes. The wheels were turning again. This did not compute. I hadn't been staring at my phone for two weeks, waiting for his call. I had a life when he wasn't looking.

I watched closely, waiting to catch a whiff of steam swirl out of his ears.

"The salad is very tasty," I said. "Did you really make it yourself?"

The laughter came more forcefully now—relief at the change of subject. "With a little help from Whole Foods."

On my first visit, he hadn't greeted me with a meal. He'd answered the door barefoot, a hole in the knee of his jeans, a baby blue Oxford shirt untucked, the top couple of buttons undone to reveal a tuft of hair in the cleft of his chest. He offered me a beer and we drank quickly, on the way into the bedroom. He was a passionate lover that night, each moment another seduction to lead me to the next. His touch alternately gentle and rough, he leaned in and pulled away with a rhythm calibrated to keep the tension rising.

It had gone on that way for a few weeks, meeting at his house or mine and spilling into bed within minutes, plans for the night put on hold until our bodies were satisfied. Our bodies were in charge of the relationship, minds patiently waiting to get on with it. But over time, the ratio gradually reversed, and we began to spend those evenings talking, hanging out. Once our bodies had answered all their questions, they grew less interested, the initial excitement giving way to routine. And without sex as a distraction, a raison d'être, the real effort began.

I could use a change of subject now. "Brendan thinks I should sell the condo," I told him, slicing into an anchovy.

"Sell? And do what?"

"I don't know. Retire to Palm Springs, I suppose."

"Oh." His shoulders relaxed.

I tried to tamp down my own satisfaction in watching the emotions fluttering over his face faster than his mind could keep up.

"I don't know," I said. "I think he's crazy."

Damien's fork hovered over the plate like a divining rod. "I can't imagine you anywhere else," he said. "You love San Francisco."

"Well, it's changing."

"But still."

"Maybe I'm changing, too," I said.

He smiled. "I guess we all are. That's what life is, right?"

I set my fork down. I'd had enough. "That was delicious," I said. "Thank you."

He pushed back his chair. "I'm glad you liked it." He took both plates and placed them on the kitchen island, just behind him. "Why don't you pour yourself another drink and sit in the living room? I'll just be a minute. I want to clean up before …"

Before he could finish the sentence, I got up, too. He was opening the dishwasher when I grabbed my bag out of the foyer.

I took another sip of my mimosa and laid the glass on the coffee table. The living room was defined by a wide window that looked out onto the back of the complex—palm trees vying with ginkgos for attention along a winding path beside a manicured lawn.

The bag looped over my shoulder, I made my way into the bedroom. Everything looked so tidy—the bed neatly made, the navy comforter spilling symmetrically over each side; the dresser gleaming.

I quietly pulled open the bottom drawer. I hadn't left much stuff there—a few pairs of boxer briefs, a couple of polo shirts, a light jersey. I scooped them up in a single armful and laid them on the bed. I coughed forcibly as I unzipped the bag. Pushing my book to the side, I scooped out the clothes. The lining of the sweatshirt felt luxurious against my fingers as I laid it gently in the drawer. A couple of pairs of underwear—tighty whiteys, as Damien called them; socks; a wool sweater. I nestled the deodorant and toothbrush on top of it all.

I closed the drawer, tucked my own things into the bag, and zipped it up. I was back in the living room, holding my nearly empty glass and looking out the window, when Damien finally emerged from the kitchen.

"It's a beautiful day, isn't it?" Suddenly, his arms were around my waist. "We should go for a hike."

"I'm sorry," I said, "I can't stay."

His arms released me and I turned around to face him. "I have plans tonight. In fact, I really should get back soon."

"Plans? What are you up to?" His raised eyebrows tried to convince me it was just idle curiosity.

"Oh, dinner plans with the guys."

"That sounds fun."

I squinted. "Does it?"

"Sure. Your friends are great."

Now I knew he was lying. "Anyway," I said, "I have errands to run, so I might as well get started soon. As it is, I won't be home for an hour."

"I could drive you," he said.

"No, thanks. With the bridge traffic, that's not any faster. Besides, I kind of like the train." As long as I can block out images of the Titanic, I thought.

"Okay." He backed away. His arms looked empty. "Well, call me."

I nodded. "It was good to see you," I said.

And I kissed him. His lips opened, soft, moist. As he reached around to embrace me, I pulled away with a big smile. "Okay," I said, hoisting the bag back onto my shoulder. I could feel that brick of a book jockeying for room with my Calvins.

He walked me to the door. His lips parted as if to say something, but the words didn't come.

I was all the way down the hall before I heard the door close behind me.

CHAPTER 16
CIRCUMSTANTIAL
EVIDENCE

My mother was obsessed with soap operas. They brought into the house all the drama that was missing from real life—girl meets boy, girl loses boy, girl stabs boy to death in a jealous rage. On summer afternoons I would watch one or two of them with her, learning to identify the passions that drove people—love, sex, greed. For her, these stories were an escape from real life. For me, they were an introduction to it.

The alleged heroines—the dowdy housewives who never put a foot wrong except to protect their children from harm—bored me. I was much more interested in the women torn between the squeaky-clean hero and the tempting villain, each of whom brought out a different side of herself. Our favorite show was *Guiding Light*, in which not one but two heroines fell into the same snare—in love with the gentle Ed, yet unable to resist the sexy and dangerous Roger.

Years later, I was still living in their world, still filing the men I met into one fictitious camp or the other. Like Holly and Rita, I was never clear on what I was looking for. After a date or two, I would find myself labeling—this one was a Roger, that one an Ed. Or too much of one and not enough of the other. I was always drawn to Roger's darkness, slightly terrified of Ed's earnestness. I craved the passion—night after night of bodies coming together, leaving hearts to be figured out later. I made a rule to have sex within the first three dates: if we weren't compatible in bed, we wouldn't be compatible anywhere else. I was suspicious of the guys who wanted to put it off for a while, who wanted to "get to know" me first, assuming that having things in common was the real key to success. The Eds who brought me flowers and ended the night with a chaste kiss. Their charms were effective, but they wore off quickly. There was one in particular, a sweet guy named Beau, who proclaimed on the fourth date, "I could fall in love with you." My eyes bugged open so that when he leaned in for a kiss, I imagined that those gently parted lips were about to devour me. I backed away and covered my embarrassment with a cough that sent me running to the kitchen for a glass of water. Beau was living in his own soap opera, but it wasn't mine.

As I boarded the train back to San Francisco, I tried to figure out which bucket Damien belonged in. At first, he'd carried hints of Roger, or brought out the Roger in me. But the Ed parts had never felt genuine. He presented me with flowers a few times, on each instance holding them gruffly, at arm's length, as if he didn't know quite what to do with them. I pictured him grabbing the first bouquet off a sidewalk stand, foreign objects that spoke a language he couldn't comprehend.

◻

The Lone Star was not one of my usual haunts. Not because I didn't like the atmosphere—there was something old-school charming about the sawdust on the floor and the wooden keg of peanuts beside the pool table. It was more a question of geography. Bars were no longer destinations for me. Somewhere along the way they had become mere conveniences, and the most convenient ones, by definition, were closer to home.

I grabbed a beer and found a spot against the wall with a view of the door and the pool table. I'd never been interested in the game, but there was something soothing about watching others play—the dance of balls across the green felt, the satisfactory thump as each ball dropped into a pocket.

A barrel-chested guy with a thick beard scanned the table in search of his next shot. Decided, he bent toward the table, back arching elegantly. He peered over his shoulder before extending the stick behind him and then, turning back to the table, lined up the shot. The cue ball cracked against a pair in the middle, sending one rolling toward the far corner. It slid against the wall for a second before spilling into the pocket. The guy rose back to his full height, his face betraying no sign of triumph, and slinked to the other side of the table to scope out his next move.

His opponent—wiry by comparison, every ab outlined by a tight black t-shirt—held his stick vertically against the floor and peered at the table. With one hand, he pushed long, curly hair over his ears—a nervous tic disguised as an afterthought—and waited his turn.

"Who's winning?"

I turned away from the table to see Oscar sidling up beside me, eyes on the game as he unbuttoned his sport coat. His pink tie, knot loosened over an open collar, caught the light from a lamp over the bar and seemed to glitter.

"A little overdressed for this joint, don't you think?"

He smirked. "Sorry, I didn't have time to change into my chaps."

I peered around him, toward the door. "Where's Rafe?"

"Parking the car. This neighborhood is becoming impossible." He gestured toward my beer. "What are we drinking?"

"I don't know," I said, "something wheaty."

"Ever the connoisseur." He headed for the bar.

The burly guy had evidently missed his shot. The wiry one was up now, gangly body extended over the table as he angled his cue. The resulting crack sounded more like a thud. I could see a couple of balls spinning on the table, but there was no successful plunk. He grimaced and straightened up, then made his way back into the corner like a child sentenced to the dunce cap in grade school.

Oscar reappeared and tapped his glass delicately against mine. "Cheers." His beer was darker, with a centimeter of foam on top.

"So what happened?" he asked. "With Damien."

"Oh," I said, watching the rounded butt of the bearded guy as he bent over the table, "that."

"Did you see him?"

"Oh yeah." I sighed. I'd tried not to think about it once I got home. I knew I'd be reliving the whole thing right now, with Oscar, so I'd felt no need to process, no need to punish myself with memories and second thoughts.

"So? Did he propose or something?"

I laughed. "A proposal of sorts, you could say. I'll give you a direct quote."

Oscar gazed at me with pursed lips in anticipation.

"I decided I'm happier with you than without you."

"How romantic."

"Then you agree," I said. "I was afraid I was being too sensitive."

[216]

"That depends. What else did he say?"

"Nothing."

"Nothing?"

"Well, we talked about work and how expensive anchovies are at Whole Foods."

"That's it? I mean, no follow-up to 'I'm happier with you'?"

"Nada. It was like he'd done his duty. He welcomed me with a mimosa and assumed we were back to normal. It was kind of sad, actually. He asked if I was seeing anyone, and you should have seen the way he squirmed when I refused to give him a straight answer."

"*Are* you seeing anyone?"

I laughed. "I had one trick," I said. "Actually, we were *in flagrante* when Damien texted that he wanted to see me."

"Ooh, irony's a bitch." Oscar paused. "So did you fuck him?"

"Who?"

"Damien."

I shrugged, practiced my newfound nonchalance. "No, I didn't fuck him. I made a polite exit an hour or so later, and that was that."

"Did you break up with him?"

There was a hint of orange in the beer that made it taste almost like a dessert. "Yes," I said. "But he doesn't know it yet."

"How mature of you."

"Really?" I said. "I'm supposed to be the bigger man? I'm sick of being the bigger man."

Beside me, a cute blond turned with a start. He smiled and winked.

"So what if he calls?" Oscar asked. "What are you going to say?"

"I don't know. I'll cross that bridge when I come to it." I

paused. "But I did leave him a hint."

Oscar tilted his head and leaned in.

"I took all his shit out of my house—clothes, toothbrush, deodorant, whatever—and brought it with me. And while he was in the kitchen washing dishes, I snuck into the bedroom and dumped it all into a dresser drawer. And brought my own stuff home."

"And he didn't catch you?"

"No. I don't think he had any idea what was going on."

"That's almost like theft," he said.

"In reverse. It's more like a surprise gift."

We were clinking our glasses when Rafe appeared, eyes bright. "What are we drinking to?" he asked. "Are you and Damien back together?"

"No," I said. "Quite the opposite. I dumped him."

I repeated the gist of the story once Rafe had his drink. He stared at me, stunned. "That's a little passive-aggressive, don't you think?"

"Oh honey, I'm an expert at passive-aggressive. I learned it from my mother."

"Minnesota nice," Oscar said. "Smile to your face and stab you in the back."

"You know me so well."

I gazed around the room. If most bars in the Castro catered to 25-year-olds, the average age here seemed to teeter around 40. After this, it was just the geriatrics at Twin Peaks. And that was where we were in life, one foot in each camp, stuck between worlds.

"I can't believe I'm 51 years old and still resorting to such foolishness."

Oscar smiled mischievously. "Well, age doesn't necessarily

bring maturity."

"Who said that?"

"Confucius. Maya Angelou. I don't know. Just drink."

It was good to laugh. With the second round, we moved toward a far corner of the room, safe from the vagaries of pool cues.

"I never liked him anyway," Rafe confessed at last.

"Why didn't you tell me?"

He shook his head fiercely. "First rule of friendship: Never tell someone what you think of his boyfriend."

A couple of hipsters came in, wool caps pulled back on their heads, slender bodies easily squeezing through the crowd.

Oscar rolled his eyes. "Youth is wasted on the ridiculous."

I smiled. "*Life* is wasted on the ridiculous. I wonder if we just resent them for being young."

"What?" Rafe said.

"Seriously. Here we are, falling apart already, and they're all around us—young, vital, smooth skin."

"Bad fashion."

I watched the hipsters ordering drinks at the bar—glowing shots that they downed quickly before turning to their drafts.

"Do you ever think about what the previous generation thought of us when we were that age—taking over the town? When I first moved here, it seemed to me that everyone over 35 had this wisdom in their eyes that I didn't see in anyone else's, certainly not in my own. They'd lived through something that I was only ever on the edge of. They knew something I couldn't fathom, no matter how much I read about it, no matter how much I told myself it defined my world."

I gazed off into the dark corner. "In reality, it hadn't defined my world. I had escaped it. That was a luxury people hadn't had just 10 years before." I turned back to look at them. "I think they hated us for it. We were free. Our world wasn't falling apart, it was just beginning."

"I remember one guy," Rafe said. "I met him through one of those phone lines—remember those, 976-something or other? We chatted, he seemed really nice, so I went over. He kept the apartment dim. I thought it was romantic, but when I got close to him, when we kissed, I saw how thin he was, his face kind of sunken. He was okay, no lesions or dementia or anything like that. But it was coming. He knew it was coming. We fooled around—safely. I told myself not to be scared. My strategy was to assume that everyone was positive, anyway, so it wasn't like I had to take any extra precautions with him."

Rafe's eyes narrowed, as if physically peering into the memory. "What really struck me was how angry he was. Not at me, but I still felt it—like he was angry at what I represented. I remember him looking out the window—his apartment was on a high floor right near Castro and Market; you could see the whole neighborhood. He looked out the window and kind of raged at what he saw—people parading down the street, going about their lives, bouncing from one bar to another. And he scoffed. They weren't taking it seriously, he said. They were having fun, playing a fiddle while Rome burned around them. That was when he scared me. I felt like I was part of what he was railing against. I was just having fun, living my life. And that seemed shameful now."

We got another round to drown the downer mood and spent the rest of the evening reminiscing about youthful exploits. Rafe laughed and shook his head as Oscar and I traveled down our private memory lane.

"Remember that Scottish guy who was hitting on you at the Sun that night?"

It was 20 years ago, but the memory was crystal clear. I turned to Rafe. "He was drunk off his head, and I just chatted him up. Not really interested, but I loved the way he talked."

Oscar interrupted. "And then, while he went to fetch a drink, Craig started talking to some other guy. Sure enough, when ol' Sean Connery comes back and spots him, he yells out in the thickest brogue, 'Crrraig, ya whorrrrrre!'"

Rafe and I were still howling with laughter when Oscar put a hand on my shoulder, his expression strangely sober. "Fuck Damien," he said softly. "You don't need anyone."

He kissed me on the cheek. His lips were warm, his hand on my shoulder steadying. And I tried to believe him.

CHAPTER 17
GREY GARDENS

Brendan called it an adventure. "We're just exploring," he said. "You can't make a decision without knowing what's out there, right?"

I stared ahead as he cruised down Judah, the avenue numbers steadily clicking up. I had only the vaguest idea where I was.

"It's nice out here," he assured me. "You know Irving, right? All those restaurants. Cool neighborhood. And look," he said, gesturing as a MUNI train zipped past us on the street, "you won't even have far to walk to get downtown."

"Or to the Castro," I said. Already, I was measuring every new neighborhood by its proximity to the old one.

Brendan turned onto a side street and pulled into the driveway of an ecru house, thick steps leading up to a double entrance.

"There are only two units in this place," he said, getting out of the car, "so you won't have to worry so much about neighbors."

Urban living, I thought, was all about neighbors. It was only in the suburbs that you tried to avoid them. What the hell was I doing?

The door on the left was hanging open, and a young couple emerged just as we reached the stoop. The woman turned her head to say something inaudible to her husband, long brown hair snapping over one shoulder. "I don't know," he said, "I kinda liked the kitchen." She waved a hand dismissively and skipped down the steps.

The tiny entry opened onto a square living room, bay window poised over the driveway, a Persian rug defining the space. The furniture was otherwise nondescript—glass tabletops, a white couch and chairs—obviously staged to make the place look bigger than it was.

Brendan greeted the realtor, who was standing beside a vase of flowers on the sidebar, tidying up a pile of flyers. I always assume that people in a given profession all know one another, but it seemed that there were more realtors in San Francisco then grocery store clerks. Introducing himself, Brendan exchanged cards with the other man—thin, young, overdressed in a dark suit and patterned tie.

The condo was nice enough, certainly larger than my current place, but there was an unmistakable coldness to it. Maybe it was just the staging, but I couldn't imagine anyone living here, sealed in by these white walls, the narrow blond planks of the hardwood floor.

The long hallway bordered a lightwell, where a couple of tall plants sat in red ceramic pots. This was apparently the solution for the lack of side windows.

We moved through the space languidly, Brendan pointing out features—the wainscoting in the dining area, the delicate crown molding. It all washed over me, just a series of images barely piercing my consciousness. I felt like I was sleepwalking in someone else's dream.

"Well?" he asked as we made our way back to the car.

"It was interesting," I said.

"Ooh, damning with faint praise."

"What's next?" I strapped myself into the passenger seat and resolved to keep an open mind.

"A couple of other places around here, and then I thought we'd look closer to the beach." He backed out of the driveway and sped back toward Judah. "If nothing else," he said, "you're doing me a favor. I don't have time to see every new listing when it comes open for brokers, so this is my chance to get a little more familiar with what's available."

"For your less reluctant clients."

"Precisely," he said. "So pretend we're just on a Sunday joyride."

We went through a few more condos that all looked pretty much identical on the inside. Given the similar architectural style of the neighborhood, the layouts were bound to be the same, but the staging only enhanced the feeling: in their effort to leave each place open to the imagination, the realtors had effectively drained any trace of character out of them. By the fourth one, I was beginning to believe that the whole world was made of glass tables and blond wood.

Things changed when the ocean came into view, its immensity demanding a different approach to architecture as well as life. Brendan brought me to a single-family wood-framed house, its exterior weatherworn but not without a certain charm.

"I hear this one is a bit of a fixer-upper," he said, leading me inside, "but it's kind of a steal for the location."

The wide windows let a great wave of light into the living room. I made a mental note not to fall for that, knowing that fog was the default weather for this part of town. The floor creaked as we made our way through, the noise granting the place a lived-in quality that belied the requisite staging. I stopped in the kitchen for a few minutes, taken by the quirky construction—cabinets everywhere, an impressive wine rack almost hidden beside the staircase to the upstairs bedrooms. Brendan was right: the place would need a lot of work, but I was starting to understand what he meant by "good bones."

We wended our way through the house—two tiny bedrooms on the upper floor and a bath whose fixtures were rusty and grimy in turn—and I found myself paying more attention than I had to the stylish boxes of the Inner Sunset. While Brendan returned to the kitchen to inspect things more closely, I lingered in the living room. A couple of other househunters meandered back and forth through the space as I drifted toward the large plate-glass window. The Great Highway was just a few yards away, cars sailing back and forth on either side of the median. Just over the dunes, the ocean breathed in the distance, a gentle rise and fall that pulsated against the sky. In this light, it was hard to mark the different shades of blue, the precise line where the one ended and the other began. Instead, together sea and sky comprised one huge expanse, indifferent to whatever was going on on this side of the road.

On the morning after the election, I had come down to the beach, very near this spot. I remembered standing on the sand, eyes focused on the waves, the enormity of the ocean. I'd been drawn there, but I didn't understand why until I arrived. I'd needed to see something larger than myself, larger than the country that had disappointed me, larger than the thing I called civilization that was quickly destroying itself. The ocean was at peace. The ocean knew it would survive us.

"Ready?" Brendan said, suddenly at my side. We stood together before the window for a moment, watching the waves.

"I like it," I said at last.

"Really? That's surprising. It's the most remote place we've seen today."

"Maybe that's why. If I'm going to leave, it should be for something completely different. Not a pale imitation. Those other places think they're still part of a city. This place seems to know better."

It was on the edge of the world, as far as you could go and still have your feet on the ground.

We ended up back at Brendan's, winding down in the quiet of the garden. He always looked calmer here, the greenery stripping away the world's drama and with it any need for vigilance. He sat across the table, the rustle of the leaves above his head moving the shade back and forth so that his face always seemed striated into moving strips of light and dark.

"So, what did you learn today?" he asked, lounging back, wine glass cupped in one hand.

"What an interesting question," I said. "I guess I'm more open to change than I thought I was."

"Oh good," he said. "When you stop wanting change, you're dead."

"Does it seem to you like I'm stuck in my ways?"

"Of course," he said. "Aren't we all, after a certain age?"

Little Edie slinked under the table and wove herself around my feet.

I'd been coasting for a while, that much was true. "You get so comfortable," I said.

"Until you don't. Until life throws you a curve ball."

"Isn't it supposed to get easier as you get older? I mean, you don't need as much, you don't care as much."

"Absolutely. It should be easier." He closed his eyes for a moment, as though waiting for a magic elixir to take effect. "But age just brings a different set of issues. Just when you're beginning to relax and let go of ambition, let go of perfectionism, other shit comes in to take its place."

I sat back in my chair, echoing his position, cradling the glass, relishing the breeze. Brendan, several years older than me, than anyone else in our group, was supposed to be the wise old man. He'd been there before, always a few steps ahead, equipped to warn us of the loose stones in the road.

"Hopefully," he said at last, "we've already been through the worst. I know I have, anyway."

The worst, of course, was the plague. The worst was losing Stan.

"Every night, he would sit right where you are now," Brendan said. "This was his favorite place in the world." He glanced around, taking in the entire yard. "It didn't matter where else we went, he always wanted to come home to this spot. In Stan's eyes, even Florence couldn't hold a candle to this ramshackle garden."

"It's a lovely garden."

He laughed. "Don't bullshit a bullshitter. There's a reason I call the cats Big and Little Edie."

His smile softened and his gaze got lost somewhere in the hedge behind me. "This is how I got through it all, you know. When I moved in, the yard was a mess. Stan may have loved the idea of it, but tending to it wasn't his forte—it was all patchy grass, weeds, not much else. I did my best to keep it trim, but mostly I just sat here with him and enjoyed the wildness."

There was a long pause. Brendan's chest visibly rose with a deep breath. "And then, one day I came home from visiting Stan in the hospital. He was declining fast. I knew he wasn't going to last the week. As soon as I walked through that gate, I bent down to rip out some weeds. And I couldn't stop. There, on my hands and knees, I was tearing at the earth. Violently. Attacking it. The weeds became a stand-in for the virus—nature turning on us. So I fought back. Crawling around the whole yard, pulling them up by the root. At some point, I realized I was crying. And then I was screaming, surrounded by piles of raggedy plants, uprooted, dying all around me."

His expression was remarkably impassive, as if he were simply reciting a historical fact—the Civil War from a distance.

"After that, I decided to focus on sprucing it up. I started planting flowers, those hedges in the corner. Every time someone died, I would make a trip to the nursery and find something that seemed appropriate."

He pulled himself out of the chair. Like a tour guide, he began pointing out the sights. "The hydrangeas over there were for Lenny."

I followed his gesture toward the side of the house, heliotrope petals bunched together into balls, a tight clump of color trimmed to knee height.

Brendan paced through the garden, studying each bush, each patch of flowers, and calling out names one by one—lantanas for Kevin, a rosebush for Aaron and Gil. I wondered if I should stand up and join him, follow behind on the tour. But it seemed to me that he was in a world of his own now—less identifying things for my sake than sauntering through a field of memories.

He was just completing a round of the yard, heading back toward the table, when he stopped at a potted plant by the door—bright white petals opening toward what was left of the sun. "Stan's favorite flower," he said, and he turned to me suddenly. "Do you have any idea how hard it is to grow gardenias in San Francisco? They like sun, but not too much. Warm days, cool nights. But not too cool. San Francisco summers can freeze the damn things overnight. So I keep moving the pots around to catch the right amount of sun. Half the time I just keep them indoors. Constant effort, like raising a child. But look at them! Smell them!"

I looked, focused on the oval petals swirling around the center of each flower, open around the edges but tightly closed toward the middle. I didn't need to lean in to catch the scent. It reminded me of my mother's perfume. There was something old-fashioned about it, something eternal.

"It's chaos," he said, gazing around. "But I love that. I could never have one of those French gardens, with the neatly trimmed hedges and everything laid out in clean little squares. I like the mess. It's more like life."

The sun was still shining on the right side of the yard, lighting up the patch from the hydrangeas to the roses. It would fall below the hill soon and leave everything in shadow.

Brendan's face softened and a subtle smile took over his lips as he took his seat again. "Stan and I would sit out here every night," he said. "This is where we would wind down at the end of the day. Just like this—a glass of wine while we waited for the work amnesia to kick in. I get pissed now when the weather doesn't cooperate. Sometimes I sit out here in a parka, just because I'm stubborn. It's my version of church, I suppose."

"Were you ever religious?" I asked.

"God no," he said with a laugh. "I went to temple, of course, got the bar mitzvah. But once I got a little older, I realized it was the culture that appealed to me, not the God thing. Fortunately, I always saw Judaism as more about the human level, how we treat one another, and less about the big guy in the sky. I've always wondered what it must be like to be raised in a religion that focuses so much on an afterlife."

"It's not everything it's cracked up to be, take it from me."

"Who needs more than this, right? One world is enough."

"Too much, sometimes."

He drained his glass and reached for the bottle. "Have you ever been to Rome?" he asked. "You walk around the Forum and the Coliseum, and it's a few splintered columns surrounded by patches of grass and all this glorious dirt. And you realize that you're walking on history, that every stone at your feet used to be part of something bigger, that the dirt itself is what's left of something that used to be beautiful and alive." He was staring into the wine again. "I was in my twenties then, visiting Italy for the first time. And that was when I learned there was no point in mourning the past. We don't have time for it. We have to live. And nothing fully disappears, anyway. It just changes into something else. Like these flowers."

We sat in silence for a while, until the wine was gone. Little Edie had settled at my feet, gently snoring, her gray fur tickling my ankle.

By the time I wended my way back home, the sky had turned royal blue and, like a falling curtain, brought a hush upon the world. I hadn't eaten since breakfast, so the wine had gone directly to my head. Everything looked oddly peaceful—even when I turned to take in the extent of Castro Street and the endless bustle as it approached Market. I stopped on the corner and watched for a few moments, as the traffic light in the distance changed and cars and buses made their way across one another's path. I suddenly felt a warmth rising up through my body, as if I had dipped into a bath. I was back in my bubble. Home for now.

CHAPTER 18
FRIENDS LIKE THESE

On Monday the trial moved from circumstantial to direct evidence, from the technical to the personal. When the prosecution called Vasquez's ER nurse to the stand, I was expecting further testimony about the wound—with more grotesque photos to accompany it—but the questioning led in a completely different direction.

"Nurse Williams, you spent a good amount of time alone with Mr. Vasquez, did you not?"

"Yes." The nurse, thin and visibly nervous, tugged at her hair, as if getting used to a new cut.

Harmon affected a casual demeanor. The day had just begun. "Now you had given him painkillers. Was he still fully conscious, aware of what he was saying?"

"Objection!" called out Crews. "Goes to state of mind."

Harmon sighed. "The witness is an ER nurse, Your Honor. She is an expert in this area."

"I'll allow it," said the judge.

Harmon smiled sympathetically at Ms. Williams. The nurse turned a confused look toward the judge and back. Finally realizing she could just answer the question, she did. "Yes, he seemed fine."

"Did he tell you what had happened to him?"

Crews jumped up a second too late, his own line—"Objection; hearsay!"—overlapping with the witness's response.

"No," she said, and Crews sat down sheepishly.

"Didn't he ask you about his injury? The prognosis? The pain?"

"Not really. He complained about the pain for a while, but once the drug kicked in, he didn't have any questions about the injury."

"Nothing?"

"No," she said. "Nothing."

"What *did* you talk about?"

She bit the corner of her lip and looked toward the jury. I had the distinct impression that she had turned to us less to be responsive than to ensure she didn't meet Vasquez's eye. "At one point, he asked me if the police were still there."

"Did he explain why he was asking that?"

"Yes. He wanted to talk to them. He asked me to go find Officer Turner."

Harmon leaned in and locked eyes with the nurse, wordlessly encouraging her to speak further, perhaps reminding her what they had rehearsed.

"He got pretty agitated at that point. 'Get me the cop,' he said. 'They told me I could go home if I just changed my story, if I said I'd shot myself. Get him.'"

Crews sat tall in his chair, a taut expression on his face, feigning indifference. Beside him, Vasquez wore the same lack of affect as ever, features slack, stunted.

"He wanted to change his story?"

Finally, Crews shot up with an objection.

"Withdrawn," Harmon said, not waiting for a ruling. "Did you find the officer?"

"No," the nurse replied. "I offered, but then he changed his mind. I remember standing up to leave, and he got this look in his eye."

"Look?"

"Like he was terrified."

"Objection!"

"No further questions," said Harmon and turned back to her table.

Crews's cross-examination focused on credibility, questioning the nurse's ability to read Vasquez's expressions or to imagine what he was thinking.

"Did he say he wanted to change his story?"

"He said he wanted to see the officer who'd made him the offer."

"But did he say *why* he wanted to see him?"

"Not specifically."

"So, he might have just forgotten to tell the officer something. For all you know, he might have wanted to borrow a stick of gum."

Harmon objected that he was badgering the witness, but that was it. Crews had made his point and sat down.

The next witness was a striking woman named Sofia. She was dressed in black, her hair pulled back into a petite ponytail. Her fingers trembled as she straightened the lapel of her jacket.

"You joined Mr. Vasquez and two others that night, didn't you? For drinks?"

"Yes," Sofia responded faintly. The judge asked her to move closer to the microphone. "Yes," she repeated.

Harmon asked a series of simple questions, and Sofia responded with one-syllable answers. They were at a bar on Mission Street that evening. They started with beer and then began to alternate with tequila shots.

"And you left after midnight."

"Yes."

"Right after midnight?"

"I'm sorry?"

"I'm just looking for a more specific time. Was it 12:15? 1:00?"

"I'm not sure."

"2:00?"

"I don't recall."

"Well, did you close the bar?"

"I don't recall."

"You don't recall whether the lights came on?"

"No," Sofia said, fumbling suddenly. "It wasn't that late."

"So it could have been anytime between 12 and 2."

"Yes."

"Why can't you be more specific?"

"We were drinking," she said. "I was a little intoxicated."

I blanched at the word. Her language seemed as artificial, as scripted, as the cop's.

"Did you all leave together, Mr. Vasquez included?"

"I don't think so."

"But you're not sure."

Sofia paused. "Not really, no. As I said, I was intoxicated."

The rest of Harmon's questioning followed along similar lines. The only thing Sofia was sure about was that she'd been intoxicated. She didn't see a gun, didn't hear a shot on the street, didn't see a car speeding by. But she didn't dispute any of it, either. If someone had asked her if a spaceship had landed on Mission Street that night, she wouldn't have denied it.

The next witness, Lara, told much the same story. *Intoxicated* was the word of the day, their excuse for not being able to answer any substantive questions. I began to wonder why it was the prosecution that was calling these people. They added nothing to the case, except the suspicion that someone was hiding something. But it was the defense's job to seed doubt, not the other way around. Perhaps, I thought, Harmon was getting the jump on Crews, again.

I imagined them all out that night, Vasquez and his friends, drinking their problems away in a dark bar. No doubt, some of my fellow jurors saw suspicion enough in that alone. Shirley, a few seats past me in the front row, looked like she hadn't drunk anything stronger than V8 in years.

What were they talking about that night, as the tequila shots piled up? I knew nothing about them beyond the fact that they had spent that evening together. Were they old friends, or had they only recently met? What did they have in common? Were their ties close enough to justify lying for each other? Or were they just innocent friends bemoaning their problems and drinking too much in order to forget them for a night?

I had forgotten a night or two myself. One minute I was at Badlands, downing shots with Oscar at the bar. The next, I was waking up in bed, hours having passed with no memory of how I'd gotten myself home. I called Oscar in the morning, and he told me that I'd seemed fine, a bit drunk but by no means incapacitated. He had walked me home and watched until I got inside, and that was that. But would he have covered for me if something bad had happened, something I couldn't remember? Would he have protected me from myself?

I pictured Vasquez and his crowd at the bar, or talking the next day, getting their stories straight. That's what friends do: they look out for each other.

At the break, we filed back into the jury room. Shirley dug

into her bag for a square Tupperware container. "I made these last night," she said, removing the lid to reveal a couple of dozen chocolate chip cookies. "I thought we might need some sugar."

She was met with a series of *oohs* and *ahs*, and I felt a sudden pang of guilt for what I'd been thinking about her.

I was just biting into my cookie when Nancy made her way to my end of the table. "What did you do this weekend?" she asked.

The cookie was surprisingly tasty. I savored it and took a moment to answer. "I went house hunting, actually. One of my friends is a realtor. He's trying to convince me that I could afford more space if I left the Castro."

She raised her eyebrows. "Don't do it, man. I'd kill to live in that neighborhood."

I laughed. "And what did you get up to over the weekend?"

"Oh, I'm not really sure." She paused, flipping the cookie between her fingers. "I was intoxicated."

We both started laughing and looked away from each other to get control over ourselves. Don scowled from his corner.

When we marched back into the jury box, my attention was drawn to Vasquez's mother, in her usual spot, hands in her lap, shoulders high, apparently unmoved while we were gone. I looked away quickly. It seemed intrusive to witness her confusion and pain, her anger and disappointment. There was a hopelessness in her eyes—a sense, perhaps, of inevitability, as if she'd always known that seat was waiting for her.

The mood changed with the arrival of the next witness. A broad-shouldered man more than six feet tall, Roland Talbott lumbered through the courtroom in a tight sport coat, its sleeves nearly bursting at the biceps. He appeared to be in his late twenties at most—a little young, I thought, for a name like Roland. His head drooped after he'd taken his seat. He wanted to be anywhere else but here, and made no secret about it.

Harmon wasted no time. After verifying his name, she charged in with questions, her tone more severe than before. "Mr. Talbott, you were at the Peppermill with Mr. Vasquez on the night of October 6th, correct?"

"Yes," Talbott said, bass voice booming through the microphone.

"Did you leave the bar together?"

"No."

"But you're the one who drove him to the hospital—is that correct?"

"Yes."

"How did that come about?"

Talbott looked up with a jolt. "He got shot," he said, sneering.

"No, Mr. Talbott. I meant how is it that you drove him to the hospital?"

Talbott paused, gazing toward the back of the room. "I found him on the street," he said. "Raul left the bar a couple of minutes before me, and by the time I got out there, he was lying on the sidewalk."

"Did you hear the shot?" Harmon asked, arms once again folded. I came to think of it as her warrior stance.

"No," he said.

"What about other people? Did anyone else look upset? Was anyone running?"

"I didn't notice," he said. "I was just worried about my friend."

She pushed for details, but got little more than Vasquez writhing in pain and Talbott depositing him into the back seat of his car.

"So it was your car? You drove him to the hospital in your own car?"

"Yeah, it was mine."

"Then what happened?"

It's a fairly short drive from the Mission to San Francisco General. Talbott pulled up to the emergency room entrance in a few minutes, parked the car, and helped Vasquez inside. While Vasquez was being seen by the medical staff, a police officer approached Talbott.

"And he asked to search the car?"

"He wanted to look at it, yeah."

"And you gave him permission?"

"Sure. I got nothing to hide."

"What did Officer Turner find in the car?"

Talbott remained silent.

"Did he find a gun?"

Talbott shifted in his seat and grunted. "Yeah."

"Was it your gun, Mr. Talbott?"

Talbott hesitated.

"Was it your gun?"

"No," he said at last, "I don't have a gun."

"Then was it Mr. Vasquez's gun?"

"I don't know anything about a gun."

Harmon paused, arms folded more tightly, and arched her back. It was beginning to look like an episode of *Wild Kingdom*, competitors signaling a fight for dominance.

"The gun was found in your car," she said. "Is it your testimony that you don't know how it got there?"

"Yeah."

"You didn't see your friend with the gun. You didn't see a gun at all. You didn't hear a shot. You didn't see a car pulling away. You sure missed a lot, didn't you, Mr. Talbott?"

He squirmed, the coat constricting him, perhaps, imprisoning his shoulders.

"I'd had a few drinks," he said at last. "I don't remember everything clearly."

"Were you intoxicated?" Harmon asked.

"A little."

Why not? I thought. Everyone else was.

"And yet you drove the car."

"He was hurt," Talbott said boldly, pushing out his chest. "I didn't want to waste time calling no ambulance."

Harmon paused, looking down at a stack of papers on her table. When she straightened up again, her features were softer, her tone almost casual. "How well do you know the defendant, Mr. Talbott?"

"We're friends," he said gruffly.

"Good friends?"

"Pretty good."

"And you trust him?"

Crews's voice squealed its way across the room, but I was busy watching Talbott's face go through a dance of grimaces.

"Withdrawn," said Harmon. She drew a few steps closer to the witness stand. "Where did you meet Mr. Vasquez?"

"A while ago."

"Not when," she pursued. "Where?"

"Objection!"

Talbott rolled his shoulders uncomfortably. I imagined that he was desperate to race out of the room and pull off the suit.

"Sustained," said the judge. She gazed down at Harmon. "Move on, counselor."

"No further questions, Your Honor."

She had what she needed.

It felt clear to me now. Half the reason she was calling these people was to point out the absurdity of their stories. But, I thought, the defense didn't need a counternarrative. Technically.

Crews asked two or three perfunctory questions, trying to humanize Talbott a bit. He focused on Talbott's concern for Vasquez, the trauma of seeing his friend on the ground with a bullet wound.

"You were concerned about your friend," Crews said, "weren't you?"

"Yes."

"And that was all you were thinking about, all you really registered from what was going on."

"Yeah."

"Thank you, Mr. Talbott. No further questions."

Talbott was already pulling out of his chair when the judge formally released him. He marched quickly across the room, looking only forward, craving the door like a desert hiker craves an oasis.

CHAPTER 19
THE MILLENNIAL
WHISPERER

It was a relief to get to the bookstore. I needed the distraction of work, the reassurance of routine—straightening up displays, unpacking new titles, running my fingers along the spines of books to align them on the shelves. Even the obnoxious groan the credit card reader emitted to register approval was a comfort.

"Wow," Joel said, "you're really in the zone today."

I laughed. "Zoning *out* is more like it."

We were alone toward the front of the store. Dave was in back, packing up a box of unsold books for returns.

"How are you doing?" I asked. I moved on to the front bookcase, where we arranged "Staff Picks." Tom had selected a Robert Ferro novel. Dave's card lavished purple prose on the latest graphic best-seller. Cassandra's round but precise handwriting extolled the importance of a 500-page tome on the dangers of capitalism. And Joel, with the simple description, "The best book I've ever read," highlighted *Tess of the d'Urbervilles.*

"I'm okay," he said. "Just the usual stuff—like what am I going to do with my life?" He laughed self-deprecatingly.

"Worried about the store?" We had spoken only briefly about the sale. Nothing was final yet, so I hadn't wanted to add any drama to the situation.

"Not just," he admitted. "That's only one piece of it. I'm still finding my way, you know? Trying to make friends, trying to date. I'm still getting to know the city."

"I remember the feeling. It's glorious, but it can be overwhelming. Everything you do is a choice that means you're not doing something else."

His eyes lit up. "Exactly! I'm free for the first time in my life—no family, no school. I can make my own decisions, and I'm paralyzed half the time."

"Freedom is scary," I said. "It means you're free to make mistakes, too."

"And I hate mistakes."

I folded my arms and gazed at him with faux sternness. "Well, that has to change. Mistakes are just a given. If you're too afraid to make any, then you won't take any risks, and one day you'll wake up my age and wonder what the hell happened."

He looked stunned in that way children do when they learn that adults don't have all the answers, after all.

The bell clattered as the front door swung open.

It took me a moment to recognize Wayne, his bag slung over his back, tipping his body awkwardly to one side. It was always an adjustment, seeing someone in a new context. Wayne had never come to the store before. I imagined he was the kind of person who read everything on his phone.

"Hi," I said.

His eyes were wide open, and in this light I made out the honey glow within the brown of his irises. He wasn't looking for a book. He had come to see me, and yet his eyes registered surprise, as if he'd been hoping I wasn't there and he could just turn away instead.

"Hi," he said, the syllable sharp as a razor.

"Are you okay, Wayne?"

He affected a smile, dimples slashing each cheek. "Yeah. Umm, do you have a minute?"

I turned toward Joel, just to acknowledge the interruption. "Sure," I said. I gestured for Wayne to follow, and we made our way through the store and into the office.

I leaned against the desk as Wayne closed the door softly behind him. "What's up?"

He stood silently before the door, his face half in shadow. His lips twitched jarringly, as if words were trying to force their way out. "I'm sorry," he said at last. "This was probably a bad idea."

"Sit," I said, as forcefully as I could muster. I gestured toward the seat beside me. This seemed my day to be stern with youngsters.

Wayne came forward, shaking his head with a self-conscious grin. "I'm just being ridiculous," he said, taking the proffered seat.

"We're all entitled to be a little ridiculous now and then."

He took in a deep breath, which turned his smile into a nervous chuckle. "Yes," he said, "I suppose you're right."

I smiled down at him, silently waiting.

"I just—it seems wrong to come here, but—well, I'm not sure who else to talk to."

There was something uncomfortable, inappropriate, about standing before him. I slunk into the other guest chair and met his gaze head on.

"None of my friends would understand. And well, to be frank, among John's friends, you're the only one who's ever actually been kind to me."

A shiver of guilt went through me. Though I had felt more

empathy for him recently, I had started out no better than anyone else. Whatever kindness I'd shown him in the beginning was a polite cover, Minnesota nice. But now there was an undeniable fragility in his expression, even more than he'd shown me at the coffee shop. I had cast him as a one-dimensional character— John's inappropriate boy toy—and now, suddenly, a real person was breaking through the mold.

He played with the cuff of his shirt, fingered the white buttons that put the purple stripes in relief. And when he looked up again, he spoke quickly, as if the downcast look had given him a moment to string the words together, to find verbal coherence in emotional chaos.

"John asked me to marry him."

"Oh." I found myself surprised by the words, and surprised by my surprise. I'd never thought John would actually go through with it, my doubt growing with each passing day of postponement until I'd begun to forget it had ever been an option.

"Did you know?" Wayne asked. "Did he tell you he was planning to propose?"

The question brought me out of denial. I was only fooling myself at this point. "Yes," I said, "he mentioned it."

Ordinarily I would ask for details. How did he pop the question? Were they sitting before a fireplace, as I'd imagined, or in an intimate restaurant, or at the beach? Was there a ring? But, under the circumstances, only one question was called for.

"What did you say?"

He sighed. "I told him I would think about it." He bit his lip. "I was stunned, to be honest. I didn't see it coming. I had no idea he felt that strongly."

I wanted to ask the obvious question next—*Are you in love?* But again, I waited. My job right now was to listen.

"Don't get me wrong," he said. "We get along great. We have fun together. He's a wonderful man, and I really care about him."

"Did you tell him that?"

"I didn't tell him much of anything. I've never been so tongue-tied in my life. I just told him I wanted to think about it, and I got out of there as fast as I could. To think."

"When was this?"

"Last night. He invited me for dinner and brought it up over dessert. I've spent most of today walking around."

"Where's your head at now?"

He laughed. "I wish I knew. I'm usually so focused, so logical. But not now. Now I'm just … lost."

Shoulders hunched, he went back to worrying his shirt cuff. A day's growth of stubble encircled his throat, beneath the perfectly trimmed beard that ended crisply at the jawline.

"Walking always works for me," I ventured. "Did anything come of it?"

He threw his head back and gazed at the ceiling. Anywhere but at me. "Not much." He paused before bursting out, "Resentment, I think. I mean, I had everything laid out, you know? The company, my life. I'm on top of things. I know what I'm doing. I know where I want my life to go. And now, all of a sudden, it's all thrown into turmoil."

His cheeks were flushed, the blood crimsoning his ears.

"I'm sorry," he said. "That sounds mean. I don't want to be unsympathetic. I just—I'm not prepared to deal with this right now. I have too much going on."

"Well," I said, "maybe that's what you should tell him."

He let out a sigh that drowned the ticking of the clock on the far wall. "Maybe." He gazed over my shoulder at the Matisse poster I'd picked up at MoMA.

The dim windowless room seemed suitably clandestine. I had no right to even listen to him behind John's back. John was my friend. Wayne just needed an ear.

He turned back to me. "I'm sorry for putting you in this position. It's not fair to you."

"That's okay," I said. "I'm a good listener."

At least I wanted to be. We all delude ourselves from time to time into thinking we are what we want to be.

But there was no more listening to do. We sat together in silence for a long moment, our eyes drifting around the room. When we stumbled upon each other's gaze, we ended up giggling, the drama of the situation striking us both as absurd. We were in a Chekhov play, waiting for a gun that would never go off.

"Thank you," he said at last. "It's good to have someone to talk to." He rose from the chair and made his way to the door. "I hope I didn't make you uncomfortable."

"Not at all," I said. "Don't worry about it." I wanted to tell him to call me if he needed to talk more, but that seemed like overstepping. It was one thing for him to come to me on his own. It was another to invite him.

Still, as he wrapped his hand around the doorknob, I rose from my seat and began to speak hurriedly. "I understand," I said. "At the risk of sounding like the wise old man, I think I know what you're going through."

He turned and dropped his hand to his side as I went on.

"I'm no expert at this. I don't have all the answers. I probably have no business giving advice to anyone, considering."

"Considering what?"

"Well, you don't see a ring on this finger, do you?" I held up my bare hand and chuckled. "I've never been terribly successful

[246]

at love."

He just looked at me, head tilted slightly to one side, eyes dark and soft.

"Some people get lucky," I said. "Oscar and Rafe, for example. They're so right for each other, and they knew that from the start. I've never been that brave."

I didn't know why I was saying all this. I didn't know where the words were coming from. "I think I let a lot of chances go through my fingers. I was always looking for Mr. Right. I had an image—standards, if you want to put it crassly. But mostly, I think, I didn't give my relationships a chance. Most people aren't like Oscar and Rafe: most of us have to give a relationship time, get to know each other. It's not like choosing a cereal at Safeway."

Wayne nodded, and the tension in his face seemed to relax. "Well," he said, "I'm sure you'll find him."

I laughed. "I'm not looking anymore."

"Don't say that. It sounds defeatist."

"It's the truth," I said. "I'm content. If it happens, it happens, but … I've never been good at recognizing it."

He smiled. "Well, maybe you'll get lucky and someone'll sweep you off your feet."

"Maybe." We laughed together, and I watched his eyes—lively for once. In my mind, Wayne had always been thinking about something—first his work, today the conundrum with John—but now, for a moment, all of that seemed to float away. He was just present, and I felt like I was seeing him for the first time.

CHAPTER 20

FEELINGS

As time passed, I found myself looking forward to the trial. In its ritual—the rules of evidence, the silent attention it demanded, the certainty of finding each person in the same space day after day—it offered an order severely lacking in what I still thought of as the "real world." The content of what I witnessed each day— the evidence offered, the people taking the stand—may have been unpredictable, but the format wasn't. There was an inviolate structure. In this room, with its dark paneled walls and the trappings of government, there was at least the promise that we were heading toward resolution, a sense that the process itself was what mattered, and the process would work. I trusted that there was truth somewhere beneath the obfuscation, between the conflicting stories, and that I would be able to find it. Here, at least, things would eventually make sense.

The real world was about the future: What would I do after the store closed? Should I leave town one of these days? By contrast, in court all I needed to focus on was one discrete moment in the past: What had really happened on the night Raul Vasquez arrived at the hospital with two holes in his leg?

It was a jigsaw puzzle, a math problem. There was an answer, a single answer. This had happened, then that, then that. There were no variables involved in the past. The only variables were right here, in the present, in the question of whom to believe.

Today's first witness looked like she had stepped into the wrong room.

When Harmon called her name, Charlotte Gardiner, blonde and lithe, rose calmly from the last row of the gallery and, keeping her eyes focused firmly forward, made her way to the witness stand. Poised on four-inch heels, she walked with deliberation, as if the courtroom were a runway at New York Fashion Week. Her clothes—white silk blouse, knee-length black skirt—looked sharp and expensive, and her makeup was subtle. The contrast with the other witnesses—whether law enforcement or the rest of Vasquez's friends—was stark.

"Ms. Gardiner, how do you know the defendant?"

She leaned toward the microphone and spoke into it with a husky voice. "He's my boyfriend," she said.

"How long have you been dating?"

"Two years."

Even now, Vasquez's face was expressionless. I tried to picture them together, wondering at the extent of the romance. After two years, there had to be something, unless it had already faded away. They didn't exchange a glance throughout her testimony.

She said she had been with them all at the bar that night, but had left early. "I had to be at work at 8:00 the next morning, so I just had one drink and went home."

"When did you find out about the shooting?"

"Not until the next night, when Raul called me."

"So Ms. Sanchez didn't call you? Or Mr. Talbott?"

"No."

"Where was Mr. Vasquez when he called you?"

She hesitated and tilted her head to one side so that her straight hair fell toward one shoulder. "Jail," she said.

"He called you from jail. And what did he tell you?"

"Objection, Your Honor. Hearsay."

Harmon threw a sharp glance toward Crews. "I could just play the recording," she said flatly.

"Overruled," said the judge. Crews sat down like a deflated jack-in-the-box.

Harmon turned back to Charlotte. "Did he tell you how he'd been shot?"

"Yes. He said it was a drive-by, in the Mission."

"Did that surprise you?"

Charlotte squinted. "Of course," she said. "Who expects their boyfriend to get shot?"

"Did you know of anyone who might want to harm Mr. Vasquez?"

"No."

Harmon paused, perhaps weighing how far she could go to turn implication into evidence. She took a few steps back, breaking the mood. "Did he mention the gun?"

"The gun?"

"Yes."

"I don't remember anything about a gun."

"He told you he was shot, but mentioned nothing about a gun." Harmon was in warrior pose again.

"Not that I recall."

I wanted to glance at Nancy, but controlled myself. At any moment now, we'd hear that she'd been intoxicated.

"Your Honor, I would like to play for the jury the recording of the phone call in question."

The judge nodded and turned toward the jury box. "Ladies and gentlemen, just to clarify, all jailhouse calls—except when a lawyer is present—are recorded as a matter of course." She looked back at Harmon. "You may proceed."

Harmon clicked something on her laptop and a crackling sound emerged from the speakers in the courtroom. The audio quality was somewhat hampered by ambient noise, as well as the muffled effect of the telephone.

There were no niceties. As soon as she'd said hello, Vasquez launched in.

"I got shot last night."

"Shot? Are you okay?"

"Yeah, I'm fine."

"Are you in the hospital?"

"No, they released me this morning. It's not bad."

"What happened? Where are you?"

"I'm in jail."

"What? Why?"

"Because of the shooting."

"But you're the one who got shot. Did you—"

Immediately, he jumped in, talking over her. *"The cops are crazy. They think I shot myself."*

"On purpose?"

"No." He sounded frustrated now. *"It doesn't matter. They're just making up some bullshit."*

I threw a glance toward Vasquez's mother, whose lips began to twist.

"They found a gun. And they think it's mine."

"They found it?"

Again he cut her off. *"Stupid,"* he said. *"I'm done, I'm done. Stupid. I fucked everything up."*

"Raul, what—?"

His desolate tone quickly shifted back. *"Look, could you go see my mom? I don't want to have to tell her about this on the phone."*

[251]

There was an abrupt click and the recording stopped. Harmon was hunched over her laptop. She rose and walked back to the witness stand.

"Ms. Gardiner, what did you mean by *it*?"

Charlotte cocked her head again, exposing a silver ear cuff. "I don't understand the question."

"Right there, toward the end of the call, you said, 'They found it?'"

The witness remained silent.

"That *is* your voice on the recording, is it not?"

"Yes."

"So what were you referring to?"

"I don't know."

Harmon affected a faint smile. Flies with honey. "Mr. Vasquez refers to the police having a gun. And immediately, you ask, 'They found it?'"

Charlotte shrugged. "I guess I meant the gun. They found a gun."

"But you didn't say *a* gun. You said *it*."

Charlotte's face, so porcelain a moment ago, turned sharp, lips sneering. "It's a pronoun," she said. "I learned it in grade school."

Harmon was unmoved. "So you weren't referring to a particular gun? A gun you were familiar with?"

"I'm not familiar with guns."

"Have you ever seen Mr. Vasquez with a gun?"

"I don't know anything about guns."

"I'll repeat the question. Have you ever seen Mr. Vasquez with a gun?"

Charlotte sighed, a long drawn-out breath, and her features returned to normal—skin smooth, lips flat to highlight the pink gloss. "I don't recall."

◼

Dean Sanborn was probably in his early thirties, though he looked older. The furrowed brow and crow's feet could be dismissed as the product of anxiety and confusion, the stress of being in court. As he walked toward the witness stand, he slouched a bit, perhaps self-conscious of his height, uncomfortable being watched. He wore khakis and a heavy cream shirt—a uniform that, according to Damien, passed for formal wear among the tech crowd.

He was sworn in and took his seat quietly, looking straight ahead the whole time.

Harmon started gently, friendlier than she had been with the previous witnesses. Immediately, I could tell that Sanborn was not one of Vasquez's friends.

He had moved to San Francisco a couple of years ago, he said, for an IT job with a start-up in SoMa. He lived in a duplex in the Mission. On the night in question, he had gone to happy hour with friends after work. They were having a good time, so they got a bite to eat and continued to hang out together. He walked home alone at around midnight.

"And then what happened?" Harmon asked, her expression suddenly changing, sympathy turned to hard concern.

Sanborn was surprisingly soft-spoken. As he leaned into the microphone, he reminded me of a DJ from the seventies. "I was nearly at my front door when I … I sensed someone behind me. I turned around and, before I knew what was happening, I'd been thrown to the ground."

He paused, and Harmon let the silence sit for a few seconds.

Sanborn continued. "I was on my stomach and I felt someone reaching into my back pocket. That's where I carry my wallet. I know I shouldn't. My girlfriend says that's the most dangerous place to carry it. Anyway, I rolled over and someone was standing over me."

"Did you get a good look at the person?" Harmon asked.

Sanborn grimaced apologetically. "Not really. He was standing in the shadow of a tree on the sidewalk. His baseball cap was tilted down. I couldn't see his face, but I did make out his hands."

"His hands. Was he holding something?"

He paused. "Yes. In one hand, he had my wallet. And in the other, he was holding a gun."

"What kind of gun?"

"I don't know. A handgun."

"Like this?" Harmon retrieved the gun from the table and held it before Sanborn.

"Maybe. I can't be sure. I was too scared to really look that hard."

"Okay," she said. "Then what happened?"

"He was waving the gun at me. I remember kind of curling in on myself and just saying, 'Take it! Take it!'"

"Take what?"

"The wallet. I just wanted him to take the wallet and leave."

"And did he?"

Sanborn nodded.

The judge looked down at him. "You need to answer the question verbally, Mr. Sanborn."

Sanborn turned his eyes toward the judge. "Yes," he said. "Yes, he took the wallet and left."

"You saw him leave?"

"Yes. He put the wallet in his pocket and started running, toward Mission Street."

"And what did you do?" Harmon asked.

He redirected his attention toward her. "I ran up the stairs and unlocked the door to my building. I remember fumbling with the keys; I was shaking."

"That's understandable." She nodded. "Then what happened?"

"Well, I had just opened the door when I heard a loud noise."

"What kind of noise?"

"I can't be sure. It was kind of like a truck backfiring, or ..."

"A gunshot?"

The jack-in-the-box popped up again. "Objection, Your Honor. Leading the witness."

Harmon lifted her gaze and smiled wanly. "Did it sound like a gunshot, Mr. Sanborn?" she asked.

"It might have been," he said. "I don't think I've ever heard a gunshot outside of the movies."

"So you heard the noise. Then what?"

"Well, it scared me all the more. I slammed the door and ran up to my apartment and called the police."

He stared straight ahead, at Harmon. He seemed to be making a conscious effort not to look in Vasquez's direction.

"Now, before you got inside," Harmon said, "you said that you saw the assailant running away."

"Yes."

"Can you describe how he ran?"

"He just ... ran."

"Was he doing anything else as he ran?"

Sanborn paused again. "Well, he seemed to be putting something in his pocket."

"Didn't you say earlier that he put your wallet in his pocket before running away?"

"Yes."

"So this was something else. Do you know what he was putting in his pocket?"

Sanborn's eyes were locked on hers. "It looked like the gun," he said.

Harmon paused for a long moment. She paced away and then, at the midpoint of the jury box, turned around to face the witness again. "Were you able to identify the person who attacked you, Mr. Sanborn?"

"Not definitively," Sanborn said. "It was dark. And like I said, the brim of his cap was turned down."

"What about his silhouette? Were you able to tell how tall he was, how much he weighed?"

"More or less. As I told the police, he was about 5'7", maybe 170 pounds."

"Like the defendant?" Harmon swiveled toward Vasquez, and Sanborn's eyes reluctantly followed.

"I can't be sure, but yes, the same general build."

When it was his turn, Crews rose nimbly to his feet, like a boxer approaching the ring.

"How much had you had to drink that night, Mr. Sanborn?" he asked, while still walking toward the witness box.

"I'm not sure," Sanborn said. "A couple of beers before dinner, maybe a couple more after."

"It was Friday, right?" Crews asked. "A hard day? The end of a long week?"

Sanborn nodded.

Crews didn't wait for a verbal response. "And over the course of the evening, you had four or five beers?"

"I think so," Sanborn replied. "I wasn't counting."

"And then you walked home from the bar. How long of a walk was that?"

"About 20 minutes."

"And you were alone by then."

"Yes."

"Was there anyone on the street? On *your* street."

"I didn't see anyone, until—"

"Yes, until you were assaulted."

"That's right."

"And no one saw you."

"I can't know that for sure." He smiled—reveling, I thought, in the nerdish literal logic of his response.

"You said that just before the assault, you turned around. Why?"

"I sensed someone behind me."

"Sensed. Did you hear someone? See them from the corner of your eye?"

"I don't know. I just had a feeling."

"You're a scientific man, aren't you, Mr. Sanborn? Computer science and all that."

"Yes."

"So do you believe in extrasensory perception? Do you believe in 'feelings'?"

"Maybe I heard something. Or maybe there was a sudden blocking of the wind. I don't know what it was, but ... I turned around to look."

Crews let that sit for a moment. "Do you often turn around at your front door?" he asked at last.

Sanborn hesitated. "I suppose so."

"Because you 'sense' someone behind you?"

"I don't know."

"Then why?"

"It just seems like the prudent thing to do, I suppose. At night."

"In a rough neighborhood."

"I didn't say that. I don't consider my neighborhood rough."

"Well, that's good." Crews nodded. "Now you told Ms. Harmon that you didn't get a good look at the person who assaulted you, is that correct?"

"As I said before—"

"Yes, as you said before, he was 5'7" and 170 pounds. Very specific."

Sanborn gazed down for a moment.

"How long have you lived in the Mission?" Crews asked.

"Two years, since I arrived in San Francisco."

"And you came here from …?"

"Iowa."

Crews nodded. "Iowa. That must have been an adjustment."

"I don't know what you mean."

"Well, such a different environment. Iowa."

"I suppose so. But I love San Francisco."

"Don't we all," Crews said. He paced for a moment and then spun around, closer now to the witness box. "Do Latinos all look alike to you, Mr. Sanborn?"

Sanborn, clearly flustered, furrowed his brow. "What are you suggesting? No, no, of course not."

"Well, living in the Mission after all those years in Iowa."

"Are you calling me a racist, Mr. Crews?" Sanborn straightened up in his chair.

Harmon jumped up. "Objection. Badgering the witness."

Crews drew a deep breath. "Just to clarify, Mr. Sanborn, you were not able to identify your assailant. Correct?"

"Yes."

"So the truth is that you can't say whether it was Mr. Vasquez who robbed you."

"No."

"And you had been drinking."

"A few beers. I was wide awake, fully cognizant."

"Fully cognizant," Crews repeated, eyebrows raised in lieu of finger quotes. "But not able to identify the person who attacked you. Which is it, Mr. Sanborn? Did you know what was happening, or didn't you?"

He might have been talking to me.

CHAPTER 21
SIDEBAR

Every table was already taken when I walked in. Waves of conversation lilted across the room, pierced by the occasional laugh.

My phone buzzed amid the uproar. A text from Brendan: *Look up.*

And there he was, waving from the balcony. I waved back and stopped at the bar to pick up a drink.

The balcony, the size of a small bedroom, had a welcoming, cozy feel. With only one tiny window and a scarily low ceiling, it was also fairly dark. I joined Brendan at a small table by the balustrade.

His glass was nearly empty, the cherry floating in a shallow pool. "How long have you been here?" I asked.

"Just a few minutes." He gestured toward the crowd downstairs. "What is it, a holiday?"

"Yes," I said. "It's called happy hour. Where's Oscar?"

Brendan cocked his head with a wink. He pointed downstairs, where Oscar was making his way to the bar. As he looked up, we both waved like schoolgirls. He rolled his eyes and leaned over to talk to the bartender.

"I saw John," Brendan said. "The question has been officially popped."

"Oh?"

I was spared the need to feign surprise by Oscar's appearance at the top of the stairs. "Why are you hiding up here?" he asked, sliding into the chair beside me, the one with a head-on view of the room below.

"We're not hiding," Brendan said with a laugh. "There was no space downstairs when I got here."

"Really?" Oscar said. "Haven't you been here since breakfast?"

"Bitch." Brendan drowned a smile in the remains of his Manhattan.

Oscar laughed. "So what's going on? Regale me with your stories. I've been up to my eyeballs in depositions all day. You would not believe how brazenly people lie."

"How can you tell?" I asked.

"They're breathing." His smile flattened into a sneer. "I shouldn't complain; it was probably the most entertaining part of my week. Rafe wants to drag me to some fabric store this weekend to look at swatches."

"What now?" I asked. "The kitchen isn't even finished yet."

"Tell me about it. But next he wants to redecorate the bedroom. New curtains, maybe wallpaper. Welcome to my life."

"At least he has goals," Brendan said. "When you stop making plans, you're as good as dead."

"Well," I said, "that's cheerful."

Brendan winked. "How about I get everyone a refill?"

Oscar gestured toward his nearly full glass. "Jesus, man, I just got here. Besides, I doubt you can get three drinks up those stairs without a major catastrophe."

"I am a man of many talents," Brendan said, attempting to rise from his chair.

"Later," Oscar insisted. "Now tell me what I missed."

"When?"

"Well, clearly you two were gabbing about something."

"Oh, nothing," Brendan said, sitting back down with a melo-dramatic sigh. "Only that John got engaged."

"No, he didn't," I said automatically. I felt myself blushing and stumbled for an out. "I mean, you didn't say that Wayne accepted."

Brendan didn't notice. "No, you're right. As a matter of fact, John said he was still thinking about it."

Oscar shook his head. "We all know what that means."

"Well," Brendan said, "John seems to think he'll say yes. For a guy who was so afraid to broach the subject in the first place, he now seems absolutely cocky."

"Or delusional."

"I guess the hardest part was getting the nerve to ask," I said.

"Trust me," Oscar said, "that's not the hard part. He's in for a surprise."

"Why are you so certain?" Brendan asked.

"Come on, you've seen them together. I don't think I've ever seen them so much as shake hands. There's nothing there."

I remembered Wayne's words: *He's a wonderful man, I really care about him.* The kiss of death.

But it was none of my business.

"Even if it did work out," Oscar said, "don't you think Wayne would resent him after a while? I mean …" His lips twisted into a grimace.

"Wasting all that nubile flesh?" Brendan asked.

"Always the poet." Oscar shut his eyes for a moment and took in a breath. "I wish Rafe and I had met in our twenties. When I look at his old photos, I'm jealous of whoever he was with then. He was so beautiful."

"He still is," I said.

Oscar dipped his head. "No, now he's handsome. Distinguished. But then, he was beautiful. In that clean, innocent way that only the young can be beautiful. And I just wish I could have been there. To touch that smooth, barely lived-in skin. To listen to all his dreams, before I turned them into reality."

I dutifully chuckled. "Well, you have him now."

Brendan drew a hand through his hair. "So you think Wayne just isn't ready yet, is that it?"

"Or maybe he worries that John *thinks* he's not."

"Isn't that what we all think?" I said. "I mean, Wayne's so focused on his work, making his way in the world. And it's a world that's kind of foreign to the rest of us." I paused, remembering the look on Wayne's face, the confusion, like he was lost on a dark street he didn't recognize. "It wouldn't be the worst thing, for either of them, if this relationship didn't work out."

"What John needs to learn," Oscar said, "is that it's not the end of the world to be alone." He plucked an olive off with his teeth and pulled the swizzle stick dramatically away from his lips.

Over his shoulder, I gazed down at the main floor. A tall young man stood at the bar, his hair glowing in a pool of light from the window. His head was tipped down, so I could barely make out his face, but something in his stance struck me as familiar—a show of arrogance in the way he clutched his drink, a lifeline against discomfort.

My heart fluttered abruptly when I realized it was Roland Talbott—Vasquez's friend, the man behind the wheel. I turned away quickly, averting my face in case he looked up toward the balcony.

I couldn't tell if I was afraid of Talbott or merely concerned about maintaining objectivity. If jurors weren't allowed to read news reports about the case, then surely we weren't allowed to observe the parties in real life, outside the courtroom. I adjusted my chair to face away from the balustrade and pretended there was nothing downstairs to see.

"What's wrong with you all of a sudden?" Oscar asked.

"Nothing. Why?"

The table in the corner was clearing out, and someone bumped into my chair on the way to the stairs. As they passed, I inadvertently swerved my neck away and found myself gazing over the balcony again. Talbott had taken a seat at the bar, in the narrow alcove by the north windows. He was chatting with an older man whose hands embraced a beer glass. They were sitting close to each other, Talbott bending his lips toward the man's ear as he spoke.

In court, I hadn't gotten the slightest vibe from him. Maybe my gaydar shut down in that context, blocked by the formality of the situation. Even now, I couldn't quite see it. But the younger generation was less classifiable than ours. Their sexuality didn't reveal itself in the visible ways that ours did—fashion, music, manner of speech, shared cultural references. They could melt more easily into the mainstream. Perhaps, feeling less rejection from it, they were less willing to turn against it in favor of something distinct and isolating. I could understand the attraction of that. If I'd had more respect for mainstream culture, I might have embraced it myself.

"Are you all right?" Oscar tapped my shoulder with his own, pulling me back to the conversation.

"Yeah, sorry."

"He's probably just cruising somebody downstairs," Brendan said.

"No," I said quickly. "Nothing down there interests me."

"You may have to lower your standards," Oscar said. "At your age."

"Bitch."

"Bitch Esquire to you."

Downstairs, the older man laid several bills on the bartop. He and Talbott rose from their stools and collected themselves.

"We're just a bunch of old farts," Oscar murmured. "We've seen it all. Nothing impresses us anymore, not even romance."

Talbott pushed the door open and held it for the other man. They paused on the sidewalk and then abruptly turned, walking side by side along 17th Street, past the plate-glass windows and out of sight.

CHAPTER 22

ALTERNATIVE FACTS

The defense called only one witness, and it wasn't Vasquez.

Amos Burden had been the head of the forensics lab in Yolo County before retiring several years ago. He marched to the stand, surprisingly spry for a man his age, which I estimated at about 70. He was dressed in a green tweed jacket, which he un-buttoned as he took his seat, a tight professional smile on his lips under a bushy white mustache.

This was the defense's expert witness, their answer to the aca-demic scientists and people from Quantico who had made the case for the prosecution. His particular expertise was in bullet trajectory and residue.

After a few preliminary questions, Crews got to the heart of the matter. He handed Mr. Burden the now all-too-familiar photo of Vasquez's wound. "What can you tell me about this wound, in terms of the trajectory of the bullet?" he asked, standing back and turning a three-quarter profile to the jury.

"Say again?" Burden asked, leaning forward.

Crews seemed startled and turned back to the witness. "In your expert opinion, Mr. Burden, is this wound consistent with self-infliction?"

"Ah," Burden replied, nodding his head in relief. "No, I wouldn't say so."

"And why is that?"

"The quality of the residue doesn't support that theory," he said. He went into a long description of the color of the ring around the wound. "In my opinion, Mr. Vasquez was shot from a distance."

"How much of a distance? One foot? Six? Twelve?"

"Yes," Burden responded.

Crews smiled. "Can you be more specific? In your opinion, the gun was … how far away?"

"Oh, I'd say at least six feet."

"Six feet." Crews pursed his lips, apparently deciding a smile was inappropriate.

That was about the gist of it. "No further questions," Crews said and moved back toward his table.

Burden rose from his seat, but settled back with a look of humble surprise when Harmon moved toward him. "Good morning, Mr. Burden."

"Good morning." He might have been greeting her at WalMart.

"You retired from your position in 2006, is that correct?"

"Yes, ma'am."

"And how many cases did you review over the course of your career, regarding bullet trajectory?"

"Oh, dozens, I'd say."

"Dozens." Harmon's neck arched as she uttered the word, her chin hovering in the air for a ponderous moment. "And did you examine Mr. Vasquez's wound directly?"

"Beg pardon?"

"How did you examine Mr. Vasquez's wound?"

Burden's lower lip burst forth. "They showed me the photographs," he said.

"So you didn't see the wound itself, on Mr. Vasquez?"

"No, ma'am."

"You spoke at length just now about the color of the ring around the wound. It wasn't as dark as you'd expect it to be, is that correct?"

"Yes, ma'am. If the gun was that near the leg, then the ring should have been much darker, nearly black."

She passed him the photo again. "Mr. Burden, please take a closer look at this photo for me. How would you describe the overall color of the skin, say the top of the leg, beyond the wound?"

He peered at the photo, and back again at Harmon, looking more confused by her than by the picture. "It's skin color," he said.

"My skin color?" she asked. She moved closer, holding out her pale hand.

Burden's lip protruded again as he shrugged. "More or less, I suppose."

"Now, Mr. Burden, please look at the defendant for me." She gestured toward the defense table. "Would you say the skin in that photo looks more like his or like mine?"

"Objection!" Crews called out.

"I'll allow it," said the judge, still focusing on Burden.

"Hmm," Burden said. He glanced back at the photo.

Harmon went on. "We've established that this photo is indeed of Mr. Vasquez's leg. But could it be perhaps a bit overexposed?"

"Objection," Crews repeated, rising this time. "Mr. Burden is not a photography expert."

"Sustained."

Harmon tried another tack. "Mr. Burden, if this picture is overexposed enough to make Mr. Vasquez's skin so much lighter, wouldn't that also make the ring around the wound lighter?"

He paused, staring at the photo for several seconds. "I suppose so," he said at last. "I suppose that's possible."

Harmon nodded and drew back a few feet. "Now, Mr. Burden, turning to the question of trajectory. You're an expert in the trajectory of bullets, aren't you?"

"Yes." Burden smiled now, perhaps relieved to be on more solid ground.

"And, given that expertise, you argue that the alignment of the entrance and exit wounds on Mr. Vasquez's leg is not consistent with a vertical shot, perhaps from his pocket?"

"Correct," Burden replied. He held up the photo and pointed. "As you can see, in this photo the leg is extended straight, and the exit wound is angled differently from the entrance."

"So your contention is that the shot must have come from another angle, while Mr. Vasquez's leg was bent, say in walking."

"Yes." He nodded firmly.

"Mr. Burden, what happens to a bullet as it travels through the body? Could it change course, say when it hits a bone?"

Burden narrowed his eyes. "Yes, but—"

"Can you tell the court how much experience you have with bullets passing through a body?"

"I'm sorry?"

"How many previous cases have you analyzed in which an exit wound was present?"

He scrunched his chin. "It doesn't happen that often," he said.

"It doesn't?"

"Well, not in my experience. Most of my work has been more straightforward. Entrance wounds, bullets that hit walls, that sort of thing."

"So how much training do you have in human anatomy?"

"Anatomy?"

Harmon nodded.

The pause lingered.

"Do you have specific training in anatomy? Or in exit wounds?"

"Not specifically," Burden said, "no."

"I see. Then you can't really be sure that in Mr. Vasquez's case, the wound was not self-inflicted."

"Well, as I said before, the markings—"

"Which, you agreed, were no doubt darker than the photo suggests."

Burden pulled away from the microphone, his shoulders slightly slumped.

"Thank you for your help, Mr. Burden." Harmon turned away. "No further questions."

And that was it. The defense rested. Or, as was clear to me at this point, surrendered.

■

Closing arguments were pretty much a repeat of the opening ones, but with more drama.

Harmon started with another explanation of circumstantial evidence, emphasizing that, contrary to popular belief, it tended to be more reliable than eyewitness testimony, and she then proceeded to list it all. She gestured with an open palm, turned up to the ceiling, and as she itemized the evidence—the angle of the wounds, the gun found in the car, the shot Sanborn heard as his assailant ran away—her hand dropped more and more, struggling under the weight of accumulated incrimination.

"The defense wants you to believe that Raul Vasquez is an

innocent man, that he was merely walking home from a bar that night when an unidentified car passed by and an unidentified person in the car stuck a gun out the window and shot him for no reason."

I didn't know the part of the Mission she was talking about. My experience of the neighborhood didn't extend far beyond the clump of taquerias around 16th Street. After days of this evidence coming to us piecemeal and out of order, I began to paint a picture of it myself—the empty storefronts lit by streetlamps on a weekend midnight, the neon sign in the bar window, the people strolling in every direction, on their way to or from home.

"But the evidence has shown that that was not the case. Aside from the fact that no one—not even Roland Talbott, who claims to have found Mr. Vasquez on the sidewalk and taken him to the hospital—heard the shot or saw Mr. Vasquez fall to the ground in front of the bar, it is clear that the wound on Mr. Vasquez's leg was caused by a gun going off not only at close range but from *inside* his pocket. The wound was self-inflicted. There's no credible alternative explanation. Therefore, Mr. Vasquez was in possession of a gun at the time. The gun that was found on the backseat of Mr. Talbott's car, in the parking lot of the hospital."

She was pacing back and forth in front of the jury box, making eye contact with each of us in turn. Finally, she stopped.

"That's enough," she said quietly. "The wound itself, the burn marks and residue in the pocket of his jeans, the location of the gun. That's enough to prove that Mr. Vasquez had possession of the gun and shot himself with it." She paused. "But let me offer a version of what happened that night, a version far closer to the probable truth than the one Mr. Vasquez presented to the police that night."

Her eyebrows furrowed with a sudden intensity. "Just around

the corner from the bar where Vasquez and his friends were spending the evening—on the other side of the same block—Dean Sanborn was coming home from his own night out when he was assaulted and robbed at gunpoint. He then saw the assailant run away and heard a gunshot. In fact, Mr. Sanborn is the only witness you've heard from who actually *did* hear a gunshot that night."

I snuck a peek at Vasquez as she spoke, looking for a sign of recognition. His neck hung forward, appearing to focus his gaze on a spot on the floor just in front of the jury box.

"This trial," Harmon said, "is not about whether Raul Vasquez mugged Dean Sanborn. You are not being asked to decide that issue. Mr. Sanborn's testimony, however, does provide context. Mr. Vasquez was not shot in front of the bar on Mission Street, but a shot *was* fired around the corner as a mugger was running down the street with a gun in his pocket. I submit to you that that man was Raul Vasquez."

She was leaving something unsaid. I'd gotten used to that in the past several days. *This* trial wasn't about the mugging. She seemed to be leaving open the possibility that he would be charged with it separately. I tried to put the pieces together myself, all the tidbits Harmon was using to layer her case. Common sense, the judge had said. We could use common sense as well as tangible evidence.

Harmon ended by playing a snippet from the jailhouse recording, Vasquez talking to his girlfriend:

"They found a gun. And they think it's mine."

"They found it?"

Harmon clicked a button on the computer and paused for a long moment. "Yes," she said at last, "we found it. Ladies and gentlemen, the evidence is strong that there was no drive-by shooting, that Raul Vasquez shot himself with the gun found in Mr. Talbott's car. Upon deliberation, I am confident that you will return a verdict of guilty."

She made her way back to the prosecution table, heels clicking on the floor.

Now it was Crews's turn. I sat up and reminded myself to be open-minded.

As Crews unfolded himself and wended his way past the defense table, there was a stiffness in his limbs, as if they were attached by bolts rather than ligaments. He moved toward the jury box with a deliberate, even pace.

He stepped around the prosecution table and stopped directly in front of Harmon, blocking her from the jury's view. His gaze glided across the jury box.

He paused for a long moment before finally arching his back, straightening up to a height I hadn't quite noticed before.

"Reasonable doubt."

His legs firmly planted, he cupped one palm in the other like a priest about to deliver a homily. "What exactly does it mean?" he asked. "Judge Reilly will provide a definition for you shortly, but at this point, I want to emphasize it for you. Reasonable doubt. The evidence is scant and circumstantial. With what degree of certainty can we say that Raul Vasquez was in possession of the gun in Roland Talbott's car? Not much. That he accidentally shot himself with it? Again, not much. No fingerprints on the gun. No DNA. No witnesses. Nothing except the prosecution's theories."

As he spoke, his lips were twisted in a combination of offense and disgust. "And with what degree of certainty can we say that Raul Vasquez assaulted Dean Sanborn that night?" He paused. "Again, not much. In fact, none at all."

His voice grew louder as he went on, booming after a couple

of minutes.

"Nothing places Mr. Vasquez at the scene of that so-called crime. No evidence even supports the existence of a crime. Only Mr. Sanborn's words. Mr. Sanborn, who admits to drinking quite a bit that night." He took a deep breath, like a yoga teacher preparing the class for a new pose. "But Mr. Sanborn isn't on trial here. I don't know if he was mugged that night. He may very well have been. But there is no reason to believe that Raul Vasquez had anything to do with what may or may not have happened to Dean Sanborn. That whole scenario is nothing more than an accident of geography, the prosecution's fantasy. In even bringing it up, they're grasping at straws, showing the weakness of their case."

Crews paused for a long, uncomfortable moment. "As for the shooting of Mr. Vasquez—well, that crime went uninvestigated. The police asked the bartender whether he'd heard a gunshot, and that was that. And why? Why was the victim in this case—the man lying in a hospital bed with a bullet hole in his leg—treated as a criminal? Why all the concern for a well-off young white man who may have simply left his wallet at a bar after a night of drinking, and none for a working-class Latino who was shot on the street?"

Crews's face was flushed by now, a vein suddenly prominent in the middle of his forehead, like the Sierra cutting through an aerial photo of the desert.

"Reasonable doubt, ladies and gentlemen. The prosecution's story may be more appealing—to Ms. Harmon, at least. But is it any more convincing? Mr. Sanborn couldn't even identify his own alleged assailant."

He paused for a moment, took in a deep breath. And then, in a veritable whisper, he said once again, "Reasonable doubt."

"Does anyone want to do it?"

Nancy was sitting at the head of the table, trying to make eye contact with each of us. Most looked away. The alternates had been dismissed as soon as closing arguments ended, both of them disappearing quickly with sympathetic smiles—glad to go, but resentful of wasted time—like contestants snuffing their torches on *Survivor*.

"I'll do it," I said at last, "if no one else wants to."

And that's how I became foreman of the jury.

The bailiff had given us a list of instructions and a verdict sheet, the sight of which was enough to terrify me. As foreman, I would have to write down the verdict on the sheet and sign it when the time came.

But first things first. "Shall we just take the temperature before we dive in?" I asked. "See where we all are?"

"You mean vote?" asked Madge. "Now?"

"Well, a preliminary vote, yes. Just as a baseline."

Half of the room assented with a variety of groans, the others quietly staring at the table.

"Okay," I said. "Let's do it on paper so no one feels pressured."

I reached toward the stack of loose sheets in the center of the table, counted out twelve, and passed them around. Meanwhile, Nancy reached for a stack of pens and distributed them.

It took only a few minutes to vote. I noticed just a couple of people obviously pondering the question. I counted aloud as I unwrapped the papers: 7 guilty, 5 not guilty.

"I don't really get it," Chet said when we were done counting.

"Why is possession of a gun a crime?"

"Because he's a convicted felon," Madge said. "They're not allowed to have guns."

"What was he convicted of? That was never mentioned."

"It's not relevant," said Don.

"It's not?" Chet's lips curled in disbelief.

"Apparently he served his time. The slate is clean."

"Hardly clean," Chet pursued. "I mean, they won't let him have a gun."

Nancy was tapping her pen against the table. "They don't want us to be unduly influenced by his previous crimes," she said.

"You mean if we knew he'd previously committed armed robbery we'd be more likely to convict him this time?"

"Maybe."

"So now we're just left to wonder. It could be anything from shoplifting to murder."

"I doubt it's murder," said Don. "He'd still be in jail."

"Not these days," Bonnie said. "They let all kinds out on the street." Her neck stiffened, eyes wide through her glasses.

This was not going to be easy. As foreman, I supposed it was my job to focus the conversation, but for now I decided to sit back for a while and observe.

The people who had been just bodies in comfy chairs for a couple of weeks now were suddenly emerging into full-fledged personalities. Chet, who had seemed so quiet before, was revealing wells of suppressed anger. Perhaps, I thought, he'd grown frustrated with the process: he'd pegged Vasquez as guilty from day one; every day since had been confirmation, and ultimately a waste of time.

"I can picture him doing it," he said now. "Holding that poor guy up with a gun. What's wrong with people?"

"Just because you can picture it doesn't mean it happened," Nancy said in a charmingly calm tone. I imagined she'd had to talk down angry men before.

We spent the rest of the day going over the evidence, trying to piece it together into a coherent story. The judge had given us the option of going home at the usual hour, but everyone agreed to keep deliberating in the hope that we could finish up by the end of the day.

"It's pretty cut and dry to me," Chet said. "I mean, they found the gun in his car. And clearly he shot himself." Like him, I'd been surprised that nearly half of us had initially voted not guilty. I wasn't looking forward to moving the needle on a close vote, but at least I knew I wouldn't have to fight Chet on it.

"We don't know that." Don had been leaning back in his chair, propping the back against the wall so that the front legs were up in the air. Suddenly he dropped it back down and rested his hands on the table. "It's just speculation," he said.

"What is?"

"The gunshot, for one. It could have been a drive-by."

"From that angle?" Chet said. "Maybe from an airplane above his head."

"Look," Don said, "the residue on the wound was not consistent with the gun being so close to his leg."

"What are you basing that on?"

"The expert witness."

Chet's neck jerked involuntarily. "The expert witnesses said precisely the opposite."

"Not the last one. I thought he was very convincing."

Chet scoffed. "You mean Grandpa Walton? He was clueless."

"How can you say that? A man with all that experience."

"All that experience from the twentieth century," Chet said flatly.

"Well then, why don't you tell me your analysis, since you're so smart?"

I raised a hand and my voice. "Let's try to do this without arguing and name-calling, okay?"

"I was just—"

"I know, Don," I said, "we're all a little emotional right now. This is a stressful situation."

"I'm not emotional," he snapped. "I'm being completely rational here."

I let the subsequent silence speak for itself.

There was only one person on trial, so I tried to tamp down my desire to judge anyone else, but Don was testing my resolve. It felt like Thanksgiving dinner with a Republican relative, dodging conspiracy theories about the "deep state" as you passed the gravy. After the 2016 election, I had reluctantly gone home for the holiday, but only because I'd bought the tickets in October. I was in no mood to argue with Uncle Rex, who, according to my mother, was a fierce supporter of the orange menace. As much as the rest of us strived to steer the conversation toward apple pie and fall foliage, Rex kept coming back to border walls and guessing how big Hillary's prison cell would be. I'd put an end to it then with an expletive-laden rant that made my mother blush and move the carving knife out of my reach.

Uncle Rex was not a worldly man. He had never owned a passport and got all his information from Fox News and Facebook. He believed any conspiracy theory that suited his ideology. When the conclusion came first, evidence was only a distraction. He had once said that fossils were planted in the ground by the Devil to confuse human beings about the age of the planet.

It didn't help that Don, though younger, had a slight physical resemblance to Rex—something in the shape of the nose and the veins splintering out across it. The disconnect came in the fact that, while Rex believed everyone arrested was guilty (especially a person of color), Don was choosing the opposite side here.

"Reasonable doubt," he said. "I have reasonable doubt."

He might have been the chorus behind Crews's closing speech.

"Well, let's walk through it, then." I looked around the table. The only way to shut Don up was to get other people to speak. "Sandra, what do you think?"

Sandra, elbow on the table, was cradling her face in her hand. She looked up at me suddenly. "I don't know what to think. It's all so upsetting. I mean, maybe it was his gun. I don't know."

So much for Sandra.

Chet took the opportunity to chime in again. "Okay, let's itemize the evidence, then. For me, it begins with the fact that they found a gun in the car. The guy in the passenger seat has a self-inflicted gunshot wound and there's a gun in the back. That can't be a coincidence."

"Maybe," Don said, "but we don't know for sure."

Chet rolled his eyes. "The term is *reasonable* doubt, not *shadow* of a doubt. The only way to be 100% sure is if we were in the car ourselves."

"Well, what's-his-name was. The gun could have been his."

"Talbott," I said.

"Yeah, him."

"He said it wasn't his gun," Chet retorted.

Don sighed. "Ah, I didn't believe a thing out of his mouth. He seemed like a real low-life."

"But you believe Vasquez? His best friend?"

"They're cut from the same cloth," Sandra murmured.

"We never heard from Vasquez," Don said.

"We heard from his lawyers."

"That's not the same thing. They don't have to prove anything. And he doesn't have to say anything."

"What about the wound?" Ellen asked. "It was clearly self-inflicted, right?"

Everyone nodded. Everyone except Don.

"Obviously," said Dylan, a skinny young guy sitting next to Nancy. I'd barely heard him speak before. "I didn't believe that drive-by story for a second."

Dylan rose from his seat and walked toward the corner of the room where the cart of evidence had been rolled in for us. There was a box of blue gloves on top. He put on a pair and picked up Vasquez's jeans. "Look at this," he said, turning the pocket inside out. I finally saw the burn marks up close, but I was distracted by the wide spatter of dried blood. "Who thinks this could have been done from a distance? The gun was clearly in his pocket."

"The guy's a liar and a felon," Chet said. "It's a ridiculous story."

"I tell you what I believe," said Shirley. "I believe his girlfriend in that taped phone call. She knew he had a gun."

The conversation went on like this for a while—comments ranging through various pieces of evidence, but only occasionally veering toward an attempt to string them together. It was frustrating but, I decided, necessary. People needed to air their concerns as they came up. Maybe later we could organize the points together to construct a narrative.

The judge had instructed that no discussion of the case was permissible unless all twelve of us were together. Each time someone went to the bathroom, we had to fall silent or change the subject to something innocuous and unrelated—the weather, the Giants' chances for the World Series.

In those quiet moments, I scanned the room, trying to get a read on the other jurors. At this point, I was less concerned with how they were leaning than with how they thought.

Chet was no-nonsense: like a scientist, he was inclined to just look at the facts and ignore any emotional baggage. Shirley was the opposite: her first instinct was to consider the human aspect of a situation, and she used people's behavior and feelings as a guide toward the truth. The tone of Vasquez's girlfriend on that call seemed to say as much to her as the words.

We all came from different backgrounds, and I guess that was the point. We were supposed to be a representative cross-section of the community, with varying skill sets and approaches to life. Neither Chet's head nor Shirley's heart was necessarily the better route to assessing the case. I was beginning to see that the hope was that such differing paths could be more effective when joined.

Don was pontificating again on reasonable doubt when I got up to use the bathroom. "Hold that thought," I said, squeezing past him. "I'll be right back."

We had a small private bathroom right next to the jury room. I shut myself in and stared into the mirror for a minute. The reflected image sadly matched how I felt inside—drained, frustrated, a bit lost. I did not want to do this. More and more as time went on, I did not want to do this.

What struck me most, suddenly, was how focused I'd become. All day I'd been thinking only about the trial. The chaos of my life outside this room seemed to have drifted away. I hadn't remembered any of it until now.

I splashed water on my face, hoping to wash away the discomfort. It was hard enough accepting that someone's fate was in my hands. Having to fight with these strangers only made it worse.

I stood still, closed my eyes, and breathed deeply, tracking the air on its way through my body. The breath pushed away some of the anxiety, leaving me surprisingly relaxed. I told myself to hold on to the feeling and opened the door.

The room looked like a diorama, figures frozen silently in place, caught in a moment just before destruction—Pompeii, Lot's Wife. Even Don was seated quietly, staring into his third cup of coffee. During our lunch break, I'd seen him dash around the corner, away from the building entrance, to smoke a cigarette. Being stuck inside was probably killing him.

"It's getting late," I said. "Shall we see where we are? Another vote?"

No one was enthusiastic, but no one objected, either.

"Can we just do it by hand this time?"

Again, no objections.

"Okay. Guilty?"

Nine hands rose tentatively into the air.

"Not guilty?"

Don's hand shot up. I looked around the room, waiting for the others. Nancy grimaced and arched her arm over her head so that it was more horizontal than vertical. I hadn't seen that coming.

I locked eyes with her, trying to invite more than intimidate. Finally, she spoke. "I'm not sure," she said. "I think he's probably guilty, but I'm not quite sold yet."

In the corner, Don let out a triumphant sigh.

I had to lean forward, around my neighbor, to see who the third hand belonged to. Billie, a woman around 70, straight gray hair hanging down to her shoulders in a cut I imagined her maintaining for 50 years. She hadn't said a word yet, but her eyes suggested painful deliberation, thoughts behind them rattling toward a conclusion.

"I need to think some more," she said in a soft voice.

I nodded sympathetically. "How certain is everyone else?"

We went around the room, each person giving just a sentence or two—less about the case than about the clarity of their positions.

"Rock solid," said Chet.

"I'm pretty clear, too," said Dylan.

When we got to Don, he scowled. "Absolutely not guilty," he said.

"Well," I said when the circle was complete, "it looks like we have 9 solid guilty votes, 1 solid not guilty, and 2 on the fence. Aside from Nancy and Billie, does anyone see wiggle room?"

Don shook his head firmly. The others didn't respond.

"Okay. Let me send a note to the judge and ask what we should do."

In the envelope the bailiff had given us there was a form for communicating with the judge. I wrote that we were concerned that we were deadlocked and asked for guidance.

I peeked out the door and found the bailiff in the hall. He took the envelope from me and I returned to the room.

It seemed that everyone was exhausted, worn down by hours of concentration and argument. Watching Don stew in the corner, arms folded across his chest, I felt certain he would never budge. The only way out of here was for everyone else to agree with him.

Billie was making a cup of tea, dipping the bag methodically in and out of the water, which didn't reveal any steam. I pored over the remnants of pastry beside her.

"Slim pickings at this point," she said with a chuckle.

"I'm not really hungry, anyway," I replied. "Just looking for some carbohydrate comfort, I guess."

"There's wisdom in that," she said. She smiled at me through pale blue, almost gray eyes and whispered, "You're doing a very good job, you know."

I felt a sudden shiver. Only now did I realize what a disastrous job I thought I'd been doing. "Thank you. That's nice to hear."

"I don't envy you. Herding cats is a thankless task." She dropped the tea bag into the wastebasket and drew the sugarless cup to her lips.

"Do you live in the city?" I asked.

"Yes," she said, smiling. I was sure it was from the memories, not the tea. "I moved here from Colorado as soon as I turned 18."

"Wow. That was brave."

Her smile widened, revealing teeth that were surprisingly bright and straight. "It was the Summer of Love," she said. "You couldn't keep me away."

"Oh, that sounds wonderful."

She nodded. "San Francisco in its heyday. So much has changed since then."

"I didn't move here until the nineties, and I can say the same thing."

"Sure. But some things are constant, if you look for them."

Her lips stretched into a gentle smile. Both hands wrapped around the cup, she said, "The city still has a lot of heart. People still care about each other, about doing the right thing."

"There's nowhere else like it." That's what kept coming back to me, whenever I thought about leaving. There was nowhere else like it.

"I spent my career in nonprofits," she said. "You learn a lot about the world by helping the less fortunate. You learn a lot about yourself."

She told me about a civil rights group she'd joined in the sixties, another place that provided training to help lower-income women find jobs, the homeless shelter she'd run for 15 years. It was a portrait of the city I'd never seen. She described the work as invisible supports, the bones that helped the world stand up.

"I retired a few years ago, but I'm still on a couple of boards. I can't seem to pull myself away."

I wanted to ask more, but the door squeaked open behind her, and the bailiff was standing in the doorway. He handed me a piece of paper and left again. At the bottom of the form, below my note to the judge, was a simple statement. *Keep trying. I suggest you break for the day and come back in the morning, refreshed.*

I read it aloud to everyone else. A sigh went around the room, like an audible wave in a football stadium. Relief to call it a day, but frustration that it wasn't over. Now we would have to spend the night with this decision still hanging over our heads.

I hoped the air on the walk home would clear the cobwebs out of my head. Only one day of deliberations, and it was already the worst part of the trial. I would gladly have sat through another eight hours of testimony on powder burns rather than return to that stuffy room and argue with Don again.

Just outside the building, I spotted two people standing silently side by side—Vasquez's mother talking to a young man. She turned her head and locked eyes with me for a moment. Every day, all day, she had watched the defense table more than the witness stand, more than the jury box, and yet she seemed to recognize me as well as I did her. Her eyelids drooped beneath a furrowed brow. In the breeze, her hair crisscrossed her face, gray interwoven with black, and she didn't bother to push it back.

I looked quickly away. She knew nothing about me other than

that I was sitting in judgment of her son. Even that was too much. I wanted to be anonymous, invisible, imaginary.

Propelled by her eyes, I dashed across the street, to the sunny side, where the light could warm me.

I hated this. Suddenly, all the excitement I'd felt before, all the ways the trial had pulled my attention and grabbed my interest, felt cold to me. I didn't want to do this anymore. I didn't want to do this ever again.

CHAPTER 23

NOTHING BUT THE TRUTH

I was walking down Market Street when my phone chimed, a text from Brendan:

I need a drink. Care to join me?

No, I thought. Right now, what I needed was peace and quiet—or at least peace and the white noise of traffic whizzing by and disjointed voices tossing non sequiturs toward me as they passed on the sidewalk. Two young women at the Octavia off-ramp: "I just, like, couldn't believe it. I mean, I don't even like, *like* him." A gay man on a cell phone: "Girl, he's such a slut, he has stirrups on his ears."

I laughed—more than the line deserved, grateful for the distraction.

It had turned into a surprisingly nice day while I'd been cooped up inside. The sky was still a crisp, cloudless blue, light bouncing off the gold trim of a Victorian on the corner—doomed, no doubt, to be replaced by another plastic condo.

My phone rang. Assuming it was Brendan losing patience with my delayed response, I answered without looking.

"Hi, Craig. Am I calling at a bad time?"

"No, Angela, it's fine. I'm just walking home from the trial."

Her voice grew lighter. "Ooh, did you fry him?"

"There's a moratorium on the death penalty in California," I replied. "We're still in deliberations. I expect we'll wrap up tomorrow." Wishful thinking, I told myself. "Cassandra and the boys are doing fine."

"That's good."

I bounced on the balls of my feet, waiting for the light to change.

"So, I have news," Angela said after a long pause.

The walk light finally came on and I made my way across Church. A stream of hipsters emerged from the subway and splintered in all directions. A small group of them made their way into an elegant bar on the corner, one of the upscale joints Wayne liked so much. I had to admit that I liked it, too, but I still resented the fact that it had displaced a gay bar, albeit a pretty run-down one.

"The sale's going through," Angela said as a couple passed cackling by.

"The yoga studio?"

"Yeah, I think that's what she wants to do with it."

A hollowness opened up in my chest, where my fantasy had lived, my hope that nothing would change. "When?" I asked.

"The deal should close in a few weeks. I asked for time to get things in order, see what we can do about getting rid of the inventory. We should have a big sale. Fifty percent off the whole store, something like that."

"And the staff?"

She seemed distracted. When she returned to the phone, I heard a long exhale and imagined her lighting a cigarette. "What we talked about before. They should be happy."

"A bonus if they stay til the end?"

"Sure," she said, and puffed again. "Whatever you think is reasonable."

All those books, I thought. Now they were just something to get rid of, something in the way.

"Look," Angela said, "I gotta go. Let's talk tomorrow." I heard a splash in the background.

"Okay. Good night, Angela."

A streetcar squeaked to a halt at Noe, and more people streamed past at the corner. The intersection—five spokes splintering off at disjointed angles—was bustling with a rainbow of commuters. Waiting for the light, I scrolled back to Brendan's text.

Maybe later, I typed. *Can I come over in an hour?*

Sure, he said. *I'll be here.*

I turned north on Castro, legs straining at the angle of the climb. I veered onto States for some relief and, at the end of the block, continued up toward Corona Heights. The park might have been another planet. On either side of me, wildflowers and tall grass swayed in the breeze as I made my way up the narrow path. The plants thinned out the higher I got, until I emerged onto a moonscape, two piles of boulders framing a plateau that offered an expansive view of the city.

I called it Mount Castro. Despite the view, it tempted only a few random tourists each day, the vast majority preferring the more famous—and drivable—lookout at the top of Twin Peaks. To me, Twin Peaks was a bar, not a view. I had steered more than one tourist wrong by misinterpreting their request. I consoled myself by considering it payback for the trip to New York when I had asked the cabbie to take me to the Met, and found myself at the museum instead of the opera house.

I passed by the outcrop and traced the jagged edges of the rocks, the places where some adolescent couple had carved their initials to commemorate a love that had long since gone.

The sky was a striated blue, pale toward the ground, darker as it reached higher, with only a filmy streak of cloud here and there. Closer to the edge, I studied the downtown skyline, steel and glass that might easily be mistaken for New York or Tokyo. On either side, the small, familiar boxes of the neighborhoods spread around, undulating over hills.

That was more like it, I thought, turning slightly to keep the skyscrapers out of my sightline. I had fallen in love with the San Francisco of cable cars and pastel Victorians, sea lions sunning on the dock, and the dizzying sensation of winding my way down steep twisted streets. Any building over six stories was uninteresting to me, because it was not uniquely San Francisco.

I grew up in a place no one ever leaves and moved to a place no one is from. In all this time, I'd met only a handful of people who'd been born here. Maybe it was just the circles I traveled in—the gays, the artists, the recent college grads, the hungry youngsters who make up a large portion of any cosmopolitan center—but I continued to be surprised when someone introduced himself as born and raised in the City (the capital imposed by the immortal Herb Caen). I didn't envy them. For me, growing up was largely tied to rebellion: I thought it was perfectly natural to want to leave wherever you came from. So what did you do if you came from paradise?

On every visit back to Minnesota, I would inevitably run into a friend from high school, most of whom still lived just a few miles from their childhood homes. Even if, on the surface, their lives had changed dramatically—lawyers and doctors spun from working-class parents—they still embodied the values they'd been raised with, still felt connected to their origins. They were grounded in a way I'd never been able to understand.

My father tried to convince me we were all invested with Viking spirit. What I'd never been able to appreciate, though, was the stoicism that went with it. The adults around me went about their business—whether the bus driver who dropped us off at school, my mother doing her housework on the same schedule every week, or my father coming home from work without sharing a word about his day, just a grim, inscrutable expression on his lips—with an air of fatalism and duty that became stranger and stranger to me over time.

I was the sensitive one in the family. That was how they put it when a horror movie scared me, when I cried over a skinned knee. I felt things more gravely than others, but I would get over it. The Viking spirit would kick in, and I, too, would learn to bury my feelings in action. I watched them all in their constant motion and realized that that was the key: they were so busy raising children, raking leaves, shoveling snow, they didn't have time to waste on *feeling* anything.

It wasn't until senior year of high school, when I started researching colleges, that I decided I could emulate the other Viking trait—adventure. The only schools I applied to were on one coast or the other—far from the too comfortable uniformity of home. California was another world, everything about it dramatically different from what I had been raised with. Palm trees lining the campus, relentless sun for 12 months of the year, and faces of every size, shape, and color. In California, with my tousled hair and Nordic cheekbones, I was the weird one. And I loved it.

My trips home, twice a year during college, retracted over time to Christmas visits only—a week or so of intense family gatherings, too much food, and reveling in the snowfall. Winter was what I missed most. My friends in California thought I was crazy. They couldn't imagine temperatures lower than 50, days when even a lined leather coat would earn you frostbite. But as the plane came in over Minneapolis, coasting over wide patches of white interrupted only by roadways and large frozen lakes, I felt my breath quicken, my eyes widen to take it all in. I didn't care about the cold. With enough layers—thermal underwear, a heavy sweater under my down coat, a thick wool cap under the hood—I was always fine. A bulky, multicolored snowman who couldn't be touched by the cold.

That was part of it. Hidden behind all that clothing, I was essentially anonymous, an unrecognizable figure treading through the snow. Every year, I would take a break from the duties of family to walk around the lake on my own, admiring the far shore in a way you never could in summer, when leaves got in the way. The snow absorbed all sound, even the traffic hurtling by on the parkway. I knew the path by heart, the spots where the thin trees were clumped together, reaching into the white sky, the patches where they opened to provide access to the lake. Inevitably, there was a tent on the ice, several yards from shore, a couple of men sitting in front of it, dropping fishing lines into a hole they'd drilled there. And in another spot, a makeshift hockey rink, kids skating wildly around one another, sticks slapping against the ice like castanets.

But mostly it was silent. The snow covered and embraced everything. If you didn't fight against it—plowing the streets, dusting off your coat—it would blanket everything. It would take over, its silence enveloping the world. In the snow, there was a kind of peace I'd never found anywhere else.

The closest I came in San Francisco was up here, where the wind devoured the voices of fellow pilgrims, where the life below—the towers and apartment buildings and bridges and cars—was all silenced by distance.

From here, the easiest landmark was the rainbow flag over

Harvey Milk Plaza, its colors whipping in the wind. The Castro stretched beneath it, fanning out to the south. The bold colors of the Victorians—blue, purple, green, a dash of pink—rode the hill like the spiky fins of a neon fish. Just to the left, in its own bright patch of sunlight, I spied the Mission—flatter, less ornate if more colorful—the part of the city that was changing now more rapidly than any other, but on a quieter scale than the downtown areas that had been razed for behemoth glass towers. In the Mission, it was less architecture that was evolving than culture. The buildings remained; it was the people who were different.

Somewhere down there, the hipsters who had displaced Raul Vasquez strolled from their SoMa offices to a trendy bar, shopped for fair-trade coffee and veggie burgers, and got their arms sleeved in dragons. Looking back first, they would pass through their front doors and lock them securely behind them. They'd walk up the steps and into their spacious, sterile apartments—white and black Pottery Barn and Crate & Barrel showrooms, an espresso machine where a Mr. Coffee might have been before. They'd put some hip hop on the stereo and pretend for a minute that they weren't white. They didn't see the destruction they were leaving in their wake. It wasn't destruction in their minds; it was reinvention. They were changing the world for the better. In the echo chamber of their generation, their slice of the culture, it never occurred to them that someone else might have liked the world the way it was.

A lot had changed somewhere along the way—the reasons I had moved to San Francisco no longer seemed as prominent, things I loved about the city no longer on ready display. It wasn't completely gone, of course, and I maintained a measure of faith that it never would be. San Francisco was still—would always be—the refuge of the weirdo. That was the problem, ironically.

Yesterday's weirdos—hippies, artists, sexual outlaws—had been supplanted by new types. The new misfits were the awkward young men who dreamt in code, sealed in their left-brain heads, unable to relate to their own bodies or the rest of the world. They were the single-minded twentysomethings who thought time was running out to join the C-suite, the rebellious ones who struggled to find something to rebel against. They, too, had let their weirdness come alive in San Francisco, and it had welcomed them. And in turn, they had drained its blood and were intent now upon ripping the flesh away and building cold castles from the bones.

I tore my eyes away from the view and found the tilted path beyond the rocks, along the chain-link fence that wound its way past the more perilous part of the hill. Finally the path opened onto a wide staircase overlooking the dog run, planks of wood anchored to the ground. I stopped for a moment and watched a Golden Retriever speeding around, playing tag with a black Lab. They nuzzled playfully, dancing in the air, barking with gentle delight.

◘

Brendan was in the garden when I arrived. As I creaked open the gate, I could hear the cocktail shaker.

"I heard you coming," he said with a laugh, continuing to rock the shaker as I closed the gate behind me.

When Oscar left the neighborhood, Brendan became my go-to for emergency cocktails, those nights when all you need is a stiff drink and a warm shoulder. I saw it in his eyes now. He looked tired, drained, and I wondered if I were actually looking at myself.

I took a seat at the patio table, behind a martini glass with my signature olive-and-onion spear angled neatly to the left. The spear danced in the glass, the drink swirling like a mild tornado.

He poured his own—dirty, a pool of olive juice blending with the gin—and sat across from me. "Cheers," he said.

His face, partly shaded by the tree to my left, suddenly took on a peaceful glow. "Gin agrees with you," I said.

"Mother's milk."

"So what's going on?"

"It's just been one of those days," he said. "I woke up with a backache that wouldn't quit, and that just put me in a mood." He took another sip. "Mmm, I feel so much better now. I should have done this at 9 a.m."

"Has it come to that?" I asked.

"Soon enough. You know, I went to the doctor last week, and he said—very earnestly, my doctor is nothing if not earnest—*What's bothering you, Brendan?* And I took out my list. Seriously, it's gotten to the point that I make a *list*."

"What was on it?"

"Well, the backache, of course. Indigestion. This weird tingling sensation in my thigh. Oh, and most fun of all, diminished libido."

"Diminished libido? *You?*"

He laughed. "I know. Who'd have thunk it? I'm fine when I need to be, but I really miss spontaneous erections." He plucked an olive off the spear. "I used to get them at all times of day, for no apparent reason. Just—*boing*, there it is. Now it's basically just morning wood, and it's inconvenient because all I want to do at that hour is pee."

"At least you still *can* pee."

"Oh, that's coming, trust me." He sighed. "Anyway, the earnest doctor leans in and whispers, *It's fine. You're just getting older.*"

"That's it?"

"Yeah. What I didn't get was why everything's happening at once. I mean, do we really just start to fall apart at a certain age?"

I grimaced, suddenly aware of a crick in my neck. "Do we?"

Brendan lifted an eyebrow and hid his face behind the glass.

"So what did he tell you to do?"

"Get exercise. Eat lots of fiber. And drink water." He lifted the glass in the air.

"That doesn't count."

"Baby steps, dear." He leaned back in the chair. "How's the trial going?"

I shook my head. "Almost over. I'll tell you all about it soon."

I swirled the spear in my drink. The tip of my finger got wet, and I licked off the gin.

"Angela's selling the store," I said.

"It went through?"

"Apparently. A couple of months from now, a gaggle of girls will be doing sun salutation in the self-help section."

"I'm sorry. Are you okay?"

I thought about it for a moment, suddenly realizing that I hadn't thought about it much until now, now that it was definite. Perhaps I'd been too much in denial to admit the possibility of unemployment.

"Yes," I said at last. "I think it's time. I need a change."

"Good for you. There's no point in fighting the inevitable." And suddenly his eyes widened.

"Oh god, what now?" I laughed nervously.

He leaned over the table, cradling his drink. "Wayne dumped John."

"What?" I was getting used to feigning surprise.

Brendan grimaced. "Poor bastard. I was hoping John would be the one to call it quits. Now Wayne gets to feel like the powerful one."

"What happened?"

"I don't know," said Brendan. "We just spoke briefly on the phone. He didn't give me any details."

"How did he sound?"

"Numb. Maybe we should take him out, see if we can cheer him up a bit."

"He'll be better off in the long run," I said. "I just hope he can see that." It was what I'd told myself about Damien, about all of them.

Brendan pulled his seat out from the table. "Let's keep the mood going," he said. "I'll mix another round."

"I'm not quite done here," I said, swirling.

"You will be." He smiled and carried the cocktail shaker inside. "I'll be right back."

I slunk in my seat and threw my head back. Through the full leaves of the tree overhead, I could see the sky darkening in patches. A breeze wafted through, ruffling the leaves, sending a sudden chill to the back of my neck. I found myself trembling slightly.

Eyes closed, I was suddenly aware of a creaking sound behind me. I turned to find Bette shutting the gate. She moved forward calmly. In the dimming light, she seemed to float a millimeter above the grass.

I rose from the chair and embraced her. I was craving that minty smell again, the soft touch of her curls against my skin.

As we pulled apart, I murmured apologetically, "Brendan's inside, refilling the cocktail shaker."

"Of course he is." She smiled knowingly.

I gestured toward the table, but Bette moved in the other direction, and I followed her, strolling slowly through the garden. She reached out to caress the petals of a pink rose. "I do love it here," she said. "I hope Brendan never gets sick of me, because I couldn't survive without these flowers."

"No danger of that," I replied.

She bent her nose toward the bud and breathed in the scent. Rising back up, she turned a gentle gaze to me. "And how are you?"

I shrugged, knowing that Bette was not one for couching emotion under politeness. "It's been a rough day."

"Just the day?" She chuckled.

I was grateful to smile. "The month? The year?" *Life*, I wanted to say, but that sounded pathetic.

She just looked at me, head tilted a bit so that her hair danced lightly on one shoulder.

"The trial," I said at last. "We're in deliberations now, and"—I parsed my words, wondering what I could say, how far I could go—"it's all coming home to me."

"What do you mean?" Her voice was soft, almost swallowed by the breeze.

"I can't say much. But I'll tell you one thing: I can't wait until I *can* talk about this!"

She leaned in closer and placed a hand on my shoulder.

The words tumbled forth of their own accord. "I just—I can't. … I know I need to be objective, but that's so damn hard. You have to put all the pieces together, and in the back of your mind is the knowledge that your decision will affect someone's life. A complete stranger."

I looked into Bette's eyes, and a sudden image came back—

Vasquez's mother on the sidewalk, watching me.

"It was exciting in the beginning. Like a play I was watching—a mystery I had to solve. But it's not like that now. Suddenly, once the testimony ended, it became personal."

I heard the jailhouse tape again, spooling in the back of my brain—Vasquez's voice, nearly crying, as he repeated again and again, *I'm done, I'm done.* He'd tried to get his life back together after being released from prison. He'd gotten a job, tried to make something of himself. And now, here he was again, and I had to decide what would happen to him.

"He's somebody's son," I said. "His mother is there every day—"

Maybe it was Bette's hand on my shoulder, but at that moment, something released the tension and my belly was wracked, the sobs cutting through my words. I didn't have time to wonder why this was happening, why the wall had broken so abruptly.

Finally, I slowed down, breathed deeply. Opening my eyes, I looked down at the ground, the deep green of the grass beneath my feet. "I'm not in the audience anymore," I heard myself saying. "Now I'm one of the actors."

Bette said nothing, but her grip tightened on my shoulder. Her body blocked the wind.

"Who am I to determine what happens to someone else? How do I know what to do?"

"That's the process," she said softly. "It's not just you. There are 12 of you. You'll do the right thing."

I didn't care about Raul Vasquez. If he wasn't guilty of this offense, he was guilty of others. The world would not suffer if he were locked away for a few years. This wasn't about Raul Vasquez.

"I don't like the power," I said. "It's safer having no one to worry about but a cat." Elsa, whom I'd never really had to worry about. Elsa had been perfectly capable of taking care of herself.

"I understand," Bette said. "But that's life. That's the best part of life. Even when we fuck it up."

I had fucked it up too often, even when it really mattered. "Did you ever meet Garrett?" I asked. "We dated several years ago."

Why was he here now, in my mind? Why did he never leave?

She thought for a moment. "Tall redhead?"

I nodded.

"Yes, he was very sweet. What happened?"

"I let him go."

Bette's hair, caught by a sudden breeze, swayed toward one side of her face.

"No," I said, "I pushed him away."

The end had lasted a year—a year of me hemming and hawing every time he suggested moving forward, living together. And then he stopped asking.

"He was a huge Sondheim fan," I told Bette.

Her eyes lit up. "No wonder I remember him."

And I told her. The night he had made me dinner and put *Into the Woods* on the stereo. "No One Is Alone"—his favorite song. And he looked at me, his eyes moist in the candlelight, and said he was tired of being alone. The worst thing, he said, is not to be alone. It's to feel alone when you're with someone else.

His eyes pleaded. I couldn't answer. And he smiled, slowly put down his drink, and disappeared into the bedroom.

In a minute or two he came back. I was standing at the window now, watching the lights of the neighborhood flutter on. When I turned, he was holding a paper bag in his hands. *Here*, he

[300]

said, *I think you should take this.*

My deodorant, a pair of underwear, a toothbrush. Our relationship fit into a Safeway bag. But at least he was more direct than I'd been with Damien.

"What did you say?" Bette asked. The images fell away, and I was back in a deepening dark with her, the wind cool on the nape of my neck.

"I don't know what I said. I'm sure I muttered something about how we should talk some more, how I just wasn't ready. But I took the bag and walked down the stairs and into the night. You know the walk of shame?"

She smiled, nodded.

"That's the only time I ever walked home from another man's house and really felt shame."

Her eyes softened, her face aglow in the diffused light from the open door.

"I was too humiliated to call him after that. I knew in my heart that whatever I said he wouldn't believe. And I wasn't sure I could believe it, either."

We stood in silence for a while, her eyes all the language I needed. She understood. I searched her eyes, hoping their wisdom would miraculously spill back onto me.

She waited a long moment. Finally, her eyes narrowed and she said, in a whisper that was almost a song, "You did what felt right in the moment. I think you're torturing yourself because you think he might have been the one, as they say. But, in that moment, he wasn't. And if the reason he wasn't was simply that you weren't ready, then so be it. That doesn't change anything. You can live in only one time zone, hon, and in that one, he wasn't right."

"The thing is, I'm not sure I'm any better at it now."

"We all make mistakes," Bette said. "Sometimes the same one over and over, until we get it right. The young don't have a monopoly on screwing up."

I let myself laugh and was instantly afraid the eruption would make the tears return. I breathed hard and gazed down again. She took hold of both shoulders and ducked her head to look into my eyes. "Are you all right?"

"I'll be fine," I said, wiping my eyes on my sleeve. "You're right. This is just something to get through. I'll be fine."

And suddenly, Brendan was there, shaker in one hand, a fresh glass in the other. "Dinnertime!" he called from the table as he placed them down. "You two take this and I'll get some nibbles for us." And he vanished back into the house.

Bette draped an arm through mine and we made our way to the table.

"Are you okay?" Brendan asked when he settled down beside us again, a plate of cheese and crackers now displayed on the table. He leaned in close. I must have looked a mess.

I told him what Bette and I had been talking about, pretending it was all behind me, but he continued to gaze gently into my eyes. Then he lifted his glass, dismissing the evil spirits.

That second martini didn't hurt. It numbed everything, as martinis are intended to do. We changed the subject, and changed it again. We laughed over silly things, stories from the past that were becoming more and more the content of the present. And for a moment—here, in the encroaching darkness, surrounded by green life—the chaos of the world felt out of reach. This moment, with its laughter and kindness and the cool evening air, was all there was.

CHAPTER 24
ANOTHER ROUND

After a rough couple of hours in bed, watching the clock and dreading the next day, I finally managed to sleep. I woke early, surprisingly calm, save for a constant queasiness. I told myself to ignore it, to forge ahead. I would blow through this day, and in a matter of hours, my life would get back to normal.

The best course, I decided, was to go into the jury room with an agenda. Over breakfast, I wrote out a few ground rules—no sidebars, no monopolizing the conversation, no interruptions, no belaboring things we'd already decided—and determined that I would make a concerted effort to steer back anyone who was going off-topic.

I walked into the room that morning like a substitute teacher—fake smile and a no-nonsense attitude. All I needed was a blackboard to write my name on.

Most of the jurors looked well rested, as if they hadn't given a single thought to the case overnight. I envied anyone for whom that was true, but part of me assumed they were all faking it as much as I was.

I presented the ground rules and asked for feedback or additional items. Everyone agreed. I counted that as the first accomplishment of the day, but it didn't necessarily bode well for the other decisions we'd have to make.

Then I jumped into the task at hand. "As I see it, there are two things that play into our decision: Do we believe Vasquez's wound was self-inflicted? And do we believe that the gun in custody is the one he used?"

Chet piped up. "I still don't get why it has to be that gun."

"Well, as we heard, that gun was stolen from somebody in Arizona," Nancy said.

"So what?" Chet pursued. "He's a felon in possession of a gun, no matter where the gun comes from."

Ellen fidgeted with a stray lock of hair. She'd worn it long and free in the courtroom, but today she'd wound it into a bun atop her head. Getting down to business. "Let's stop avoiding the obvious: the reason the feds are after him is that he's a gang member."

"We don't know that," Billie said. Her voice carried the same calm as a therapist's.

"Don't we?" Ellen lifted her hands with a dramatic sweep.

"Well, it's not in evidence."

"The neck tattoo is."

Chet rose up in his chair, his chest widening. "The judge told us to feel free to use our common sense. We're not just computers that the lawyers feed their data into. I didn't need them to tell me who that guy is. I could tell for myself. All those ridiculous friends of his. They're complete low-lifes, criminals. How did this prick get a felony conviction in the first place? Was he jaywalking?"

I decided to let it play out. They weren't talking over one another, they were just arguing. Arguing was good. Arguing was what this was all about.

"I don't think that's relevant," said Nancy. "If they wanted us to know what he'd done before, they would have told us. The implication, actually, is that it shouldn't matter. His being a felon is relevant only because felons can't have guns."

"And the reason felons can't have guns is also irrelevant?" Chet asked flatly. "This guy is a piece of crap."

"I don't disagree," Nancy said. "I'm just trying to keep it to the side."

"Well, good luck with that."

There was a brief smattering of laughter. At this point, we were willing to jump at the slightest sign of humor.

"So," I said, "to the question of the wound. Was it self-inflicted?"

"Of course," said Madge. Others nodded around her.

So far this morning, Don had been quiet. If I was the schoolteacher, he was the scolded kid sulking in the corner. But now he looked up, arms folded across his chest, and said, rather softly, "I'm not sure."

"Still?" asked Chet.

Don's eyes narrowed. "As I said yesterday, I believe that last expert witness. The shot could have come from a distance."

"And the hole in his pocket?" said Chet with a sneer.

We'd been through all this before, but this morning felt like the opening of a TV drama, when you get clips of the previous episode just to refresh your memory.

Nancy met my eye with a slight smile. "For the record," she said, "I've had a change of heart. I'm voting guilty."

Don's face sank. The dominoes were falling in the wrong direction.

"So, just as a check-in, who thinks he's guilty?"

Ten hands shot into the air—more decisively, less patiently than before. Ten people who clearly wanted to get this over with.

That impatience brought on more conversation, and soon it

was flowing. People consulted their notebooks, brought up specific pieces of evidence, parsed witness testimony. In my own notebook, I began to list evidence of guilt on one side, open questions on the other. Within minutes, the list was completely lopsided.

As the others talked, Don sat silently in his spot. He seemed to have checked out. He was immovable. Everything going on around him was mere noise. But his expression was less smug than resigned. He knew he wasn't going to win. He knew his intransigence was punishing him as much as the rest of us.

I thought again of Uncle Rex, how we're stuck with certain people in our lives—family, colleagues, fellow jurors. Friends are the only people we really choose, and the only ones we can walk away from with minimal guilt. That was the source of my frustration with Don: I was stuck with him—for the time being, at least. I couldn't just turn my back and push him out of my life. For a while yet—until he surrendered, or until the judge lost patience with our indecisiveness—we were locked in this room together. And there was no easy way out.

A few chairs away from him, Billie sat quietly in a silky lavender blouse with tiny blue flowers at the neckline. She was directly across from me today, so I didn't have to shift in my seat to see her. I imagined her wearing the same blouse decades ago, dancing in Golden Gate Park, listening to Janis. She carried those days with her, the peace and hopefulness of an era when everything seemed possible. I envied the sense of calm she exuded. While the rest of us hopped from point to point and Don scowled in his corner, she was quietly contemplating.

"What about the girlfriend?" Ellen asked, turning the subject away from the gunshot wound for a moment. "That conversation in the jailhouse. What does she say?"

Dylan adjusted his wool hat and flipped through his notebook. "He tells her the cops have a gun and she says, 'They found it?'"

"Exactly," Ellen said. "*It*. Not 'a gun,' but *it*. She knew he had a gun."

"And the way he shuts her up immediately is telling. He knew the call was being recorded."

Finally Billie moved her head, just a faint flicker to one side. I didn't realize how still she'd been sitting until then—so still that the tiniest gesture captured my attention. Her lips parted and I spotted her tongue resting hesitantly just behind her front teeth. "Let's talk about the gun for a minute," she said.

I nodded, welcoming her thoughts.

"I don't think there's any doubt that he shot himself," she said. "I hesitate to imagine why, what kind of circumstance he might have been in—whether the mugging story is true or not. But I trust my eyes, and it's clear to me that he did it. But for whatever reason, they need us to be sure that he used the gun they found. And that's where I'm struggling."

Her lips sealed back into a faint smile, and she tapped the table lightly with unpolished fingernails.

"I can see that," said Arnold from the corner. "But for me, the fact that the gun was found in the car is enough. I mean, it's common sense."

"We don't really know that," Billie said. "It might have been Talbott's gun, and he just denied it because he knew it was stolen. For all we know, Vasquez threw his own gun out the window."

"Does it matter?" asked Shirley with a frustrated sigh. "It's completely arbitrary, if you ask me. It's like being at the grocery store. You pick up one apple or another one. They're both in the same bin. In any event, you're still reaching for an apple."

Billie's smile looked pained now. "But this isn't about apples. It's about a man's freedom."

Chet glowered. "Frankly, I think we're all better off with someone like him behind bars."

Nancy frowned. "Sadly, we can't lock up someone because of what they *might* do in the future."

Billie folded her hands on the table. "It's *all* sad. There's no good way out of this."

When no one responded, she went on. "He may be a bad egg, as my mother used to say. But I have to wonder how he got that way. No one starts out wanting to be a criminal. And this trial is a reminder of that. We know he's a felon, but we've been told in no uncertain terms to leave that off to the side. It's relevant only because felons are subject to this particular law, about not having a gun. If any of us had our own hands on a gun, there would be no charge. He did something wrong in his past, and that mistake continues to haunt him. And unless he's shown some kindness along the way, it always will. He'll never get out from under it. It's a tragedy."

The room was silent for a long moment. I wanted to be on her side. I wanted to let kindness rule the day. I'd always considered myself a compassionate person. That was the ethos of San Francisco, the reason I'd moved here all those years ago. This was supposed to be a tolerant place, a place where people were allowed to be what they wanted to be. It had been true for her generation, the hippies in the park living free and protesting war. And it had been true for the next group, the gays who came to liberate themselves and build their own sense of community. And my generation had benefited from both legacies.

I wanted to be on her side, but instead I found myself in opposition. I wasn't making a statement. I wasn't denying Billie's vision of the world. Nor was I condoning the implicit racism I saw in Chet, just because we happened to see this particular crime the same way. Still, here I was, aligned with the hipsters and the businessmen and the suburban housewives, everyone I raged against outside, in my real life.

We talked for another hour or so, revolving around the same issues again and again, like a ship circling a whirlpool. Don was steering, and he was determined to bring us all down with him. "I have reasonable doubt," he said at the end of one harangue. "That's all it comes down to, and there's no evidence that's going to change that."

"Look," Chet said, "none of us was there. We didn't see him do it with our own eyes. That doesn't mean that that stack of evidence"—he gestured toward the cart, towering with files, bloody clothing, and even the gun itself—"doesn't count for something. I'm perfectly willing to say that I have a measure of doubt. But not a *reasonable* measure."

What he didn't need to add was that the principle of reasonable doubt is predicated upon jurors demonstrating reason. Billie was still struggling—engaged in the conversation, thinking about every angle. But in Don's case, the capacity for reason was debatable.

"Okay, fine," I said at last. "I'd like to take another poll."

Madge reached for the stack of paper in the middle of the table.

"No," I said, "not a vote. I think we're beyond that. What I need to know—what I think we owe to the judge—is confidence that we've done the best we can. So, I'd like everyone to think about these questions: Can you vow that you're being open to both sides? That you're voting your conscience and that you can live with yourself after the vote? And are you certain that nothing will change your vote?"

Madge stared at me, eyes wide. She looked slightly terrified.

The room was quiet for a long moment.

"Chet?" I asked, watching him.

Chet pushed his glasses up. "Yes," he said. "Yes to all of that."

From him, I circled the room. Everyone seemed fully engaged and thoughtful. They clearly understood that this time, we weren't just shooting the shit. This time really counted. I felt the weight of the air around us. The energy had shifted, we'd entered the eye of the storm.

In turn, everyone confirmed their feelings—even, of course, Don, though his expression read more anger than gravity.

I removed another form from the packet and penned a note to the judge.

The courtroom felt colder now, without the hubbub of the proceedings. There were no boxes of evidence on the prosecution's table, all of it still sitting on the cart in the jury room. And the audience was minimal—a smattering of faces I'd seen before, the only truly recognizable one belonging to Vasquez's mother. Her expression hadn't changed in all this time. No matter what was happening here, which witness was testifying, which lawyer was grandstanding—even when I'd seen her outside that day, rushing past as if I were the criminal—her forehead remained flat, undisturbed, her eyes black and empty, her lips level and unrevealing. I imagined that she knew as well as I that her son was guilty. And of course, I knew that this was not the first time she'd had to sit in a courtroom and wonder whether the next time she saw her son it would be behind glass. I pictured her doing just that not long ago, holding a phone against her ear and a hand on the glass, that cold transparent slab the closest she could come to touching her son's skin.

Her expression was matched by his, though his face was unmarred by lines, its hardness firmer, less inscrutable. Unjaded by time, he was less skillful at hiding his anger, a seething hatred evident in the stiffness of his jaw, his energy focused on keeping his teeth together so he wouldn't scream. This entire process was an affront to him, these twelve people just interfering strangers with no right to judge.

With no verdict to present, the proceedings had lost their TV glamour.

Judge Reilly leaned forward. "On the charge of possession, the jury has not reached a unanimous verdict. Is that correct?" She was looking directly at me, bidding me with her eyes to stand.

I rose in the box. "That's correct, Your Honor."

She nodded. She knew all of this. It was just a formality, performance. "Have you polled the jury?"

"Yes, Your Honor."

"And everyone agrees that you are hopelessly deadlocked?"

"Yes, Your Honor."

She turned her eyes now to the rest of the jurors. A few heads nodded.

"Very well, then. Ladies and gentlemen, the Court thanks you for your time and your hard work. You are dismissed."

And it was over. In an instant, like the flipping of a switch, this episode of my life was done. I suddenly felt like I'd done something wrong, like I'd wasted everyone's time. The jury had been useless, and now the judge couldn't wait to get rid of us, like a singer who couldn't hold a note or a date who used the wrong fork.

The bailiff led us back to the jury room and collected our badges. As I pulled the lanyard over my head, I spotted Nancy on the other side of the table. We drifted toward each other and silently drew in for a hug. With my head on her shoulder, hers on mine, I felt my eyes welling up. It might have been the gravity of the situation, or just the disappointment, regret that we were letting a criminal go free. I hadn't fought hard enough—that was the thought rushing through my head now. I had given up too quickly, let Don's stubbornness intimidate me. I knew what was right, and I'd let him block it.

As the tears spilled onto my cheeks, I felt my whole body relax, and I was suddenly aware of how rigid it had been—throughout the morning, throughout the past two weeks. As the tension dripped away, it left my entire body trembling. I held on to Nancy a beat longer than appropriate, a second or two after I felt her begin to pull away. I held on because I didn't trust my feet.

Over Nancy's shoulder, I spotted Billie buttoning her sweater, gathering her purse. She smiled gently, eyes crinkling, sealed lips curling toward her cheeks.

As Nancy and I released each other, I saw Don's back rushing through the door— escaping like an able-bodied man barging past a child toward a lifeboat, hoping no one would notice as he returned to his craved-for invisibility, and his cigarettes.

The others moved through the room to say goodbye, the relief clear on their faces, the same trouble in their eyes that I felt behind my own. The men shook hands, the women lightly tapped shoulders, everyone making a conscious effort to look one another in the eye. It had suddenly become a strangely intimate affair. We had shared an experience, an all-encompassing experience, and felt momentarily bonded, like survivors of a crisis, an accident, a war.

Billie came up to me, adjusting her purse strap. She gave me a quick hug and, drawing away, looked me piercingly in the eye. "We do what we can do," she said. "It's okay if it's not perfect. We just do what we can do."

And she smiled again.

Instantly, I was ashamed of my tears, but when I felt a matching smile on my own face all those feelings washed away. I believed her. We touched hands softly as she pulled away, and I watched her go.

CHAPTER 25

REASONABLE DOUBT

I was already on my second martini when the boys started to arrive. My limbs felt light, jelly-like, and I realized I hadn't eaten anything since leaving court. In my thirties, I'd had no trouble downing three strong drinks over the course of a couple of hours. These days the effect was happily rapid, though it was easy to cross the line. Before long, the delightful buzz would turn into nausea and I'd have to switch to water or just call it a night.

I'd found a table just before the overhang, affording a convenient view of the entire room. The top half of the Dutch door was open, letting cool air waft through. I spotted Oscar and Rafe as they arrived, letting the bottom half swing shut behind them like something out of *Green Acres*. Rafe, arching his neck, scoped the room from side to side until he caught sight of my hand waving subtly from the corner.

"Are we incognito this evening?" Oscar asked.

"Yes," I said, "the FBI is after me. They're looking for the well-hung juror."

"Ooh, is it over?"

I nodded. I was about to speak when the waitress came by, holding her empty tray vertically against her chest. "What can I get you?" she asked.

The boys ordered martinis of their own. I decided to nurse

mine, and asked for a glass of water to make it last longer.

"So what happened?" Oscar said. Elbows on the table, he opened his hands as if waiting to catch something.

I described the case to them in broad outline. Rafe took it all in, eyes narrowed in concentration, while beside him, Oscar shook his head. He'd heard it all before.

"So did you convict the little shit?" he asked when I was done.

I laughed, toying absently with the stem of my glass. "No. We deadlocked, 10 to 2 guilty."

"You were in the 10, I assume?"

"Yep, that's me. Heartless bitch."

Rafe looked puzzled. "That's insane," he said. "All you had to do was find that he had the gun in his possession, right? And there he is, with a self-inflicted bullet hole in his leg and a gun in the car. Two plus two equals four."

"Not in court," Oscar said. "Sometimes two plus two equals three."

"This one guy, Don, was obsessed with reasonable doubt," I told them. "He wouldn't shut up about it, and clearly he didn't understand what it means."

Oscar sighed. "Some jurors get full of themselves," he said. "It's a big deal, sitting on a jury, especially for people who lead otherwise obscure lives. This was probably the most exciting thing that's ever happened to your Don."

The waitress appeared and carefully laid down the drinks.

"He reminded me of someone in my creative writing class in college," I said. "She was the worst writer in the class. It was like reading juvenile Danielle Steel. But whenever it was someone else's turn to be workshopped, she'd spill out all these *rules*. What's 'at stake' for the character, she'd ask. And then she'd complain that the story didn't follow a three-act structure. Or that it was all 'tell' and no 'show.' If someone had brought in a manuscript of *Mrs. Dalloway*—which, believe me, she never heard of and probably still hasn't read—she'd think it was a complete mess and talk about how the writer would be better off modeling *The Other Side of Midnight*."

Oscar laughed. "So you know exactly what I'm talking about. A little knowledge is a dangerous thing."

"I feel terrible," I said. "We let this obviously guilty guy back on the street."

"They're all guilty," Oscar said. "That's why I moved to corporate."

"Right," Rafe said. "Because god knows corporations never do anything wrong." He laughed. "What about the other half of the two?"

I sighed. "Heart of gold," I said. "I think she felt sorry for the guy."

"Oh, Christ," said Oscar. "The kiss of death on a jury. Like an Evangelical in a science class."

Brendan suddenly appeared behind him, John in tow.

"Hey guys," Brendan said, patting Oscar on the shoulder. "Talking about us?"

John was smiling broadly, but there was a dullness in his eyes. He was putting up a good front. He hadn't said a word to anyone except Brendan, but we all knew. And he knew we all knew. Our crowd was quite efficient at gossip. It made things easier: you never had to tell your story twice.

"What's everyone drinking?" John asked, a painfully forced pertness in his voice.

"The usual," Oscar said, "fire and brimstone."

I nodded. Though the waitress was hovering only a couple of tables away, John made his way to the bar while Brendan took a seat beside me.

"Well," Oscar said, "welcome back to the real world."

"What happened?" Brendan asked.

"The trial," I said.

"It's over? Why didn't you call me?"

"I had an appointment with a martini."

John returned with drinks for Brendan and himself, and we scooched our chairs around to make room at the table. "What are you guys talking about?" he asked.

"My trial," I said. Already I was tired of reliving it, so I summarized as concisely as I could.

John looked distracted. I'd hoped my story would get his mind off Wayne, but so far it wasn't working.

"What's everyone doing for Pride?" Rafe asked.

Brendan shook his head. "Pride is over."

"It's not even June yet!" Rafe persisted.

"No," Brendan said, "I mean it's *over* over. I don't even recognize the damn thing anymore. It used to be about celebrating who we are. Now all we do is celebrate the corporations that pander to us for one month of the year."

"I think all those nearly naked boys dancing on the floats would disagree."

Brendan shook his head. "What I used to look forward to was Pink Saturday. You know, just us, the neighborhood, getting together for a little street party of our own before the excess of the parade. But they've taken that away from us now, too. It's like Halloween—the streets full of straight people with strollers pretending to be hip."

Oscar laughed. "I have to agree. When was the last time Pride was fun?"

"The late nineties," Brendan said. "AIDS slowed down and

the calls for marriage began. When the oppression ended, so did the party."

Clearly, Oscar was in no mood for another Brendan rant. He turned back to John. "So what happened?"

"To what?"

"Wayne."

John froze in his seat for a moment before finally reaching for his glass. "It's complicated," he said. His jaw was set, the rest of his face as smooth as ice. He took another sip, and when he drew the glass away a calmness had returned to his expression. He placed the glass back down on the table, in the dead center of his napkin.

"What did he say?" asked Rafe softly. Rafe, the only one of us who could calm someone down with a look, the only one whose eyes could naturally, effortlessly, convey compassion.

John looked directly at him, ignoring the rest of us. "The usual excuses. He blamed his work. It's so intense right now, he said, he wasn't able to give the relationship what it deserved. He was sparing me."

"*It's not you, it's me,*" Brendan said with a sly smile.

"So what do you think is really going on?" Rafe asked.

John shrugged—just the tiniest lift of a shoulder, like brushing off a bug. "I don't know. Maybe his heart wasn't in it."

"We've all been there," Brendan said. "On both sides."

I saw again that shell-shocked look in Wayne's eyes at the bookstore—stumbling into a landscape he'd never seen before, where there were no markers to navigate by.

John recovered quickly and cast us an almost-smile. "Well, no point in wallowing. Life is too short."

"Ain't that the truth," said Oscar.

Brendan's face softened. "But still," he said, tapping John's hand, "you have to grieve. For a bit, anyway."

John's smile was more forced than ever, cheeks straining against gravity.

Brendan continued. "Relationships aren't the only answer." He winked at Oscar and Rafe. "I used to think the top priority in my life was love. A good relationship would make me happy, and nothing else could compare. And, of course, I had that. Stan made me happy. Those years with him were terrific." He turned his eyes toward his fingers, drumming silently against the table-top. "And when he died, I thought I would, too. But I didn't." He looked up, but his eyes were focused on the distance, as if he saw something there, something essential.

"I kept going," he said. "And eventually, *I* was enough. Just me."

John touched Brendan's shoulder, pulled him back into the room. "Wow," he said, "this has gotten awfully heavy. Sorry to bring back all that."

"No," Brendan replied, shaking his head. "No, it's all good."

Oscar straightened up in his chair. "Who needs another drink?"

The nervous laughter erupted, followed by a chorus of "Me!" and the downing of every glass on the table.

My heart lifted as I watched them. We'd sat here so often to-gether—mulling over problems, celebrating successes, reliving a past that grew more vivid by the day. Our nights together were built into the fabric of my life, like a given. And every now and then, it would hit me—how crucial the ritual was, how much love was at the base of it.

They seemed constant to me, unchanged over the years, while I saw myself as fumbling all the way to this point—still haunt-ed by every misstep, every regret. I could see the changes in my character but struggled to forgive myself for the mistakes, no matter how long ago or frivolous they were.

In the past, there had always been a reason to quit a relationship, a job, a favorite hangout. But the person who had left Barry and let Garrett slip through his fingers, who had let friendships die from lack of tending, was someone else. I knew it in the abstract—the immaturity, the fear that had driven so much of my life then, the implacable effect that lack of experience had had on my ability to understand what was happening at any given moment and what to do about it. Maybe *that* Craig couldn't have behaved any differently, couldn't have chosen another path. Maybe I hadn't even known that a different path was available until now, when I could look back and see where the two diverged. You can only see life backwards, but you have to live it in the other direction and continually plunge yourself into darkness.

I had trouble now taking my eyes off John's face—that combination of equanimity and defeat, as if nothing surprised him anymore, as if the future didn't matter, as if the past were enough.

And then Wayne's face came to me, eyes glittering because the future was everything, because it was so much bigger than the past.

And I wondered which side I was on.

CHAPTER 26
SAFE LANDING

Cassandra didn't stick around to see the sky fall in. Shortly after the announcement of the sale, she took a receptionist job at a tattoo parlor in the Mission. So by the time the fire sale at the store started, she was checking in hipsters who wanted Chinese ideograms and Disney characters (ironic, of course) painted on their bodies.

The sale was pretty easy to prepare. All we had to do was put up signs that read *50% off! Everything must go!* Business was brisk every day, but we kept pulling inventory out of the storeroom to replenish the shelves, so it took a while to notice the growing emptiness.

When the realization finally came—a week before the doors would close for good—it hit with a thud.

The shelves were growing more and more disheveled. Without a tight alignment to keep them vertical, books were toppling against one another and forming little pyramids. The display tables had become an untidy mess that I kept rearranging. There was no point anymore in being a stickler about separating genres, let alone alphabetizing. At this point, the place looked more like a bargain basement, where the whole point seemed to be plundering for hidden gems.

I meandered through the store, trying to keep the place from looking too much like Dresden. One by one, dozen by dozen, books disappeared, color draining from the displays, leaving only bare slabs of dusty wood behind. This—the place I'd often had to drag myself to over the years—in its decline took on an unexpected aura, revealing itself as something my heart had been secretly in love with, cheating on my mind. It felt like a major ending—not just of my job, or the store. Something was passing away, something crucial, leaving yoga mats in its wake.

I was wandering through the remains of the fiction section—tall bookcases lining an entire wall—when I spotted her. A familiar swirl of gray hair piled up in a bun, and a tie-dyed loose blouse, a riot of color.

"Billie?" I said, approaching cautiously. I couldn't be sure until I caught her eye.

She lifted her head from the book cracked open in her hand. "Craig. I was hoping I'd find you here." She came in for a brief embrace. "I heard the store was closing and I remembered you saying you worked here, so I thought I'd take a look around."

It was odd to see her in this context—no cold paneled walls, no pretending to like bad coffee. "Thanks for coming. It's wonderful to see you."

"It's a shame what's happening," she said. "Bookstores of all things, just dying everywhere." She looked around the room, shaking her head piteously. "There's magic in bookstores. Don't people know that anymore?"

I desperately wanted to change the subject. "How have you been?" It had been nearly two weeks since the trial.

"Oh, I'm fine. A few aches and pains, but life is good. As long as you're breathing, life is good."

I forgot for a moment that we had disagreed at the trial. What mattered was that we had come through it together. Like a plane crash, or college.

"So what's next?" she asked. "For you."

I shrugged. "I don't know. Just take some time off, I think, and see what I want to be when I grow up."

She paused thoughtfully, fingers delicately grazing the back of the book, a black-and-white photo of Toni Morrison. "You know, I may know of something. Are you familiar with the Harrison Foundation?"

"For queer youth? Yes. Don't they have an office on Market Street?"

She nodded. "Just a few blocks away. I'm on the board, and we're about to lose our executive director. She's moving on to a new job in Portland. I think you might be a good fit. Do you have any nonprofit experience?"

"Well, the bookstore never turned much of a profit, if that counts." I looked around the store. Joel was trying to make sense of a display table, which seemed to have become a dropping-off point for books people decided against.

"But really," I said, "executive director? That seems like a big responsibility for a newbie. I'm not sure I'm qualified."

She chuckled. "It's a very small nonprofit. And from what I saw in the jury room, you definitely have the management skills. And heart. Those are the most important qualities. I'll put in a word if you like."

"That would be wonderful."

"It's so rewarding, working with young people. They really need the support of mentors, especially these days."

On cue, I heard a pile of books tumble to the floor. When I turned, Joel was standing sheepishly behind the display table. He quickly bent down and started to pick up the mess.

"Thank you," I said to Billie. "I could use a new adventure."

We exchanged contact information and she turned back to the shelves. "Do you have any Forster left?" she asked. "I let someone borrow my copy of *Howards End* ages ago and, of course, they never returned it."

"Let's see. God knows where anything is anymore. It could be in the gardening section at this point."

Miraculously, I found a copy, and Billie beamed. "It's one of my favorites," she said, "and I think the time is ripe to read it again. I've always had an affinity for Mrs. Wilcox. Now that I've gotten older, I wonder if my perspective will be any different."

She trundled away with several books and Joel rang her up. With a wave from the doorway, she disappeared into the evening.

I was struggling with the Graham Greenes when a nasal voice whispered at my shoulder: "I think books are so decorative, don't you, Mrs. Burnside?"

I snorted out a laugh and turned to find Brendan, eyebrows arched, a lopsided grin on his lips. "How's it going?" he asked.

"It's fine," I said. "If we'd sold half this many books on a regular basis, Angela wouldn't be getting rid of the place."

"It looks good." He moved in closer as someone pushed past to reach for a *Harry Potter*. I was surprised we had any left at this point. Above it, I spotted a clump of Dostoevsky volumes gathering dust. "Can I buy you a drink?"

"Always."

With a smaller staff, I'd decided to start closing at 7:00 each night, so there were only a few minutes left in the workday. I put Joel in charge and led Brendan back to the office to fetch my bag.

Even the office looked different. I still had personal things lying around—a Newton's cradle on the desk, a Rubik's cube I'd never been able to figure out—but there were fewer papers, and a clump of empty boxes in the corner, ready for returns on the books we wouldn't be able to sell.

"Are you going to miss it?" Brendan asked. He fingered a parachuting doll hanging from my desk lamp, a gift from Garrett. A reminder, he'd said, that somewhere there's always a soft place to land.

"Sure," I said. "A bookstore is a pretty civilized place to work." I grabbed my jacket from the back of the chair. As we made our way out through the store, I imagined what the last day would be like—the shelves completely empty, dust bunnies having races on the floorboards.

It was a gorgeous evening, a full moon glowing over the city and making the streetlights almost superfluous. I left my jacket open to the brisk air as we strolled past colorful Victorians, turning on Castro and dipping down the incline toward 18th Street.

"I have a quick stop to make," I said as we reached John's office. Eyeglass frames sat in the window in a smorgasbord of colors and shapes. The light was dim inside, no sign of life.

"What are we doing here?" he asked. "Isn't he closed for the day?"

"Not to me," I said, pushing the door open. "My new glasses are finally ready, and John said I could stop by after work." The frames had been out of stock when John placed the order, so the glasses were weeks late in arriving.

A bell tinkled gently as we stepped inside and closed the door.

"Be right out!" called a voice from the back.

Brendan was scanning the display of frames when John appeared. "Finally breaking down and getting glasses?" he asked.

"No," Brendan said, quickly turning around. "I can't stand the things. That's why I got LASIK years ago."

I scoffed. "You find glasses uncomfortable, but you had no problem letting a laser slice through your eye?"

"It's all about vanity, my dear."

John gestured with the black glass case he'd carried in from the back. "Speaking of vanity," he said, "you're going to look quite dashing in these, Craig." He gestured toward a small table near the window.

Sitting across from me, he slid the glasses onto my face. "Look at me," he said. He peered back and forth, adjusted one side of the frame. "Is the bridge too tight?"

"No," I said, "they feel fine."

"Good." He drew away and angled the standing mirror on the table toward me.

The frames were more dramatic than I remembered—neon blue, thick on the sides but thin around the lenses, narrow rectangles that just covered my eyes. Holding my head straight, I glanced across the room and then down at the paperwork on the table, testing the progressive lenses. Everything—near and far—looked shockingly clear.

"They'll take a little getting used to," John said, noting my hesitation. "So much better than having to switch between glasses."

"Yes," I said. "I can see that."

"Literally," said Brendan, forcing a laugh from us all.

For now, though, it wasn't how I saw that concerned me, but what I saw. The frames were bold, the color drawing attention. In the past, when I'd slipped on my wireframes—lightweight, nearly invisible—my appearance barely changed. Even the tortoiseshells hadn't stood out too much. But these glasses were a statement. They seemed to alter the shape of my face. Instead of blending in, they defined—like a uniform or a trendy haircut.

I stared at my reflection, searching for something familiar—the old me, the me I was used to.

"Are you free now?" Brendan asked John. "We're going to get a drink."

"Sure." John paused, and I felt his eyes on me. "Are you okay there?"

I turned away from the man in the mirror and smiled. John's face looked sharper than before, my eyes shifting easily from him to the wall in the distance, bringing everything into focus at will. "Absolutely," I said.

CHAPTER 27
ONLY ONE IS A WANDERER

I hardly knew what to do with myself now that the trial was over and the bookstore was dying. I drifted through the next week, as the closing sale sputtered to an end while the neighborhood ironically bloomed with Pride signs and the steady influx of tourists that swarmed in every June. Pride was our Christmas and New Year's rolled into one. It had always seemed like the beginning of something. But this year, I felt disconnected, a crasher at my own party.

I wandered more. Whenever I was between things—lovers, jobs, projects—I wandered. At first, I wanted to be alone, just because I was sick of talking about all the thoughts wreaking havoc in my brain. But after a while, the solitude itself became the desired thing. I craved it so I could get to know myself again before venturing back to the world of obligations and other people's expectations.

In my head, there were still only two reasons to go to a bar: to hang out with friends or to pick someone up. So on those occasions when I did venture in alone, I often brought a book as cover—a signal that I was just here for a relaxing drink. The stratagem wouldn't have worked anywhere else. Twin Peaks was the only place where the light was good enough to read anything more than the labels on the bottles behind the bar.

Volume 2 was as physically heavy as its predecessor, albeit lighter in tone. I plopped it down on the bar, splayed open like a corpse on the slab.

"That looks serious," the bartender said, settling my drink beside the book.

Today, for the first time in ages, I was craving a cosmo. The bartender had squinted at me, wondering perhaps if I was really serious—a middle-aged man in 2019 asking for a drink to catapult him back to his youth. Even Sarah Jessica Parker didn't drink those poofy things anymore.

But now, he'd produced it with the ritualized nonchalance I'd come to expect here—the old San Francisco, where quirkiness was something to be admired rather than judged.

"It is," I replied. "And this isn't half of it."

"There's another one like that?"

"Five," I said.

"Wow, that's commitment."

I smiled. "One thing I can commit to is a book."

He laughed. "Well, books probably don't break your heart or give you a headache."

"Not usually."

We were in the sweet spot of the day, before rush hour would bring the crowds, so the bartender was hanging out at my end, wiping down the bar, organizing the tray of garnishes—olives, shiny cocktail onions, perfectly formed lime wedges.

"How long have you been here?" I asked.

"This bar? Don't remind me. About 12 years now."

"You must like it."

"I love it," he said. "Nice people, quiet. It feels exactly the same as it did the day I started. Nothing else in this neighborhood is recognizable, so it's like an oasis."

[329]

I'd taken a spot on the north side of the bar. Only when the room became very crowded would people fill in the narrow space between the bar and the window. There was a feng shui comfort in knowing that the only people behind me were on the other side of glass. A couple of men took up stools at the bar, a few more dotted at various tables by the window, whispering, laughing. No attitude, no scowls. Nobody came here to nurse their troubles or vaunt themselves over the world.

"I've seen you here a lot," the bartender added.

"A lot?"

"Don't worry, I don't think you're an alkie or something. Standing here, I just get to know the regulars."

I'd never been a regular anywhere, and suddenly here I was, nursing a drink in my favorite spot, with the same view out the window, familiar faces all around, furnishings that never changed. It seemed sudden, anyway, in the way something—snow on the sidewalk, an age spot on your hand—accumulates gradually until it reaches a tipping point and you become abruptly aware of its presence and shocked by the fact that you hadn't noticed it creeping up on you all along.

A heavyset guy at the other end of the bar raised a hand. The bartender excused himself and drifted away—no doubt to pour something a bit more manly.

He was right, I thought: I had become a regular, and I wasn't quite sure what that meant. An acknowledgment of my age? Surrender of expectations? In the old days, a bar had been a transitory place—act 1 of the evening, where you met someone you'd spend act 2 with in the dark. I gazed down at the book and realized that it wasn't just a cover, a way of keeping conversation at bay. It was a marker. The chase was over. And sometimes a drink was just a drink.

I turned my attention to the unnaturally pink liquid in the glass. The bartender had gone overboard with the triple sec; the drink was cloyingly sweet. Or maybe I'd just forgotten what cosmos were like. They'd been our regular drink, Oscar's and mine, back when our youthful arrogance wouldn't allow us to even glance through these windows on our way to someplace trendier.

I'd never wanted to have a regular hangout, whether a bar or a vacation spot. A regular place would take time away from all the other things life had to offer. As much as I loved Paris, I had gone there only once. Money and time were limited, and other places beckoned—Rome, Prague, Barcelona—each of which I visited exactly once. I hadn't even bothered to drop a coin in the Trevi Fountain, as if that were too much like tempting fate—ensuring a return trip at the expense of somewhere else, somewhere perhaps just as exciting. I'd left every city satisfied but wanting more. The unfinished nature of each vacation made it all the more delicious, kept the desire alive long after I'd returned home to an unavoidable routine.

The Castro was still full of bars, even if most of the ones I'd grown up on were long gone. I'd tried the newer ones, the hip places that had sprung up recently on the sites of old favorites—Edison lightbulbs hanging over shiny bartops where there had once been worn wood, initials scratched in the surface beside water rings that would never go away, shadows of the glasses held by thousands of strangers over dozens of years—but, inevitably, a couple of visits were enough to prove that I didn't belong.

I returned to the book, one hand grazing the page while the other lay gently on the bartop. I was giving the new glasses a workout—training myself to look through the bottom of the lenses as I read, back to the top when I raised my head. At first the transition was a bit vertiginous, but I was getting used to it.

The bartender had been right: the book was a commitment. But, like love, there was something hypnotic about it—whole pages dedicated to peeling potatoes or setting a table. Or maybe it was just the exoticism of the culture, the contrast Knausgaard drew between his native Norway and his wife's Sweden. Despite our origins, no one in my family had ever been to Scandinavia. That whole world had always seemed monolithic to me, a cliché.

My ancestors had come from Sweden in the 1870s. Aside from the blond hair and blue eyes everywhere in my family, there were no real signs of their origin—no family recipes handed down from the old country, not a word of Swedish spoken. I was the only one who seemed to take much interest. In my twenties I had obsessively absorbed Bergman. When I mentioned one of his films to anyone in the family, describing the plot, they would look at me in disbelief. That's what our ancestors had tried to get away from, they seemed to say. Why would I want to dredge any of it up now?

After each page, I looked up from the book. The room was starting to fill up. A couple of stools away I spotted a familiar face, but one I couldn't quite place.

He was older, a full head of white hair flying every which way over his brow. Young men created such unkemptness deliberately, forming unnatural peaks in their hair with overpriced substances that left a greasy sheen. They would have envied him if he weren't invisible to them.

His thick fingers, slightly gnarled, wrapped around a tall glass, but his eyes were focused behind the bar, a gentle smile on his lips. He was watching the bartender mix a drink, studying every motion like a painter working on a portrait.

The sun was bright behind his head, a last gasp before settling in for the night. When he finally turned to me, his face was hard to read, my eyes slightly blinded by the sharp light through the window. I caught a polite smile and a nod of acknowledgment.

"I love these long days," he said, "don't you?"

I fumbled for a response.

"Sorry," he said with a soft chuckle. "I noticed how you were squinting into the sun. You should enjoy it."

I laughed. "I should switch to my sunglasses." I'd tried transition lenses before, but they tended to turn uncomfortably dark on hazy days, fooled by the UV rays peeking through the fog.

As my eyes adjusted to the light—or the sun fell deeper behind the hill, it was hard to tell which—the old man's features grew more and more familiar. And suddenly, with a shock of recognition, I knew who he was.

"You get used to it," he said. "The glare of sunlight is the price we pay for refusing to hide."

He'd been in the same spot when I'd seen him before, but not alone. He looked a bit older up close, the lines on his face deeper, the eyebrows bushier and more wiry. At the same time, his eyes—which I'd been unable to see from my perch in the balcony—were lively, a bright blue that belied the haggard appearance of his skin.

At the moment of placing him, an anxious quiver ran through my belly. I imagined Roland Talbott returning, taking the space between us. If they were still in touch, if they really even knew each other at all. Even now, with the trial relegated to the past, it seemed inappropriate to be within two degrees of separation from Vasquez. But if this old man was indeed still involved with Talbott, I wondered if I should warn him, let him know the kind of circles his friend traveled in.

"I've never seen you in here before," the man said. "Do you

live in the neighborhood?"

"Yes," I stammered. "I just don't get out much." It was funny, I thought, how I could be a regular to the bartender but a stranger to another regular.

"At your age? That's a shame."

"I used to go out a lot more," I confessed. "Middle age doesn't agree with me."

"Oh, that's absurd." The man shook his head. "You're in the prime of life."

Who was I to argue, I thought. This man had 20 years on me, and he was fucking someone half my age.

"You're as young as you feel, that's what the doctors keep telling me." He hunched over his beer, smile broadening. "I'll let you in on a little secret."

"What's that?" Now seemed the time to stop being coy. I slid my drink toward him and moved onto the adjacent stool.

"When I force myself to stop worrying about the aches and pains and how gray my hair is, I feel a hell of a lot better. I focus on the world around me, the way it is now as opposed to how it was in my day—the young people, the storefronts that have changed hands, the buildings going up everywhere. And inside I feel like I'm still 25 years old. It's the world that's changed; I'm still me." He lifted his eyebrows with the confidence of a magician pulling a rabbit out of a hat.

"That's lovely," I said. "Because I have to tell you, things have changed a lot, inside and out."

"I've lived in this neighborhood for over 40 years now," he said. "From its heyday." His smile grew warmer. "We've been through a lot here."

"It must have been so different then."

"It was. But the heart of it is still here."

"I don't know. Sometimes it feels like everything I loved is fading away."

"Some of it, maybe. But we thought that before. You missed the eighties, hunh?"

"Yeah," I said. "I came here in the nineties, right after college."

"Well, the neighborhood survived that. We can survive whatever this is." He gestured toward the window, a street that, in his day, had probably teemed with young shirtless men, pioneers staking their claim on every street corner.

I bought him another drink, and he started to tell me his story. It was a story I'd heard before, a cliché by now—a young man moves to the city, discovers himself in a place where all the limits of his earlier life shatter in one fell swoop. It was my story, too, albeit a couple of decades removed. It was the story of this neighborhood, this unique place that had been charted by his generation and had nurtured everyone who'd come here since. He talked about the exciting moments, the people, the street parties, drag queens marching proudly through the neighborhood, men making out in doorways in the middle of the afternoon. He gave just the highlights of the rougher patches—the obituaries piling up in the paper, the faces that vanished unexpectedly. When they did, he said, when you realized there was someone, a regular feature of the neighborhood, whom you hadn't seen for days, then weeks—you knew, and you didn't ask what had happened. There was no need to ask.

"Cultures are like people," he said. "They have a life cycle, just a much longer one. Even the worst things fade away, and new waves of people come in to replace what's been lost. The world goes on."

We toasted to that, his glass still nearly full, untouched while he'd told his stories.

"So," he said, "what about you? You married? Everyone your age is married these days."

I laughed. "No," I said, "I don't see that happening anytime soon."

"Still playing the field, then."

"Not really. I'm reassessing. I broke up with someone recently, and I'm not quite sure why I was ever involved with him."

"Been there!" he said. "Lust does crazy things to your head. And love is even trickier."

"Oh no," I said quickly, "it wasn't love."

He looked me in the eye—scoping my expression, searching, perhaps, for a truth beyond words. "So what do you want now?" he asked.

"Do I have to want something?"

His eyes, pale azure, opened wide. "Yes," he said. "You always have to want something."

To change the subject, to veer off the minefield of my love life, I told him other stories. He was upset to hear that the bookstore was closing; he said he'd been going there for years. But I'd never noticed him browsing the shelves. Perhaps I was as guilty as anyone else of being blind to men I wasn't attracted to.

"Well," he said, "at least some institutions are still here." He tapped the bartop. "The bartenders don't even ask what I want anymore. They can tell from my mood whether it's a Blue Moon or a margarita."

His eyes sparkled when he laughed. I imagined him being a real charmer in his day.

"I used to go to all sorts of places," he said, "but priorities change. Now all I really want is a quiet place to relax."

"So you don't get out much either?"

"No," he said with a laugh. "No husband, no boyfriend. I'm

too tired to put in the effort." He leaned toward me conspiratorially and whispered, "The truth is, it's much easier to just pay for it."

"Where do you meet them—online?" I asked.

He leaned back and shook his head disdainfully. "God, no. One of the pleasures of being my age is I can opt out of all that folderol. No, I meet them here and there, the old-fashioned way." He tilted his head suddenly as an idea struck him. "As a matter of fact, not long ago I met one right here, just where you're sitting."

I made a show of looking down toward my stool. "Really?"

He smiled. "Lovely young man. Broad shoulders, kind of a chiseled face. Not much of a conversationalist, though. It was pretty much strictly business. In fact," he added, leaning in again, "he was obviously straight. He didn't do anything more than open his pants for me. But I couldn't find fault with that. What red-blooded male wouldn't want to get his dick sucked and collect 50 bucks into the bargain?"

We laughed together. I wondered about Talbott being gay for pay, and what Vasquez and his other friends would think of it.

"Did you ever see him again?" I asked now.

"Franco?" he said. Of course, I thought, he'd used a sexy pseudonym. "No."

I tried to hide my sense of relief. "Just be careful," I said.

He laughed. "No worries there. It doesn't happen very often, anyway. I have too many other things going on in my life to worry much about sex. Besides, you'd be surprised how seldom the subject comes up at my age. Pun intended." He winked again.

He kept busy with other things, he said—staying in touch with friends, reading all the books he'd put off during his working years, volunteering at a nearby hospice.

"So no," he said, "I don't need a man. What I do need is somewhere I can fit in. Some place where the drinks aren't watered down, and neither is the conversation."

"I'll drink to that," I said, and our glasses clinked once more.

CHAPTER 28
NO FURTHER QUESTIONS

We met for coffee at a Starbucks south of Market. I had seldom taken the metro this far before, past Embarcadero station, where the train emerged from the tunnel and followed the curve of the bay. Here, on the edge of the neighborhood, the buildings were mostly new, but only a few stories high, in a maroon and cream palette that felt consistent with old San Francisco. The other side of the street was dominated by the Bay Bridge and the ball park, whose name changed every time a new sponsor came along. If I'd cared more about sports, I might have been better able to keep track.

I rode the train to the end of the line, just across from the Cal-train station, which commuters were already scurrying to for the afternoon ride home to the peninsula. As I strode down the platform, I could see them crowded inside, anxious to get back to their lawns and two-car garages, to push their children on swing sets in the backyard.

The opposite side of the street was lined with condo complexes, and I marveled at the reverse evolution, homes coming before all the reasons that people traditionally moved to a neighborhood—restaurants, shops, nightlife. Aside from the occasional sandwich shop and the Safeway on the corner, there was nothing to draw anyone here. It was still a work in progress, I supposed.

Those square homes were no doubt here merely for their proximity to the start-ups dotting the neighborhood and the trains that could whisk people to Silicon Valley without the nightmare of 101. Work and sleep. Until they had kids and needed the lawn.

When I'd first moved to the city, not long after the earthquake led to the removal of the Embarcadero freeway, this whole area had been full of warehouses, which I'd known only because they were occasionally transformed into decadent party spaces. Unlike the Castro, SoMa had never had much character to begin with. I felt like a tourist here: I had no ties to what had come before, so I could simply accept what I found.

I located the café and pushed my way inside. The place was fairly empty, rush hour no doubt draining it quickly. I ordered a latte and brought it to a table along the side wall.

Caffeine was probably the last thing I needed, considering that I was feeling a little anxious about this meeting. His text had come out of the blue, but it was so empathetic I couldn't resist. With all that had been going on, he said, he wanted to see how I was doing. Despite everything, he wanted us to be friends.

I cracked open my book, once again peering through a peep-hole at someone else's life, albeit one that he had laid bare for me to see.

"How's the book?"

I looked up at the end of a sentence. Holding a cup, he was smiling broadly, raised cheeks amplifying the crisp trim of his beard.

"Great," I said. "Just long." I shut the book as Wayne took the seat across from me.

"It's awfully heavy," he said. "You should get a Kindle."

I shook my head. "Never."

He laughed. "Moving must be a bitch."

"It is. Half the weight of my apartment is in books."

"But you love them," he said coyly. "The scent of mildew, the decaying pages, the splatter of mold spores on the binding."

"Exactly!" I said, laughing. "A Kindle is too antiseptic. Every time you pick up an old book, you're reminded of your own mortality."

"Well, that's cheerful." He pried off the lid of his coffee and emptied a pack of Nutrasweet into it.

"It is," I said. "I think it's important to be reminded of that. It makes you appreciate things while you can."

"You're an interesting man, Craig Amundsen."

"Thank you."

"So, the store," he said, snapping the lid back on. "It's all over?"

"Yes. Case in point: everything dies." I was tired of talking about the store, tired of worrying about myself. "What about you?" I asked. "Are you okay after …?"

"John? Yeah, I'm fine. It was the right thing to do." His eyes, bright with that golden glint, seemed to be smiling despite the downturn of his lips. "How is he? You must have seen him since."

"Yeah. He's okay. I think he understands."

"He's a really good man. He deserves someone who can give him what he wants."

"And what's that?"

He smiled. "Damned if I know. That was part of the problem. He didn't ask for anything. He was kind, very kind. We did the things I like to do, or he gave me space to do them on my own." He sighed. "It sounds cruel, but there were times when I felt I wasn't in a relationship, that it was just me making all the same decisions I'd have made if I were alone, only he was there."

"Maybe he was just afraid. I think he cared about you a lot, and he didn't want to push you away."

"It's ironic. That's exactly what he ended up doing."

I thought suddenly about Damien, who had never asked to be in charge of our relationship. I had thrust the power upon him, and became a witness to my own life.

Part of me wanted to protect John, or at least explain him. If I could explain him, maybe I could understand myself. "Some people find it hard to verbalize what they want."

"That fear of rejection thing again."

"Yeah, maybe." I tried to make light of it. "I was just raised to be passive-aggressive. My mother seemed to resent that other people couldn't read her mind."

He laughed. "Too bad you aren't psychic."

"How do you know I'm not?"

A lock of hair drooped over Wayne's forehead. "What am I thinking right now?"

The eyes again—still, hypnotic. I decided to change the subject.

"So," I said, "was *your* family dysfunctional?"

He laughed. "Immensely." He crossed his arms, and his head tilted as though to capture a memory. "My father's a workaholic, and my mother … well, she's an alcoholic. They like the rhyme."

"That must have been difficult."

"Oh, she was never falling-down drunk or anything like that. Just a few too many cocktails when her bridge club came over in the afternoon. We did get a lot of take-out. And the maid had the run of the place while she was passed out."

"The maid."

"I told you my father was a workaholic. Have you heard of Percy Financial? That's him. Money was something we were never short of."

"Where was this?"

"Greenwich, Connecticut. He put us up in a lovely big house and then took the train to the city every day. Saturdays included."

"I didn't even know you were from there," I said.

"You guys never asked."

"No," I said. "No, we didn't."

He spoke quickly, cutting off the possibility of a fainthearted apology. "It's okay. I was John's boyfriend. That was enough of an identifier, I suppose."

"It shouldn't be."

He lifted his eyebrows. "It makes it easier to dismiss people, don't you think? If you don't see them as … three-dimensional."

I had no answer for that one.

"Anyway," he said, "I escaped to boarding school and then college. Rutgers—close enough to go home when I wanted, far enough to have an excuse not to."

"And here?"

"I moved to the Bay Area for the work."

"Not to be gay?"

He laughed. "No. It's the center of new technology. And that, for good or ill, is me." He danced his cup on the tabletop. "Did you move here to be gay?"

"Oh yeah." I rested my chin in my hand, elbow against the table.

Wayne leaned forward. "I'm no poster child for my generation, but I have to say it was never that difficult for me. I never felt the need to define myself that way."

"Did you date girls?"

"No," he said swiftly, pursing his lips. "Well, does the prom count? And there was this girl in college who had a real crush on me and practically raped me one night." He rolled his eyes. "It didn't work."

The world had changed. Somehow, when I wasn't looking, the world had changed, and this was the result. He wasn't the antichrist, I thought. We had just wanted him to be.

We lingered at the café for a while, until rush hour slowed on the other side of the window and the sky began to take on a vaguely violet tint. I decided to forgo the subway, so we walked together, through SoMa and into the Mission. I could use the exercise, I thought, and the air was so inviting, as it often is in summer. The air in San Francisco, when it was cool, coming in off the ocean, tasted clean, delicious. I drank it in like water.

Wayne pointed out his favorite taqueria and shops, huge and colorful murals that defined the neighborhood. He'd moved to Mountain View when he first arrived in California. It was the place to be, but he'd soon tired of it. The suburban life, he said, reminded him too much of home. And there was nothing more different from home than San Francisco.

"I like the bustle," he said. "All these people running around, doing their own thing, I feed off their energy."

"How long have you been here, in the city?"

"Five years."

"Ah," I said, "a native."

He laughed.

"No, I mean it. That's what they say: if you've lived here five years, you're an honorary native. I mean, no one's *from* here, after all," I said with a wink.

I'd never been a winker.

As we talked, there was another conversation going on—the one inside my head. In the first, I was getting to know this particular man; in the second, I was trying to reconcile him with the image, the caricature, I'd carried around all these months. Yes, he was exceedingly clever, a little nerdy, a little naïve. But he was also surprisingly mature and personable, and I wondered whether John—or the rest of us—had restrained that. The few times we'd gotten together, those nights when John could pull him away from his work, he'd never said much. He'd tried to jump into our conversations, give his perspective on whatever topic was at hand, but he'd seldom talked about his own interests, his past, who he was. And no one had asked.

When John spoke about him—trying to justify his affection—everything he said sounded false, as if there were two Waynes, the one we all saw with our own eyes and the one John simply imagined and tried to pass off as real. I wondered now which of us had been deluding himself—John or me.

We rounded the corner onto Mission, fully alive at this time of day, with people streaming into restaurants, checking out the sidewalk sales in front of colorful shops. We passed one whose bright wall abutted a darker building—incongruous, cold—and I felt a sudden shiver.

My body seemed to get the message before my mind did. I stopped on the sidewalk, Wayne going on ahead for several paces before realizing I wasn't beside him. He backtracked and found me.

"What is it?" he asked. "Are you okay?"

I couldn't take my eyes off the black wall, the grimy windows, the orange neon. *Peppermill.*

"This is where it happened," I said, finally meeting Wayne's gaze.

"Where what happened?"

I hadn't told him much about the trial, beyond the circumstances of the charge and my disappointment at the result. Now, standing in the very spot, I told him the rest as I scoured the street.

I told him Vasquez's story about leaving the bar, standing where we were now when a car came by—there, between us and the barbershop across the street—a gun aimed out the passenger window, a finger pulling the trigger, Vasquez stunned and falling to the ground.

Looking down, I instinctively checked the sidewalk for blood stains, foolishly wondering if they could seep through pavement and become embedded, still visible all these months later.

I laughed at myself, at the insane sense inside me that if I just looked hard enough, the truth would be revealed—the images of that night lingering in the air like ghosts, and all I had to do was prime myself to feel them.

I shook my head to drive it all away, but the images lingered, the what-ifs. Vasquez's story, and an alternative version, the one I believed—Vasquez running away from Sanborn's house, the gun jangling in his pocket just before it went off.

I didn't realize I was frozen in place until Wayne's hand gently touched my shoulder. "Are you okay?"

I tried to smile. Something tumbled inside me. It all came rushing back—Sanborn's fate in Vasquez's hands, Vasquez's in mine. At any moment, a gun could come out of hiding. At any moment, a heart could be ripped open.

"Let's walk," Wayne said, draping an arm across my back. I strode in lockstep with him, the energy and the momentum entirely his.

When we turned the corner, my head noticeably cleared. A couple of blocks down the street, we stopped in front of a duplex, white wooden steps leading up to a pair of doors, bay windows on either side. In its own way, the house looked perfectly suburban. He identified it as his.

"Well," I said, "good night. I'm glad we could do this."

He strengthened his grip on my side. "No," he said, "come in. You're as white as a ghost, Craig. I'm not letting you walk home by yourself like this." He jerked his head toward the entrance. "I'll make you some coffee. Or a whiskey."

I let myself laugh. "Good whiskey?"

"I got it in Edinburgh."

"Okay, deal."

I followed him inside, into a surprisingly large apartment, artwork on every wall—original paintings he said he'd gotten for a steal at various galleries over the years, posters from the Musée d'Orsay, a Vermeer reproduction from the Rijksmuseum.

"Quite the collection," I said softly.

"See? I'm not just a computer geek." He smiled and headed for the sideboard. My side suddenly felt cold where his hand had been.

The room was lit by a single lamp near the front door, coaxing a golden glow from the dark furniture, pulling highlights from the creases in Wayne's violet shirt. When he guided me toward the couch, I nearly fell into it, sinking into soft cushions. The whiskey warmed me, filtering through every limb.

Wayne settled in beside me, curling a leg under himself so he could face me. "Feeling better?" he asked.

"Yes," I whispered, "thank you. I'm sorry about that. It's weird how this whole thing has affected me."

"The trial?"

I caught myself before responding with a kneejerk *yes*. "No," I said, "more than that. There's just been so much lately. The store, of course."

"And?"

"I had a break-up of my own a while ago," I said.

"Damien."

"Yes." I couldn't even remember whether Wayne had ever met him. I'd barely talked about him in the group, relegating our travails to one-on-ones, mostly with Oscar. There was no reason for him to even know Damien had ever existed.

"I'm sorry to hear that."

"It was for the best," I said. "We weren't really a good match."

"Why is that?"

"No common interests."

"He was a nerd like me, wasn't he?"

"Not quite," I said. "He's a computer guy, but without the ambition or the creativity of an entrepreneur." I looked around the room. "And no Vermeers on the wall."

I realized all at once that I hadn't yet articulated it all, even to myself. "Mostly, he just didn't feel, you know? He knew how to go through the motions. He knew how other people looked when they were feeling something. But I'm not sure he every really experienced the emotions he was expressing. Does that make any sense?"

Wayne said nothing. And I realized I wasn't asking him. I was asking myself. And yes, finally, it made sense.

When he spoke, his voice was a whisper, almost a draught in the air. "Did you ever realize that I had a crush on you?"

The room felt tighter suddenly, the walls closer. "I don't always notice those things," I confessed. "But I did wonder sometimes."

"Well, I did." His hand, beside mine on the couch, lifted slowly and settled on my thigh. "I do."

We kissed tentatively at first, like friends greeting each other at a party. In that moment, he was still John's boyfriend, something I wasn't allowed to touch. And in the next moment, with the next kiss, he was just Wayne, a gentle, handsome man who opened his lips to mine.

Later, in the bedroom, he cradled my head in the crook of his shoulder, and his hand—soft and smooth as pearls—slipped gently along my bare skin. His body was firm but a little soft in the belly, covered in fur darker than his beard. I longed to touch it, but he wouldn't let me linger, always directing things back to my pleasure. And in the darkness, the warmth, I let him. He kissed me from cheek to toe, his fingers exciting nerve endings I barely knew I had. And finally, I shuddered inside, a rush like waves ebbing and flowing, building in strength and intensity. I hadn't experienced it like this in a long time, my whole body alive, trembling under the skin. I stared up at the ceiling as the waves began to slow, and suddenly I was aware of Wayne's hand lying gently on my thigh—grounding me, holding me close.

CHAPTER 29
THE DEFENSE RESTS

The new kitchen was beautiful—ivory cabinets replacing the walnut that had stood there for years, sparkling new appliances, and a long island made of white granite, gray striations branching in multiple directions like arteries. I sat on a high stool on the outer side of the island, nursing a glass of Pinot Grigio while Rafe sliced tomatoes.

He gestured around the room with his knife. "Brendan took one look at the kitchen and his only comment was how much we'd increased the resale value of the house. As if the point of the renovation was to immediately turn around and sell the place."

I laughed. "He has a one-track mind, that one."

When I'd arrived, Rafe had given me a detailed tour of the renovations—the spice shelves that disappeared into the wall through pocket doors, the wifi-enabled refrigerator that somehow tracked what was in it. And it looked like you needed a degree from MIT to figure out the fancy faucet. The space was beautiful but intimidating. I'd be afraid to spill anything here. That was why, when asked, I'd opted for white wine.

Rafe scooped the tomatoes into a large wooden bowl that was already full of torn lettuce and purple onions. The room smelled of oregano from the lasagna baking in the oven.

"This is now officially my favorite room in the house," Rafe added. "Cooking is my meditation. I spend most of my days negotiating with other people, trying to argue without arguing, if you know what I mean. But when I come home, I can walk in here and be completely in charge and make something delicious. It's reassuring somehow."

"I know what you mean." But I didn't, really. Watching him mix the dressing—the slow pour of olive oil as he whisked—I suddenly felt a wave of envy, wondering if there was an equivalent in my own life. I enjoyed cooking, but not to the same degree. For me, it was a social thing—a way to entertain friends. Sitting quietly in this fresh space, this shrine to Rafe's passion, I was struck by the absence of a passion in my own life. At best, the things I enjoyed—books, music, theater—were passive activities. I had no creative outlet at my disposal. I was always an audience.

"If it were up to Oscar, we'd get take-out every night. He's so exhausted when he gets home, the last thing he wants to do is cook. It's too much like work for him, whereas for me it's rejuvenating."

In all these years, Rafe and I had had few occasions to be alone together, just the two of us. Oscar was the thing we had in common. Oscar was always there.

I hadn't wanted to like Rafe at first. I'd always been quick to judge my friends' lovers. Protectively, I would assess every word, every gesture, to make sure they were worthy of my friend, looking for signs of incompatibility, spying out evidence of cruelty or insensitivity. I would give them little tests—ask their opinion of my friend's favorite movie, evaluate their politics, their understanding of current events.

In Oscar's case, that effort had been critical. Oscar was opinionated. I told myself that he needed someone who cared about things as much as he did, someone who got upset at injustice and ignorance, someone who agreed that art was essential to life, that a city without good museums and an opera house wasn't worth living in.

Rafe understood all that, but I'd never sensed the same fire in him. He shared a lot of Oscar's interests, but none with the same enthusiasm. When Oscar went on a tirade about Tucker Carlson or Kim Kardashian, Rafe would sit quietly beside him, a pale grin on his face, and say nothing.

But over time I came to realize that that was exactly what Oscar needed. He needed someone to listen, to let him be himself, not to goad him on. They were yin and yang—gentle and angry, peaceful and impatient, enacting a graceful balance. Rafe, it turned out, was good for Oscar in ways I'd never even considered, and now he was the exception to the rule, the only partner of a friend for whom I felt the same degree of unconditional love.

"How has Oscar been lately?" I asked. "He seems stressed with work."

Rafe retrieved a wedge of Parmesan from the fridge and began to grate it. "He's always stressed with work. He loves the drama of being stressed with work."

Rafe had always been the quiet one. Every relationship assigns roles to people, and since Oscar was such a larger-than-life person, I'd assumed that was simply how it worked for them: Oscar gulped in the bulk of the oxygen, and Rafe sat back, silent and supportive.

"Do you ever feel drowned out?"

"Constantly," he replied, chuckling. "Don't you? Isn't that what we love about Oscar? But would you really want to be with someone who's exactly like yourself? He does his stuff and I do mine, and we're grateful for the things we can share. A nice meal, a bottle of wine, good friends. I don't ask him to evaluate swatches, and he's learned not to care that I can't tell *La bohème* from *Aïda*."

"I should tell you something," I said. "Before Oscar gets here." I'd never confided in Rafe before. I'd never had a secret I didn't share with Oscar.

He lifted the grater away, revealing a tall mound of cheese in delicate tatters. He looked me straight in the eye, his own softening, welcoming. His hands, freed at last of the work of chopping, grating, mixing, settled awkwardly on the countertop, as if inaction, rest, were foreign to them.

"It may be crazy," I began, "but I'm kind of seeing someone."

"There's nothing crazy about that."

I toyed with the stem of my glass, willing myself not to look away from his eyes. "It's Wayne."

Rafe gasped, his back straightening sharply. "Wow. When did that happen?"

"Last week. It's too soon to make much of it, I know, but if I'm being honest, there's been something there for a while. And now that I've gotten to know him better. … Well he's much more complex and kind-hearted than I gave him credit for."

Rafe smiled.

"There's more to him than his work and … being young," I said. "We just never listened."

"How could we," Rafe asked, "when Oscar and Brendan do all the talking?"

I laughed. "So you don't think I'm nuts?"

He scraped the cheese into a bright orange bowl. "Not at all," he said. "To tell you the truth, I always kind of liked him. He never said much, but I always saw the spark in his eyes."

I could feel my heart rate slowing down and was suddenly aware of how tense I'd been, afraid to put my feelings into words.

Rafe poured himself a glass of wine. "Has he told you much about John? It always looked so awkward between them—on both sides—like they weren't really connecting."

"No," I said. "I don't think they were, after a while, and John was just unable to notice. Wayne went into it in good faith. John can be charming, but a relationship is something else. I think John was constructing something that wasn't really there. And the more invested he got in his fantasy, the harder it became for Wayne to untangle himself without hurting him."

"I get it." Rafe tapped his wedding ring against the glass. "I've been there. When I was young. We're all stupid when we're young."

I laughed. "Oh, does it stop after a while?"

Our quiet reverie was suddenly interrupted by the clamor of the front door and Oscar's baritone. "Hello!"

"We're in the kitchen," Rafe sang out.

Oscar appeared in the doorway and leaned his briefcase against the wall. He pulled off his jacket and draped it over the back of a stool before rounding the island to kiss Rafe. "Have you had enough time to talk about me, or am I home too early?"

"No worries," I said. "I'm sure you'll give us more ammunition before long."

"What are we drinking?"

I gestured to the wine bottle on the island. Oscar scrunched up his nose. "Oh no," he said, "I need the hard stuff." He crossed to a cabinet on the far side of the room and pulled out a cocktail shaker. "Martini, anyone?"

"Not for me," Rafe said. "But I will want to switch to red for dinner. Could you find a nice Cabernet?"

It was like so many other nights, and exactly what I needed— the casualness of a few friends getting together spontaneously, no expectations, no frills. Rafe had texted me in the afternoon and asked if I was free. He didn't plan an elaborate menu, just the sort of thing he could whip up from staples. Lasagna may have been a big deal for some people, but Rafe could manage a meal like this on autopilot.

I helped Oscar set the table in the breakfast nook, surrounded by windows looking out on the garden. The density of the greenery and the peace it foretold was enough to explain why they'd left the hubbub of the Castro for this quiet oasis. The house, despite its size, felt homey, filled with mementos—photos of places they'd visited or smiling faces at weddings and parties and street fairs, souvenirs from every corner of the globe. Their lives, I thought, were in those things, in these walls, where the past was honored and protected.

Rafe, both hands in oven mitts, carried the bubbling lasagna to a trivet on the kitchen island. He freed his hands and laid one empty mitt against each side of the pan—a reminder that the danger had not yet passed.

Walking silently behind him to grab something out of a drawer, Oscar gently touched Rafe's hip, his fingers lingering for a moment. He laid a corkscrew and foil cutter on the far end of the counter and bent down to assess the wine rack by the doorway. He pulled a bottle out and glanced at the label before straightening back up. While Rafe pulled plates from a cabinet, Oscar twisted the foil cutter smoothly over the neck of the bottle and dropped a perfect ring onto the counter. A few seconds later, he removed the cork with a satisfying pop and carried the bottle to the table, where Rafe had already settled the glasses.

They moved around the kitchen like well-choreographed dancers, going through their steps automatically, sensing each other's presence and continually making room. The space itself may have been fairly new, but after years together they seemed to have learned how to anticipate every move, flowing around each other seamlessly.

We made small talk over dinner, none of us in the mood for anything heavy—no rehashing of the trial, the bookstore, Oscar's latest case, Rafe's frustration with a client. Instead, we talked about the books we were reading, and waxed rhapsodic about how Ryan Gosling was more than just a pretty face.

It wasn't until after dinner, before the light of the gas fireplace in the living room, that a melancholy tone fell over the conversation. Oscar had distributed huge snifters of brandy, and we sat in our separate chairs nursing them. I held mine up and swirled the brandy, watching the color change from maroon to orange before the flames.

I focused on the fireplace for a while, the repetitive leaps of color, like a video on loop. I missed the crackle of normal fireplaces, but nobody in the city burned wood anymore.

"I heard from an old friend today," Rafe said. "Oscar, do you remember Mason? We used to work together."

"I think so," Oscar replied. "How is he?"

"Not good. He's on chemo. Pancreatic cancer. Nothing's working. He may have only a few months left."

"My god, I'm sorry."

"We haven't been in touch in ages. It felt like he was making the rounds. Saying goodbye."

"We're not young anymore," Oscar said. "Sure, most of us have two or three decades left, but it's starting. I used to go to the doctor once a year at most. Unless I had chlamydia or something." He chuckled lightly. "But now, there's something every couple of months. And you get paranoid, you know? What was just an ache when you were in your forties now could be the beginning of the end."

"My grandmother used to tell me not to get old," I said. "And I would argue, 'Well, Nana, it beats the alternative.' She wasn't convinced."

"We're all on the exit ramp," Rafe said.

"That's a little morbid." I straightened up in my chair, hackles raised against mortality.

"I'm just saying, we should get used to the idea. I'm an orphan now. Next in line."

"We shouldn't complain," I said. "I mean, there was a time when gay men just assumed they wouldn't grow old."

Oscar shifted in his seat. "Well, Mother Nature's taken over now. Welcome to death and debility by natural causes." He sipped his brandy and shut his eyes for a long moment.

They sat in almost identical positions, legs crossed symmetrically over knees, bookending the fireplace. They hadn't started to dress alike—there still seemed little chance that Rafe's fondness for cool colors and Oscar's for warm ones would ever merge into tepid neutrality—but they clearly fit together. More, I thought, than they ever had before.

I'd seldom seen them quite like this—or perhaps I was just watching more closely now, entranced by the serenity, the hypnotic ripples of flame in the fireplace. This, I told myself, a voice spontaneously echoing in my head, is how it's supposed to be. It wasn't about romance or the melodrama of perceived slights, the weight of expectation. I searched for recent memories of the two of them kissing in public or holding hands as I walked behind them on the street. That had never really been their thing. But the grace was everywhere. Even their public tiffs—the contradictions and eyerolls when one of them said or did something off color— played out with a smooth cadence, a rhythm they had mastered over time.

"Is this how you imagined it?" I asked, cutting through the silence, stifling the voice in my head.

"Imagined what?" asked Oscar. He shared a look with Rafe—wondering, perhaps, if he'd missed something.

I told them what I'd been thinking, the way they had come to fit each other. I wanted to know if there had been a moment when they saw it themselves, a moment when something clicked in their minds and they knew everything was going to be all right.

"There's nothing perfect here," Rafe said at last. "Besides my hair."

"And my 32-inch waist," added Oscar with a conspiratorial smile.

"Maybe that's the secret, then," I said. "Not expecting perfection."

Rafe nodded. "It's certainly a good start."

After the drama—the romance, the excitement of each early date—when the sex peters out, when the gourmet dinners meant to impress give way to pork chops—there's the quiet, the imperfect quiet. I had always feared silence. It signified the death of something.

"I've never been good with all that," I said. "When things start to go wrong, I run."

"And sometimes you should." Oscar leaned forward, cradling his brandy. "You weren't wrong about Damien, you know. The way you ended it may have been—"

"Immature?"

He smirked. "I was going to say childish, but it did have to end somehow."

"Better luck next time," Rafe said and winked.

"You have enough on your mind these days," said Oscar.

"Just relax."

Rafe let out a satisfied, calming sigh. "In the meantime," he said, "we have nights like this." Cradling his glass, he caught my eye with a gentle smile. The three of us comprised a little triangle in the room, the stablest of shapes. We toasted, three glowing orbs lifted toward the light.

And I turned my eyes back to the fireplace, the persistent stasis of its artificial logs, like some modern-day biblical bush, burning but never consumed.

CHAPTER 30
THE VIEW FROM TWIN
PEAKS

"I was nervous the first time. I didn't know what to expect. I'd seen pictures on the news, but they were only quick snippets, and they had their own agenda. The image I recalled best was of a couple walking down the street, hands in each other's back pockets. The camera lingered on their butts—it was half-eroticism, half-indictment. The straight world has always had, let's say, an ambivalent relationship with us. They're creeped out by us, but they're intrigued. They define us by the sex we have, and then they condemn us for being defined by sex. After a while, I grew convinced that the main reason for their disdain was envy. All men are driven by sex. All men want it as often as possible. But when *we* look for it, we get it. There's no one to say no. They hate that."

I was sitting up in bed. Wayne's head rested on my shoulder, his beard gently grazing my skin. We had drawn the curtains. The room was in almost complete darkness. If he'd fallen asleep, I wouldn't have known it. But the stillness of his body, the way his hand rested firmly against my leg, told me he was wide awake, listening.

"I felt like Persephone," I said, warming to my own story,

"emerging from the underworld. The escalator seemed so slow, I swear it took five minutes to move ten yards. First, I could just see the tops of the buildings across the street—then, as in the slow lowering of a camera lens, people's heads, bodies moving busily back and forth. Finally, the escalator reached the surface, and there I was. I remember walking off and having to remind myself to get out of the way of the people behind me. I stood off to the side and just watched for a couple of minutes, to make sure it was real. It wasn't like the stories on the news. Nobody was making out on the corner or smoking pot in a doorway. They were just normal people going about their business—carrying grocery bags, coming out of the movies, grabbing a cup of coffee, chatting with friends. The difference was that they were mostly men, and the couples were men, and they weren't looking over their shoulders to make sure it was safe. It was magical."

He had asked for this story. He wanted to know what it was like when San Francisco was a paradise, when we were here because there was simply nowhere else to go. He'd told me his own story, visiting the city with friends when he'd lived in Silicon Valley. Even then, just a few years ago, he'd had to come up here to find a decent gay bar, to be in a place where you could assume people were gay. It sounded transactional, like how you go to one store for shoes and another for groceries. He had come up to the Castro when he wanted sex. I had come here for everything.

"Do you still feel that?" he asked. "I mean, with everything that's changed, do you still feel the magic?"

I exhaled. "Every day."

He squeezed my leg. "I'm glad."

"Don't you?" I asked. "Is it magical now?"

"I don't know." He giggled, an innocent, delightful sound. "I'm a very practical guy. I've never really believed in magic."

I stroked the hair off his forehead. "Well, as long as it believes in you."

It had been like this for nearly a month now—one or two nights a week. Dinner, theater, maybe a movie, then tumbling into bed. For once, I was in the moment, enjoying his company but not expecting anything, not looking beyond today. And we talked in bed. We talked everywhere. So much, I thought, had been bottled up inside him on those other nights, when John had dragged him along, turning him into a bystander to our life.

For now, I was keeping Wayne to myself. We were our own oasis.

"Shall we do something special for Pride?" he asked.

"Like what?"

"Watch the parade."

"Watch the parade?" I asked with a laugh. "That would be special?"

"I've never seen it."

"Oh. Well then, we have to." I gazed down, testing my vision in the darkness. "God, really? You've never seen the parade? That's like living in New York and never seeing the Statue of Liberty."

"Come on, Craig. No New Yorker I know has ever been to the Statue of Liberty. They think it's gauche."

"Point taken." I kissed his brow. "Then we'll go. We'll have to pack a lunch, though."

"Pack a lunch?"

"It's an all-day affair."

"Oh, maybe—"

"No no no," I said with a maternal scold, "you can't back out now. It's a ritual. Like a bris."

He laughed, his breath rippling against my chest. "Well, if

you insist."

□

I crept quietly into the room and grabbed a chair by the wall, hoping to remain invisible. I was still in the learning phase.

A boy by the window, shoulder-length hair, barely 16, was talking animatedly, punctuating every sentence with a self-conscious laugh. "They have no idea," he said. "No idea what it's like."

"Say more about that." Rosita, the counselor, leaned forward in her chair, fingers interlaced and subtly pointing. I'd watched her in action a couple of times now. She had a talent for getting the kids to talk, assuring them that they were in a safe space.

The boy continued for a minute or so. He was thinking out loud, deciding what he needed to say in the process of saying it. A girl a few seats away nodded enthusiastically, finally jumped in to build on his story with her own experience—the father who'd abandoned the family long ago, the mother who'd kicked her out when she told her she was a lesbian.

There were dozens of stories like that—kids thrown to the street by parents who forgot their responsibilities once their offspring revealed the truth, as if parenting stopped the moment a child failed to live up to their expectations. Other kids didn't wait to find out. They just left to spare themselves the moment of rejection. One had slipped out of the house in the middle of the night, right before his parents planned to take him to a conversion camp. Possessed of only what he could carry in his school backpack, he had hitchhiked from Idaho, not stopping until he reached San Francisco.

San Francisco was Shangri-La to the runaways. They'd never seen it, but the name itself conjured sanctuary, freedom. They knew that if they couldn't fit in anywhere else, they could fit in here.

Some kids in the group were still living at home and came to these meetings just for a sense of community and to blow off steam. San Francisco may have been a refuge for outsiders, but apparently coming out here wasn't any easier than it was anywhere else.

My eyes swept the circle slowly, taking in the rainbow of kids. They ranged in age from 14 to 24—male, female, trans, nonbinary. And the stories they told, while unique to their own experience, were all of a piece. The battles were different, but the war was a shared one.

Rosita turned her attention to the corner opposite, a chair pulled slightly out of the circle, long dark hair hiding most of a face. "Lila, we haven't heard from you yet today. What have you been up to lately?"

Lila lifted her head, revealing a tight smile. Her legs were crossed, tapered jeans ending in black tennis shoes. She swept her hair awkwardly over one ear. "I've been good," she said softly. "My mom bought me these new earrings." She turned to the side to reveal a long dangling hoop.

"That's great," Rosita said. Her eyes brightened. "And they're beautiful."

"Very girly," said Shonda.

Lila blushed and her smile now bloomed. "She said she thought I needed something pretty." She paused, caught her breath, pink-tipped nails splaying her flat chest. "She said her daughter should have something pretty."

Cheers went up in pockets around the room. Rosita's eyes

looked full, but she held back the tears. "That's fantastic, Lila. I'm so happy for you."

I sat up in my own chair, a sudden chill flowing through my body. It wasn't a miracle, I knew, but clearly it felt like one to Lila, and that was why we were here, so that what now seemed like miracles could one day become expectations.

I slipped out as quietly as I'd entered, under cover of the loud, excited conversation that swirled around Lila. Her face was a welter of emotions, revealing a habitual fear of attention breaking into bliss at finally being the center of it.

The office was a warren of narrow hallways and cramped workspaces, every wall plastered with posters, pictures of community icons. The furniture was old, donated from a variety of sources, and the whole space smelled a bit damp. Not unlike the musty smell of a library, I thought, or the back of a bookstore. I was right at home.

My own office was at the far end of the hall. There were only a couple of other employees. Most of the people around me, aside from our young clients, were volunteers. In one room, a group was planning this month's main event—a poetry slam to be held in the café downstairs, which was donating the space and refreshments. On the other side of the hall, Jamal, the volunteer coordinator, was giving an orientation to the latest recruits. There was always a steady stream of conversation throughout the office, often peaking in screeches of laughter and excitement. No one here was waiting for the sky to fall. No one here was just putting in time.

I settled into my office and closed the door halfway, enough for privacy but not enough to intimidate people from knocking. So far, I hadn't spent much time in here at all. I was too busy shadowing the staff, attending events, meeting potential donors, drinking in the energy. I was in the honeymoon stage, Oscar warned me. Soon enough it would begin to feel like a job.

The truth was that I'd been hesitant. I thought I'd be over my head, or that the work would be thankless, disheartening. But the opposite had turned out to be the case. Without the pressure of the commercial world, we were free to focus on the work for its own sake. Enough money to support our efforts was the goal. No one was going to get rich from this. No one wanted to.

The chair wobbled furiously as I sat down, the spring connecting the seat to the base letting out a piercing shriek. Like a dog howling, Jamal had said more than once, urging me to get some WD40 for it, or to tighten up the bolts before I leaned back too far and went flying through the window. "I've played it safe too long," I told him. "It's time to live a little dangerously."

I had a window now, though its view was restricted largely to the backyard of the house behind us, rough patches of grass competing with broken pavement. The front of the building was given over to conference rooms, wide windows welcoming sunshine and the towering palm trees that lined the Market Street median. But at least my office had a view of something, unlike the cave at the bookstore.

When the knock came at the door, I was going through the donor list again, trying to learn who everyone was, thinking about who else we might approach. I looked up with a smile and saw Brendan in the doorway.

"What about your agency?" I asked. "Think you could persuade them to help the kids?"

They didn't like to be called kids. I'd learned that the hard way. They were clients, but in private, when I mooned about them with my friends, I felt they would always be my kids.

Brendan scowled. "You do know that real estate is a greedy

[366]

business, right?"

"Of course. But it's a competitive one, too. You have to do something to make yourselves look less like snakes in the grass."

"And vultures," he said. "Don't forget the vultures."

I tossed my papers back into one of the dozens of manila folders on my desk. "Is it 5:00 already?"

"It is somewhere," he said, looking facetiously at his watch.

"Very funny."

"You know we have to get started early. Those streets are going to be a madhouse in another hour."

It was Fag Friday, as we called it—to distinguish it from all the other Fridays of our gay year—a ritual evening out before the onslaught of Pride weekend left us little room to breathe.

I shut off the desk lamp, Garrett's parachute man spinning in circles at my touch, and followed Brendan out.

"Happy Pride!" called out Teena as we passed the front desk.

"Happy Pride," I said. "See you Monday."

"I'll do my best," she said with a laugh. "You never know what's going to happen this weekend."

We skipped down the stairs and out, a gust of warm air surprising me as I pushed through the door. "Gee," I said, fanning myself, "you'd almost think it was summer."

"Summer?" Brendan said. "What's that?"

I rolled my eyes and headed down Market Street. I stopped at Sanchez. "Can we go back to my place first?" I said. "I want to drop off my stuff."

"Sure," he said, "I haven't seen your place in a while. I could—"

"I'm not leaving," I said firmly. "I don't care what the condo's worth. It'll only be worth more when I'm ready."

My phone buzzed as we bounced down the street. I slipped

it out of my pocket and read the text at close range, through the bottom half of my glasses.

Happy Pride! Looking forward to spending the weekend with you. xox

I would respond later, I thought, in the safety of the bar, where I wouldn't draw attention.

Rafe was still the only one I'd told. Even Oscar, who knew everything else about me, from my stories of grade-school humiliation to my middle-aged aches and pains, was out of the loop. Even Brendan, who'd seen me weep over broken hearts, knew nothing about the way mine was healing.

As we approached the building, I suddenly wondered if there were any telltale signs of Wayne's presence—his scarf draped on a chair, his toothbrush in the holder in the bathroom, the post-it notes he liked to leave for me to find when he left in the morning.

For once, my secret wasn't about shame. I was doing it to protect John. I felt like a woman who doesn't reveal her pregnancy until the second trimester, just in case anything goes wrong. There was no point in letting this out until I was more certain. Still, the secrecy added unearned weight to the situation. It exerted its own sort of pressure.

I waited until we got inside. Dropping my bag on a chair, I turned to face Brendan, who was quite consciously not assessing the bones of the place.

"I have to tell you something," I said. "It's preliminary, but it has to come out sometime."

"Oh dear. You're a Republican."

"No," I said. "But we can start with that. Anything else will be easy to take."

I considered fortification, but the guys were probably waiting for us at the bar by now.

"I'm dating someone," I said.

Brendan smiled broadly.

"It's Wayne."

His mouth was hanging open. It was shocking to see him speechless for once. Too shocking.

"Rafe told you."

"Rafe? No." He paused, his smile growing positively mischievous. "Oscar."

"Oh my god! He must be furious at me for not telling him myself."

"Don't worry. He's too stunned by the news to feel slighted."

"When did Rafe—oh, that little shit!"

And suddenly my whole body relaxed.

"It's fine, Craig. We all could see something. Hell, there was one night months ago when Oscar pulled me aside and said, 'Half the trouble with Wayne is that he's dating the wrong guy. He should be with Craig.'"

"He didn't."

Brendan raised his hand in the air like an oath. "So tell me, what were we missing?"

"A lot," I said. "I don't want to make too much of it. It's early, and you know my history. But it's good. It's very good."

"Well, then I expect to get to know him a lot better."

"Absolutely. I'm not going to make the same mistake that John did. I'm not going to hide him from you guys or make him hide himself. I won't foist you on him too often, but I do want you to see that there's more to him."

"Fine with me," Brendan said. "This old dog is willing to learn a new trick or two."

We headed downstairs. Outside, I turned to Brendan. "Please tell me John doesn't know yet."

"No," he said, "I don't think anyone would go that far. That's your job, my friend. But don't worry. John will be fine. The truth is, I think he's completely over it. At some level, he knows it would never have worked. But he cares about you both, so why shouldn't he want *this* to work?"

As we turned onto Castro, I spotted the figures in the distance, the rainbow flags rippling on either side of the street. In the fading sunlight, it was all a blaze of color—that first glimpse of Oz through the black-and-white doorframe. It seemed especially appropriate at the moment, my head still spinning from learning that my secret was out. Everything had a film of unreality over it. It was too easy. I wasn't accustomed to easy.

It was a relatively quiet night, before the weekend festivities would erupt in full, making the sidewalks nearly impassable. As we approached 18th, the crowd grew thicker, in the brief valley where two slopes met, just one dip in a street that ran the length of town—but the most important one, the one that gave the street its reputation, the tiny stretch of pavement that marked its fame in the world. All these people converged here, as though the slopes of the hill compelled them, that soft pull of gravity bringing them to a shared space.

Beyond, nearly at Market, the theater sign had flickered on, one letter at a time announcing the neighborhood in pink and blue neon.

"It never gets old," I said.

"What?"

I swept the air with an elongated arm. "All of it."

Brendan laughed. "Too bad we can't say the same for ourselves."

"Isn't that really what it's about, though?" I said. "I mean, are we upset because the city's changing, or because we are?"

"A little of both, I guess."

I studied the faces that flowed past. Many were younger, of course, but there were still enough like me, like Brendan, like that old man at Twin Peaks. We weren't dead yet. My generation had come in the nineties to replace so many who had moved on before their time, and now others were here, waiting to replace us. It was constant, natural, even good.

Different people lived here now, I told myself, but the spirit remained. Harvey Milk had walked along this street. Every gay tourist in the world had made a pilgrimage here. Thousands were gone, but the street was still alive, still beckoning, despite the competing noise, the unrelenting pull of change.

We passed by a sandwich shop that had once been a burrito joint that had once been a camera store. The tile beneath the windows suddenly struck me as ancient. I could picture it there through each incarnation of the building, the same black squares easing into triangles to accommodate the slope of the hill, despite the completely different scenes behind the glass above. Architectural pentimento.

I slipped an arm through Brendan's and we made our way together, up toward Market, pilgrims charging into the Emerald City.

As we passed the theater, I spotted Oscar and Rafe standing outside the bar. We raced up to meet them. I had an urge for us all to go in together, like a posse.

We were regulars. We weren't going anywhere.

www.ingramcontent.com/pod-product-compliance
Lightning Source LLC
Chambersburg PA
CBHW030630020726
47493CB00006B/1653